A TEXT BOOK OF

PRINCIPLES OF PROGRAMMING LANGUAGES

FOR
SEMESTER – II

SECOND YEAR DEGREE COURSE IN COMPUTER ENGINEERING

**Strictly According to New Revised Credit System Syllabus
of Savitribai Phule Pune University**
(w.e.f June 2016)

Mrs. PRITI P. JORVEKAR - KUMBHAR
ME. (Comp. Engg.)
Assistant Professor,
Comp. Engg. Deptt.,
NBN Sinhgad School of Engineering,
Ambegaon (Bk.), PUNE.

Mrs. SHILPA N. BHOSALE
ME. (Comp. Engg.)
Assistant Professor,
Comp. Engg. Deptt.,
NBN Sinhgad School of Engineering,
Ambegaon (Bk.), PUNE.

SACHIN P. GODSE
ME. CSE (IT),
Assistant Professor,
Comp. Engg. Deptt.,
Sinhgad Academy of Engineering,
Kondhwa (Bk.), PUNE.

NIRALI
PRAKASHAN
ADVANCEMENT OF KNOWLEDGE

N3580

PRINCIPLES OF PROGRAMMING LANGUAGES (SE COMP.)   **ISBN 978-93-86353-01-6**

First Edition	:	**January 2017**
©	:	**Authors**

Published By :   **Polyplate**
NIRALI PRAKASHAN
Abhyudaya Pragati, 1312, Shivaji Nagar,
Off J.M. Road, Pune – 411005
Tel - (020) 25512336/37/39, Fax - (020) 25511379
Email : niralipune@pragationline.com

☞ **DISTRIBUTION CENTRES**

PUNE

Nirali Prakashan   :   119, Budhwar Peth, Jogeshwari Mandir Lane, Pune 411002, Maharashtra
Tel : (020) 2445 2044, 66022708, Fax : (020) 2445 1538
Email : bookorder@pragationline.com, niralilocal@pragationline.com

Nirali Prakashan   :   S. No. 28/27, Dhyari, Near Pari Company, Pune 411041
Tel : (020) 24690204 Fax : (020) 24690316
Email : dhyari@pragationline.com, bookorder@pragationline.com

MUMBAI

Nirali Prakashan   :   385, S.V.P. Road, Rasdhara Co-op. Hsg. Society Ltd.,
Girgaum, Mumbai 400004, Maharashtra
Tel : (022) 2385 6339 / 2386 9976, Fax : (022) 2386 9976
Email : niralimumbai@pragationline.com

☞ **DISTRIBUTION BRANCHES**

JALGAON

Nirali Prakashan   :   34, V. V. Golani Market, Navi Peth, Jalgaon 425001,
Maharashtra, Tel : (0257) 222 0395, Mob : 94234 91860

KOLHAPUR

Nirali Prakashan   :   New Mahadvar Road, Kedar Plaza, 1st Floor Opp. IDBI Bank
Kolhapur 416 012, Maharashtra. Mob : 9850046155

NAGPUR

Pratibha Book Distributors :   Above Maratha Mandir, Shop No. 3, First Floor,
Rani Jhanshi Square, Sitabuldi, Nagpur 440012, Maharashtra
Tel : (0712) 254 7129

DELHI

Nirali Prakashan   :   4593/21, Basement, Aggarwal Lane 15, Ansari Road, Daryaganj
Near Times of India Building, New Delhi 110002
Mob : 08505972553

BENGALURU

Pragati Book House   :   House No. 1, Sanjeevappa Lane, Avenue Road Cross,
Opp. Rice Church, Bengaluru – 560002.
Tel : (080) 64513344, 64513355,Mob : 9880582331, 9845021552
Email:bharatsavla@yahoo.com

CHENNAI

Pragati Books   :   9/1, Montieth Road, Behind Taas Mahal, Egmore,
Chennai 600008 Tamil Nadu, Tel : (044) 6518 3535,
Mob : 94440 01782 / 98450 21552 / 98805 82331,
Email : bharatsavla@yahoo.com

niralipune@pragationline.com | www.pragationline.com

Also find us on 🅕 www.facebook.com/niralibooks

Dedicated to ...

My husband **Mr. Rushikesh S. Kumbhar**,
   for their infinite patience and inspiration.

...... *Priti P. Jorvekar*

Dedicated to ...

My husband **Mr. Nikhil D. Bhosale** &
Mother in law **Ms. Pushpa D. Bhosale**
   for their infinite patience and inspiration.

...... *Shilpa N. Bhosale*

Dedicated to ...

My lovely son, **Avanish** & daughter, **Devashree**
   for their infinite patience and smiles.

...... *Sachin P. Godse*

PREFACE

It gives us great pleasure in publishing this text book on "**Principles of Programming Languages**" for the students of Second Year Degree Course in Computer Engineering. This book is strictly written according to **New Revised Credit System Syllabus** of Savitribai Phule Pune University (2015 Pattern).

As per the policy of the University, Engineering Syllabi is revised every five years. Last revision was in the year 2012. New revision is coming little earlier, as university has introduced **Online System of Examination** from year 2012.

As per the **New Credit System**, the **Online Examinations** Phase–I will be conducted based on First & Second Units and Phase–II on Third & Fourth Units. The **Online** examinations will have objective types of questions with multiple choices. End Sem. Theory Examination will be based on all the six units and that will be conducted in traditional way and the Theory Course will have 4 credits.

It is our objective to keep the presentation systematic, consistent, intensive and clear presentation of concept through explanatory notes and figures. So we are sure that this book will cater for all your needs for this subject.

Main feature of this book is, **Complete Coverage** of the New Credit System Syllabus with large number of **Worked (Solved) Programs, Examples and Exercises.**

We have given Separate Book of Multiple Choice Questions (MCQ's) which will be very useful to the students especially for Online Examinations.

We would also like to thanks Dr. R. S. Prasad, Principal, NBN Sinhgad School of Engineering, Ambegaon (Bk) and Dr. K. P. Patil, Principal, Sinhgad Academy of Engineering Kondhwa, Pune, for their valuable guidance and timely reliving us for performing this task.

We take this opportunity to express our sincere thanks to Shri. Dineshbhai Furia, Shri. Jignesh Furia, Mrs. Nirali Verma and Shri. M. P. Munde and entire team of Nirali Prakashan namely Mrs. Deepali Lachake (Co-ordinator), who really have taken keen interest and untiring efforts in publishing this text.

The advice and suggestions of our esteemed readers to improve the text are most welcomed, and will be highly appreciated.

Pune   **Authors**

SYLLABUS

Unit I: Programming Language Syntax and Semantics   **07 Hours**

Software development process, language and software development environments, language and software design methods, languages and computer architecture, programming language qualities, languages and reliability, languages and maintainability, languages and efficiency, a brief historical perspective and early high level languages, a bird's eye view of programming language concepts.

Syntax and Semantics: language definition, syntax, abstract syntax, concrete syntax, and pragmatics, semantics, an introduction to formal semantics, languages, language processing, interpretation, translation, the concept of binding, variables, name and scope, Type, l-value, r-value, reference and unnamed variables, routines, generic routines, aliasing and overloading, an abstract semantic processor, run time structure. Case study- run time structure of C.

Unit II: Structuring the Data, Computations and Program   **07 Hours**

Structuring of Data: Built in and primitive types, Data aggregates and type constructors, Cartesian product, Finite mapping User-defined types and abstract data types, Type systems, Static versus dynamic program checking, Strong typing and type checking, Type compatibility, Type conversions, Types and subtypes, Generic types, monomorphic versus polymorphic type systems, Case Study- The type structure of C++, Java.

Structuring of Computations: Structuring the computation, Expressions and statements, Conditional execution and iteration, Routines, Style issues: side effects and aliasing, Exceptions, Case Study-Exception handling in C++.

Unit III: Structuring of Program   **07 Hours**

Structuring of Program: Software design method, Concepts in support of modularity, Encapsulation, Interface and implementation, Separate and independent compilation, Libraries of modules, Language features for programming in the large, Program organization, Grouping of units, Encapsulation, Interface and implementation, Abstract data types, classes, and modules, Generic units, Generic data structures, Generic algorithms, Generic modules, Higher levels of genericity.

Programming Paradigms: Introduction to programming paradigms, Introduction to four main Programming paradigms- procedural, object oriented, functional, and logic & rule based.

Study of Java as Object oriented programming language.

Unit IV: Java as Object Oriented Programming Language-Overview   **07 Hours**

Java History, Java Features, Java and Internet, Java and Word Wide Web, Web Browsers, Java Virtual Machine, **Data Types and Size** (Signed vs. Unsigned, User Defined vs. Primitive Data Types, Explicit Pointer type).

Arrays: one dimensional array, multi-dimensional array, alternative array declaration statements.

Control Statements: Revision of identical selection Statements in brief (if, else if, Nested if, Switch, Nested Switch), Iterative Statements for Each version of For Loop, Declaring Loop Control Variables Inside the for loop, Using comma in for loop), Jump Statements (Labeled Break and Labeled Continue).

String Handling: String class methods.

Unit V: Inheritance, Polymorphism, Encapsulation using Java   07 Hours

Classes and Methods: class fundamentals, declaring objects, assigning object reference variables, adding methods to a class, returning a value, constructors, this keyword, garbage collection, finalize() method, overloading methods, argument passing, object as parameter, returning objects, access control, static, final, nested and inner classes, command line arguments, variable-length arguments.

Inheritances: member access and inheritance, super class references, Using super, multilevel hierarchy, constructor call sequence, method overriding, dynamic method dispatch, abstract classes, Object class.

Packages and Interfaces: Defining a package, finding packages and CLASSPATH, access protection, importing packages, interfaces (defining, implementation, nesting, applying), variables in interfaces, extending interfaces, instance of operator.

Unit VI: Exception Handling in Java   07 Hours

Fundamental, exception types, uncaught exceptions, try, catch, throw, throws, finally, multiple catch clauses, nested try statements, built-in exceptions, custom exceptions (creating your own exception sub classes).

Managing I/O: Streams, Byte Streams and Character Streams, Predefined Streams, Reading console Input, Writing Console Output, Print Writer class.

Applet: Applet Fundamental, Applet Architecture, Applet Skeleton, Requesting Repainting, status window, HTML Applet tag, passing parameters to Applets, Difference between Applet and Application Program.

CONTENTS

✠ ✠ ✠

PROGRAMMING LANGUAGES SYNTAX AND SEMANTICS

1.1 INTRODUCTION

Software

- Software is nothing but automation of business process. Now days in every activities of daily life routine automation takes place or in progress.

- Automation means whatever manual activities previously done by human beings are now done by software. e. g. for banking operations, traditionally we need to visit bank and manually required to perform all operations like withdraw amount, transfer money, checking balance etc. but now days we are using net banking software or mobile banking software.

- Technically we can define software as set of instructions which when executed then certain task is happen.

- Software size is varying depending on scope of business processes. If we are implementing code/software for small program which will perform simple mathematical operation like addition, subtraction, multiplication, division it will required only few lines of instructions of particular programming languages. But if scope is bigger like, shopping mall management software, it may contain multiple modules and each module may contain multiple programs and each program may contains thousands of line.

- Like other engineering domains software engineering becomes important for solving society problems by automation. It is necessary to understand software development process for effective software development.

1.2 SOFTWARE DEVELOPMENT PROCESS

- Software is developed it is not manufactured mechanically like other products.

- To carryout software development systematically, software development processes are come in to exist.

- There are different process models are available to carry out software development work.

For Example : Waterfall model, spiral model, Rapid application development model etc.

- There are some common framework activities which involve in each and every process model.

- Activities are as below :
  - ➢ Communication
  - ➢ Planning
  - ➢ Modeling
  - ➢ Construction
  - ➢ Deployment

Consider waterfall model for software development process :

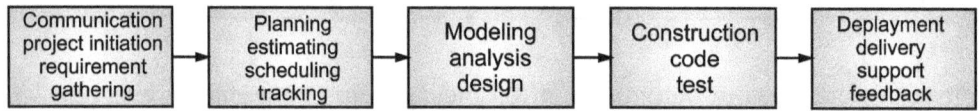

Fig. 1.1 : Water fall model

So software development process based on waterfall model map in to following phases :

- **Requirement Analysis and Specification :** In this phase communication between customer and software developer take place. Requirements are collect from users by software developer team, requirements are processes by team. Processing may involve feasibility study, need of requirement, remove unwanted requirements, assigning priority to requirements, estimating cost of requirements etc.

  The result of this phase is a requirements document stating that what the system should do. It does not specify how the system is going to meet its requirements.

- **Software Design :** Requirement phase gives what the problem is but not giving how to solve the problem. Design phase give how to solve the problem. Problem can be decompose into modules that will meet stated requirements. Each module functionality are visually represented by diagrams, there are different tools available for creating diagrams. The design method followed in this step can have a great impact on the quality of resulting application in particular on its understand ability and modifiability. It can also affect the choice of programming languages to be used is system implementation. The result of this phase is a design specification document identifying all of the modules in the system and their interfaces.

- **Implementation :** Starting with the design specification software developers implement the system. Design gives visual representation of problem in hand. Steps or strategy for solving problem is stated in this phase. The goal of implementation step is to select suitable platform, language for implementation. The result of implementation phase is fully executable code with required documentation.

- **Verification and Validation :** These are quality assurance activities carried out in parallel with every phase of software development. It checks that intermediate deliverables of software development process satisfy their objectives or not.

Verification is all about "Are we building the product in right way". Validation is all about "Are we building the right/quality product".

Testing is tool for verification and validation. Different kinds of testing can be used to check different aspect of system.

- **Maintenance :** After delivery of software to customer, changes or error may be identified by users of the software. These changes to software become necessary because of detected malfucuntions, a desire to add new capabilities or to improve existing ones, or the need to accommodate changes in operational environment. All these works comes under software maintenance phase.

1.3 LANGUAGES AND SOFTWARE DEVELOPMENT ENVIRONMENT

- As we seen that software development process involves different phases from requirement gathering to maintenance.

- Each phase of development should supported by computer aided tools. Currently for coding activity sufficient tools are available like different editors, compilers, linkers, libraries. These tools used to semi automate the process of coding which help to reduce manual work and save time for coding.

- Other phases of software development also need support of such semi automated tools to increase productivity.

- A software development environment is an integrated set of tools and techniques that aids in development of software.

- Current scenario of environment shows different tools are available for different phases of software development like for requirement gathering and processing work computer specialist and user of application interacting with the environment developed system requirements.

- For Design process visual paradigms, Easy draw, Star UML etc. tools are available different notations are available to model diagrams.

- Implementation of requirements is done by using different editors, compilers, linkers interpreters and debuggers.

- For testing different tools are available like QTP (Quick Test Professionals), QF Test, silk Test etc. which can provide facility to write test cases, generate test data as per requirement, to write test script, to execute test.

For working of all these; tools must be compatible and integrated with tools used in other phases.

For Example : The programming languages must be compatible with the design methods supported by the environment at the design stage and with design notations used to document designs.

- The editor used to enter programs might be sensitive to the syntax of the language, so that syntax errors can be caught before they are even entered rather than later at compile time.
- A facility for test data generation can also available for programs written in the language.

1.4 LANGUAGE AND SOFTWARE DESIGN METHODS

- Designing software is important phase in software development process. As we seen that requirement analysis gives what will be in the system. However how it can be possible is specified in designing phase.
- There are different methods of designing software; structured design and object oriented design.
- Different approaches are followed for designing software; top down approach and bottom up approach.
- Structural designing follows top-down approach and object oriented designing follows bottom up approach.
- Designing methods provide guideline to developer for visualizing system in the form of models and their details steps/operations.
- Software designers decompose system into logical components, which then coded into languages.
- In structural design system is treated as whole for implementation. Requirements are split in to functions. Each functions give one or more requirements.
- In object-oriented design system is divided into classes of objects. Each class provide one or more requirements.
- Languages are also categorized depending on their design method like structural languages, object oriented languages.
- To understand the relationship between a programming language and a design method, it is important to realize that programming languages may enforce a certain programming style, often called a programming paradigm. For Example, Small talk and Eiffel are object-oriented languages. They develop the system by dividing it into classes and objects. Similarly, FORTRAN and Pascal are procedural languages. They develop programs based on routines.
- Languages enforcing a specific programming paradigm can be called paradigm-oriented. Some languages, in fact, are paradigm neutral and support different paradigms. For Example, C++ supports the development of procedural and object-oriented programs.
- If the design method and languages paradigm are the same, or the language is paradigm neutral, then the design abstractions can be directly mapped into program components. If these two are not same then programming effort increases. So, the design methods and the paradigm supported by the language should be the same.

1.5 LANGUAGES AND COMPUTER ARCHITECTURE

- Computer architecture has influence on language designs to decide what can be implemented efficiently on current machines.

- Languages have been constrained by the ideas of Von Neumann, because most current computers are similar to the original Von Neumann architecture.

- The Von Neumann architecture is as shown in Fig. 1.2. It contains three units Input/Output unit, memory unit and CPU. Memory contains instruction and data in it. Input/Output unit used to take input and display output to user. The CPU is responsible for taking instructions from memory one at a time. Instructions are very low level. It takes data from memory, manipulated via arithmetic or logic operations in the CPU, with the results copied back to some memory cells. Thus, instructions execution changes state of machine which is represented by the contents of memory.

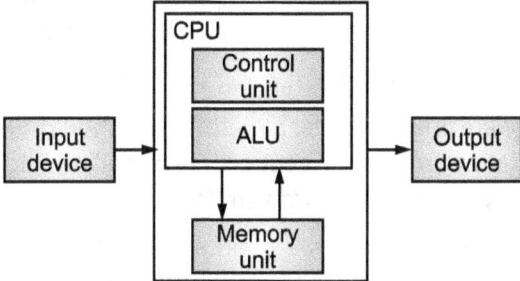

Fig. 1.2 : Von-neumann architecture

- Von-neumann architecture is the basis for imperative programming language. Imperative language simply give abstractions of the instructions in standard von Neumann machines. These included assignment statements conditional statements and branching statements. Assignment statements provided the ability to dynamically update the data store, while conditions and branching statements allowed a set of statements to be either skipped or repeatedly executed. Using this three kinds of statements any program can be written.

- Many kinds of abstractions were later invented by language designers, such as procedures and functions, data types, exception handlers, Classes and concurrency features.

- Language designers try to simplify programming languages for easier to use by humans. They followed von Neumann architecture only. It shown in Fig. 1.3. Some programming languages, namely, functional and logic languages have von Neumann computational model both are based on mathematical foundations rather than on the technology of underlying hardware.

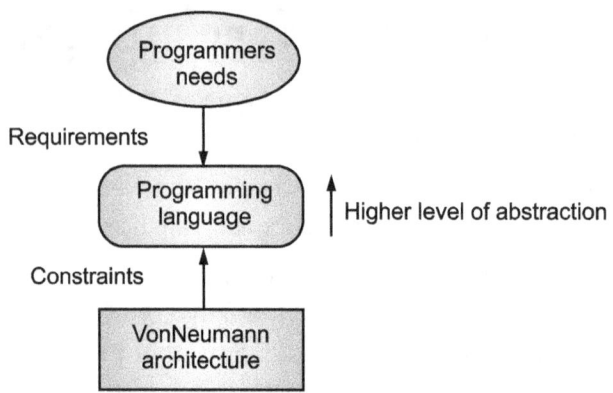

Fig. 1.3 : Requirements and constraints on a language

1.6 PROGRAMMING LANGUAGES QUALITIES

- Programming languages are used to implement the software. So qualities of programming languages directly affect the qualities of software.

- Software is called as quality software if it posses following features.

  ➢ **Reliability :** Software must be reliable, Software should work properly in different situation occur during program execution. For that it should be fault tolerant system should not affect by software or hardware failures.

  ➢ **Maintainability :** Software must be maintainable. After the delivery of software to customer, he may suggest changes in existing functionality or ask for additional functionality, he may come up with error occurs during execution. All such type of rework comes under maintenance. Many time cost of maintenance is more than cost of development. Software should be easily maintainable i.e. modifiable, easy to recover from errors.

  ➢ **Efficiency :** Software should be efficient. Efficiency of software measure in the form of time required for execution and space required for storing data. All above features i.e. requirements reliability, maintainability and efficiency can be achieved by adopting suitable methods during software developments and tools used in the software development environment.

1.7 LANGUAGES AND RELIABILITY

- **Languages and Reliability :** Programming Language, reliability is achieved through following qualities of programming languages.

  ➢ **Writability :** Program writing should be easy for programmer. Language should provide easy conventions/notation to write a program so that programmer can express their view/ logic instead of concentrating on languages details.

    High level languages like c++, JAVA are more writeable than lower level languages like assembly or machine language.

- ➢ **Readability :** Program should be readable as it is gone through multiple users, may be for testing by tester, for future modification by developer, error detection and recovery. Programming languages should have provision of comments, rules of data types declarations, rules to define new operations which enhance readability of language.

- ➢ **Simplicity :** Language should be easy to understand and learn. It should allows expressing algorithm easily. Simplicity can be achieved by minimizing the features of a language.

- ➢ **Safety :** The language should not provide feature which if used in the program, program becomes harmful. E.g. Feature like goto statements or pointer variable which cause untraceable errors in the program.

- ➢ **Robustness :** The language support robustness means program should handle data overflows, invalid input, recovery from error etc. That is such event should he trapped and messages corresponding to events should be given to users. In this way behaviour of the program becomes predictable.

1.8 LANGUAGES AND MAINTAINABILITY

- • Programs should be easily maintainable means changes should be easily adaptable, error tracking and recovery should be easy. Deletion of particular function/operation should be easy and so on. Two features that languages can provide to support modifications are factoring and locality.

  - ➢ **Factoring :** The language should allow programmer to factor related features into one single unit. If any operation is used at many places of program. Instead of writing logic/code again and again it can be factor in to a routine and replace its use by routine call. Due to this program become more readable and if any change in operation, only need to reflect change in routine.

  - ➢ **Locality :** The effect of a language feature is restricted to a small, local portion of the entire program. Otherwise, if it extends to most of the program, the task of making the change can be exceedingly complex, for e.g. in abstract data type programming, the change to a data structure defined inside a class is guaranteed not to affect rest or program.

1.9 LANGUAGES AND EFFICIENCY

- • From early days, efficiency of language affect the design of programming languages. Many languages have efficiency as a main design goal either implicitly or explicitly.

- • Traditionally speed (Time required for execution) and space (Memory required for program) are main parameter to measure efficiency but now days effort required to produce a program, maintenance effort are also the parameters for efficiency.

- Efficiency is often a combined quality of both the language and its implementation. The languages affects efficiency if it disallows certain optimization to be applied by the compiler. The implementation adversely affects efficiency if it does not take all opportunities into account in order to save space and improve speed.

For example in general, statement like.

$$X = Fun\ (y) + z\ Fun\ (y) :$$

In c cannot be optimized as

$$X\ =\ 2*\ Fun\ (y) + z;$$

- Which would be more efficient as it called function Fun (y) just once. The language feature that allows functions to modify global variables (like z) disallow optimization.

- Another example, the language can affect implementation efficiency by allowing multi-threaded concurrent computations. An implementation adversely affects efficiency if it does not reuse memory space released by the program.

1.10 A BRIEF HISTORICAL PERSPECTIVE AND EARLY HIGH LEVEL LANGUAGES

A Brief History of Programming Languages

- The first programming languages were the machine languages of the earliest computers, designed in the 1940s. Several hundred programming languages are developed since that time.

- Most languages have had a limited life span and utility, while few languages enjoyed success in one or more application domains. Many languages have played an important role in influencing the design of future languages.

- A general overview of the history of a few of the most influential programming languages is summarized as in Table 1.1. The languages, dates and paradigms characterized in Table 1.1 provide only a general overview of this history and most of the players in the design of programming languages.

Table 1.1 : A Summary of Some of the Major Programming Languages

Languages	Year	Originator	Predecessor Language	Intended Purpose
Fortan	1954	J. Backus		Numeric computation
ALGOL-60	1958	Committee	Fortran	Numeric computation
COBOL	1959	Committee		Business data processing
APL	1956	K. Iverson		Array processing
LISP	1956	J. McCarthy		Symbolic computation

Contd...

SNOBOL4	1962	R. Griswold		String processing
PL/I	1963	Committee	Fortran	General purpose
Simula-67	1967	O.J.Dahl	ALOGOL-60	Simulation purpose
ALGOL-68	1963	Committee	ALOGOL-60	General purpose
BCPL	1970	Committee	ALGOL-60	General purpose
Forth	1970	C. Moore	Fortran	General purpose
ML	1970	R. Milner	LISP	Functional programming
Bliss	1971	W. Wulf	ALGOL-68	System programming
Pascal	1971	N. Wirth	ALGOL-60	Educational purpose
Prolog	1972	A. Colmerauer		Artificial intelligence
C	1974	D. Ritchie	ALGOL-68	System programming
Mesa	1974	Xerox PARC	Pascal	System programming
SETL	1974	J. Schwartz		Very high-level programming
Concurrent Pascal	1975	P. B. Hansen	Pascal	Concurrent programming
CLU	1974	B. Liskov	Simula-67	Methodology abstraction
Euclid	1977	Committee	Pascal	Verification programming
Gypsy	1977	D. Good	Pascal	Verification programming
Modula-2	1977	N. Wirth	Pascal	Real-time programming
Ada	1979	J. Ichbiah	Pascal	Real-time programming
Fortran-77	1979	J. Backus	Fortran	Numeric computation
Icon	1980	Committee	C	General purpose
Elf	1980	Committee	Prolog	Logic programming
Miranda	1980	D. Turner	LISP	Functional programming
REBOL	1980	Committee	LISP	Functional programming
Scheme	1980	G. L. Steele	LISP	Functional programming
VAL	1980	W. Ackerman		Data-flow programming
C++	1980	B. Stroustrap	C	Object-based programming
Smalltalk	1980	A. Kay	Simula-67	Personal computing
SR	1982	G. R. Andrews	C	Concurrent programming
CLOS	1984	Committee	LISP	Object-based functional

Contd...

Common LISP	1984	Committee	LISP	Functional programming
Blue	1985	Committee	C++	Object-based programming
Eiffel	1987	B. Meyer	C++	Object-based programming
Oberon	1988	N. Wirth	Modula-2	General purpose
Haskell	1989	Yale University	LISP	Functional programming
Ada 95	1989	J. Ichbiah	Ada	Concurrent programming
HTML	1989	Committee		Web programming
Occam	1989	Inmoc Company	Ada	Distributed programming
Java	1980	Sun Microsystems	C++	Object-based programming
Visual Basic	1990	Microsoft		Windows programming
Fortran-90	1990	Committee	Fortran	Scientific computing
Linda	1991	Scientific Computing	C	Concurrent programming
C*	1991	Thinking Machine	C++	Concurrent programming
Concurrent Prolog	1992	Committee	Prolog	Concurrent logic for AI
MultiLISP	1992	Committee	LISP	Parallel functional language
Perl	1994	Committee	C++	Object-based programming
Python	1995	G. V. Rossum	C	Object-based programming
UML	1998	G. Booch	C++	Modelling language
Modula-3	1999	Committee	Modula	Concurrent programming
Ruby	2000	Y. Matsumoto	Python	Object-based scripting
Dylan	2000	Apple	C++	Object-based dynamic

- COBOL and FORTRAN have evolved greatly since their emergence in the late 1950s. These languages built a large following and have remained fairly autonomous in there evolution and influence on the design of other languages over the last 40 years.

- On the other hand, the Algol languages design has had a tremendous influence on the development of several of its successors, including Pascal, Modula, Ada, C++ and JAVA.

- In the functional programming area, Lisp was dominant in early years and continues its influence to the present dates, motivating the development of more recent languages such as scheme, ML and Haskell.

- In the logic programming area, only one language Prolog, has been the major player but Prolog enjoys little influence on the design of languages outside that area. The event-drive and concurrent programming areas are much earlier in their evolution and only a few languages are prominent. Some of these like High performance Fortran (HPF).

1.11 EARLY HIGH-LEVEL LANGUAGES

- Early day's computer hardware is with limited power. Early languages are designed considering machine; they are very much close to machine.

- High level languages in early days are designed considering both needs for expressiveness and limitation of machine power.

- Several high level languages have been designed, but few of them become popular and affected the development of new programming languages.

- Brief description of some high-level programming languages, in order of development.

  ➤ **FORTRAN (Formula Translator) :** Developed by IBM as the first high-level programming language introduced features such as symbolic expression and subprograms with parameters. Fortran can be used for scientific and engineering applications that require complex mathematical computations.

  ➤ **COBOL (Common Business-Oriented Languages) :** A highly structured languages was specifically designed for business applications and emphasized data representation. COBOL is used primarily for commercial applications that require precise and efficient manipulation of large amounts of data.

  ➤ **ALGOL (Algorithmic Languages) :** It was designed with a well defined and machine independent structure and inspired most of the subsequent theoretical work in programming languages. ALGOL-60 introduced the concept of block structure. Where by variables and procedures could be declared in a program whenever they were needed. ALGOL-68 contained additional features for parallel processing.

  ➤ **LISP (List Processing) :** It was designed for problem with irregular data structures that are well represented as lists. LISP has been used for symbolic calculations in differential and integral calculus, electrical circuit theory, mathematical logic, game playing and artificial intelligence. An extension of LISP designed for parallel processing is called MultiLISP.

  ➤ **APL (A Programming Language) :** It is geared towards array but is much higher level language than FORTRAN. APL supports numerous powerful aggregate operators that act on arrays. APL has 66 high-level operators compare with 6 in FORTRAN.

  ➤ **PL/1 (Programming Languages 1) :** It is a large language that combines many features of FORTRAN, ALGOL and COBOL. The IBM version contains parallelization primitives that allow the creation and termination of parallel tasks for parallel processing.

  ➤ **Simula :** It was developed at the Norwegian computing centre by the Royal Norwegian council for scientific and industrial research. Simula was system descriptive language, for discrete event networks and was designed to simulate situations such as queues at a supermarket, response times of emergency services, and chain reactions of nuclear reactors, developed for simulations.

➢ **SHOBOL (String Oriented Symbolic Languages) :** It was developed by david Farbar, Ralph Grisworld and Ivan polonsky at bell laboratories and was designed primarily to process string data. The successor to SHOBOL called TCon was developed by Grisworld.

➢ **Pascal :** Named after the seventeenth century mathematician and philosopher Blasic Pascal, was designed for teaching structured programming in an academic environment Pascal became the preferred introductory programming languages at most universities and has influenced nearly all recent languages, Pascal emphasizes safety with a simple input/output (I/O) mechanism and strong typing component.

➢ **C :** It is evolved from two earlier languages, BCPL (Basic combined programming language) and B. BCPL was developed in 1967 by Martin Richards as a language for writing operating systems and compilers. Ken Thompson modelled many features of his language B after their counterparts in BCPL. Both BCPL and B were type less languages, and every data item occupied one word in memory. C is developed by Dennis Ritchie at Bell Laboratories in 1972 as general-purpose language, C is commonly used for system programming. The empharis in C is on Flexibility and lack of restrictions. Its ability to access hardware makes it a better choice that other programming languages for writing operating systems.

➢ **Smalltalk :** It was designed to be a self-Contained, interactive programming language, in which programs would be characterized by a high degree of modularity and dynamic extensibility. The environment consists of windows, several of which can be on the screen at one time. Smalltalk is a pure object oriented language.

➢ **Ada :** It was developed under the sponsorship of the U.S. Department of Defence as a general-purpose programming language for numerical computations. System programming and applications with real-time and concurrency requirements. Pascal was influential as the basis of the languages, which supports both shared memory and message passing for parallel computation. Ada is the best available example of a state of the art concurrent programming language.

➢ **Modula :** Combined the block-and-type structure of Pascal with module Constructs for defining abstract data types. Modula is a general-purpose language that has enough of the underlying hardware visible to be useful in operating system design.

➢ **Prolog (Programming in Logic) :** It is a high-level languages whose heritage is logic notation and automatic theorem proving. Concurrent Prolog is a well-known parallel variant used in expert systems.

➢ **ML :** It was developed as a functional programming languages by Robin Milner at Edinburg university in the 1970s with a syntax and a mechanism for type checking similar to that of pascal-but much more flexible. In ML, the basic program is the same, as in scheme in defining and applying functions. ML has a rich set of data types, from enumeration types to records to lists. It supports higher order functions that is, functions that take functions as arguments.

➤ **C++ :** It is a popular object oriented language. Bjarne stroustrup, motivated by simula, added classes to C in a pre-processing compiler step. The success and widespread use of C, coupled with the lack of any sort of support for abstract data types in C, has prompted widespread use of C++. More important thing is that C++ provides object Oriented programming capabilities. Unlike Smalltalk, which is a pure object oriented language C++ is a hybrid language, meaning that programming can be done in a c like style, an object oriented style or both.

➤ **HTML (Hyper Text Markup Language) :** It is developed to build a web address or web page by Tim Berners –Lee in 1989 in Switzerland, It is an easy-to-understand language HIML Controls the appearance of a web page and Consists of hyper text and hypermedia. In hypertext, pointers or links area used to jump to other parts of a document or to other files or web sites. Hypermedia allows the addition of other items to text documents including images, animations and sound.

➤ **Visual Basic :** It is evolved from BASIC, which was developed in the 1960's. Development of the Microsoft windows graphical user interface (GUI) in the late 1980s and the early 1990's spurred the evolution of visual Basic by Microsoft in 1991. Visual Basic greatly simplifies windows application development and the latest version, visual Basic 6 was released in 1998.

➤ **Java :** It is emerged as the name of a C and C++ based language when a group of sun microsystems programming language designers visited a local coffee shop. Sun formally announced Java at a major conference in 1995 ant it generated immediate in the business community.

1.12 BIRD'S EYE VIEW OF PROGRAMMING LANGUAGES CONCEPTS

• In this section we look at the kinds of facilities that a programming language must support and the different ways that languages go about providing these facilities.

1.12.1 A Simple Program

• As programmer we try to convert requirements into executable code of lines. Program should be simple. It should clear about what to do and how it does it. Our motivation in this subject is to learn about the concepts and structure of programming languages. We are interested in the kinds of things one can do with programming languages rather than the specifics of a given program. What are the inherent capabilities and shortcomings of different programming languages ? What makes one languages fundamentally different from another, and what makes one language similar to another, despite apparent difference?

- Consider simple C++ program to add two integers using add( ) function and display addition in main ( ).

```
# include < iostream.h>
using namespace std ;                                    }   Part 1 : organization


    // Function prototypes (declaration)
    int add ( int, int);                                 }   Part 2 : environment
    int main ( )
    {
        int num1, num2, Sum;
        cout<< "Enter two numbers to add :";             }   Part 3 : Computation
        cin >> num1 >> num2;
    // Function call
    Sum = add (num1, num2)
    cout << "Addition of number is ="<< Sum;
    return 0 ;
    }
    // Function definition
    int add (int a, int b)
    {
    int result ;
    result = a + b;                                          Part 3 : Computation
    return result ;
    }
```

- Program is divided into three parts. First part consist of one header file include and name space; the second part consist of function prototype declarations and third part contains main function code and user defined function add ( ) definition.

- First part defines the organization of the program. It contains various files that constitute the program.

- The second part defines the environment in which the program will work by declaring some entities that will be used by the program in this file.

- The third part deals with the actual computation. This is the part we most often associate with a program. It contains the program's data and algorithms. Some of the data and processing in this part may use the entities defined in the environment established in the second part.

1.12.2 Syntax and Semantics

- Any programming language specifies a set of rules to write valid programs in that language. For example, in the above program of addition, we see that many lines are terminated by a semicolon.

- We see that there are some special characters used, such as "{" and "}". We see that function is followed by a parenthesized expression. The syntax rules of the language state how to form expressions, statements, and programs that look right. The semantic rules of the language tell us how to build meaningful expressions, statements, and programs. For example, they might tell us that before using the variable request in the add function, we must declare that variable. They also tell us that, the declaration of a variable such as request causes storage to be reserved for the variable. On the other hand, the presence of the extern in the declaration of the variable num1 , num2, result indicates that the storage is reserved by some other module and not this one.

- Characters are the ultimate syntactic building blocks. Every program is formed by placing characters together in some well-defined order. The syntactic rules for forming programs are rather straightforward. The semantic building blocks and rules, on the other hand, are more complex. Indeed, most of the deep differences among the various programming languages stem from their different semantic underpinnings.

1.12.3 Semantic Elements

- In this section, we will look at some of the basic semantic concepts in programming languages. The idea is to examine these notions not from a programmer's point of view but from the language designer's point of view. We want to see what choices may be available to a language designer and how the designer's decisions affect the programmer.

1.12.3.1 Variables

- A variable is the name given to memory location.
- A value of variable can be change during program execution.
- We refer to a variable by its name.
- The syntactic rules specify how variables may be named, for example, that they may consist of alphabetic characters. But there are many semantic issues associated with variables.
- A declaration introduces a variable by giving it a name and stating some of its semantic properties.

- Among the important semantic properties are :

  ➢ **Scope :** Part of program where variable can be accessible is called as scope of that variable. For example, in the addition program, the scope of the variable result is within the add function; while num1 and num2 variable scope is within main. That is, the variable may be referred to in any part of the program from the declaration of the variable to the end of the function main. Usually, the location of the variable declaration determines the start of the scope of the variable.

  ➢ **Type :** what kinds of values may be stored in the variable and what operations may be performed on the variable? The variable num1, num2 and result all are of type int. Usually there are a number of fundamental types defined by the language and there are some facilities for the user to define new types. Languages differ both in terms of the fundamental types and in the facilities for type definition. The fundamental types of traditional languages are dictated by the types that are supported by the hardware. Typically, as in C++, the fundamental types are integer, real, character. Pascal also has boolean types. There is a large body of work on data types that deals both with the theoretical underpinnings as well as practical implications.

  ➢ **Lifetime :** when is the variable created and when is it discarded? As we said, a variable represents some region of memory which is capable of holding a value. The question is when is a memory area reserved, or allocated, for the variable? Some possibilities are : when the program starts, when the declaration is encountered at execution time, when the unit in which the declaration occurs is entered, or there could be a statement that explicitly requests the allocation of storage for the variable. Indeed, C++ has all of these kinds of variables : automatic variables are allocated when the unit in which they are declared is entered and deallocated when the unit terminates; static variables live throughout the execution of the program; some variables may be created and destroyed explicitly by the programmer using the operators new and delete.

1.12.3.2 Values and References

- Having defined some basic issues concerning variables, let us see a simple question : what is the value associated with a variable? Well, there are at least two answers to this question. Consider an assignment statement of the form :

$$x = y;$$

- The value referred to by the name y is of a different kind from that referred to by the name x. We have defined a variable as a region of memory. On the right hand side of this assignment statement, we need the contents of that memory and on the left hand side we need the address of, or a reference to, that region. To enable us to refer to both of these kinds of values, we define two notions: an l-value is a value that refers to a memory location, and therefore, may be used on the left hand side of an assignment statement; an r-value is a value that refers to the contents of a memory location, that is, a value that may be used on the right-hand side of an assignment statement. Referring to the assignment statement above, we need an r-value for y and an l-value for x.

- In most languages, the conversions from l-values to r-values are implicit. Some languages, such as C++, also have explicit operators to do the conversions when necessary. For example, the & operator in C++ is the address-of operator, which obtains the l-value of its operand. Therefore,

$$x = \&y;$$

- Stores the address of y into x. The & is necessary because the default rule is that on the right-hand side, the r-value is used. Some contexts require a particular type of value. For example, the left-hand side of an assignment statement requires an l-value. Therefore :

$$3 = y; //error, left-hand side requires l-value$$

is an error because literals in C++ do not have l-values. Instead,

$$y = 3; is legal since the literal 3 is an r-value.$$

1.12.3.3 Expressions

- Expressions are syntactic constructs that allow the programmer to combine values and operations to compute new values.

- The language specifies syntactic as well as semantic rules for building expressions. Depending on the language, an expression may be constrained to produce a value of only one type or of different types at different times.

- In the program of addition, we see several expressions of different types. For example, result = num1+num2, is an expression of type arithmetic. For example, in C or C++, an assignment statement produces a value and therefore is also an expression and may be used as a constituent of another expression.

  Consider :

$$a = b = c + d;$$

- which assigns (first) to b the value of the expression c+d and then assigns the same value to a. The language Pascal does not allow an assignment statement to be used as part of an expression.

- As seen from this example, the order in which operations are performed in an expression may influence the value of the expression.

- Some languages specify the order strictly, for example right-to-left, and others leave it to the implementer to decide the order. Leaving such issues to the implementation requires the programmer to be more careful because a program that produces the correct result may not necessarily do so when compiled with a different compiler.

- The major semantic issue surrounding expressions is the allowable kinds of expressions. Specifically, does the language support expressions that produce only r-values or can expressions also result in l-values.

1.12.3.4 Program Organization

- Programs that implement software systems and applications consist of thousands, hundreds of thousands, or even millions of lines of code. These lines together implement a particular system design that consists of many inter related components, or modules.
- A programming language can provide mechanisms to help the programmer in managing this complexity. To some degree, the structure of the design may be reflected in the structure of the program. As we mentioned, this is straightforward whenever the design method and the programming language paradigm match.
- As an example, a program in C/C++ consists of a number of files. By convention, a programmer may implement each design module in one file. Even more, some files may contain modules that are more generally available, referred to as libraries. In the example of addition program includes a file called iostream.h, which provides the declarations to use the standard input output library provided by C/C++.
- The language does not have any particular facilities for supporting input-output. Instead, a collection of routines make up a library that support input-output operations.
- Programs that want to use input/output include iostream.h. The other file included by the program is called namespace std; contains information, such as type definitions, that are shared by different modules of the program.
- Being able to break a program into a number of independent parts has many advantages. First, if the parts are independent, they may be implemented and validated by different people. Program debugging and maintenance is also simplified because changes may be isolated to independent modules.
- Second, it is more practical to store the program in several files rather than one big file. The ability to compile separate parts of the program is important in writing large applications.
- In C/C++, the inclusion of files imposes an ordering relationship among the modules of a program. The main program includes some files which may in turn include other files and so on.
- Obviously, the included files must be written before the files that include them. This relationship imposes a hierarchy among the files that constitute the program. There are files that need no other files. These are at the lowest level of the hierarchy—level 0.
- At the next level are files that only include files from level 0. This file inclusion facility support the direct implementation of hierarchical designs. Finally, if C++ is chosen, the language provides support both to procedural and object-oriented programming.
- The program structure can therefore match a design method based on both decomposition into abstract operations and hierarchies of abstract data types. Similar considerations hold for Ada. Whereas the correspondence between design modules and program files in C/C++ is rather loose and by convention, in Ada this correspondence is emphasized.

- Each module has a specification and an implementation. Once the specification of a module is written, other modules that use this module may be written and compiled. This approach reduces the dependence among programmers in that more work may be done in parallel.

- Ada also supports the concept of a library where module specifications are stored. The language requires that interfaces across independently compiled modules must be checked to ensure that the called and the calling modules agree. On the other hand, the FORTRAN language also supports independently developed (procedural) modules but does not require type checking across such modules.

- The program organization facilities provided by a programming language are dependent on the goals of the language. If the language is intended for writing small programs, for example for the writing of mathematical algorithms to be run on a calculator, such facilities are not crucial.

- If on the other hand, the language is to be used to develop very large programs, these facilities are indispensable. Most modern languages today support at least the notion of a module for breaking up a large program into several independent parts. Where the languages differ is in the way the different modules have access to each other's internal entities and in the types of entities that may be imported from other modules. They also differ in the treatment of modules, e.g. whether they can be instantiated, whether they can be separately compiled, etc.

1.12.3.5 Program Data and Algorithms

- Programming languages provide facilities for implementing algorithms. The algorithms operate on some data to produce some results. This is where programming languages differ the most from each other.

- The majority of programming languages, including C++, are imperative. As we can see in addition program, the main program consists of some variable declarations and some statements that operate on these variables. There are also input-output statements. The execution of statements modifies the values stored in the memory of the underlying machine; i.e., it modifies the state of the computation. We will deal with these in the next section. For now let us look at the issues relating to data and computation.

Data

- There are many issues surrounding the idea of data. Look at the simple variable num1 declared in our example program. It has a type, which in this case is int. It tells us what kinds of values it may hold. Where can such a variable declaration occur in a program? Only at the beginning of a program or anywhere? When is the variable created? Does it have an initial value? Is it known to other procedures or modules of the program? How can variables be exported to other modules? Given some elementary data items such as variables, are there mechanisms to combine them? For example, C++ provides arrays and records for building aggregate data structures. What are the kinds of components that a data structure may contain? Can a function be an element of a record? In Pascal the answer is no and in C++ the answer is yes.

- Sophisticated mechanisms for data definition allow the programmer to modularize the data in the program similarly to the way that the algorithms are modularized. For example, in our program of addition, we use a function add to store the basic definitions concerning addition of two integer variable data that are used by all other modules. Object-oriented programming languages draw much of their power from the mechanisms to define and refine complex data items.

Computation

- We have already seen expressions as a mechanism for computing values. Expressions are usually made up of elementary values and have a simple structure. Control structures are used to structure more complicated computations. For example, mechanisms such as various kinds of loops provide for repeated executions of a sequence of statements. Routine calls allow for the execution of a computation defined elsewhere in the program. Combining expressions, statements, control structures and routine calls in C++ and other conventional languages allows the programmer to write algorithms using an imperative computation paradigm.

1.12.3.6 External Environment

- Programs are seldom self-contained implementations of algorithms. The data they need and the results they expect to compute are normally transferred to and from the program to the external environment.

- Program might need to access an external database; a device driver program might need to acquire the value of a particular signal. How do programs communicate with the external environment?

- Some languages define specific constructs for input/output. Other languages, such as C/C++, do not provide such facilities. Instead, they rely on libraries external to the language to provide such facilities. For example, iostream.h is the header file that allows the input/output library to become accessible by the program of addition, allows the program to interact with the user.

- The same happens for accessing an external database. The advantage of language-supported facilities for communication with the external environment is that the programmer has a complete model of the environment and the compiler can do consistency checking.

- Supporting the facilities in a library makes the language simpler and allows more flexibility. For example, different libraries may be added as new devices, such as graphical ones, become available.

1.13 SYNTAX AND SEMANTICS

- Programming languages are act as a intermediate languages between computer and human being. As computer understand only binary i.e. 'o' or '1'. For representing English written algorithms in the form of programming languages.

- It provides various notations. A programming language has two major components. Syntax and Semantics.

- The syntax is a set of formal rules that specify the composition of programs from letters, digits and other characters. For e.g. the syntax rules may specify that each open parenthesis must match a closed parenthesis in arithmetic expressions, and that any two statements must be separated by a semicolon.

- The semantic rules specify "the meaning" of any syntactically valid program written in the language.

  ➤ **Languages Definition :** When you read a program, how do you know if it is well formed? How do you known what it means? How does a compiler know how to translate the program? Any programming language must be defined in enough detail to enable, these kinds of issues to be resolved.

- Language definition should enable a person or a computer program to determine whether a program is in fact valid and if the program is valid what its meaning or effect is. In general two aspects of a languages must be defined syntax and semantics.

1.13.1 Syntax

- Syntax is a set of rules that define the form of a languages. They define how sentences may be formed as sequences of basic constituents called words. Using this rules we can tell whether a sentence is valid or not.

- The syntax does not tell us anything about meaning of the sentence, the semantic rules tell us that.

- As an example, C keywords like if, else, for , do, while etc. identifiers, numbers, operators, etc. are words of the language. The C syntax tells us how to combine such words to construct well formed statements and program.

- Words are not elementary. They are constructed out of characters belonging to an alphabet. Thus the syntax of a language is defined by two sets of rules : lexical rules and syntactic rules.

- Lexical rules specify the set of characters belonging to an alphabet of the language and the way such characters can be combined to form valid words. For example. Pascal consider lower case and uppercase characters to be identical but c and Ada consider them to be distinct. Thus according to the lexical rules, "Memory" and "memory" refer to the same variable in pascal, but to distinct variable in C and Ada. The lexical rules also tell us that < > (or ≠) is a valid operator in pascal but not in C, where the same operator is represented by !=..

- The distinction between syntactic and lexical rules is somewhat arbitrary, They both contribute to the "external" appearance of the languages.

- Defining the syntax for language is nothing but way to define an infinite set using a finite description.

Syntactic Elements of a Languages

- Syntactic style of a language is set by the choice of the various basic syntactic elements most widely use element description is given as below :

  ➢ **Character Set :** Choice of character set is one of the first to be made in designing a language syntax. There are several widely used character sets, such as the ASCII set, each containing a different set of special characters in addition to the basic letters and digits.

  ➢ **Identifiers :** The basic syntax for identifiers a string of letters and digits beginning with a letter is widely accepted.

  ➢ **Operator Symbols :** Most languages use the special characters + and – to represent the two basic arithmetic operations, but beyond that these is almost no uniformity.

  ➢ Primitive operations may be represented entirely by special characters as is done in APL. Alternatively identifiers may be used for all primitives, as in the LISP, PLUS, TIMES and so on.

  ➢ **Keywords and Reserved Words :** A keywords are an identifier used as fixed reserved words of the syntax of statements. Example. 'if' used for conditional statement in 'C', for beginning a C iteration statement.

    Syntactic analysis during translation is made easier by using reserved words.

  ➢ **Noise Words :** Noise words are optional words that are inserted in statements to improve readability. COBOL provides many such options. For example, in the goto statement, written GOTO label. The keyword Go is required, but to is optional; it carries no information and is used only to improve readability.

  ➢ **Comments :** Comments in a program is an important part of its documentation. A languages may allow comments in several ways.

    Delimited by special markers, such as the c /* and */ with no concern for line boundaries.

    Beginning anywhere on a line but terminated by the end of line as the ---- in Ada, // in C++ or ! in FORTRAN go.

    Comments make program more readable and user friendly.

  ➢ **Blank (Spaces) :** Different languages interpret blank space differently. In 'C' blanks are not significant anywhere except in literal character string data. Other languages use blanks as separators so that they play an important syntactic role.

> ➤ **Delimiters and Brackets :** Delimiter is a syntactic element used simply to mark beginning or end of some syntactic unit such as a statement or expression. Example, Brackets are paired delimiters.
>
>   Delimiters serve the important purpose of removing ambiguities by explicitly defining   the boundaries of a particular syntactic constructs.
>
> ➤ **Statements :** Statements are the most prominent syntactic component in imperative languages. Using this syntactic elements languages create their syntax styles.
>
>   **Example :** Fortran was defined by simply stating some rules in English. ALGOL 60 was defined with a context free grammar developed by John Backus. This method known as Backus-Naur form or BNF. BNF provides a compact and clear definition for the syntax of programming languages.

- Extended version of BNF is (EBNF). EBNF is a meta language that is used to describe, other languages. EBNF described First, and then it can be used to describe the syntax of a simple languages.

Example :

(a) Syntax Rules

```
< program > : : = { < statement > * }
<statement > : : = < assignment > | < conditional > | < loop>
< assignment > : : = < identifier > = < expry>;
<conditional > : : = if < expr > { < statement > + } |
if <expr > { <Statement > + } else {<statement > + }
< loop>  : : = while <expr> {< statement > + }
<expr > : : = < identifier > | < number > | (<expr>) | <expr>
<operator > <expr>
```

(b) Lexical Rules

```
<operator > : : = + | – | * | /| ≠ | < | > |  ≤ | ≥
< identifier > :  : = < letter > < id > *
< id > :  : = < letter > | < digit >
< number > : : = < deigit > +
< letter > : : = a  |  b | c | ... | z
< digit > :  : = 0 | 1 | .... | 9
```

- Syntactic description of a language has two primary uses. It helps the programmer know how to write a syntactically correct program.

> ➢ **Abstract Syntax :** The abstract syntax of a language is a formal device for identifying the essential syntactic elements in a program without describing how they are concretely constructed. Language constructs in different programming languages have the same conceptual structure but differ in their appearance at the lexical level.

Example : The following pascal and C/C++ looping statements.

Pascal	C/C++
while i<n do begin	while (i < n) {
i : = i + 1	i = i + 1;
end	}

- This two loops are designed to accomplish the same result their syntactic differences are nonessential to the fundamental looping process that they represent.

> ➢ **Concrete Syntax :** When two constructs differ only at the lexical level we say that they follow the same abstract syntax but differ at the concrete syntax level. That is they have the same abstract structure and differ only in lower level details.

- Although conceptually concrete syntax may be irrelevant, pragmatically it may affect usability of the language and readability of programs for example the symbol $\neq$ is more readables than != .

- while statements and the branches of conditionals to be bracketed by { and }. Other languages, such as c or pascal allow brackets to be omitted in the case of single statements.

For example in c one may write

  while (x ! = y)

  x = y + 1;

- Pragmatically, however this may be error prone, If one more statement needs to be inserted in the loop body, one also needs to add brackets to group the statements constituting the body.

1.13.2 Semantics

- Syntax define well formed programs of a language. Semantics defines the meaning of syntactically correct programs in that language. For Example the semantics of C helps us to determine that the declaration.

  int array [20]

- Causes space for 20 integer elements to be reserved for a variable named array.

- Another example, the semantics of C states that the instruction.

```
if (a > b)
max = a ;
else
max = b;
```

- Means that the expression a > b must be evaluated and, depending on its value one of the two assignment statement is executed.
- So syntax rules tell us how to form this statement. For example, where to put a " ; " and the semantic rules tell us what the effect of statement is.
- All systemically correct programs may not have a meaning. Thus semantics also separates meaningful programs from merely syntactically correct ones.
- In many cases, semantic rules of syntactically correct programs can be verified before a programs execution; they are called static semantics, as opposed to dynamic semantics, which describes the effect of executing the different constructs of the programming language. In such cases programs can be executed only if they are correct with respect to both to syntax and to static semantics.

1.14 AN INTRODUCTION TO FORMAL SEMANTICS

- **Languages :** Languages is act as intermediater between computer and user of the computer. We seen in detail history of programming languages, its feature and application domain.

  We also seen basic classification of programming language i.e. low level /machine languages and higher level languages. In this section we are going to study processing aspect of languages. Means how the languages get processes by computer.

- **Language Processing :** Machine languages are designed on the basis of speed of execution, cost of realization and flexibility in building new software.

  High languages are designed on the basic of user friendliness, ease of writing program, ease of maintenance of S/W and reliability of programming.

  It is main issue that how a higher-level language eventually can be executed on a computer whose machine language is very different and at a much lower level.

  There are two important choices for an execution of program i.e. interpretation and translation.

- **Interpretation :** In this type of execution of program, action implied by the constructs of the languages are executed directly. For each specific action there exist a subprogram written in machine language which execute the action directly. Program is executed line by line, It is more faster than other executions methods.

- Interpreter is a program that repeatedly executes the following sequence.
  - ➢ Get the next statement
  - ➢ Determine the actions to be executed
  - ➢ Perform the actions.

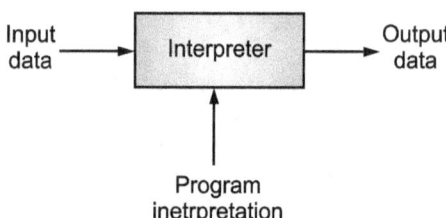

Fig. 1.4 : Interpreter

- **Translation :** In this type of execution of program, high level language program are translated into an equivalent machine language version through several steps.

  The general term translator denote any language processor that accepts program in some source language as input and produces functionally equivalent programs in another object language as output several specialized translator have particular names like compiler, linker and loader respectively.

  In some cases, the machine on which the translation is performed (host machine) is different from the machine that is to run the translated code (the target machine). This kind of translation is called cross-translation.

  A program may be translated into an intermediate code that is then interpreted.

  Several specialized types of translator are as below :

- **Assembler :** It is a translator which take assembly language program as source program and translates' into machine code.

- **Compiler :** It is a translator whose source language is a high level language and whose object language is close to the machine language of an actual computer, either being an assembly language or some variety of machine language. For example, C program is first complied into an assembly language which is then converted into machine language by an assembler.

- **Loader or Link Editor :** It is a translator whose object language is actual machine code and whose source language is almost identical; it consist of machine language programs in relocatable form. It actually link subprogram and library functions in sequence to become truly executable.

- For example, subprogram A might be compiled for addresses 0 to 999, and subprogram B might be, complied to use address 0 to 1999. In addition these subprograms may use library functions that are defined for addresses 0 to 4,999. Loader's function is to create a single executable program whose addresses are compatible. As shown in below table.

Subprogram	Complied Address	Executable Addresses
A	0-999	0-999
B	0-1,999	1000-2,999
Library	0-4,999	3,000-7,999

The executable program is now look as single program using addresses from 0 to 7,999.

- **Macro-Processing :** It is a special kind of translation that may occur as the first step in translation of a program. Through macro-processing, macro names in a text are replaced by the corresponding bodies. In C one can write macros which are handled by a pre-processor, which generates source C code through macro expansion.

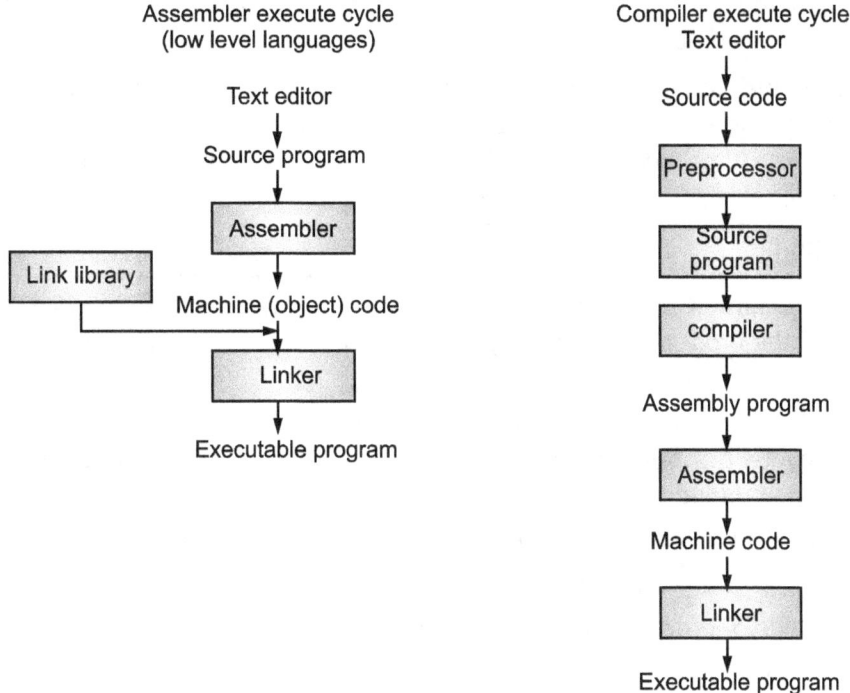

Fig. 1.5: Assembler and compiler execute cycle

1.15 THE CONCEPT OF BINDING

- Program contains different entities, like variables, routines and statements, Each entity have certain properties called attributes. For example, a variable has a name, a type, a storage area where its value is stored. Function has name, return type, formal parameters of certain type, parameter passing convention. A statement has associated actions. The values of attributes must be set before they can be used. Setting the value of an attribute is known as binding. For each entity, attribute information in contained in a repository called a descriptor.

- Some attributes may be bound at language definition time others at language implementation time, other at program translation time (or compile time) and other at program execution time (or run time). Binding can occur at three specific times which give them their names.

  ➢ **Compile Time Binding :** It also known as static binding and sometimes referred to as early bindings. It occurs when the program is translated into machine languages. Name and type binding take place at compile time when declarations are encountered by the compiler and cannot be changed later.

  ➢ **Load-Time Binding :** It occurs when the machine code generated by the compiler is being stored to memory locations. Location binding occurs at load time. At this time, all the hypothetical address used by the compiler, are actually bound to physical locations in the computer.

  ➢ **Run Time Binding :** It also known as dynamic binding and sometimes referred to as late bindings, occurs when the program is being executed. Value binding occurs at run time. Run time decisions are the choices made during the execution of the program. For example, when a value is equal to zero.

1.16 VARIABLE

- Variable is name given to memory location. In program various data objects are defined and named by the programmer explicitly. A simple variable is an elementary data object with a name.

- Memory location consisting of elementary cells. Each of which is identified by an address. The content of cell is an encoded representation of a value. A value at memory cell can be read and modified during program execution.

  Formally, a variable is a 5-tuple < name, scope, type, l-value, r-value> where

- Name is a string of character used by program statements to denote the variable.

- Scope is the range of program instructions over which the name is known.

- Type is the variables type

- l-value is the memory location associated with the variable

- r-value is the encoded value stored in the variable's location.

1.17 VARIABLE, NAME AND SCOPE

- Name of the variable is come under declaration part of program. Different programming languages have different rules for declaring variable. Depending on data types of value hold by variable, convention of variable names are different.

- The scope of a variable is the range of program instructions over which the name is known. Program instructions can use or modify a variable through its name within its scope.

Consider program in 'C'

```
# include <stadio.h >
main ( )
{
    int a , b, c,
    Printf ("n enter value of a & b);
    Scanf (" %d %d", & a,&b);
    C = a + b;
    Printf ("%d",c);
}
}
```

- In this program, scope of variable a, b, c, is within the main, It called as local variable of main. Global variable scope is outside the main also. It is declared before main.

1.18 TYPE

- Depending on type of value hold by variable its type is declared. For example, if we want integer data object type of variable will be integer if we want character data object variable will be declared under character (char) data type.

- When the language is defined, certain type names are bound to certain classes of values and set of operations. For example type integer and its associated operator are bound to their mathematical terms.

- In some languages the programmer can define new types by means of type declarations. For example in Pascal one can write.

- type vector = array [1 ...10] to integer. This declaration establishes a binding at translation time between the type name vector and its implementation.

- Most languages, including FORTRAN, COBOL, Pascal, C, C++ Modula-2 and Ada, bind variables to their type at compile time and the binding can not be changed during execution. This is called static typing. In these languages, the binding between a variable and its type is specified by variable declaration, For example, In Pascal one can write.

```
    Var x, y, : integer ;
    C : character;
```

- By declaring variables to belong to a given type, variables are automatically protected from the application of illegal (or nonsensical) operations.

- In the example, the compiler can detect the occurrence of illegal assignments like.

```
    x : = C;
    y : = not y ;
```

1.18.1 Type Checking

- It is the process a translator goes through to verify that all constructs in a program are valid for the types of its constants, variables, functions and other entities.

  Consider following statements in c languages

$$Y = x * 10 + z ;$$
$$\text{Addition } (Y, x + z)$$

- x must be of a type that permits multiplication by an integer, (x * 10). Similarly, the types of the actual parameters for the call to function Addition must be checked for compatibility with the types of the formal parameters.

- Type checking by the translator can help to detect and prevent errors.

- Type checking can occur at compile time, at run time, or not at all.

- The type checking process involves the application of a type, equivalence test that consists of rules for determining whether two types are the same; it is used to detect and prevent execution errors.

- **Compile Time Checking :** The type can be checked at compile time. It can be viewed as static type checking in which type information is maintained and checked at compile time.

- **Translation Time :** This type of checking is easy to implement and inexpensive in memory and run time.

- **Run-Time Checking :** The types can be checked at run time, which means that type checking must be performed every time a data object is accessed. It can be viewed as dynamic type checking, in which type information is maintained and checked at run time.

- This method of checking can be expensive in memory use and run time because a check must be performed every time a data object is referenced and type indicator must be part of every data value.

- A language is said to be strongly typed language if all feasible type checking is performed at compile time and all other type checking is done at run time.

- **l-Value :** l-value is the memory location associated with the variable. Storage area/memory location bound to the variable during execution. The lifetime or extent, of a variable is the period of time in which such binding exists.

- The action that acquires a storage area for a variable and thus establishes the binding between the variable and its l-values called memory allocation.

- The lifetime extends from the point of allocation to the point in which the allocated storage is reclaimed. In some languages, for some kinds of variables, allocation is performed before run time and storage is only reclaimed upon termination (Static allocation). In other languages it is performed at run time (dynamic allocation)

- **R-Value :** R-value is the encoded value stored in the variable location. The encoded representation is interpreted according to the variable's type. For example, a certain sequence of bits stored at a certain location would be interpreted as an integer number. if the variables type is int; it would be interpreted as a string, if the type is an array of characters. Consider x = y in C. The variable appearing at the left-hand side of the assignment denotes a location (i.e. the variables l-value). The variable appearing at the right-hand side of the assignment denotes the contents of location (i.e. the variables r- value)

- The binding between a variable and the value held in its storage area is dynamic, the binding is established by an assignment operation. An assignment such as b=a; cause a's r-value to be copied into the storage area referred to by b's l-value. That is b's r-value changes.

- Functional and logic programming languages beat variables as their mathematical counterparts. They can bound to a value by the evaluation process but once the binding is established it cannot be changed during the variables life time.

- Some conventional languages, however, allow the binding between a variable and its value to be frozen once it is established. The resulting entity is in every respect a userdefined symbolic constant. For example is C one can write.

- Constant float pi = 3.1415 (The variable pi is bound to the value 3.1415 and its value cannot be changed.

1.19 REFERENCES AND UNNAMED VARIABLES

- Some languages allow variables that can be accessed through the r-value of another variable. Such an r-value is called a reference (or a pointer) to the variable. Variables that are accessed via pointers may even be unnamed variable is through some other named variable.

- The only way to access an unnamed variable is through some other named variable. In general an object can be made accessible via a chain of references (called an access path). Reference variable provide alternative name to previously defined variable.

Example of Reference variable in c++ :

int a = 50;

int &b = a;

cout<<a;

cout<<b;

- Here variable a and b are holding same value. If we print the value of a and b it gives 50. Syntax '&' telling the compiler that 'b' is a reference variable.

> ➢ **Unnamed variable** is an anonymous variable given no name. Anonymous variables in C++ have "expression scope", meaning that they are destroyed at the end of the expression in which they are created. Consequently, they must be used immediately.

Example of unnamed variable in c++ :

```
#include <iostream.h>
int add(int x, int y)
{
   return x + y;
}
 int main()
{
  std : :cout << add(5, 3);
   return 0;
}
```

- When the expression x + y is evaluated, the result is placed in an anonymous, unnamed variable. A copy of the anonymous variable is then returned to the caller by value.

1.20 ROUTINES

- Program is composed of a number of units called routines. Here routine term is general without committing to any specific featured offered by an individual language. Assembly language subprograms,FORTRAN subroutines, Pascal and Ada procedure and functions and C functions are well-known examples of routines.

- In the programming languages world, routines usually come in two forms, Procedure and functions. Functions return a value; procedure do not. Some languages example c and C++ only provides functions but procedure are easily obtained as function returning the null type void. Example of a C function definition.

- Like variables, routines have a name, scope type l-value and r-value. A routine name is introduced in a program by a routine declaration. Usually the scope of the name extends from the declaration point to some closing construct which is determined either statically dynamically, depending on language. Example in C function declaration extends the scope of the function till the end of the file in which declaration occurs.

- Routine activation is achieved through a routine invocation i.e. routine call. Since routine is activated by call, the routine's scope.

- Besides having their own scope, routine also define a scope for the declarations that are nested in them. Such local declarations are only visible within the routine. Depending on the scope rules of the language routines. Routines can also refer to nonlocal items (e.g. variables) other than those declared locally.

- Non local items that are visible to every unit in the program area called Global items. The header of the routines define the routines name its parameter types, and the type of the returned value .

1.21 GENERIC ROUTINES

- Routines factor a code fragment that is executed at different points of the program in a single place and assign it a name. The fragment is then executed through invocation and customized through parameters. However, similar routines must be written several times. Because they differ in some detail that cannot be factored through parameters. For example, if program needs a routine to sort both arrays of integers and arrays of strings, two different routines must be written, one for each parameter types.

- Generic routines, as offered by some programming languages, provide a solution to this problem. A generic routine can be made parametric with respect to a type.

- A generic routine is a template from which the specific routine is generated through instantiation, an operation that binds generic parameters to actual parameter at compile time. Such binding can be obtained via macro-processing, which generates a new instance for each type parameter.

E.G. generic swap routine in C ++

int i , j;

swap (i, j);

//will instantiate an integer swap routine.

float f, g;

swap (f, g);

//will instantiate a float swap routine.

Template <class t> ;

void swap (T & A, T & B)

//* function is generic with respect to type T: a,b refer to same locations as the actual parameter */

Swap

{

T temp = a;

a = b ;

b = temp

}

1.22 ALIASING AND OVERLOADING

- In program variable and function/routines are denoted by some names. The languages uses special operator names such as + or - to denote certain predefined operations, so far we have assumed that at each point in a program a name denotes exactly one entity, based on the scope rules of the languages.

- Since names are used to identify the corresponding entity, the assumption of unique binding between a name and an entity would make the identification unambiguous. This restriction, however, almost never holds for existing programming languages.

For example in C

int i, j, k;

float a, b, c;

- -

i = j + k;

a = b + c;

- In this example, the operator + in the two instructions of the program denotes two different entities. In first expression, it denotes integer addition in the second, it denotes floating point addition.

- Although the name of the operator is the same in the two expression, the binding between the operator and corresponding operation is different in the two cases, and the exact binding can be established at compile time, since the types of the operands allow for the disambiguation.

- We can generalize the previous example by introducing the concept of overloading. Consider another example, if the second instruction of the previous example is changed to

a = b + c+ b ( );

- The two occurrences of name b would (unambiguously) denote, respectively, variable b and routine b with no parameters and returning a float value. Similarly, in C++, if another routine named b with one int parameter and recurring a float value is visible.

a = b ( ) + c + b (i);

would unambiguously denote two calls to the two different routines.

- Aliasing is the opposite of overloading. Two names are aliases if they denote the same entity at the same program point. This concept is especially relevant in the case of variables. Two alised variables share the same data object in the same referencing environment. Thus modification of the object under one name would make the effect visible, may be unexpectedly under the other.

Example : Aliasing by the 'C'

```
int x = 0 ;
int *i = &x ;
int *j = &x;
```

- If a new value is assigned to *i eg. * i = 10 the change is also visible by dereferencing j and as a new value of x.

1.23 AN ABSTRACT SEMANTIC PROCESSOR

- To illustrate the operational semantics of programming languages we initiate a simple abstract processor called as SIMPLESEM.

- SIMPLESEM consists of an instruction pointer, a memory, and a processor.

- The instruction pointer is a reference to the instruction currently being executed.

- The memory is where the instructions to be executed and the data to be manipulated are stored.

- For straightforwardness, we will assume that these two parts are stored into two separate memory sections: the code memory (C) and the data memory (D). Both C's and D's initial address is 0 (zero), and both programs and data are assumed to be stored from the initial address.

- The instruction pointer (IP) is always used to point to a location in C; it is initialized to 0. We use the notation D[X] and C[X] to denote the values stored in the X-th cell of D and C, respectively. Thus X is an l_value and D[X] is the corresponding r_value.

- Modification of the value stored in a cell is performed by instruction set, with two parameters: the address of the cell whose contents is to be set, and the expression evaluating the new value.

- For example, the effect on the data memory of instruction set 10, D[20] is to assign the value stored at location 20 into location 10.

- Input/output in SIMPLESEM is achieved quite simply by using the set instruction and referring to the special registers read and write, which provide for communication of the SIMPLESEM machine with the outside world.

- For example, set 15, read means that the value read from the input device is to be stored at location 15; set write, D[50] means that the value stored at location 50 is to be transferred to the output device.

- We are quite tolerant in the way we allow values to be combined in expressions.

- For example, D[15]+D[33]*D[41] would be a an acceptable expression, and set 99, D[15]+D[33]*D[41] would be an acceptable instruction to modify the contents of location 99.

- IP is SIMPLESEM's instruction pointer, which is initialized to zero at each new execution and automatically updated as each instruction is executed.
- The machine operates by executing the following steps repeatedly, until it encounters a special halt instruction:
  - ➢ Get the current instruction to be executed i.e, C[IP].
  - ➢ Increment IP.
  - ➢ Execute the current instruction.
- Some programming language instructions might modify the normal sequential control flow, and this must be reflected by SIMPLESEM. In particular, we introduce the following two instructions: jump and jumpt.
- The former represents an unconditional jump to a certain instruction. For example, jump 47 forces the instruction stored at address 47 of C to be the next instruction to be executed that is, it sets IP to 47.
- The second represents a conditional jump, which occurs if an expression evaluates to true. For example, in: jumpt 47, D[5] > D[10] the jump occurs only if the value stored in cell 5 is greater than the value stored in cell 10.
- SIMPLESEM allows indirect addressing. For example: set D[10], D[20] assigns the value stored at location 20 into the cell whose address is the value stored at location 10. Thus, if value 30 is stored at location 10, the instruction modifies the contents of location 30. Indirection is also possible for jumps.
- For example: jump D[13] jumps to the instruction stored at location 88 of C, if 88 is the value stored at location 13.

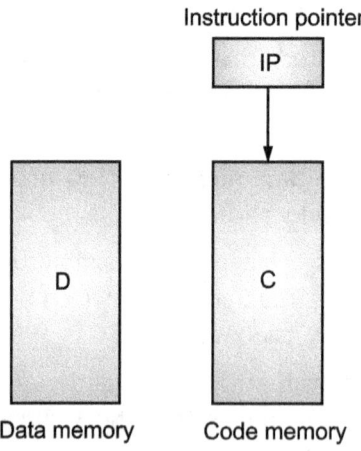

Fig. 1.6 : SIMPLESEM machine

- Above Fig. 1.6 shows SIMPLESEM machine which is quite simple. It is easy to understand how it works and what the effects of executing its instructions are.In other terms, we can assume that its semantics is intuitively known; it does not require further explanations that refer to other, more basic concepts.

- The semantics of programming languages can therefore be described by rules that specify how each construct of the language is translated into a sequence of SIMPLESEM instructions.

1.24 RUNTIME STRUCTURE

Run Time Structure

In this section, we will move through a hierarchy of languages that are based on variants of the C programing language. They are named Case 1 through Case 5.

- Languages can be classified in several categories according to their execution-time structure.

Static Languages :

- In static languages all the needed memory can be allocated before program execution.
- Clearly, these languages cannot allow recursion, because recursion would require an arbitrary number of unit instances and thus memory requirements could not be determined before execution.
- Languages Case 1, Case 2, and its variant Case 2', all of which fall under the category of static languages.

Stack-Based Languages :

- This class is more demanding in terms of memory requirements, which cannot be computed at compile time. However, their memory usage is predictable and follows a last-in-first-out discipline: the latest allocated activation record is the next one to be deallocated.
- It is therefore possible to manage SIMPLESEM's D store as a stack to model the execution time behavior of this class of languages. Notice that an implementation of these languages need not use a stack deallocation of discarded activation. Records can be avoided if store can be viewed as unbounded.
- In other terms, the stack is part of the semantic model. We provide for the language; strictly speaking, it is not part of the semantics of the language.
- Languages Case 3 and Case 4, which fall under the category of stack-based languages.

Fully Dynamic Languages:

- These languages have un random memory usage i.e, data are dynamically allocated only when they are needed during execution.
- The problem then becomes how to manage memory efficiently. In particular, how can unused memory be recognized and reallocated, if needed.
- To indicate that store D is not handled according to a predefined policy like a FIFO policy for a stack memory, the term "heap" is traditionally used. This class of languages is illustrated by language Case 5.

1.25 CASE STUDY ON RUNTIME STRUCTURE OF C

Case 1 : A Language with Only Simple Statements

- A very simple programming language called as Case 1, which can be seen as a lexical variant of a subset of C, where we only have simple types and simple statements there are no functions.

- Assume that the only data manipulated by the language are those whose memory requirements are known statically, such as integer and floating point values, fixed-size arrays, and structures.

- The entire program consists of a main routine i. e. main ( ), which encloses a set of data declarations and a set of statements that manipulate these data.

- For straightforwardness, input/output is performed by invoking the operations get and print to read and write values, respectively.

- A Case 1 program is shown below and its straightforward SIMPLESEM representation before the execution starts .

- The D portion shows the activation record of the main program, which contains space for all variables that appear in the program.

- The C portion shows the SIMPLESEM code.

- A Case 1 program is as follows:

```
main( )
{
    int i, j;
    get (i, j);
    while (i != j)
    if (i > j)
    i -= j;
    else
    j -= i;
    print (i);
}
```

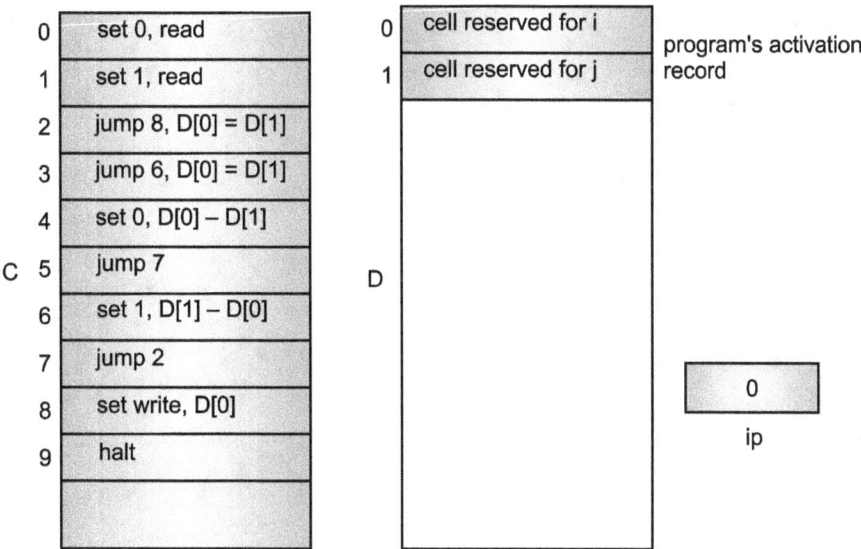

Fig. 1.7 : Initial state of the SIMPLESEM machine
for the Case 1 program in above program

Case 2 : Adding Simple Routines

- By adding a new feature to Case 1 The resulting language Case 2 allows routions to be defined in a program and allows routines to declare their own local data.

- A Case 2 program consists of a sequence of the following items:

  ➢ A set of data declarations global data

  ➢ A set of routine definitions and or declarations

  ➢ A main routine i.e main ( ), which contains its local data declarations and a set of statements, that are automatically activated when the execution starts. The main routine cannot be called by other routines.

- Following program shows example of a Case 2 program, whose main routine gets called initially, and causes routines beta and alpha to be called in a sequence.

```
int i = 1, j = 2, k = 3;
alpha ( )
{
    int i = 4, l = 5;
    ...
    i+=k+l;
    ...
};
```

```
beta ( )
{
    int k = 6;

    ...

    i=j+k;
    alpha ( );

    ...

};
main ( )
{

    ...

    beta ( );

    ...

}
```

- Following Fig. 1.8 shows the state of the SIMPLESEM machine after instruction i += k + l of routine alpha has been executed.

- The first location of each activation record is reserved for the return pointer. Starting at location 1, space is reserved for the local variables.

- In general, for an instance of unit A, the return pointer will contain the address of the instruction that should be executed after unit A terminates. This does not apply to main, which does not return to a caller.

- On real computers, main is called by the operating system, and after termination main must return control to the operating system. Also notice that we maintain an activation record to keep global data at the low address end of store D.

- Case 2 the main program and its routines are compiled in one monolithic step. It may be convenient instead to allow the various units to be compiled independently. This is illustrated by a variant of Case 2 which allows program units to be put into separate files, and each file to be separately compiled in an arbitrary order.

- The file which contains the main program may also contain global data declarations, which may then be imported by other separately compiled units, which consist of single routines.

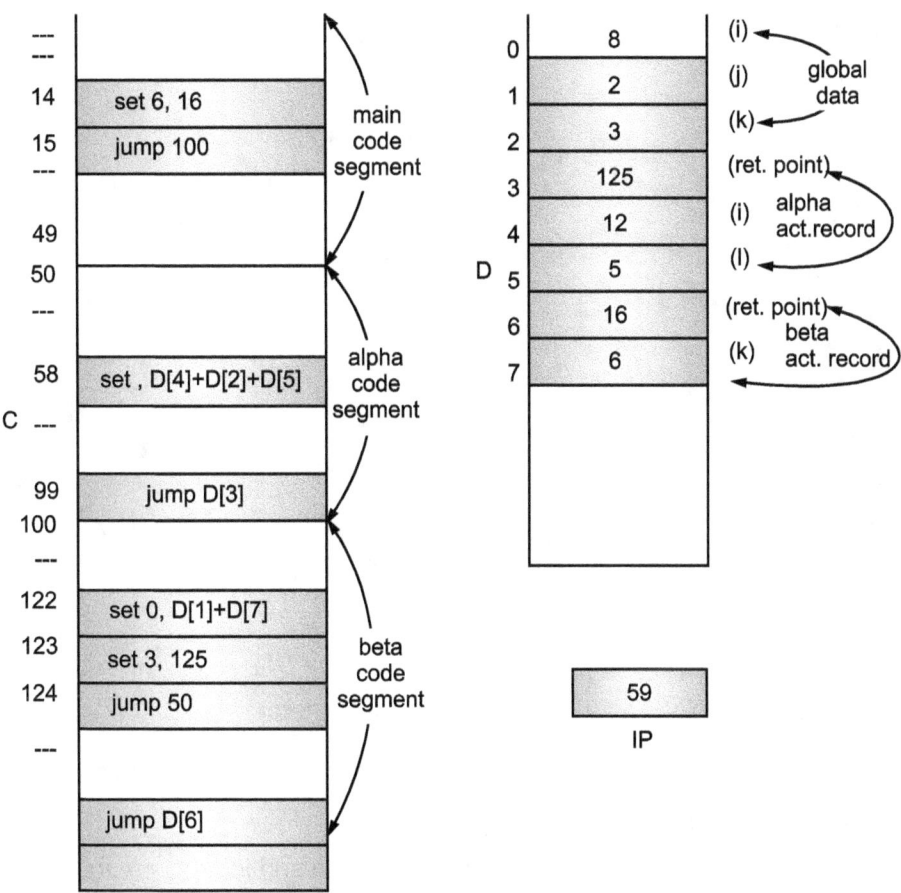

Fig. 1.8 : State of the SIMPLESEM executing the program Case 2

- If any of such routines needs to access some globally defined data, it must define them as external. Following program shows the same example of Fig. 1.8, using separate compilation.

```
file 1
int i = 1, j = 2, k = 3;
extern beta ( );
main ( )
{
    beta ( );

    . . .

}
    . . .
```

```
file 2
extern int k;
alpha ( )
{
}
. . .


file 3
extern int i, j;
extern alpha ( );
beta ( )
{
}
. . .
alpha ( );
. . .
```

Case 3 : Supporting Recursive Functions

- Let us add two new features to Case 2: direct recursion and indirect recursion..

- These extensions define a new language Case 3, which is illustrated in following Fig. 1.9 through an example.

```
int n;
int fact ( )
{
        int loc;
        if (n > 1)
        {
            loc = n--;
            return loc * fact ( );
        }
        else
```

```
        return 1;
}
main ( )
{

        get (n);
        if (n >= 0)
            print (fact ( ));
        else
            print ("input error");
}
```

A Case 3 Example :

- Let us first analyze the effect of the introduction of recursion. Although each unit's activation record has a known and fixed size, in Case 3 it is not known how many instances of any unit will be needed during execution.

- As an example, for the program shown above, at a given point of execution two activations are generated for function fact if the read value of n is greater than or equal to two.

- All different activations have the same code segment, since the code does not change from one activation to another, but they need different activation records, storing the different values of the local environment.

- As for Case 2, the compiler can bind each variable to its offset in the corresponding activation record. However, as opposed to Case 2, it is not possible to perform the further binding step which transforms it into an absolute address of the D store until execution time.

- An activation record is allocated by the invoking function for each new invocation, and each new allocation establishes a new binding with the corresponding code segment to form a new activation of the invoked function.

- Consequently, the final binding step which adds the offset of a variable–known statically–to the starting address called base address of the activation record–known dynamically–can only be performed at execution time.

- To make this possible, we will use the cell at address zero in D to store the base address of the activation record of the currently executing unit. Following Fig. 1.9 provides an intuitive view of SIMPLESEM's D store.

- Activation records are allocated one on top of the previous, and the allocated memory grows from the upper part of the store downwards.

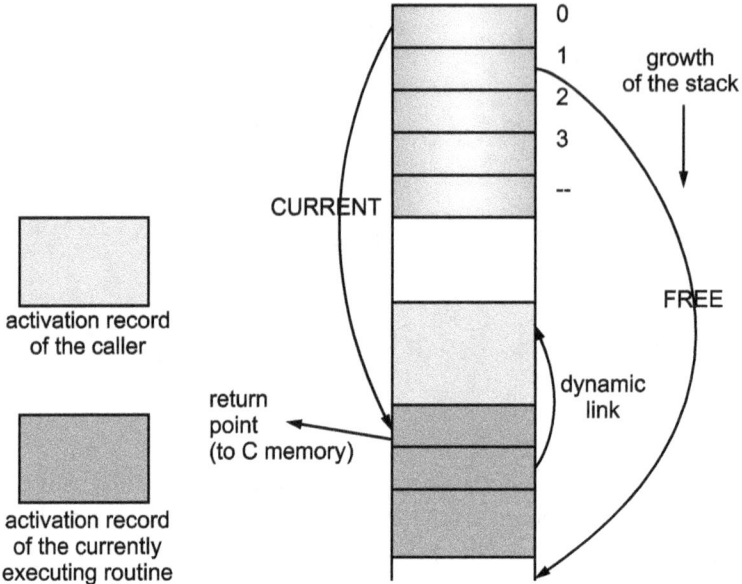

Fig. 1.9 : Structure of the SIMPLESEM D memory implementing a stack

- As recursive routines are the main additional features of Case 3, we now show how the semantics of routine call and return are specified in terms of SIMPLESEM instructions.

Case 4 : Supporting Block Structure

- The structuring facilities offered by Case 3 allow programs to be defined as a sequence of global declarations of data and routines. Routines may call themselves in a recursive fashion.

- The family Case 4 contains two members: Case 4' and Case 4".

- Case 4' allows local declarations to appear within any compound statement.

- Case 4" supports the ability to nest a routine definition within another.

- Conventionally, the new features offered by Case 4' and Case 4'' are collectively called *block structure.*

- Block structure is used to control the scope of variables, to define their lifetime, and to divide the program into smaller units. Any two blocks in the program may be either disjoint i.e.they have no portion in common or nested i.e. one block completely encloses the other.

Nesting via Compound Statements

- In Case 4', blocks have the following form of compound statement, which can appear wherever a statement can appear:

{<declaration_list>; <statement_list>}

- It is easy to realize that such compound statements follow the aforementioned rule of blocks: they are either disjoint or they are nested.

- A compound statement defines the scope of its locally declared variables: such variables are visible within the compound, including any compound statement nested in it, provided the same name is not redeclared.

- An inner declaration masks an external declaration for the same name. Following program shows an example of a Case 4' function having nested compound statements. Function f has local declarations for x, y, and w, whose scope extends from //1 to the entire function body, with the following exceptions:

- x is redeclared in //2. From that declaration until the end of the while statement the outer x is not visible;

- y is redeclared in //3. From that declaration until the end of the while statement, the outer y is not visible;

- w is redeclared in //4. From that declaration until the end of the if statement, the outer declaration is not visible.

- Similarly, //2 declares variables x and z, whose visibility extends from the declaration until the end of the statement, with one exception. Since x is redeclared in //4, the outer x is masked by the inner x, which extends from the dec laration until the end of the if statement.

```
int f( );{              //block 1
int x, y,w;             //1
while (...)
{                       //block 2
int x, z;               //2

. . .

while (. . .)
{                       //block 3
int y;                  //3

. . .

}                       //end block 3
if (. . .)
{                       //block 4
int x, w;               //4

. . .
```

}	//end block 3
}	//end block 2
if (. . .)	
{	//block 5
int a, b, c, d;	//5
. . .	
}	//end block 5
}	//end block 1

An Example of Nested Blocks in Case 4'

- A compound statement also defines the lifetime of locally declared data. Memory space is bound to a variable x as the block in which it is declared is entered during execution.
- The binding is removed when the block is exited. A block structure can be described by *static nesting tree* (SNT), which shows how blocks are nested into one another. Each node of a SNT describes a block; descendants of a node N which represents a certain block denote the blocks that are immediately nested within the block.
- For example, the above program is described by the static nesting tree of following Fig. 1.10.

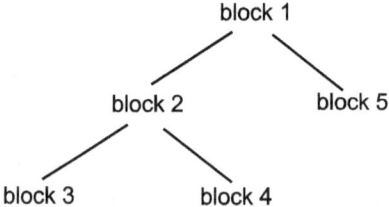

Fig. 1.10 : Static nesting tree for the block structure of above program

Nesting via Locally Declared Routines:

- As we mentioned, block structure may result from the ability to nest compound statements within unnested routines, to nest routine definitions within routines or both.
- C and C++ only support the nesting of compound statements within routines. Pascal and Modula-2 allow routine nesting, but do not support nesting of compound statements. Ada allows both.

f1 ( )	
{	//block 1
int t, u;	// 1
f2 ( )	
{	//block 2

```
int x, w;                //2
f3 ()
{                        //block 3
int y, w, t;             //3
...
}                        //end block 3
x = y + t + w + z;
}                        //end block 2
...
}                        //end block 1
main ();
{                        //block 4
int z, t;
...
}                        //end block 4
```

A Case 4 Example :

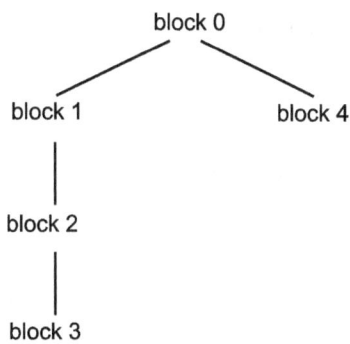

Fig. 1.11 : Static nesting tree

Case 5 : Towards More Dynamic Behaviors

- The mapping of variables to storage within the activation record can be performed at compile time i.e. each variable is bound to its offset statically.

Activation Records whose Size Becomes Known at Unit Activation

- Let us first begin language Case 5', by relaxing the assumption that the size of all variables is known at compile time. Such is the case for dynamic arrays that is, arrays whose bounds become known at execution time, when the unit in which the array is declared is activated.

- For example, in the Ada programming language, it is possible to define the following type:

  type VECTOR is array (INTEGER range <>); --defines arrays with unconstrained index and declare the following variables:

  A: VECTOR (1. .N);

  B: VECTOR (1. .M); --N and M must be bound to some integer value when these two declarations are processed at execution time

- The abstract implementation that defines the semantics for this case is rather straightforward. At translation time, storage can be reserved in the activation record for the descriptors of the dynamic arrays.

- The descriptor includes one cell in which we store a pointer to the storage area for the dynamic array and one cell for each of the lower and upper bounds of each array dimension.

- As the number of dimensions of the array is known at translation time, the size of the descriptor is known statically. All accesses to a dynamic array are translated as indirect references through the pointer in the descriptor, whose offset is determined statically.

- At run time, the activation record is allocated in several stages.

  ➢ The storage required for data whose size is known statically and for descriptors of dynamic arrays are allocated.

  ➢ When the declaration of a dynamic array is encountered, the dimension entries in the descriptors are entered, the actual size of the array is evaluated, and the activation record is extended to include space for the variable.

  ➢ The pointer in the descriptor is set to point to the area just allocated.

Fully Dynamic Data Allocation

- Now let us consider another language variation, called Case 5", in which data can be allocated explicitly, through an executable allocation instruction.

- In most existing languages, this is achieved by defining pointers to data, and by providing statements that allocate such data in a fully dynamic fashion.

- For example, in C++ we can define the following type for nodes of a binary tree:

```
struct node
{
    int info;
    node* left;
```

```
    node* right:
};
```

- The following instruction, which may appear in some code fragment:

  node* n = new node; explicitly allocates a structure with the three fields info, left, and right, and makes it accessible via the pointer n.

- According to this allocation scheme, data are allocated explicitly as they are needed. We cannot allocate such data on a stack, as do automatically allocated data.

- For example, suppose that a function append_left is called to generate a new node and make its accessible through field left of node pointed by n.

- Suppose that n is visible by append_left as a nonlocal variable. If the node allocated by append_left would be allocated on the stack, it would be lost when append_left returns.

- The semantics of these dynamically allocated data, instead, is that their lifetime does not depend on the unit in which their allocation statement appears, but lasts as long as they are accessible, i.e.they are referred to by some existing pointer variables, either directly or indirectly.

EXERCISE

1. Define Software development process and list out different approaches for it.
2. Describe differences between Top-Down and Bottom-Up approach of programming.
3. Explain the differences between compilation and interpretation? What are the comparative advantages and disadvantages?
4. What does the linker do?
5. What constitutes a programming environment?
6. List the design principles of imperative languages.
7. List the benefits of modular development approach.
8. Discuss the various approaches to evaluate the expressions.
9. Explain the significances of studying the principle of programming languages?
10. Explain software design methodology.
11. List out the programming language qualities and their role to make language better.
12. Define Binding and Binding Time.
13. Take one or two languages you have used and discuss the types of expressions you can write in the language.
14. Explain concept of binding with classification.
15. Difference between static and dynamic semantics.

16. What do you understand by procedure and function? Differentiate between two with suitable example.

17. What do you understand by scope of variable? Describe along with its different type.

18. Discuss desirable features and design issues of programming languages.

19. What are the different factors that influences the evolution of programming languages?

20. Explain various syntactic elements of language with the help of examples.

21. Explain the characteristics of good programming language.

22. Explain in detail various stages of language translation.

23. Explain functional programming with small program.

24. Discuss the feature of prolog.

25. Explain reference and unnamed variables.

✠ ✠ ✠

Unit II

STRUCTURING THE DATA, COMPUTATION AND PROGRAM

2.1 STRUCTURING OF DATA

- Program is nothing but set of instruction which when executed in sequence, particular task is takes place.
- Size of program depends on number of task expected by user from software. Program may contain multiple functions.
- Functions take input data, process it and give desire outputs. This function is evaluated through a sequence of steps that produce intermediate data that are stored in program variables.
- For effective utilization of computer resources like memory, CPU etc. Structuring, organizing and computation of data in efficient manner are important. This unit gives detail study of structuring the data and mechanisms provide for combining the data and computation structure into a program.
- Programming languages organize data through the concept of type. Types are used as a way to classify data according to different categories.
- A type is defined as a set of values and a set of operations that can be used to manipulate them.
- For example type Boolean of languages such as Ada and Pascal consist of the values TRUE and FALSE; Boolean algebra defines operators NOT, AND and OR for BOOLEANS. BOOLEAN values may be created, for example, as a result of the application of relational operators ($<,\leq,>,\geq,=,\neq$) among INTEGER expressions.

2.2 BUILT – IN TYPES AND PRIMITIVE TYPES

2.2.1 Built in Types

- Programming language is equipped with a finite set of built in types, also referred as predefined types. It's reflecting the behavior of the underlying hardware.
- The built in types of a programming language reflect the different views provided by typical hardware.
- Examples of built in types are :
  - ➢ **Booleans:** i.e. Truth values TRUE and FALSE, along with the set of operations defined by Boolean algebra.
  - ➢ **Characters:** The set of ASCII characters.

➢ **Integers :** The set of 16 bit values in the range <−32768, 32767>

➢ **Reals :** Floating point numbers with given size and precision.

Advantages of using Built in Types in a Programming Language :

• Hiding of the underlying representation help to achieve programming style and modifiability.

• Correct use of variables can be checked at translation time.

• Resolution of overloaded operators can be done at translation time

• Accuracy control

2.2.2 Primitive Type (Elementary Type)

• These types of data type are not built from other types. Their values are atomic and cannot be decomposed into simpler constituents. In most cases, built in types coincide with primitive types.

• It is also possible to declare new types that are elementary. An example is given by enumeration types in Pascal, c or Ada.

Example :

in pascal

type color = (white, yellow, blue, red, green, black);

in Ada same example as

type color is (white, yellow, blue, red, green, black);

similarly in c

enum color {white, yellow, blue, red, green, black};

• In above three examples, new constants are introduced for a new type. The constants are ordered, i.e. White<yellow<blue<red<green<black.

2.3 DATA AGGREGATES AND TYPE CONSTRUCTORS

• Programming languages allow the programmer to specify aggregations of elementary data objects and recursively aggregations of aggregates; it is also called as Composite Data Types. They do so by providing a number of constructors. Such constructed objects are called Compound Objects.

Example: Array which aggregates of homogenous type elements. Each single component from aggregates can be accessible and we can manipulate it like compare, assign etc.

2.4 CARTESIAN PRODUCT

- The Cartesian product of two sets are obtained as A $\times$ B. suppose A = {a, b, c} B = {p, q, r}. Then A $\times$ B = {(a, p) (a, q) (a, r) (b, p) (b, q) (b, r) (c, p) (c, q) (c, r)}.

- The Cartesian product of n sets A_1, A_2, ... A_n. denoted $A_1 \times A_2 \times A_3 ..... \times A_n$, is a set whose elements are ordered n-tuples (a_1, a_2, ... a_n), where each a_k belongs to A_K.

- Programming languages view elements of a Cartesian product as composed of a number of symbolically named fields.

- Examples of Cartesian product constructors in programming languages , structures in c, c++, Algol 68, and PL/I and records in COBOL, Pascal and Ada.

Example: Structure in c & c++:

```
#include<stdio.h>
typedef struct
{
   char name [20];
   int age;
   char uni_id [10];
} person;
main( )
{
   person myName = {"Rahul", 23, "1111122222"};
   printf("person info : \n");
   printf("%s%d%s", myName.name, myName.age, myName.uin_id);
}
```

2.5 FINITE MAPPING

- A function is good example of mapping, it associating (or mapping) values of one set called domain to values in another set called range of the function.

- A finite mapping is a function from a finite set of values of a domain type DT on to values of range type RT. Such a function may be defined in programming languages using routine definitions.

- The routine definition encapsulates the rules for associating values of type RT to values of type DT. In addition, programming languages provide the array constructor to define finite mappings as data aggregates.

- Array aggregates associates (maps) every index of the array to the value stored in the element that has that index. The index range therefore is the domain of the mapping and values stored in array are range of mapping.

Example : C Declaration of array

    int number[10];

Defines a mapping from integers in the domain 0 to 9 to the set of integers.

for (i=0; i<10; i++)

number[i] = 0 ;

- Here initially all values of array are initialize by zero. Value at particular location can be accessed by index. Thus the c notation number[i] can be viewed as the application of the mapping to the argument "i". Indexing with the value that is not in the domain yields an error.

- Other programming languages like pascal require the domain type to be an ordered discrete type.

Example : Days of week is ordered discrete type.

    Type weekdays = (mon, tues, wed, thu, fri, sat, sun);

- Languages that allow variables to be initialized when they are declared may also provide a way to initialize array objects. This means that the language must provide mechanism for constructing constant values of a compound type. E.g. array in C may be initialized through a compound value as shown below.

    char digits [5] = {'a', 'b', 'c', 'd', 'e'};

Example: array of 5 characters in Ada.

    X : array (INTEGER range 2.6) of INTEGER = (0, 2, 0, 5, –33);

- Array element can in turn be an array. This allows multi-dimensional arrays to be defined.

- Example in C

    int M [5][10]

2.6 USER DEFINED TYPES AND ABSTRACT DATA TYPES

2.6.1 User Defined Data Type

- As we have seen that built in data types are provided by languages. User can define new types by using built in types. These newly created data types are called as user define data types. User can give their own names to such type. Example, structure in 'C', enumerating values, union etc.

Example : C declaration

```
typedef struct
    {
    char emp_name [20];
    integer emp_id;
    float salary;
    } employee;
```

- In above example user define data type employee is created. We can create multiple instances of employee as per our requirement like employee e_1, e_2, e_3...... ;

Advantages :

- Ability to assign a type name for user defines data structure.

- Achieve classification and protection of data.

- Unstructured data to be organized as a collection of distinct categories.

- Data to be protected from undesirable manipulations by specifying exactly which operations are legal for object.

2.6.2 Abstract Data Types

- Abstract data types is a new type for which we can define the operations to be used for manipulating instances, while data structure that implements the type is hidden to the users.

- Consider C++ language. Abstract data types can be defined in C++ through the class construct. Class is extension of structure. Class can be define as collection of similar types of object.

- It acts as template for creating same type of objects. Each object has data and operations that can be perform on data.

Example : Class in C++ (Template for car's)

```
class Car
    {
        private;
        string model-name;
        double cost;
        integer average;
        public;
        void display_Carinfo( );
    };
```

- Multiple instances of car can be created.
- Each Car have its model name, cost and average attributes are private so accessible only within class i.e. to function display_Carinfo( );
- Instance can be created by following statement

Car C1;	// instance creation
C1. display_Carinfo( )	// calling function.

2.6.3 Constructors

- A newly created object whether it is instance of a built in types or a user defined type has an initial state. As we have seen that languages often provide mechanism to initialize a variable when it is created.
- A constructor is used to do the initialization for a user defined type.
- A constructor has the same name as the new type being defined.
- A constructor is invoked automatically when an object of the class is allocated.
- There are three types of constructor in C++

    (i)   Default constructor   (ii) parameterized constructor

    (iii) Copy constructor.

- Using default constructor user can assign default values to attributes in the program only. Whenever instance of class created; default values get assigned to attributes.
- Parameterize constructor take values from user at runtime and assigned to variable.
- Copy constructor allows us to build a new object form an existing object without knowing the components of the object.

Example : Constructor in C++

```
constructor in C++
#include<iostream.h>
using namespace std;
class Marksheet
{
    public :
        int maths, science, english;
        Marksheet ( )                // Default constructor
        {
            Maths = 0 ;
            Science = 0 ;
            English = 0 ;
        }
```

```cpp
    Marksheet (int M, int S, int E) // parameterize constructor
    {
        Maths = M ;
        Science = S ;
        English = E ;
    }
    Marksheet (marksheet and m) // copy constructor
    {
        Maths = m.maths ;
        Science = m.science ;
        English = m.english ;
    }
    display ( )
    {
        cout << "Maths : " << maths << endl ;
        cout << "Science : " << science << endl ;
        cout << "English : " << English << endl ;
    }
};
int main ( )
{
    Marksheet m ; // default constructor get called.
    m.display ( );
    Marksheet  m1(50, 40, 45); // parameterize constructor get called.
    m1.display ( );
    Marksheet m2(m); // copy constructor get called.
    m2.display ( );
}
```

2.7 TYPE SYSTEM

- Data types are fundamental semantic components of programming languages that try to, capture the nature of the data manipulated by the programs.

- Programming languages differ in the way types are defined and behave. We define type system as the set of rules used by a language to structure and organize its collection of types.

- Operations defined for a type are the only ways of manipulating its instance objects; they protect data objects from illegal uses. Any attempt to manipulated objects with illegal operations is a type error.

2.8 STATIC VERSUS DYNAMIC PROGRAM CHECKING

- Checking the program for syntactic and semantic errors can be classified into two types on the basis of time at which checking take place, static and dynamic. Dynamic checking requires the program to be executed on sample input data.

- Type checking is the process in which translator goes through content of program to verify that all construct in a program are valid for the types of its constants, variables, functions and other entities.

- Static checking often called compile time checking. In this, type can be checked at compile time, indicating that type checking must be performed by the compiler with regard to the declaration of data objects. It can be viewed as static type checking in which type information is maintained and checked at translation time. In this sense, the type of expressions and objects are determined from the text of the program. This type of checking is easy to implement and inexpensive in memory and runtime, but it requires rather complicated and restrictive rules.

- Dynamic checking also called as runtime checking. In this, types can be checked at run time, which means that type checking must be performed every time a data object is accessed.

- Dynamic type checking can be expensive in memory use and runtime because a check must be performed every time a data object is referenced. Static checking, though preferable to dynamic checking, does not uncover all language errors. Some errors only detect themselves at runtime e.g. If div is the operator for integer division, the compiler might check the both operands are integer. However, the program would be erroneous if the value of the divisor is zero. This possibility is general, can not be checked by the compiler.

2.9 STRONG TYPING AND TYPE CHECKING

- The goal of a type system is to prevent the writing of type unsafe program as much as possible.

- A type system is said to be strong if it guarantees type safety, i.e. if programs written by following the restrictions of the type system are guaranteed not to generate type errors.

- A language with a strong type system is said to be a strongly typed language.

- If a language is strongly typed, the compiler can guarantee the absence of type errors from programs.

- A type system is said to be weak if it is not strong. Similarly, a weakly typed language is a language that is not strongly typed.

2.10 TYPE COMPATIBILITY

- Type system verifies the types of operands while doing an operation. If an operation expects an operand of a type 'T', it may be invoked legally only with a parameter of type 'T'.

- Languages however, often allow more flexibility by defining conditions under which an operand of another type say Q, is also acceptable without violating type safety. In such a case, we say that the language defines whether, in the context of a given operation, type Q is compatible with type T.

- Type compatibility is also sometimes called conformance or equivalence. When compatibility is defined precisely by the type system, a type checking procedure can verify that all operations are always invoked correctly, i.e. the types of the operands are compatible with the types expected by the operations.

- To examine the effect of different type compatibility rules consider the sample program written in a hypothetical programming language.

- The strict conformance rule where a type name is only compatible with itself is called name compatibility. Under name compatibility, in the above example, instruction (2) is type correct, since a and x have the same type name.

- Instruction (1) contains a type error, because a and b have different types. Similarly, instructions (3) and (4) contain type errors. In (3) the function is called with an argument of incompatible type; in (4) the value returned by the function is assigned to a variable of an incompatible type.

- Structural compatibility is another possible conformance rule that languages may adopt. Type T1 is structurally compatible with type T2 if they have the same structure.

```
struct s1{
int y;
int w;
};
```

```
struct s2{
int y;
int w;
};
struct s3 {
int y;
};
s3 func (s1 z)
{
. . .
};
. . .
s1 a, x;
s2 b;
s3 c;
int d;
. . .
a = b; --(1)
x = a; --(2)
c = func (b); --(3)
d = func (a); --(4)
```

2.11 TYPE CONVERSION

- Operators involved in the evaluation of expression require one or more than one operand. Type conversion deals with two different data types in the evaluation of an expression.
- Consider example Z = X + Y;
- The right operand of the assignment operator "=" is the expression X + Y that assign a value to the left operand Z as the result of the execution. Now consider the operands Z and X is of type real and Y to be of type integer.
- Because many integers have an equivalent real representation, converting the integer operand Y to a real of equivalent value may be possible to obtain the real value for Z. In other words, in some situations two different types may be combined in certain ways to form a type that still may be correct. Type of this form called Compatible Types.

Consider example

```
void main ( )
{
    int Z, X;
    float Y;
    X = 10; Y = 2.5;
    Z = X + Y;
    printf ("%d", Z);
}
```

- In this example variable X is converted to float and the type of the result of X + Y is real. Then real value is converted to a integer and assigned to Z.

- In contrast, in a more strongly typed language like Modula 2 real and integers cannot be mixed in arithmetic expressions and reals cannot be assigned to integers, so the above statement would generate a type error.

```
    Z = TRUNC (FLOAT(X) + 2.5);
```

- The original Fortran type system rejected expression like X + I and 2 * 3.15 because one operand is an integer and the other is a real (I represents an integer variable in fortran). Most programming languages beat the expression 2 * 3.15 as if it were 2.0 * 3.15, which is the product of two real numbers. This process is called coercion, meaning that the integer 2 is coerced to a real number before the multiplication is performed.

- Converting data types may be done either implicity or explicity.

Implicitly Data Type Conversion :

- Programming languages that allow implict data type conversion provide a list of all pairs of types for which data type conversion is permitted.

- Example, In pascal Y : = X is allowed where X is of type int and Y is of type real. It's mean that integer value X converted to real to stored in Y.

- The assignment statement is not valid in Modula-2, but in Modula-2, the integer and cardial types are compatible, Thus X :=Y is of correct type if X is type CARDIAL and Y is type INTEGER.

- In C mixed types are permitted. For instance, the assignment statement X = Y + 2.5; In this y is converted to real and real value y + 2.5 truncated to an integer.

Explicit Data Type Conversion :

- When specific functions are called to perform the conversion from one type to other, the data type conversion is explicit. For example, in Ada, the function FLOAT can convert any type of data to an equivalent type float. Such conversions are normally permitted between numeric data types. Examples include trunc and round in pascal and TRUNC and FLOAT in Modula-2.

- Another kind of explicit type conversion is with a cast, meaning that a value or an object of one type can be converted to an equivalent value of another type.

Example :

```
int a;
float b = 3.5;
a = (int) b;
truncates the real value 3.5 to 3.
```

2.12 TYPES AND SUBTYPES

- Types are used to categories the data. In programming language, type is defined as a set of values with an associated set of operations.
- A subtype can be defined to be a subset of those values and the same operations.
- If ST is subtype of T, T is also called as ST's (i.e. super type or parent type). Operations defined for T are automatically inherited by ST.
- A language supporting subtypes must define the following :
  - ➢ A way to define subsets of a given type.
  - ➢ Compatibility rules between a subtype and its super type.
- Pascal was the first programming language to introduce the concept of subtypes as a subrange of any discrete ordinal type. (i.e. integers, Boolean, character, enumerations, or subranges). For example, in pascal one may define subtypes of integer type as below.

```
Type natural = 0...... maxint;
        Digit = 0...... 9;
        Small= –9...... 9;
```

- Ada provides an explicit construct for, and richer notation of, subtype than pascal. A subtype of an array type can constrain its index.

Example :

```
TYPE digit is array (integer range 1.......50) of integer;
    SUBTYPE A is integer range 1.........10;
```

- Ada subtype do not define new types. All values of all subtype of a certain type ST are of type T.

2.13 GENERIC TYPES

- In a low-level programming language you cannot process a variable without specify its type, conversely high-level programming laguages like python does. How we can facilitate this circumstance.

- Using generic types might be the best way to do. Very easy to understand, you just need to know a few new keywords, take a look :

```
#include <iostream>
using namespace std;
template<typename T>
class Adder{
public :
   T add(T first, T second);
};


template<typename T> T Adder<T> : :add(T first, T second){
   return first + second;
}


int main(int argc, char **argv){
   Adder<int> adder;
   cout<<adder.add(5, 7)<<endl;
   system("pause");
   return 0;
}
```

- As you see there is template keyword before declaration of class Adder. It indicates to compilers that class need a type parameter to be existing.

- When you create an instance object of this class with giving an int as a type name, all T marks replaces with int keyword. This is main point. After compilation, there won't be any difference between writing this and two separate class for float and integer data types.

- This technique is to read source code clearly. Now, machine accepts coding without type declaration, not as done securely and easily in python but more fast. You can also write class keyword instead of typename.

```
template<class T>
class Adder{
public :
   T add(T first, T second);
};
...
```

2.14 MONOMORPHIC VERSUS POLYMORPHIC TYPE SYSTEMS

- A simple strong type system can be provided by a statically typed language where every program entity (constant, variable, routine) has a specific type, defined by a declaration, and every operation requires that an operand of exactly the type that appears in the operation definition can be provided. For such a language, it is possible to verify at compile time that any occurrence of that constant, variable, or routine is type correct. Such a type system is called monomorphic (from ancient Greek, "single shape") : every object belongs to one and only one type.

- By contrast, in a polymorphic ("multiple shape") programming languages every constant and every variable can belong to more than one type. Routines (e.g., functions) can accept as a formal parameter actual parameters of more than one type. By examining closely traditional programming languages like C, Pascal, or Ada, however, we have seen in the previous sesions that all deviate from strict monomorphism in one way or another.

- Since polymorphic features creep in most–if not all–existing languages, a distinction between monomorphic and polymorphic languages is of no practical use. All practical languages have some degree of polymorphism. Consequently, the important questions to answer are: Can different kinds (or degrees) of polymorphism be identified? How far can we go with polymorphism, and yet retain strong typing?

- Understanding the possible different forms. Polymorphism can help us appreciate the sometimes profound semantic differences among them. Moreover, it will help us organize concepts like coercion, subtyping, and overloading, which were examined in previous sections separately, into a coherent conceptual framework.

- A first distinction is between universal polymorphism and ad-hoc polymorphism. Ad-hoc polymorphism does not really add to the semantics of a mono morphic language.

- Ad-hoc polymorphic functions work on a finite and often small set of types and may behave differently for each type. Universal poly morphism characterizes functions that work uniformly for an infinite set of types, all of which have some common structure. Whereas an ad-hoc poly-morphic function can be viewed as a syntactic abbreviation for a small set of different monomorphic functions, a universal polymorphic function executes the same code for arguments of all admissible types.

- The two major kinds of ad-hoc polymorphism are overloading and coercion.

2.15 CASE STUDY: THE TYPE STRUCTURE OF C++ AND JAVA

- C++ provides various data types and each data type is represented differently within the computer's memory.
- The various data types provided by C++ are built-in data types, derived data types and user-defined data types as shown in Fig. 2.1.

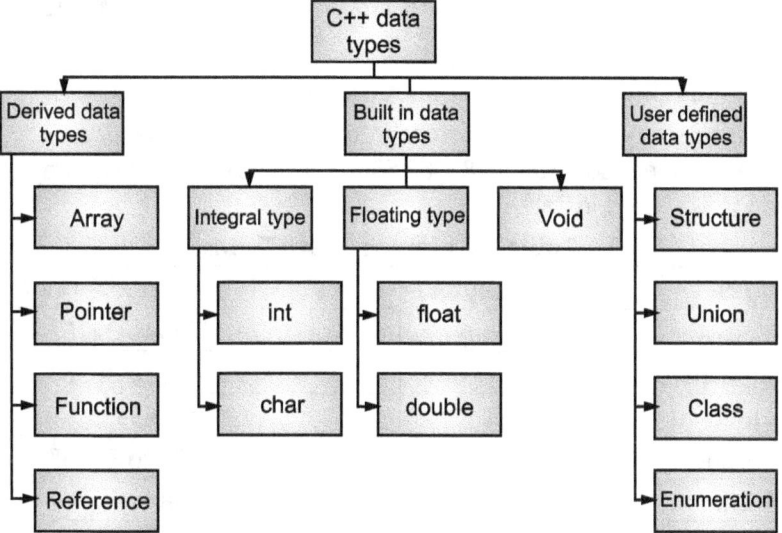

Fig. 2.1 : Classification of data types in C++

2.15.1 Built-in Data Types

- The basic data types provided by c++ are integral, floating point and void data type. Among these data types, the integral and floating-point data types can be preceded by several type modifiers. These modifiers are the keywords that alter either size or range or both of the data types.
- The various modifiers are short, long, signed and unsigned.
- By default the modifier is signed. In addition to these basic data types, ANSI C++ has introduced two more data types . bool and wchar_t.

2.15.2 Integral Data Type

- The integral data type is used to store integers and includes char (character) and int (integer) data types.
- **Char :** Characters refer to the alphabet, numbers and other characters (such as {, @, #, etc.) defined in the ASCII character set.
- In C++, the char data type is also treated as an integer data type as the characters are internally stored as integers that range in value from -128 to 127.
- The char data type occupies 1 byte of memory (that is, it holds only one character at a time).

- The modifiers that can precede char are signed and unsigned. The various character data types with their size and range are listed in Table

Table 2.1 : Character Data Types

Type	Size (in bytes)	Range
char	1	– 128 to 127
signed char	1	– 128 to 127
unsigned	1	0 to 255

- **Int :** Numbers without the fractional part represent integer data.
- In C++, the int data type is used to store integers such as 4, 42, 5233, -32, -745. Thus, it cannot store numbers such as 4.28, -62.533. The various integer data types with their size and range are listed in Table

Table 2.2 : Integer Data Types

Type	Size (in bytes)	Range
int	2	– 32768 to 32767
signed int	2	– 32768 to 32767
unsigned int	2	0 to 65535
shortint	2	– 32768 to 32767
signed short int	2	– 32768 to 32767
unsigned short in	2	– 32768 to 32767
longint	4	– 2147483648 to 2147483647
signed longint	4	– 2147483648 to 2147483647
unsigned longint	4	0 to 4294967295

2.15.3 Floating-Point Data Type

- A floating-point data type is used to store real numbers such as 3.28, 64. 755765, 8.01, -24.53. This data type includes float and double' data types. The various floating point data types with their size and range are listed in Table

Table 2.3 : Floating Point Data Types

Type	Size (in bytes)	Range	Digits of Precision
Float	4	3.4×10^{-38} to 3.4×10^{38}	7
Double	8	1.7×10^{-308} to 1.7×10^{308}	15
long double	10	3.4×10^{-4932} to 3.4×10^{4932}	18

- **Void:** The void data type is used for specifying an empty parameter list to a function and return type for a function. When void is used to specify an empty parameter list, it indicates that a function does not take any arguments and when it is used as a return type for a function, it indicates that a function does not return any value. For void, no memory is allocated and hence, it cannot store anything. As a result, void cannot be used to declare simple variables, however, it can be used to declare generic pointers.

- **Bool and wcha_t:** The bool data type can hold only Boolean values, that is; either true or false, where true represents 1 and false represents 0. It requires only one bit of storage, however, it is stored as an integer in the memory. Thus, it is also considered as an integral data type. The bool data type is most commonly used for expressing the results of logical operations performed on the data. It is also used as a return type of a function indicating the success or the failure of the function.

- In addition to char data type, C++ provides another data type wchar_t which is used to store 16- bit wide characters. Wide characters are used to hold large character sets associated with some non-English languages.

2.15.4 Derived Data Types

- Data types that are derived from the built-in data types are known as derived data types. The various derived data types provided by C++ are arrays, functions, references and pointers.

- **Array :** An array is a set of elements of the same data type that are referred to by the same name. All the elements in an array are stored at contiguous (one after another) memory locations and each element is accessed by a unique index or subscript value. The subscript value indicates the position of an element in an array.

- **Function:** A function is a self-contained program segment that carries out a specific well-defined task. In C++, every program contains one or more functions which can be invoked from other parts of a program, if required.

- **Reference:** A reference is an alternative name for a variable. That is, a reference is an alias for a variable in a program. A variable and its reference can be used interchangeably in a program as both refer to the same memory location. Hence, changes made to any of them (say, a variable) are reflected in the other (on a reference).

- **Pointer:** A pointer is a variable that can store the memory address of another variable. Pointers allow to use the memory dynamically. That is, with the help of pointers, memory can be allocated or de-allocated to the variables at run-time, thus, making a program more efficient.

2.15.5 User-Defined Data Types

- Various user-defined data types provided by C++ are structures, unions, enumerations and classes.

- **Structure, Union and Class:** Structure and union are the significant features of C language. Structure and union provide a way to group similar or dissimilar data types referred to by a single name. However, C++ has extended the concept of structure and union by incorporating some new features in these data types to support object - oriented programming.

- C++ offers a new user-defined data type known as class, which forms the basis of object-oriented programming. A class acts as a template which defines the data and functions that are included in an object of a class. Classes are declared using the keyword class. Once a class has been declared, its object can be easily created.

- **Enumeration:** An enumeration is a set of named integer constants that specify all the permissible values that can be assigned to enumeration variables. These set of permissible values are known as enumerators. For example, consider this statement.

enum country {US, UN, India, China}; // declaring an
                           // enum type

- In this statement, an enumeration data-type country (country is a tag name), consisting of enumerators US, UN and so on, is declared. Note that these enumerators represent integer values, so any arithmetic operation can be performed on them.

- By default, the first enumerator in the enumeration data type is assigned the value zero. The value of subsequent enumerators is one greater than the value of previous enumerator. Hence, the value of US is 0, value of UN is 1 and so on. However, these default integer values can be overridden by assigning values explicitly to the enumerators as shown here.

     enum country {US, UN=3, India, china} ;

- In this declaration, the value of US is 0 by default, the value of UN is 3, India is 4 and soon. Once an enum type is declared, its variables can be declared using this statement.

     country country1, country2;

- These variables country1, country2 can be assigned any of the values specified in enum declaration only. For example, consider these statements.

         country1 India; // valid

         country2 Japan; // invalid

- Though the enumerations are treated as integers internally in C++, the compiler issues a warning, if an int value is assigned to an enum type. For example, consider these statements.

                     Country1 = 3;   //warning

                     Country1 = UN;   / /valid

                     Country1 = (country) 3; / /valid

- C++ also allows creating special type of enums known as anonymous enums, that is, enums without using tag name as shown in this statement.

                 enum {US, UN=3, India, China};

- The enumerators of an anonymous enum can be used directly in the program as shown here.

                 int count = US;

2.15.6 The typedef Keyword

- C++ provides a typedef feature that allows to define new data type names for existing data types that may be built-in, derived or user-defined data types.
- Once the new name has been defined, variables can be declared using this new name. For example, consider this declaration.

typedef int integer;

- In this declaration, a new name integer is given to the data type int . This new name now can be used to declare integer variables as shown here.

integer i, j, k;

- Note that the typedef is used in a program to contribute to the development of a clearer program. Moreover, it also helps in making machine-dependent programs more portable.

2.15.7 Type Structure of JAVA

Data-Type : Java language is rich in its data types. The categories of different data-types are shown below. The two main types are Primitive and non-primitive types.

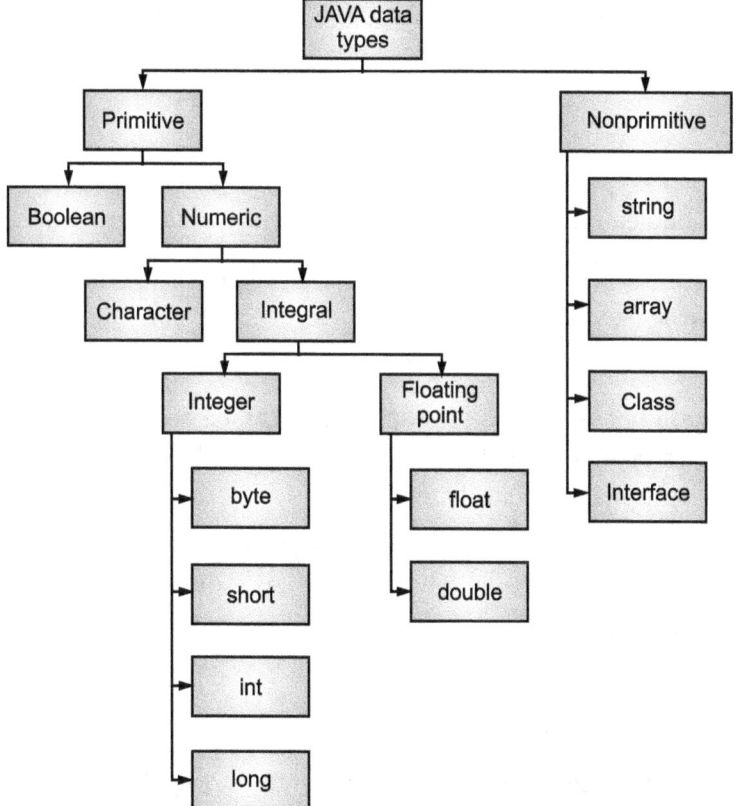

Fig. 2.2 : Classification of Data types in JAVA

2.15.7.1 Integers

Java defines 4 integer types. These include both positive and negative numbers.

byte	8 bits	byte x,y,z;
short	2 bytes	short x;
int	4 bytes	int num;
long	8 bytes	long millise;

2.15.7.2 Floating Point Numbers

- Floating point numbers are very useful when we are evaluating expressions that require fractional precisions. Java defines 2 types of floating point numbers, they are float, and double.

Float	4 bytes	float percentage;
Double	8 bytes	double distance;

2.15.7.3 Characters

- In java we store characters by using char data type. Size of character is 2 bytes.

Example :

```
char a='c';
```

2.15.7.4 Booleans

- In java we use boolean for logical values, it can represent either true or false.

Example :

```
boolean isNumber=false;
```

2.15.7.5 Arrays

- An array is a group of same kind of variables and can be accessible by a common name. In java arrays are objects. Any element in the array can be accessed by its index. Arrays can be one dimensional or multi-dimensional.

- One dimensional array is a list of same typed variables. To create an array, first you must declare an array variable of required type, the syntax is given below :

```
type variable-name[];
```

Example :

```
int account_numbers[];
```

- To allocate memory or create array object the syntax is given below :

```
variable-name = new type[size of the array];
```

Example :

```
account_numbers = new int[10];
```

- Multi dimensional arrays are arrays of arrays. To declare a multi dimensional array variable, specify each additional index using another set of square brackets. An example is given below for two dimensional array :

```
int sample[][] = new int[3][3];
```

- We can specify memory for first dimension first, and we can assign memory for second dimension later as given below :

```
int sample[][] = new int[3][];
int sample[0] = new int[2];
int sample[1] = new int[2];
int sample[2] = new int[2];
```

- The advantage of assigning memory for second dimension is your second dimension can be of any lengths, cannot be fixed length.

- **String in JAVA :** The most direct way to create a string is to write :

```
String str1 = "Hello world!";
```

- Whenever it encounters a string literal in your code, the compiler creates a String object with its value in this case, "Hello world!'.

- As with any other object, you can create String objects by using the new keyword and a constructor.

- The String class has constructors that allow you to provide the initial value of the string using different sources, such as an array of characters.

Classes in Java

- A class is a blueprint from which individual objects are created. Following is a sample of a class.

Example :

```
class Shapes
{
 Private :
  int length;
  int width;
  float radius;
  int side;
```

```
Public :
void areaRectangle()
{
}
void areaCircle()
{
}
void areaSquare()
{
}
}
```

- A class can contain any of the following variable types.

  ➢ **Local Variables :** Variables defined inside methods, constructors or blocks are called local variables. The variable will be declared and initialized within the method and the variable will be destroyed when the method has completed.

  ➢ **Instance Variables :** Instance variables are variables within a class but outside any method. These variables are initialized when the class is instantiated. Instance variables can be accessed from inside any method, constructor or blocks of that particular class.

  ➢ **Class Variables :** Class variables are variables declared within a class, outside any method, with the static keyword.

- A class can have any number of methods to access the value of various kinds of methods. In the above example, **areaRectangle(),areaCircle(),areaSquare()**are methods.

- Following are some of the important topics that need to be discussed when looking into classes of the Java Language.

Interface in JAVA :

- An interface is a reference type in Java. It is similar to class. It is a collection of abstract methods. A class implements an interface, thereby inheriting the abstract methods of the interface.

- Along with abstract methods, an interface may also contain constants, default methods, static methods, and nested types. Method bodies exist only for default methods and static methods.

- Writing an interface is similar to writing a class. But a class describes the attributes and behaviors of an object. And an interface contains behaviors that a class implements.

- Unless the class that implements the interface is abstract, all the methods of the interface need to be defined in the class.

Declaring Interfaces

- The interface keyword is used to declare an interface. Here is a simple example to declare an interface

Example :

Following is an example of an interface

```
/* File name : NameOfInterface.java */
import java.lang.*;
// Any number of import statements
public interface NameOfInterface {
   // Any number of final, static fields
   // Any number of abstract method declarations\
}
```

2.16 STRUCTURING THE COMPUTATIONS

- It is important to structure the computation part in program. Programming languages provides that structures which allow flow of controls among different components of a program.

- Basically program is nothing but set of instructions. And instructions are nothing but statements written in particular programming language.

- Statements may be expressions which play a fundamental role in all programming languages. Statements may be control flow structure like loop control type. It also contains unit level control structures like routine call and return.

- Another kind of control regime is exception handling which supports the ability to deal with anomalous situations that may arise.

2.17 EXPRESSIONS AND STATEMENTS

- Expression is combination of operands and operator. It defines how a value can be obtained by combining other values with operators. The values from which expressions are evaluated either are denoted by a literal or are the r-value of a variable.

- Operators appears in the expression denote mathematical functions. Depending on number of operands required for operations, operator are classified into unary, binary and n-ary operators.

For Example: consider unary operator in C incremental and decremental operator.

> '++' and '– –'
>
> i++ used to increase value of 'i' by 1

negation '–' can be used as a unary operator to transform positive expression into a negative value.

- Binary operator in C like '+' used to add two operand.
- Operators notation one can distinguish expression in three types infix, prefix and postfix.
- Infix notation is the most common notation for binary operators. In this operator is written between its two operands

Example :

> Infix expression : a + b.

- In postfix notation the operands appear first and are followed by the corresponding operator.
- In prefix notation, the operator appears first and the operands follow. This is conventional form of function invocation, where function name denotes the corresponding operator.

Example : postfix and prefix expression.

- Infix expression x * (y + z) Can be written in

> prefix form of given expression : *x + yz

and in postfix form as

> Postfix form of given expression : XYZ+*

- Infix notation is the most natural one to use for binary operators, since it allows programs to be written as conventional mathematical expressions.
- Programmer assign precedence and associativity by using parentheses to explicitly group sub expressions.
- In deed this is done to facilitate the programmer's task of writing expressions by reducing redundancy, but it often cause confusion and make expression less understandable.

Example :

> x * y + z%w

is interpreted implicitly as

> (x * y) + (z / w)

- In this % (division) has highest precision then *(multiplication) priority and at the end '+' (addition).

- However consider the pascal expression.

  $a = b < c$

and the C expression

  $a = = b < c$

- In pascal, operator < and = have the same precedence and the language specifies that application of operators with the same precedence proceeds left to right.

- The meaning of the above expression is that the result of the equality test (a = b), which is a Boolean value, is compared with the value of c.

- If pascal, FALSE is assumed to be less than TRUE, so expression yields TRUE only if a is not equal to b, and c is TRUE; it will be FALSE in other cases.

- In c long operator '< ' (less than) has higher precedence than "equal" (= =). Thus first b < c is evaluated. The result is then compared for equality with the value of a.

- Some languages, such as C++ and Ada, allow programmer defined operators. For example, having defined a new type set, one can define operator + for set union and for set difference.

- Programmer defined operators cause overloading, in some cases make programs easier to read and other cases make it have. Readability of program increases as user have freedom to use user define names to operator.

- Some programming language support conditional expressions, i.e. expression that are composed of sub expressions, of which only one is to be evaluated depending on value of expression.

Example :

  $(a > b) \leq a : b$

- which can be written in conventional form as below.

  if $(a > b)$

  then a

  else

  b

- for finding larger of the values of a and b, ML allows for more general conditional expressions to be written using the "case" construction.

Example :

Cases of	In the example, the value yielded
$1 \Rightarrow f_1(y)$	by the expression is $f_1(y)$ if x = 1; $f_2(y)$ if x = 2.
$2 \Rightarrow f_2(y)$	and g(y) otherwise (the value "−" denotes a catch all case not covered by
$- \Rightarrow g(y)$	any previous cases)

- Functional programming languages are based on expressions. In such languages, a program is itself an expression, defined by a function applied to operands. An assignment statement; such as x : = y + z in pascal value of y + z is computed and assigned to x. The result of the expression i.e. y + z (r value) is assigned to memory location by using the t – value OF X. Statements are executed one by one in sequence. In C, it is represented as

      Statement 1;

      Statement 2;   Sequence of

       :   execution

       :

      Statement n;

- Statements can be written inside the brackets called as compound statement. While writing routine or small unit code, or logically related statement compound statements can be used.

- In other languages such as pascal and Ada, the keywords begin and end are used instead of brackets.

- The value returned by an assignment statement is the one that is stored in the left operand of the assignment operator "=". Consider example given below.

```
int a, b, c ;
printf(" Enter the value for : a and b")
scanf("%d%d", & a, & b);
c = a + b;
if(c > 10)
{
    C = 30;
}
Else
C = 8;
```

- If you consider above example value of c is initially assigned a + b;
- But due to conditional statement value of c will be change if condition is satisfied value will be 30 if not value of a will be 8.
- In 'C' the assignment operator associates from right to left i.e. statement a = b = c = 10;
- Is interpreted as

      a = (b = (c = 10));

- Many programming languages, such as pascal require the left-hand side of an assignment operator.
- For example it can be variable name, an array element.

Example :

> (p > q) c * p : * q = 0;

- This set to zero the element pointed to by the larger of p and q.
- Sequences are simplest form of compound statements often the syntax of the language requires each statement in a sequence to be separated from the next by a semicolon.

Example :

```
begin
    statement 1;
    statement 2;
    statement n;
end
```

- Other languages instead require each statement to be terminated by a semicolon, and therefore do not need any special separator symbol.

Example in c :

```
{
    statement 1;
    statement 2;
    statement n;
}
```

2.18 CONDITIONAL EXECUTION AND ITERATION

- Programming languages provide different constructs to organize the flow of control among statements. All are explain as below.

2.18.1 Conditional Execution

- Most of the languages use "if" statement for conditional execution. Syntactically way of conditional statement are differ in different language, but meaning will be same. The syntactic appearance of a program may contribute to its readability, its ease of change and ultimately its reliability.

- Consider example of the 'if' statement as originally provided by ALGOL 60

if i = 0	if i = 0
then i : = j;	then i : = j;
	else begin i : = i + 1;
	j : = j – 1
	end

- The selection statement of ALGOL 60 raises a well – known ambiguity problem.

Example : if X > 0 then if X < 10 then X : = 0 else X = 1000. It is unclear that "else" option is part of the innermost conditional i.e. if X < 10 or the outermost conditional i.e. if X > 0. The execution of the above statement with X = 15 would assign 1000 to X under one interpretation, but leave it uncharged under the other. To eliminate ambiguity, ALGOL 60 requires an unconditional statement in the "then" branch of an "if" statement. Thus the statement must be replaced by If X > 0 then begin if X < 10 then X : = 0 else X : = 1000 end The same problem is solved in C and pascal by automatically matching an "else" branch to closet conditional without an "else". Choosing among more than two alternatives using only "if then-else" statements may lead to ambiguous constructions such as

```
        if a
            then S1
            else
            if b
                then S2
                else
                if c
                    then S3
                    else S4
                    end
        end
end
```

- To solve this syntactic inconvenience, Modula-2 has an "else-if" construct that also serves as an end bracket for the previous "if".

```
    if a
        then S1
    else if b
```

```
        then S2
    else if c
        then S3
    else S4
    end.
```

- Most languages also provides an above construct for choice selection from multiple options. For example C and C++ provides the switch case construct as shown below.

```
    Switch (operator)
    {
        case'+';
        result = operand 1 + operand 2;
        break;
        case 'x';
        result = operand 1 × operand 2;
        break;
        case '–';
        result = operand 1 – operand 2;
        case '/';
        break;
        result = operand 1 / operand 2;
        break;
        default;
        break;
    };
```

- Choice for operation will be take from user, depending on choice of operator. Control goes to that case and operation will be executed. In each case break statement is there, it take control outside the switch otherwise control will goes to next case. If user enter operator which is not in switch case control goes to default branch.

- The same example may be written in Ada as

```
Case OPERATOR is
When '+' ⇒ result : = operand 1 + operand 2;
When 'x' ⇒ result : = operand 1 × operand 2;
```

When '−' ⇒ result : = operand 1 − operand 2;

When '/' ⇒ result : = operand 1 / operand 2;

When others ⇒ null;

end case

2.18.2 Iteration

- If you want to perform same type of task for repeatedly i.e. iteratively, Iteration construct is used. Programming languages provide different types of loop construct to execute particular task iteratively.

- If number of iteration is already known before execution "for" loop is used. If number of iteration is known later word i.e. after execution "while" loop is used. In while loop depending on condition inside while iterations are set. Variation of while loop is do while statement. In this loop construct statements are executed at least once.

- Consider example of C, C++ for loop construct.

```
For (i = 0, i < 5 ; i++ )
{
    Printf("welcome");
    Printf("%d", i);
}
```

- As shown in above example welcome word is printed 5 time. Each time interation number also get printed infront oo welcome. i.e. welcome 0, welcome 1..... welcome 4.

- For loop statement divided into three parts initialization of loop, condition and increment or decrement. In above example initial value of i = 0 condition for loop execution is that i value should be less than 5 i.e. up to 4 and last part is increment of i value by 1 after every iteration.

- Pascal allows iterations where control variables can be of any ordinal type : integer, Boolean, character, enumeration, or sub ranges of them loop appears as below.

$$\text{for } i = 0 \text{ to } i < 5 \qquad \text{do statement}$$

$$\uparrow \qquad \uparrow$$

Lower bound   Upper bound

- In pascal construct has the following general form :

Repeat

Statement

Untill condition

- In a pascal "repeat" loop, the body is iterated as long as the condition evaluates to false.
- If the loop is nested within other loops it is possible to exit an inner loop and any number of enclosing loops.

```
Main_loop
    loop
    ---
    loop
    ---
        exit main_loop when A = 0;
        ---
    end loop;
    ---
    end loop main_loop;
```

- In the example, control is transferred to the statement following the end of main-loop when A is found to be equal to zero in the inner loop. The exit statement is used to effect a premature termination of loop.
- "while" loops are named after a common statement provided by languages of the Algol family. "while" loops describe any number of iterations of the loop body, including zero. They have the following general form. While condition do statement.
- Consider following pascal code describes the evaluation of greatest common divisor of two variables a and b

```
while a ≠ b do
    begin
        if a > b then
                a : = a - b
        else
                b : = b - a
    end
```

- The loop condition (a ≠ b) is evaluated before execution of the body of the loop control will come outside the loop if a is equal to b.
- In C, C++ "while" statement are similar. The general form is :

```
while (condition)
{
    statement
}
```

- Programming languages also provide variation of while loop i.e. do while loop in this case loop body executed at least one irrespective of condition written in while is true or false general form in C, C++ is

```
do
{
    statements
} while (condition);
```

2.19 ROUTINES

- Routine is generalize word. Some language called it as function, method, procedure etc.
- Routine/function used to decompose the program into smaller task/units.

Advantages of Routine :

- Routine provides reusability; if same type of operation is required in another program or in same program. Routine can be called.
- Routine provides modular approach for programming as it help to decompose program into small unit.
- Program maintainability improve as new functionality can easily add, Error can easily traceable, modification of existing content can easily possible.
- Debugging is easy as only modifiable routine can be run instead of whole functionality.
- Routine have three different parts to use it in program.
  - ➢ Deceleration of routine
  - ➢ Definition of routine
  - ➢ Calling of routine.
- **Deceleration of Routine :** Before using routine/function deceleration of it is necessary. General syntax for C, C++ is as below.
- Return type name of routine (data type P_1, data type P_2......);

Example : int addition (int a, int b);

- Consider simple program for addition routine coded in C

```
                                    # include <stdio.h>
is initialization or routine {      int addition (int a, int b);
                                    int main ( )
                                    {
                                    int x, y,x z;
```

	printf ("\nEnter the values for x & y");
Routine call	{ z = addition (x, y);
	printf ("addition of x & y, is %d, z");
routine definition	in addition (int a, int b)
	{
	int c;
	c = a+b;
	return c;
	}

- In above program main function call addition function. At the time of calling it provides input values called parameter. After calling function addition control goes to in definition of same function, execute routine and return result to main function.

- Nesting of loop is allowed. If the loop is nested within other loops, it is possible to exit an inner loop and any enclosed loop.

- Example of nested loop in C, C++

- Nesting of for loop to assign matrix elements.

```
For (i = 0; i < 3; i++)
{
    For (j = 0; j < 3; j++)
{   a[i][j] = 1;
        Print("%d", a[i][j]);
    }
}
```

Nesting of while loop as shown below.

```
while (n < 5)
{
    int i = 0, b;
    int a[3];
    while (i ≤ 3)
    {
    printf ("\nEnter value for b");
```

```
                    scanf("%d", &b);
                         a[i] = b;
        }                        i++;
                      n = n + 1;

    }
```

- Most languages distinguish between two kinds of routines : Procedure and function. A procedure does not return a value it is an abstract command that is called to effect some desired state change.

- Pascal provides both procedure and functions. It allows formal parameters to be either by value or by reference. It also allows procedures and functions to be parameters. Example is as below.

    Procedure example (Var X :T; y :Q; function f(Z :R) : integer);

- Here X is a by reference parameter of type T; y is a by value parameter of type Q; f is a function parameter that takes one by value parameter Z of type R and returns an integer.

- Ada provides both procedure and functions. Parameter passing mode is specified in the header of an Ada routine as either in, out or in out. If the mode is not specified, in is assumed by default.

- A formal in parameter is a constant which only permits reading and updating of actual parameter value. In the implementation, parameters are passed either by copy or by reference.

2.20 STYLE ISSUES

2.20.1 Side Effect and Aliasing

- Modifications of local/Global environment. Side effects provide a method of communication among program units. Communication can be established through nonlocal i.e Global variables.

- However if the set of nonlocal variables used for this purpose is large and each unit has unrestricted access to such nonlocal variables the program becomes difficult to read, understand and modify.

- Once a global variable is used for communication, it is difficult to distinguish between desired and undesired side effects.

- Side effect i.e change in the programs state caused by an expression or function cal, or modification of a global variable in a procedure or function.

Example : Java

    i = j++

Example : Java collection add (object O) returns true if the collection changed.

Example : Ada function parameters

Function sum and put Inorder (i, j : out Integer) return integer is

```
Begin
if i < j then
    Swap (i, j);
    end if
    return i + j;
    end Sum  And  Put   Inorder;
    i : Integer : = 3;
    j : Integer : = 2
begin
    Put ("Average is : ");
    Put (SumAndPutInorder) (i, j)/2);                    //change i here
    New line;
    Put ("Smallest is ");
    Put (i);
    new line;
    end;
Example : Debugging, side effects and Global variables.
    g : Integer := 1;                                    ....Global variable
    procedure do     something (P : out Integer) is
begin
    P : = 0;
    End do something;
    Procedure do     something    Else (P : in integer; q : out integer) is
Begin
    q : = 2 * P;
```

```
    end do something;
    Procedure putHeader is
Begin
    Put ("something");
    g = 0;
    end putHeader;
begin
    put(g); --- g is correct here
    putHeader;
    dosomething (x);
    dosomething Else (g – y);
    put (g); --- g is not correct here
    end;
```

- Communication via unrestricted access to nonlocal variables is dangerous when program is large and composed of several units that have been developed independently by several programmers. This difficulty can be reduced if we keep parameters as the only means of communication among units. The overhead caused by parameter passing is almost always tolerable, except for critical applications. We can restrict the set of nonlocal variables held in common by two units. Also it can be useful to specify that a unit can read but not modify some variable.

- The modification of an actual parameter that is passed by reference to a routine is also a side effect, which may produce undesired results.

- Languages that distinguish between function and procedures suggest a programming style in which the use of side effects should be restricted to procedures this should be the way a procedure sends result back to the caller side effects should not be used in functions.

```
    j : integer : = 2
begin
    put("Average is :");
    put(sumAndPutInteger (i , j)/2); // change i has
    new_line;
    put("smallest is");
    put (i);
    new_line;
    end;
```

Example : Debugging, side effects and global variables.

```
    g : Integer : = 1; --- Global variable
    procedure dosomething (p : outInteger) is
begin
    p : = 0;
    end dosomething;
    procedure putlteader is
begin
    put("something");
    g =  0;
    end putlteader;
begin
    put(g); --- g is correct here
    putlteader;
    dosomething (x);
    dosomething Else (g – y);
    put(g); --- g is not correct here
    end;
```

2.21 EXCEPTIONS

- The programmers write a program with full efficiency to make it error free and accurate. But there are many situation occur at runtime which cause failure of program at runtime. For example consider programmer written a function for division of two integers and user passed second argument 'o' for division which cause zero error. Sometime programmer declared array size limit 20 and under certain condition program trying to access higher index than 20th. Suppose program allocating memory dynamically for certain data structure or routine and memory is not available in computer storage or user given wrong input during program execution. All this thing case program failure at runtime. Program fail at runtime and come out unexpectedly by simply displaying some obsure message. This behaviour is unacceptable in many situations. To improve reliability of program it is necessary that such erroneous condition can be recognized by the program and certain action to recover from error.

- Conventional control structure are inadequate to do that. It try to fix the problem by explicit methods. Alternatively, one would like the runtime machine to be able to trap such anomalous conditions, and let the programmer program the response to the condition.

- So all the erroneous conditions which already known to programmer and can be predictable are consider as exceptional cases.

- To cope up with this problem or exceptional cases programming languages provide feature called exception handling.

2.22 EXCEPTION HANDLING IN JAVA

- When JAVA interpreter encounters an error such as dividing an integer by zero, it creates an exception object and throws it. If the exception object is not caught and handled properly, the interpreter will display an error message and will terminate program. If we want the program to continue with the execution of remaining code, we should try to catch the exception object thrown by the error condition and then display an message for corrective actions. This task known as exception handling.

- Exception handling mechanism suggests incorporation of a separate error handling code that performs the following tasks :

  ➢ Find the problem (Hit the exception)

  ➢ Inform that an error has occurred (Throw the exception)

  ➢ Receive the error information (catch the exception)

  ➢ Task corrective actions (handle the exception)

- Error handling code basically consist of two parts, one to detect errors and to throw exceptions and other to catch exceptions and to take appropriate actions.

- Some common exception that we must watch out for catching are listed as below.

Exception Type	Cause of Exception
Arithmetic Exception	Cause by math error like division by zero
Array Index Out of Bounds Exception	Caused by bad array indexes.
Array Store Exception	Caused when program tries to store wrong type of data in array.
File Not Found Exception	Caused by an attempt to access a non existent file.
I/O Exception	Caused by general I/O failures.
Null Pointer Exception	Caused by referencing a null object.
Number Format Exception	Caused when conversion between strings and number fails.

Exceptions in JAVA can be categorized into two types.

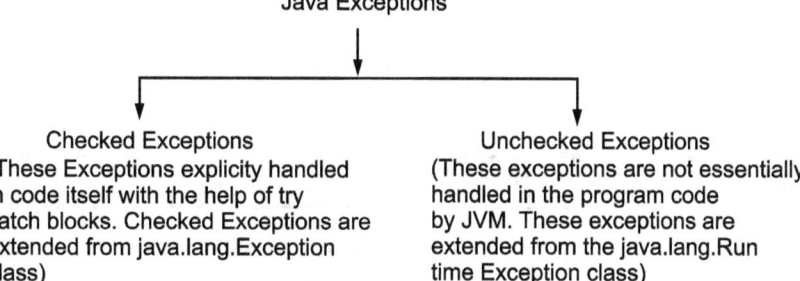

Java Exceptions

Checked Exceptions	Unchecked Exceptions
(These Exceptions explicity handled in code itself with the help of try catch blocks. Checked Exceptions are extended from java.lang.Exception class)	(These exceptions are not essentially handled in the program code by JVM. These exceptions are extended from the java.lang.Run time Exception class)

Example : Exception handling using try catch block

```
Class error 3
{
    Public static void main (string args [])
    {
        int a = 10;
        int b = 5;
        int C = 5;
        int x,y;
        try
        {
            x = a/(b – c); // Exception here
        }
        catch (Arithmetic Exception e)
        {
        System out print/n ("Division by zero");
        }
        y = a/(b + c);
        System out print/n ("y =" + y);
    }
}
```

- So program did not stop at error condition. It catch exception and display message

Output :

Division by zero

y = 1

2.23 EXCEPTION HANDLING IN C++

- In C++ exceptions may be generated by the runtime anonalies that program encounter during exception or raised explicitly by the program.

- C++ consist of 3 keywords to handling the exception they are

    Try : Code which may generate exception is written in try block exception are thrown from inside the try block.

    Throw : Throw keyword is used top throw an exception encountered inside try block. After the exception is thrown, the control is transferred to catch block.

    Catch : Catch block catches the exceptions thrown by throw statements from try block

- Multiple catch exception are allowed when user want to handle different exceptions differently.

Example : Exception handling in C++ for divide by zero exception.

```
        #include<istream.h>
        #include<conio.h>
    Void main ( )
    {
        int a, b, c;
        float d;
        cout<<"Enter the value of a :";
        cin>>a;
        cout<<"Enter the value of b :";
        cin>>b;
        cout<<"Enter the value of c :";
        cin>>c;
```

```
    try
    {
        if((a – b)! = 0)
        {
            d = c/(a – b);
            cout<<"Result is :"<<d;
        }
        else
        {
            throw (a – b);
        }
    }
    catch (int i)
    {
        Cout<<"Answer is infinite because a – b is" << i;
    }
    getch( );
}
```

Consider a = 5, b = 5, c = 30 then exception is generated as a – b =0

EXERCISE

1. Explain various primitive data types with suitable examples.

2. Explain about generic methods.

3. Explain various primitive data types with suitable examples.

4. Discuss about type-checking.

5. Explain in detail abstract data types in java with examples.

6. Define Exceptions? Discuss need & design issues of Exception Handling.

7. Define Coercion, Type error, Type checking and Strong Typing.

8. Define type compatibility? Give example of any two type compatibility.

9. Explain advantages and disadvantages of Java for loop compared to Ada for loop.

10. What is exception handling? How exceptions are handled in C++ and JAVA.

11. What is sequence control? Explain various categories of sequence control.

12. Explain Strong typing and Type Coercion with suitable example.

13. Explain design issues and their side effect in programming language.

14. Explain Conditional statements in any two programming language.

15. Explain type conversion with example in particular language.

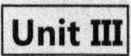

STRUCTURING OF PROGRAM

3.1 SOFTWARE DESIGN METHOD

- Software design sits at the crossroads of all the computer disciplines : hardware and software engineering, programming, human factors research, ergonomics. It is the study of the intersection of human, machine, and the various interfaces—physical, sensory, psychological that connects them.

- The process of design is founded in the systematic principles and methods. However, at times the designer is required to go beyond these principles and methods. Thus, the comfort of generic practices widely found in mathematics and traditional engineering is absent in software design. Software design consciously deploys intuitions, tacit knowledge and gut reactions of the team members and stakeholders. Software development is thus unique due to the following attributes.

  - Data available to make the estimates is scarce. Thus, the time and cost estimates arc often not reliable.

  - The number of possible solutions to a given problem is often unlimited. The possibilities are limited by the perceived complexity of implementing the solution. Working solutions are normally delivered. The perceived complexity curbs the ability to design optimal solutions.

  - Programming is individualistic. Many factors, including the psychology of the programmer need to be accounted in a team of developers.

  - Technology changes rapidly.

  - The intermediate stages of development have poor visibility. Managing the process of development is thus difficult.

- The software design is basically an exercise in managing complexity. Programming paradigms provide a variety of techniques to manage complexity. The choice of the programming paradigm is central to the design of software. There are many languages confirming to the techniques supported by a given paradigm. Paradigms help in minimizing the design errors. Programming is thus a design activity. In fact, design is the keynote in all the activities of problem solving. A study of programming languages and paradigms is aimed at providing this perspective to software development. A designer studies the following aspects of a programming language or paradigm.

➢ Support for abstraction

➢ Parameters and parameter transmission

➢ Exceptions and exception handling

➢ Expressions

➢ Support for static and dynamic storage management

- A good understanding of this aspects helps the designer in choosing a paradigm and language that best fits the needs of the problem being solved. It is the nature of the problem that determines the selection of the language and not the other way round.

- The objective of software design is to find a suitable modular decomposition of the desired system. Indeed, even though the boundaries between programming in the large and programming in the small cannot be stated severely, we may say that programming in the large addresses the problem of modular system decomposition, and programming in the small refers to the production of individual modules.

- A good modular decomposition is one that is based on modules that are as independent from each other as possible. There are many methods for achieving such modularity.

- A famous approach is information hiding which uses the distribution of "secrets" as the basis for modular decomposition. Each module hides a specific design decision as its secret. The idea is that if design decisions have to be changed, only the module that "knows" the secret design decision needs to be modified and the other modules remain as it is.

3.2 CONCEPTS IN SUPPORT OF MODULARITY

- Modularity is a general concept which applies to the development of software in a fashion which allows individual modules to be developed, often with a standardized interface to allow modules to communicate. In fact, the kind of separation of concerns between objects in an Object Orientation language is much the same concept as for modules, except on a larger scale. Typically, partitioning a system into modules helps minimize coupling, which should lead to easier to maintain code.

- A module interface expresses the elements that are provided and required by the module. The elements defined in the interface are detectable by other modules. The implementation contains the working code that corresponds to the elements declared in the interface. Modular programming is closely related to structured programming and object-oriented programming, all having the same goal of facilitating the construction of large software programs and systems by decomposition into smaller pieces, and all originating around the 1960s. While historically usage of these terms has been inconsistent, today "modular programming" refers to high-level decomposition of the code of an entire program into pieces, structured programming to the low-level code use of structured control flow, and object-oriented programming to the data use of objects, a kind of data structure.

- The key to software design is modularization. A good module characterizes a valuable abstraction; it relates with other modules in well-defined and systematic ways; it may be understood, designed, implemented, compiled, and enhanced with access to only the specification of other modules.

- Programming languages provide services for building programs in terms of fundamental modules. In this unit, we are concerned in programming language concepts and facilities that help the programmer in dividing a program into subparts modules the relations among those modules and the extent to which program decompositions can reflect the decomposition of the design.

3.3 ENCAPSULATION

- Data encapsulation is a mechanism of bundling the data, and the functions that use them and data abstraction is a mechanism of exposing only the interfaces and hiding the implementation details from the user.

- Encapsulation is an Object Oriented Programming concept that binds together the data and functions that manipulate the data, and that keeps both safe from outside interference and misuse. Data encapsulation led to the important Object Oriented Programming concept of data hiding.

3.3.1 Data Encapsulation Example

- Any C++ program where you implement a class with public and private members is an example of data encapsulation and data abstraction. Consider the following example :

Program 3.1 :

```
#include <iostream>
using namespace std;

class Adder{
public :
    // constructor
Adder(int i = 0)
{
total = i;
    }
    // interface to outside world
```

```
voidaddNum(int number)
{
total += number;
    }


    // interface to outside world
intgetTotal()
{
return total;
    };
private :
    // hidden data from outside world
int total;
};

int main( )
{
   Adder a;

a.addNum(10);
a.addNum(20);
a.addNum(30);

cout<< "Total " <<a.getTotal() <<endl;
return 0;
}
```

Output :

Total 60

- Above class adds numbers together, and returns the sum. The public members addNum and getTotal are the interfaces to the outside world and a user needs to know them to use the class. The private member total is something that is hidden from the outside world, but is needed for the class to operate properly.

3.3.2 Benefits of Encapsulation

- The fields of a class can be made read-only or write-only.

- A class can have total control over what is stored in its fields.

- The users of a class do not know how the class stores its data. A class can change the data type of a field and users of the class do not need to change any of their code.

3.4 INTERFACE AND IMPLEMENTATION

- An interface is a reference type in Java. It is similar to class. It is a collection of abstract methods. A class implements an interface, thereby inheriting the abstract methods of the interface. Along with abstract methods, an interface may also contain constants, default methods, static methods, and nested types.

- Method bodies exist only for default methods and static methods. Writing an interface is similar to writing a class. But a class describes the attributes and behaviors of an object. And an interface contains behaviors that a class implements. Unless the class that implements the interface is abstract, all the methods of the interface need to be defined in the class.

- An interface is similar to a class in the following ways :

  ➢ An interface can contain any number of methods.

  ➢ An interface is written in a file with a **.java** extension, with the name of the interface matching the name of the file.

  ➢ The byte code of an interface appears in a **.class** file.

  ➢ Interfaces appear in packages, and their corresponding byte code file must be in a directory structure that matches the package name.

- However, an interface is different from a class in several ways, including :

  ➢ You cannot instantiate an interface.

  ➢ An interface does not contain any constructors.

  ➢ All of the methods in an interface are abstract.

  ➢ An interface cannot contain instance fields. The only fields that can appear in an interface must be declared both static and final.

  ➢ An interface is not extended by a class; it is implemented by a class.

  ➢ An interface can extend multiple interfaces.

3.4.1 Declaring Interfaces

- The interface keyword is used to declare an interface. Here is a simple example to declare an interface :

Example :

```
/* File name : NameOfInterface.java */
importjava.lang.*;
// Any number of import statements


publicinterfaceNameOfInterface
{
// Any number of final, static fields
// Any number of abstract method declarations\
}
```

3.4.2 Interfaces have the Following Properties

- An interface is implicitly abstract. You do not need to use the abstract keyword while declaring an interface.
- Each method in an interface is also implicitly abstract, so the abstract keyword is not needed.
- Methods in an interface are implicitly public.

Example :

```
/* File name : Animal.java */
interfaceAnimal
{
publicvoid eat();
publicvoid travel();
}
```

3.4.3 Implementing Interfaces

- When a class implements an interface, you can think of the class as signing a contract, agreeing to perform the specific behaviors of the interface. If a class does not perform all the behaviors of the interface, the class must declare itself as abstract.
- A class uses the implements keyword to implement an interface. The implements keyword appears in the class declaration following the extends portion of the declaration.

Program 3.2 :

```
/* File name : MammalInt.java */
publicclassMammalIntimplementsAnimal
{
publicvoid eat()
{
System.out.println("Mammal eats");
}

publicvoid travel()
{
System.out.println("Mammal travels");
}
publicintnoOfLegs()
{
return0;
}

publicstaticvoid main(Stringargs[])
{
MammalInt m =newMammalInt();
m.eat();
m.travel();
}
}
```

Output :

Mammal eats

Mammal travels

3.4.4 When Overriding Methods Defined in Interfaces, There Are Several Rules to be Followed

- Checked exceptions should not be declared on implementation methods other than the ones declared by the interface method or subclasses of those declared by the interface method.

- The signature of the interface method and the same return type or subtype should be maintained when overriding the methods.

- An implementation class itself can be abstract and if so, interface methods need not be implemented.

3.4.5 When Implementation Interfaces, There Are Several Rules

- A class can implement more than one interface at a time.

- A class can extend only one class, but implement many interfaces.

- An interface can extend another interface, in a similar way as a class can extend another class.

3.5 SEPARATE AND INDEPENDENT COMPILATION

- The term separate compilation means that compilation unit can be compiled at different times, but their compilations are not independent of each other if either accesses or uses any entities of the other. With independent compilation, program units can be compiled without information about any other program units.

- The idea of modularity is to allow the building of large programs out of smaller parts that are developed independently. At the implementation level, independent development of modules indicates that they may be compiled and tested separately, independently of the rest of the program.

- This is referred to as independent compilation. The term separate compilation is used to refer to the ability to compile units individually, but subject to certain ordering constraints. For example, C supports independent compilation and Ada supports separate compilation.

- In Ada, as we will see later, some units may not be compiled until other units have been compiled. The ordering is imposed to allow checking of inter unit references. With independent compilation, normally there is no static checking of entities introduced by a module.

- The capability of compiling parts of a program without compiling the whole program is essential to the construction of large software systems. Thus, languages that are designed for such applications must allow this kind of compilation. With such a capability, only the modules of a system that are being changed need to be recompiled during development or maintenance. Newly compiled and previously compiled units are collected by a program called linker, which is a part of the operating system. Without this capability, every change to a system would require a complete recompilation. In a large system, this is costly.

- In this unit, we discuss two distinct approaches to compiling parts of programs, called separate compilation and independent compilation. The parts of the program that can be compiled are sometimes called compilation units.

- The term separate compilation means that compilation unit can be compiled at different times, but their compilations are not independent of each other if either accesses or uses any entities of the other. This interdependence is required if interface checking is to be done. We first discuss separate compilation in the context of Ada.

- To provide reliable separate compilation of a unit, the compiler must have access to information about program entities (variables, types and subprograms, including their interfaces) that the units uses but that are declared elsewhere. Information about the entities of an Ada package that can be visible in other units, which are called the exported entities, forms the interface of the package.

- The interface of a procedure includes the number, names, and types of its parameters, along with the order in which they appear. In the case of a function, the type of the returned value is also included.

- An Ada implementation maintains these kinds of unit interface information in a library that is accessible to the compiler. Every compilation causes the interface information of that compilation to be placed in a library.

- Libraries store library units, which are compiled compilation units. Compilation unit in Ada are entities such as subprogram header, package declarations, and subprogram bodies.

- During compilation of an Ada program unit, all externally declared entities that are used are type checked against their local users. In the case of subprograms, the whole interface is type checked. Not all library information is available to a particular program unit compilation.

- The name of those units that are provided required external entities are listed on with statement at the beginning of the unit being compiled. Using with, the programmer specifies the external units which the code in the compilation must access. For example, the following procedure uses entities form two external units, GLOBALS and TEXT_IO, and thus specifies those two.

```
with GLOBALS, TEXT_IO;
procedure EXAMPLE is

    ...
end EXAMPLE;
```

- Modula-2 provides separate compilation that is similar to that of Ada. FORTRAN 90 also allows separate compilation of its subprograms and modules.

- In some languages, most notably C and FORTRAN 77, independent compilation is allowed. With independent compilation, program units can be compiled without information about any other program units.

- An important characteristic of independent compilation is that the interfaces between the separately compiled units are not checked for consistency. The interface of

FORTRAN 77 subroutine is its parameter list. When a subroutine is independently compiled, the types of its parameter are not stored with the compiled code or in a library. Therefore, when another program that calls that subroutine is compiled, the types of the actual parameters in the calls cannot be checked against the types of the formal parameters of the subroutine, even if the machine code for the called subroutine is a available.

- This is not surprising in FORTRAN 77. Even when the program that calls a subprogram and the subprogram itself are compiled from the same file, they are in effect, if not actually, compiled independently. So the parameter interface between FORTRAN 77 program units is never checked for type compatibility.

- Some languages provide neither separate nor independent compilation, meaning that the only compilation unit is a complete program. FORTRAN II and the original version of Pascal are such languages.

- This is a severe restriction on the language, making it virtually unusable for industrial applications. It is clear that independent compilation, although it allows unchecked program unit interfaces, is better than having no means of compiling parts of programs. Later versions of both FORTRAN and Pascal recognized this.

3.6 LIBRARIES OF MODULES

- A library is a collection of code for functions and classes. Often, these libraries are written by someone else and brought into the project so that the programmer does not have to "reinvent the wheel." In Python the term used to describe a library of code is module.

- By using import pygame and import random, the programs created so far have already used modules. A library can be made up of multiple modules that can be imported. Often a library only has one module, so these words can sometimes be used interchangeably.

- Modules are often organized into groups of similar functionality. In this class programs have already used functions from the math module, the random module, and the pygame library. Modules can be organized so that individual modules contain other modules. For example, the pygame module contains sub modules for pygame.draw, pygame.image, and pygame.mouse.Modules are not loaded unless the program asks them to. This saves time and computer memory.

3.6.1 Why Create a Library?

- There are three major reasons for a programmer to create his or her own libraries :
  - ➢ It breaks the code into smaller, easier to use parts.
  - ➢ It allows multiple people to work on a program at the same time.
  - ➢ The code written can be easily shared with other programmers.

By separating a large program into several smaller programs, it is easier to manage the code.

- Modern programmers rarely build programs from scratch. Often programs are built from parts of other programs that share the same functionality. If one programmer creates code that can handle a mortgage application form that code will ideally go into a library. Then any other program that needs to manage a mortgage application form at that bank can call on that library.

- We know that C++ class and Ada's package make it possible to group related Things into a single unit. But large programs consist of hundreds or even thousands of such units. To control the complex difficulty of dealing with the large number of things exported by all these units, it is extremely important to be able to organize these units into related groups. For example, it is very hard to secure that all the thousands of units have unique names! In general, we can always find groupings of units that are related rather closely. A common example of a grouping of related services is a library of modules such as a library of matrix manipulation routines.

- A library collects together a number of related and commonly used services. Clients usually need to make use of different libraries in the same program and since libraries are written by different people, the names in different libraries may conflict.

- For example, a library for controlling lists and a library for manipulating dictionaries may both export procedures named insert. Machines are needed for clients to conveniently differentiate between such identically-named services.

- We have seen that the dot notation helps with this problem at the module level. But consider trying to use two different releases of the same library at the same time. How can you use some of the entities from one release and some from the other? Both C++ and Ada have recent additions to the language to deal with these issues.

3.7 LANGUAGE FEATURES FOR PROGRAMMING IN THE LARGE

- By large programs we mean systems consisting of many small programs (modules), possibly written by different people. In software development, programming in the large can involve programming by larger groups of people or by smaller groups over longer time periods. Either of these conditions will result in large, and hence complicated, programs that can be challenging for maintainers to understand. With programming in the large, coding managers place emphasis on partitioning work into modules with precisely-specified interactions.

- This requires careful planning and careful documentation. With programming in the large, program changes can become difficult. If a change operates across module boundaries, the work of many people may need re-doing. Because of this, one goal of programming in the large involves setting up modules that will not need altering in the event of probable changes. This is achieved by designing modules so they have high cohesion and loose coupling.

- Programming in the large requires abstraction-creating skills. Until a module becomes implemented it remains an abstraction. Taken together, the abstractions should create an architecture unlikely to need change. They should define interactions that have the precision and demonstrable correctness.

- Programming in the large requires management skills. The process of building abstractions aims not just to describe something that can work, but also to direct the efforts of people who will make it work.

- The concept was introduced by Frank DeRemer and Hans Kron in their 1975 paper "Programming-in-the-Large Versus Programming-in-the-Small", IEEE Trans. On Soft. Eng.

- In computer science terms, programming in the large can refer to programming code that represents the high-level state transition logic of a system. This logic encodes information such as when to wait for messages, when to send messages, when to compensate for failed non-ACID transactions, etc. A language that was designed to explicitly support programming in the large is BPEL (Business Process Execution Language).

- In this unit we look at some interesting ways that existing programming languages support or do not support the programming in the large. Every programming languages provide features for decomposing programs into smaller and largely autonomous units. We refer to such units as *physical* modules; we will use the term *logical* module to denote a module identified at the design stage. A logical module represents an abstraction identified at the design stage by the designer. A logical module may implement by one or more physical module. The closer the relationship between the physical modules and logical modules is, the better the physical program organization reflects the logical design structure. We will discuss the related aspects of all language based on the following points :

  ➢ Program organization and module groupings : How independently can physical modules be implemented and compiled? What are the visibility and access control mechanisms supported by the language?

  ➢ Module encapsulation : What is the unit of modularity and encapsulation supported by the Language, and how well does it support different programming paradigms?

  ➢ Separation of interface from implementation : What is the relationship between modules that form a program? What entities may be exported and imported by a module?

3.7.1 C

- C programming is a powerful general-purpose language. It is fast, portable and available on all platforms. C provides functions to decompose a program into procedural abstractions. In addition, it relies on a minimum of language features and a number of conventions to support programming in the large. These conventions are well recognized by C programmers and are even reflected in tools that have been developed to support the language. Indeed, a major portion of the programming in the large support is provided by the file-inclusion commands of the C preprocessor. Thus, even though the compiler does not provide any explicit support or checking for inter-module interaction, the combination of conventions and the preprocessor has proven in practice to be an adequate and popular way to support programming in the large.

- The C unit of physical modularity is a file. A logical module is implemented in C by two physical modules (files) which we may roughly call the module's interface and its implementation. The interface, called a "header" or an "include" file, declares all symbols exported by the module and thus available to the clients of the module. The header file contains the information necessary to satisfy the type system when the client modules are compiled.

- The implementation file of the module contains the private part of the module and implements the exported services. A client module needing to use the functionality of another module "includes" the header file of the provider module. A header file may declare constants, type definitions, variables, and functions. Only the prototype of the function—its signature—is given by the declaration; the function definition appears in the implementation file. Functions may not be nested. Any names defined in a file are known throughout that file and may also be known outside of that file.

- The header files are used to resolve inter-module references at compile-time. At link-time, all implementation files are searched to resolve inter-module (i.e. inter-file) references. The header file is usually named with a .h extension and the implementation file is named with a .c extension. These conventions have largely overcome the lack of any explicit support for program organization.

- Program 3.3 show the header and implementation files for a module providing a stack data structure. Language provides no encapsulation facilities. For example, the main program 3.3 has complete access to the internal structure of the stacks s1 and s2. In fact, this property is used by the main program to initialize the stacks s1 and s2 to set their stack pointers (top) to 0. There are ways to implement this program to reduce this interference between client and server but all depend on the care taken by the programmer. There is no control over what is exported : by default, all entities in a file are exported. Files may be compiled separately and inter-file references are resolved at link time with no type-checking. A file may be compiled as long as all the files it includes are available.

Program 3.3 : Stack data structure

```
//stack.h
typedef struct stack
{
    int elements[100]; /* stack of 100 ints */
    int top; /*number of elements*/
```

```
};
extern void push(stack, int);
extern int pop(stack);
/* end of file stack.h */
/*****---------------------end of file ****/
/*file stack.c */
/*implementation of stack operations*/
#include''stack.h''
void push(stack s, int i)
 {
    s.elements[s.top++] = i;
 };
int pop (stack s)
{
    return --s.top;
};
/*****---------------------end of file ****/
/*file main.c */
/*A client of stack*/
#include <stack.h>
void main()
{
    stack s1, s2; /*declare two stacks */
    s1.top = 0;
    s2.top = 0; /* initialize them */
    int i;
    push (s1, 5); /* push something on first stack */
    push (s2, 6); /* push something on second stack*/
    ...
    i = pop(s1); /* pop first stack */
    ...
}
```

- The general structure of a C file is shown below. All files have similar structure except that one of the files (only) must contain a function named main, which is called to start the program. Because functions are not allowed to be nested in C, the nesting problems of Pascal do not occur.

Structure of C Module

```
#include ...various files...
global declarations
function definitions
void main (parameters)
{
    ...one main function needed in a program
}
```

- Any names defined in the outer level of a file are implicitly known globally. These include the names of all the functions defined in the file and any other entities defined outside of those functions. There are two ways to control such indiscriminate dispersion of names.

  ➤ A module wanting to use an entity that is defined externally must declare such entities as being externally defined.

  ➤ A module wanting to limit the scope of one of its defined entities to be local to itself only may declare such an entity to be static.

- The following two lines import the integer variable maximum_length and hides the integer variable local_size from other modules.

```
extern int maximum_length;
static int local_size;
```

- There are no explicit import/export facilities. All control over module independence relies on convention and implementer competence.

3.7.2 Pascal

- Pascal is a general-purpose, high-level language that was originally developed by Niklaus Wirth in the early 1970s. It was developed for teaching programming as a systematic discipline and to develop reliable and efficient programs.

- Pascal is Algol-based language and includes many constructs of Algol. ALGOL 60 is a subset of Pascal. Pascal offers several data types and programming structures. It is easy to understand and maintain the Pascal programs.

- Pascal has grown in popularity in the teaching and academic arena for various reasons :
  - ➤ Easy to learn.
  - ➤ Structured language.
  - ➤ It produces transparent, efficient and reliable programs.
  - ➤ It can be compiled on a variety of computer platforms.

Features of the Pascal Language

- Pascal has the following features :
  - ➤ Pascal is a strongly typed language.
  - ➤ It offers extensive error checking.
  - ➤ It offers several data types like arrays, records, files and sets.
  - ➤ It offers a variety of programming structures.
  - ➤ It supports structured programming through functions and procedures.
  - ➤ It supports object oriented programming.

Why to use Pascal?

- Pascal allows the programmers to define complex structured data types and build dynamic and recursive data structures, such as lists, trees and graphs. Pascal offers features like records, enumerations, sub-ranges, dynamically allocated variables with associated pointers and sets.
- Pascal allows nested procedure definitions to any level of depth. This truly provides a great programming environment for learning programming as a systematic discipline based on the fundamental concepts.
- Among the most amazing implementations of Pascal are –
  - ➤ Skype
  - ➤ Total Commander
  - ➤ TeX
  - ➤ Macromedia Captivate
  - ➤ Apple Lisa
  - ➤ Various PC Games
  - ➤ Embedded Systems
- The only features provided by Pascal for decomposing a program into modules are procedures and functions, which can be used to implement procedural abstractions. The language thus only supports procedural programming. Some later versions of the language have modified the original version of Pascal extensively by adding object-oriented programming features.

Pascal Program Structure

- A Pascal program basically consists of the following parts –
  - ➢ Program name
  - ➢ Uses command
  - ➢ Type declarations
  - ➢ Constant declarations
  - ➢ Variables declarations
  - ➢ Functions declarations
  - ➢ Procedures declarations
  - ➢ Main program block
  - ➢ Statements and Expressions within each block
  - ➢ Comments
- Every Pascal program generally has a heading statement, a declaration and an execution part strictly in that order. Following format shows the basic syntax for a Pascal program :

```
program {name of the program}
uses {comma delimited names of libraries you use}
const {global constant declaration block}
var {global variable declaration block}

function {function declarations, if any}
{ local variables }
begin
...
end;


procedure { procedure declarations, if any}
{ local variables }
begin
...
end;


begin { main program block starts}
...
end. { the end of main program block }
```

- A program consists of declarations and operations. The operations are either the built-in ones provided by the language or those declared as functions and procedures. A procedure or function itself may contain the declaration of constants, types, variables, and other procedures and functions.

Pascal Hello World

- Following is a simple Pascal code that would print the words "Hello, World!" :

Program 3.4 :

```
program HelloWorld;
begin
 writeln('Hello World');
end.
```

Output :

```
"Hello World"
```

3.7.3 C++

- C++ provides functions as a decomposition construct to implement abstract operations. however, C++'s most important enhancements to C are in the area of programming in the large.
- In particular, the class construct of C++ provides a unit of logical modularity that supports the implementation of information hiding modules and abstract data types. Combined with templates, classes may be used to implement generic abstract data types. The class provides encapsulation and control over interfaces.

Encapsulation in C++

- Encapsulation is an Object Oriented Programming conception that binds together the data and functions that manipulate the data, and that keeps both safe from outside interference and misuse. Data encapsulation lead to the significant OOP concept of data hiding.
- The unit of logical modularity in C++ is the class. A class serves a number of purposes including :
  - ➢ A class defines a new (user-defined) data type.
  - ➢ A class defines an encapsulated unit.
- Entities defined by a class are either public—exported to clients—or private—secret from clients.
- Since a class defines a user-defined type, to use the services offered by a class, the client must create an instance of the class, called an object, and use that object. C++ supports the style of programming in which programmers write applications by extending the types of the language with user-defined types. Class derivation is a mechanism that

supports the definition of new types based on existing types. Classes may be nested. But as we saw in the case of Pascal, nesting may be used only for programming in the small and is of limited utility for programming in the large.

Program Organization

• Classes define the abstractions from which the program is to be created. The main program or a client creates instances of the classes and calls on them to perform the most wanted task. Program 3.5 shows a class implementing a stack of integers1. The implementation separates the interface and the implementation in different files.

Program 3.5 : Stack class in C++

```
/* file stack.H */
/*declarations exported to clients*/
class stack
{
    public :
        stack();
        void push(int);
        int push pop();
    private :
    int elments[100]; /* stack represented as array */
    int top = 0; /*number of elements*/
};
// the implementation follows and may be in a separate file
void stack : :push( int i)
{
    elements[top++] = i;
};
int stack : :pop (int i)
{
    return elements[--top];
};
/*end of stack.H*/
/*main.c */
```

```
/*A client of stack*/
#include "stack.h"
main()
{
    stack s1, s2; /*declare two stacks */
    int i;
    s1.push (5); /* push something on first stack */
    s2.push (6); /* push something on second stack*/
    ...
    i = s1.pop(); /* pop first stack */
    ...
}
```

- In the main program, stacks are declared in the same way that variables of language-defined types are declared. The operations exported by stack, push and pop, are called in the main program by using the dot notation and accessing the desired operation of the suitable stack objects (s1 or s2). The definitions of the operations push and pop may appear in the class body or outside of it. Finally, the compiler will try to expand the code of the member functions in-line, if possible, to avoid the overhead of a procedure call.

- C++ supports the development of independent modules (but does not enforce it) :

  ➢ A class's interface and implementation may be divided and even compiled independently from each other. The implementation must contain the interface definition and therefore must be compiled after the interface file exists.

  ➢ Client modules may be compiled with access to only the interface modules of the service providers and not their implementation modules.

  ➢ Any names defined in a class are local to the class unless explicitly declared to be public. Even so, client modules must use the class name to get access to the names internal to the class.

Grouping of Units

- C++ has several mechanisms for linking classes to each other. First, classes may be nested. As we have said before, this is a programming in the small feature. Two other mechanisms, "friend" functions and namespaces, are discussed next.

- Friend functions. A class in C++ defines a user-defined type. As a result, the operations it defines as public are operations on objects of that type. Some operations do not naturally belong to one object or another.

- For example, if we define a class for complex numbers, it may have a data part that stores the real and imaginary parts of the number, along with exported operations that let clients create and manipulate objects of type complex. But what about an addition operation that takes two complex objects to add together? Which of the two complex objects is the operation a member of? As another example, consider defining a function that multiplies a vector with a matrix. Should this function be a member of the vector class or the matrix class? To be able to execute such functions efficiently, they need to have access to the private parts of the objects they manipulate but they do not really belong to a particular object.

- Module-based languages such as Ada and Modula-2 allow these related entities to be packaged together in a single module. A class-based language such as C++ must adopt a different solution. In C++, a class can grant access to its private parts by declaring certain functions as its "friend". Friend functions have the same rights as member functions of the class but are otherwise normal global functions.

- Following syntax shows the definition of a complex number class. The class defines the type complex which is internally composed of two doubles, representing the real and imaginary parts of a complex number. These are secreted from clients. The class exports a method of constructing a complex number out of two doubles. Thus, the following declaration creates two complex numbers :

complex x(1.0, 2.0), y(2.5, 3.5);

- The other declarations state that the operator functions to be defined later (+, -, *, and /) are friends of the class complex and thus may access the private parts of the class. They are not member functions of the class and they are not exported by the class. They are simply given privileged treatment by the class. Of course, friend functions, even though not exported, are visible to clients because they are global functions.

Program 3.6 : Illustration of the use of friend declarations in C++

```
class complex
{
public :
complex(double r, double i ){re = r; im = i;}
friend complex operator+ (complex, complex);
friend complex operator- (complex, complex);
friend complex operator* (complex, complex);
friend complex operator/ (complex, complex);
private :
double re, im;
};
```

- Defining these operators as friend functions allows the clients to naturally use these functions as binary operations such as :

```
complex c = x + y;
```

- If the operation + was made a member of the class, the notation for clients would be quite embarrassed. For example, we might have had to write something like :

```
c.add(x)
```

in order to add the complex x to complex c.

- The requirement for friend functions is a direct consequence of C++'s use of classes as user-defined types. In a language like Ada where the package is used not to define types but to group interrelated entities, we would naturally group together type definitions for complex and its related functions in the same package. The functions automatically gain access to the private parts of the package because they are part of the package. In both cases, any changes to the representation of the data may require changes to the functions, whether they are part of a package or they are friend functions.

- **Namespaces :** A namespace is a declarative region that provides a scope to the identifiers (the names of types, functions, variables, etc) inside it. Namespaces are used to organize code into logical groups and to prevent name collisions that can occur especially when your code base includes multiple libraries.

- Consider a situation, when we have two persons with the same name, Zara, in the same class. Whenever we need to differentiate them definitely we would have to use some additional information along with their name, like either the area if they live in different area or their mother or father name, etc.

- Same situation can arise in your C++ applications. For example, you might be writing some code that has a function called xyz() and there is another library available which is also having same function xyz(). Now the compiler has no way of knowing which version of xyz() function you are referring to within your code.

- A namespace is considered to overcome this difficulty and is used as additional information to distinguish similar functions, classes, variables etc. with the similar name accessible in different libraries. Using namespace, you can identify the context in which names are defined. In essence, a namespace defines a scope.

Defining a Namespace :

- A namespace definition begins with the keyword namespace followed by the namespace name as follows :

```
namespace namespace_name {
  // code declarations
}
```

- To call the namespace-enabled version of either function or variable, prepend the namespace name as follows :

```
name : :code;  // code could be variable or function.
```

- Let us see how namespace scope the entities including variable and functions :

```
#include <iostream>
using namespace std;


// first name space
namespace first_space
{
  void func()
  {
    cout << "Inside first_space" << endl;
  }
}


// second name space
namespace second_space
{
  void func()
    {
    cout << "Inside second_space" << endl;
    }
}

int main ()
{

  // Calls function from first name space.
  first_space : :func();
```

```
// Calls function from second name space.

second_space : :func();


return 0;
}
```

Output :

```
Inside first_space

Inside second_space
```

3.7.4 Ada

- Ada is a structured, statically typed, imperative, wide-spectrum, and object-oriented high-level computer programming language, extended from Pascal and other languages. It has built-in language support for design-by-contract, extremely strong typing, explicit concurrency, offering tasks, synchronous message passing, protected objects, and non-determinism. Ada improves code safety and maintainability by using the compiler to find errors in favor of runtime errors.

- Ada was designed specifically to support programming in the large. It has sophisticated facilities for the support of modules, encapsulation, and interfaces. Rather than relying on convention as in C and C++, Ada makes an explicit distinction between specification and implementation of a module. A file may be compiled if the specifications of the modules it uses are available. Thus,

- Ada naturally supports a software development process in which module specifications are developed first and implementation of individual modules may proceed independently. Ada also requires the existence of a compile-time library in which module specifications are compiled. A module may be compiled if all the module specifications it needs are already in the library. This library supports the checking of inter-module references at compile time

Encapsulation in Ada

- The package is Ada's unit of modularity. An Ada module encapsulates a group of entities and thus supports module-based programming. We have already seen that the language's explicit distinction between module specification and module body forces the programmer to separate what is expected by the module from what is hidden within the module. Additionally, Ada supports concurrent modules or tasks.

- In addition to the conceptual modularity at the package level, Ada supports the separate compilation of procedures and functions as well as packages.

Program Organization

- An Ada program is a linear collection of modules that can be either subprograms or packages. These modules are called units. One particular unit that implements a subprogram is the main program in the usual sense.

- Module declarations may be nested. Consequently, a unit can be organized as a tree structure of modules. Any abuse of nesting within a unit causes the same problems discussed for Pascal. These problems can be mitigated by the use of the subunit facility offered by the language.

- This facility permits the body of a module embedded in the declarative part of a unit (or subunit) to be written separately from the enclosing unit (or subunit). Instead of the entire module, only a *stub* need appear in the declarative part of the enclosing unit. The following example illustrates the concept of the subunit.

```
procedure X ( ... ) is --unit specification
W : INTEGER;
package Y is --inner unit specification
A : INTEGER;
function B (C : INTEGER) return INTEGER;
end Y;
package body Y is separate; --this is a stub
begin -- uses of package Y and variable W
...
...
...
end X;
-----------------------------------next file--------------
separate (X)
package body Y is
procedure Z (...) is separate; --this is a stub
function B (C : INTEGER) return INTEGER is
begin --use procedure Z
...
...
...
```

```
end B;
end Y;
-----------------------------------next file--------------
separate (X.Y)
procedure Z (...) is
begin
...
end Z;
```

- The prefix **separate** (X) specifies package body Y as a subunit of unit X. Similarly, **separate** (X.Y) specifies procedure Z as a subunit of package Y nested within X. The subunit facility not only can improve the readability of programs, but supports a useful technique in top-down programming. When writing a program at a certain level of abstraction, we may want to leave some details to be decided at a lower level.

- Assume you realize that a certain procedure is required to complete a given task. Although calls to that procedure can be instantly useful when you want to test the execution flow, the body of the procedure can be written at a later time. For now, all you need is a *stub*. The subunit facility, however, does not overcome all the problems caused by the tree nesting structure.

- The textually separate subunit body is still considered to be logically located at the point at which the corresponding stub appears in the enclosing (sub)unit. It is exactly this point that determines the entities visible to the subunit. In the example, both subunits Y and Z can access variable W declared in unit X.

- The interface of an Ada unit consists of the **with** statement, which lists the names of units from which entities are imported, and the *unit specification* (enclosed within a **is... end** pair), which lists the entities exported by the unit. Each logical module discovered at the design stage can be implemented as a unit. If the top-down design was done with awareness, logical modules should be relatively simple. Consequently, the nesting within units should be shallow or even nonexistent.

- Ada does not forbid an abuse of nesting within units. Actually, the entire program could be designed as a single unit with a deeply nested tree structure. It is up to the designer and programmer to achieve a more desirable program structure.

- The last program structuring issue is how the interfaces (i.e., import/export relationships) among units are specified in Ada. A unit exports all the entities specified in its specification part. It can import entities from other units if and only if the names of such units are listed in a suitable statement (**with** statement) that prefixes the unit. For example, the following unit lists unit X (a subprogram) in its **with** statement. Therefore, it is legal to use X within T's body.

```
with X;
package T is
C : INTEGER;
procedure D (...);
end T;
package body T is

...

...

...

end T;
```

- Similarly, the following procedure U can legally call procedure T.D and access variable T.C. On the other hand, unit X is not visible by U.

```
with T;
procedureU (...) is

...

end U;
```

Interface and Implementation

- In previous Section we have seen that Ada strictly separates the specification and body of a package. We have also seen how the **use** and **with** clauses are used to import services from packages. These facilities are used also to support separate compilation. Recall that separate compilation, as opposed to independent compilation, places a partial ordering on compilation units.

- The set of units and subunits comprising a program can be compiled in one or more separate compilations. Each compilation translates one or more units and/or subunits. The order of compilation must satisfy the following constraints.

- A unit can be compiled only if all units mentioned in its with statement have been compiled previously. A subunit can be compiled only if the enclosing unit has been compiled previously.

- In addition, unit specifications can be compiled separately from their bodies. A unit body must be compiled after its specification. The specification of a unit U mentioned in the **with** statement of a unit W must be compiled before W. On the other hand, U's body may be compiled either before or after W. These constraints make sure that a unit is submitted for compilation only after the compilation of unit specifications from which it can import entities. The compiler saves in a library file the descriptors of all entities exported by units. When a unit is submitted for compilation, the compiler uses the library file to perform the same amount of type checking on the unit whether the program is compiled in parts or as a whole.

- Ada's choice of a package as an encapsulation mechanism, together with its reliance on separate compilation, and the separation of specification and body creates an interesting issue when a package wants to export a type. This issue leads to the private type feature of Ada.

- Ada's choice of a package as an encapsulation mechanism, together with its dependence on separate compilation, and the separation of specification and body creates an exciting issue when a package wants to export a type. This issue leads to the private type characteristic of Ada.

- **The Private Type :** In Program, we declared a dictionary module that exports procedures and functions only. When the client declares its intention to use the dictionary package, the dictionary object is allocated. The representation of the object is not known to the client. From the package body, we can see that the entries in the dictionary are actually records that contain three different fields.

- What if we want to export to the client a type such as dictionary_entry? This would enable the client to declare variables of type dictionary_entry. We would like to export the type but not its representation. From the language design point of view there is a conflict here.

- The Ada language specifies that a client may be compiled with the information only of the specification of the provider module. But if the provider module is exporting a type and not its illustration, the size of the type cannot be determined from the specification. Thus, when the compiler is compiling the client, it cannot determine how much memory to allocate for variables of the exported type. Ada's solution to this problem is the **private type**. The requirement must contain the representation of the type but as a private type.

- If a package unit exports an encapsulated private data type, the type's representation is hidden to the programmer but known to the compiler, thanks to the private clause appearing in the package specification. Therefore, the compiler can generate code to allocate variables for such types declared in other units submitted for compilation prior to the package body (but after its specification). When a unit is modified, it may be necessary to recompile several units. The change may potentially affect its subunits as well as all the units that name it in their **with** statements. In principle, all potentially affected units must be recompiled.

- The separate compilation facility of Ada supports an incremental rather than a parallel development of programs, because units must be developed according to a partial ordering. This is not an arbitrary restriction, but a conscious design decision in support of methodical program development.

- A unit can be submitted for compilation only after the interfaces of all used units are frozen. Consequently, the programmer is enforced to postpone the design of a unit body until these interfaces have been designed. One of the goals of separate compilation is to support production of reusable software. Certified modules can be kept in a library and later combined to form different programs.

- The Ada solution is incomplete on this point for package units exporting encapsulated (private) data types. The visible part (the specification) of such packages must contain the type's operations and a private clause that specifies the type's internal representation. This representation is not usable outside the package body; it is there only for supporting separate compilation. Logically, this information belongs in the package body, together with the procedure bodies implementing the type's operations. Besides being aesthetically unpleasant, this feature has some unfortunate consequences :

  ➢ It violates the principle of top-down design. The representation must be determined at the same time as the specification of the data type, and both appear in the same textual unit.

  ➢ It limits the power of the language to support libraries of reusable modules, unless individual care is taken in the implementation. For example, a module using FIFO queues is compiled and validated with respect to a FIFO queue package providing a specific representation for FIFO queues (e.g., arrays). The module must be recompiled if one needs to use again it in a different program in which FIFO queues are implemented by a different data structure, even though the interfaces for manipulating FIFO queues are the same in both cases.

Grouping of Units

- Ada has many features for supporting programming in the large. Two clauses, use and with, are used to import services from other packages. Child library units are used to group packages together in hierarchical organizations.

- These services are defined to enable safe separate compilation. The with and use clauses. The with clause is used by a client to import from a provider module. For example, if we want to write a module to manipulate telephone numbers and we want to use the dictionary module specified in Program, we prefix the telephone module with a with clause :

```
with dictionary;
package phone_list is
...
--references to dictionary.insert(), etc.
...
end phone_list;
```

- Now, inside the phone_list package, we may refer to the exported entities of the dictionary package. These references have to be prefixed by the name of the package from which they are imported. For example, dictionary.insert(...).To gain direct visibility, and keep away from the need to use the dotted name, Ada provides the **use** clause :

  with dictionary; **use** dictionary;

  package phone_list **is**

  ...

  --references to insert(), etc.

  ...

  end phone_list;

- Child libraries. The Ada package groups mutually a set of related entities. Clients may import either selective services from a package or all the services provided by the package by using the use clause. The package is not enough as a structural mechanism for grouping a compilation of library modules. Here are some examples of problems that could occur :

  ➢ Suppose a client uses two different libraries, encapsulated in packages A and B. as the client expects to make extensive use of both libraries, it uses the use clause to import all the library services. But if libraries A and B export entities with the similar name, the client would encounter name clashes at compile time. Ada provides a renaming ability to get around this problem.

  ➢ More serious is the case where there are no name clashes. The client compiles and works properly. But suppose that a new version of library B is released with new functionality. It happens that one of the new functions introduced in B has a name identical to a name provide by A. The next time that the client code is compiled, compilation errors will show up due to name clashes. These errors would be mainly confusing because the previously working client code appears to not work even though it may not have been changed.

  ➢ In the earlier case, after the release of the new version of the library B, the client code has to be recompiled even though it does not make use of the new functionality of the library B. The recompilation is necessary only to satisfy Ada's rules on the order of compilation.

- Ada 95 has addressed these problems by introducing the concept of child libraries which allow packages to be hierarchically organized. The idea is that if new functionality is added to an existing library package, the new functionality may itself be organized as new package that is a child of the original library. The child package can be implemented using the facilities of the parent package. But the clients of the original library are not affected by the introduction of a child package. The child package makes it possible to add functionality to a package without disturbing the existing clients of the package.

- In general, a library developer may give a number of packages organized as a tree. Each package other than the root package has a parent package. An existing library may be extended by adding a child library unit to one of its existing nodes. The parent library unit, nor any clients of the parent require to be recompiled. For example, if the library Root exists, we may add Root. Child exclusive of disturbing Root or clients of Root. The Root child may be compiled independently. It has visibility to Root and to Root's siblings.

```
package Root is
--specification of Root library
--...
end Root;
-----------
package Root.Child is
--specification of a child library unit
--...
end Root.Child;
-----------
package body Root.Child is
--implementation of Root.Child
--...
end Root.Child;
-----------
```

- Each of the above segments may be compiled independently. The clients of Root need not be recompiled if they do not use Root.Child.

3.7.5 ML

- Standard ML (SML) is a general-purpose, modular, functional programming language with compile-time type checking and type inference. It is popular among compiler writers and programming language researchers, as well as in the development of theorem provers. Modularity is not only the province of imperative languages. The notion of module is important in any language that is to be used for programming in the large. For example, ML is a functional programming language with extensive support for modularity and abstraction.

Encapsulation in ML

- A module is a separately compilable unit. A unit may contain structures, signatures and factors. Structures are the main building blocks; signatures are used to define interfaces for structures; factors are used to build a new structure out of an existing structure. The ML *structure* is somewhat like the Ada package, used to group together a set of entities.

Program 3.7 : Dictionary module in ML (types string and int are not necessary but used for explanation here)

```
structure Dictionary =

struct

exception NotFound;

val root = nil; (*create an empty dictionary*)

(* insert (c, i, D) inserts pair <c,i> in dictionary D*)

fun insert (c :string, i :int, nil) = [(c,i)]

| insert (c, i, (cc, ii) : :cs) =

if c=cc then (c,i) : :cs

else (cc, ii) : :insert(c,i,cs);

(* lookup (c, D) finds the value i such that pair <c,i> is in dictionary D *)

fun lookup(c :string, nil) = raise NotFound

| lookup (c, (cc,ii :int) : :cs) =

if c = cc then ii

else lookup(c,cs);

end;
```

- Such a structure definition corresponds to the package body in that it gives the implementation for the entities being defined. It also has the property that all the entities are exported. This structure exports an exception, NotFound, a variable root, and two functions insert and lookup. To use the structure, a client uses the dot notation :

```
val D = Dictionary.create; (*create an empty dictionary *)

val newD = Dictionary.insert ("Mehdi", 46, D); (*insert a pair*)

...

D.lookup("Mehdi", D); (*produces value 46*)
```

Interface and Implementation

- The signature of a structure definition consists of the signatures and types of all the entities defined in the structure. ML also provides a construct to define a signature independently of any structure. A signature may be viewed as a specification for a module. For example, Program gives the signature of a module that exports an exception called Not Found and a function called lookup. A signature may be used as a requirement for a structure. For example, we may use the signature of Program to restrict the exported entities of the structure of Program. The system will do type checking to make sure that the structure provides at least what the signature requires.

A signature definition for specialized dictionary

```
signature DictLookupSig = sig
exception NotFound;
val lookup : string * (string * int) list -> int
end
```

- We can use the structure and signature we have to create a new module with a limited interface and use it consequently :

```
structure LookupDict : DictLookupSig = Dictionary;
val L = LookupDict.create; (* not allowed, must be done by someone else using a different
interface *)
lookupDict.lookup("Mehdi", L);
lookupDict.insert("Carlo", 50, L); --error, insert not available
```

- We can see that the ability to define signatures means that we can provide different interfaces to the same implementation, something not possible in Ada or C++. We can also provide different implementations to meet the same interface.

- ML also supports the concept of *generic* modules or structures. The signature facility may be combined with generic structures to instantiate a structure for particular types. For example, the dictionaries that we have defined so far, both in Ada and in ML have been specific to <string, integer> pairs. In ML, we can eliminate the occurrences of the terms string and int from a signature definition for specialized dictionary. and have a generic dictionary.

3.8 ABSTRACT DATA TYPES

- An Abstract Data Type (ADT) is a data type that has been created by a programmer i.e., it is not built-in in the programming language. As any other data types, an ADT is composed of a domain (the set of values belonging to the data type) and a collection of operations to manipulate such values. The only difference is that such data type will be constructed by the programmer.

- When we build an ADT we really want to apply the principles of encapsulation and information hiding mentioned earlier. This means that, once we have finished building the data type, we wish others to use the data type exclusively through the operations we provide, and in no other way. In particular, to protect our implementation and guarantee the ability to evolve software, we want to ensure that the implementation of the ADT is hidden from other users.

- Let us make an example. We would like to create an ADT that represents fractions; the domain should be the set of all the possible fractions (since these are the values we are interested in manipulating), and the operations we would like to perform are :
  - ➢ Check if two fractions are equal
  - ➢ Read the numerator and denominator of the fraction
  - ➢ Simplify a fraction
  - ➢ Add and multiply fractions
- The result should be a new data type (e.g., called Fraction), so that we can declare variables of this type and use them in our program.

3.8.1 ADT Specification

- The first step in the creation of an ADT is the development of its Specification. The specification of an ADT is a precise description (in English) of the ADT. The description should clearly identify what is the domain of the ADT and what are the operations associated to the data type.
- For each operation, we need to clearly describe what the operation does, what kind of inputs it expects, what kind of result it will produce. Observe that the specification does not say anything about how we are going to implement the ADT.
- It just describes what the ADT does and how it can be used. The people that are interested in using the ADT in their programs (e.g., they need to operate on fractions) need to only read the specification in order to proceed with their programs (THEY DO NOT NEED TO KNOW ANYTHING MORE!). Thus, one can think of the specification of the ADT as the interface to the ADT.

3.8.2 Domain of the ADT

- We will try to follow a standard pattern in developing the specification of the ADT. The first component of the specification is the description of its domain. The domain is the set of values that we can store in objects of this type. For example :

Fraction ADT

DOMAIN : the set of all the possible fractions

- As another example, if we are building an ADT to represent points in the 2-dimensional space, then

Point ADT

DOMAIN : the set of all the points in the two-dimensional space

- Note that in both cases we are careful about providing description of the set of values, without committing to any specific internal representation (e.g., we do not say how the points are going to be represented internally – they could be represented as Cartesian coordinates or as polar coordinates...).

3.8.3 Operations of the ADT

- The second part of the specification should describe the operations that belong to the ADT. This is a very delicate part in the development of the specification. We need to ensure that

  ➢ We provide all the operations that are needed to use the ADT in a meaningful way (Completeness). Remember that the operations will be the only way to operate on the ADT, thus if we forget an important operation then the users will not be able to use the ADT in their programs.

  ➢ We provide only the necessary operations; if we provide too many unnecessary operations, we will end up making the ADT very complicated and hard to use.

- For the sake of simplicity, we will typically distinguish four classes of operations

  ➢ Constructors : these operations are used whenever we want to create a new object of that particular type. Constructors are required as the creation of a new object belonging to an ADT requires a sequence of steps

  ➢ Destructors : these are operations that are going to be executed when an object is removed from the system (because it is not used any longer)

  ➢ Inspectors : these are operations that allows one to inspect the content of an object or test properties of the object (without modifying it)

  ➢ Modifiers : these are operations that either modify an object or generate new objects.

- Modern object-oriented languages, such as C++ and Java, support a form of abstract data types. When a class is used as a type, it is an abstract type that refers to a hidden representation. In this model an ADT is typically implemented as a class, and each instance of the ADT is usually an object of that class.

- An abstract data type is a named data type defined solely through operations for creating and manipulating values of that data type. If values are available directly, they are known by name only. Any internal structure is known, and so can be manipulated, only inside the ADT.

- The associated scope rules define this distinction between public (exported) identifiers, that can be seen both inside and outside the ADT, and private (local) identifiers, that can only be seen inside the ADT. Therefore, unlike a classical block structured language, scopes are no longer strictly nested. This is known as encapsulation.

- In computer science, an abstract data type (ADT) is a mathematical model for data types where a data type is defined by its behavior (semantics) from the point of view of a user of the data, specifically in terms of possible values, possible operations on data of this type, and the behavior of these operations.

3.8.4 Good Programs Use Abstraction

- What makes a program good?
  - ➢ It works (as specified!).
  - ➢ It is easy to understand and modify.
  - ➢ It is reasonably efficient.
- The idea of an ADT is to separate the notions of specification (what kind of thing we're working with and what operations can be performed on it) and implementation (how the thing and its operations are actually implemented).

3.8.5 Benefits of using Abstract Data Types

- Code is easier to understand (e.g., it is easier to see "high-level" steps being performed, not obscured by low-level code).
- Implementations of ADTs can be changed (e.g., for efficiency) without requiring changes to the program that uses the ADTs.
- ADTs can be reused in future programs.
- Fortunately for us, object-oriented programming languages (like Java) make it easy for programmers to use ADTs : each ADT corresponds to a class (or Java interface - more on this later) and the operations on the ADT are the class/interface's public methods.
- The user, or client, of the ADT only needs to know about the method interfaces (the names of the methods, the types of the parameters, what the methods do, and what, if any, values they return), not the actual implementation (how the methods are implemented, the private data members, private methods, etc.).

Some Basic ADT :

  - • Lists   • Stacks   • Queues

3.9 CLASSES

- In the case of an ADT, encapsulation combines data (representing one entity of that type) with the operations that are used to manipulate such data. The resulting entity (data + operations) is called an object. You can think about an object as in the Fig. 3.1 below, where the data are hidden and they can be accessed exclusively through the provided methods (operations).

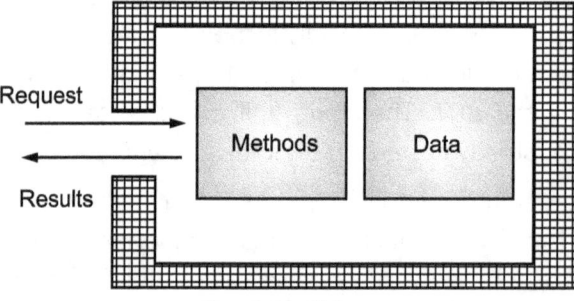

Fig. 3.1 : Object

- In Java, a class is a new data type, whose instances are objects. A class contains
  - Data fields
  - Methods
- Data fields and methods are collectively known as class members.
- Methods typically act on the data fields. By default, all members of a class are private, which means that they are not directly accessible by anybody outside of the class. If one wants to make a member accessible from outside (i.e., open a window that allows to access such member), then it should be declared as public. If we use a class to create an ADT, then we will probably want to declare as public the methods that correspond to the operations of the ADT (as we want them to be usable from outside). Note that the methods present inside a class can access all the members of the class, independently from whether they are public or private.
- You should almost always declare the data fields of a class as private. If the value of a data field is required outside of the class, then you will need to create a method (public) specifically to read the value of the data field and return it. Similarly, if there is the need of being able to change the value of a data field, then you will need to create a method specifically to perform this task.
- In short, an object is a specific combination of data and methods. Classes define the types of objects; hence, objects are frequently referred to as instances of their defining classes.
- Some important observations regarding the use of classes to build ADTs :
  - In Java, the constructor operation is represented by a special method, which always has the same name as the class. This method is automatically executed each time we request the creation of a new object belonging to the class.
  - In Java there is an automated mechanism, called garbage collector, which is in charge of discovering objects that are not used any more. This relieves the programmer from having to worry about erasing objects. It is possible to specify a method that will be executed when an object is destroyed; this method is always called finalize.

3.10 MODULES

- The main difference between classes and modules is that classes can be instantiated as objects while standard modules cannot. Because there is only one copy of a standard module's data, when one part of your program change a public variable in a standard module, any other part of the program gets the same value if it then reads that variable. In contrast, object data exist separately for each instantiated object. Another difference is that unlike standard modules, classes can implement interfaces.

- Classes and modules also use different scopes for their members. Members as defined within a class are scoped within a specific instance of the class and exist only for the lifetime of the object. To access class members from outside a class, you must use fully qualified names in the format of Object Member.

- On the other hand, members declared within a module are publicly accessible by default, and can be accessed by any code that can access the module. This means that variables in a standard module are effectively global variables because they are visible from anywhere in your project, and they exist for the life of the program.

3.11 GENERIC UNITS

- A generic unit is a program unit that is either a generic subprogram or a generic package. A generic unit is a template, which can be parameterized, and from which corresponding (non-generic) subprograms or packages can be obtained. The resulting program units are said to be instances of the original generic unit.

- A generic unit is declared by a generic_declaration. This form of declaration has a generic_formal_part declaring any generic formal parameters. An instance of a generic unit is obtained as the result of a generic_instantiation with appropriate generic actual parameters for the generic formal parameters. An instance of a generic subprogram is a subprogram. An instance of a generic package is a package.

- Generic units are templates. As templates they do not have the properties that are specific to their non-generic counterparts. For example, a generic subprogram can be instantiated but it cannot be called. In contrast, an instance of a generic subprogram is a (non-generic) subprogram; hence, this instance can be called but it cannot be used to produce further instances.

3.11.1 Generic Declarations

- A generic_declaration declares a generic unit, which is either a generic subprogram or a generic package. A generic_declaration includes a generic_formal_part declaring any generic formal parameters. A generic formal parameter can be an object; alternatively (unlike a parameter of a subprogram), it can be a type, a subprogram, or a package.

Syntax

```
generic_declaration : := generic_subprogram_declaration |
generic_package_declaration

generic_subprogram_declaration : :=
    generic_formal_part subprogram_specification;

generic_package_declaration : :=
    generic_formal_part package_specification;
```

generic_formal_part : := generic {generic_formal_parameter_declaration | use_clause}

generic_formal_parameter_declaration : :=

   formal_object_declaration

  | formal_type_declaration

  | formal_subprogram_declaration

  | formal_package_declaration

- The only form of subtype_indication allowed within a generic_formal_part is a subtype_mark (that is, the subtype_indication shall not include an explicit constraint). The defining name of a generic subprogram shall be an identifier (not an operator_symbol).

3.12 GENERIC DATA STRUCTURES

- Programs use many different data structures such as arrays, linked lists, hash tables, general trees, binary search trees, heaps etc. Each data structure is a container that holds a particular data type. Operations changes from data type to data type, for example, how you add two integers is not the same as how you "add" two tables. While we understand how to add two integers, "adding" two tables can be custom defined. Generic data types are important in designing libraries that works with "any" data type. A dynamic binding between data type and data structure occurs at run time.

- Generic data types are common in some high level languages. For example in Java 5, a generic data type can be defined using :

```
/**
*GenericversionoftheItemclass.
*/
publicclassItem<T>{
private T t;//T for type is late binding public void init (T t){
this. t = t;
}
public T get (){return t;
}
}
Item<Integer>intItem;
Item<Double>doubleItem;
```

- Hence Java allows the flexibility of late binding to types thereby allowing developers to develop generic libraries.
- In C++, a Standard Template Library (STL) provides similar facilities. For example, an example of using generic vector class for strings can be defined as :

```
#include<vector>
#include<string>
usingnamespacestd;main()
{
vector<string>V;

V.push_back("10");
V.push_back("20");
V.push_back("30"); V.pop_back();
cout<<"Loop by index :"<<endl;inti;
for(i=0;i<V.size();i++)
{
cout<<V[i]<<endl;
}
}
```

- Other modern languages such as C# provides generic classes for flexible and reusable code development. Although C does not have a built in facilities for generic data types, one can use the power of function pointers to build a good generic data structure. The following examples show building a generic data structure for a linked list and a doubly linked list structure.

Example :

- In this example we define a generic LIST_ELEM that can hold any data type as its data.

```
typedefstructLIST_ELEM
{
void*data;
structLIST_ELEM *next;
}LIST_ELEM;
```

The LINKED_LIST structure defined below contains three function pointers that define howto compare, print and free data of a particular data type. These functions can be passed during run time.

typedefstructLINKED_LIST

{

LIST_ELEM   *head;

int(*cmpData)(void*,void*);void(*printData)(void*);

void(*freeData)(void*);

} LINKED_LIST;

- The functions defined below are standard functions for LL operations not written for any particular data type, but uses the dynamic function pointers for operations specific to a particular data type.

voidinitList(LINKED_LIST*list,int(*cmpData)(void*,void*),

void(*printData)(void*),void(*freeData)(void*));

voidfreeAll(LINKED_LIST*list);/*free ALL dynamic memory in this program*/

voidinsertInOrder(LINKED_LIST*list, void*data);

voidremoveAtFront(LINKED_LIST *list   );

- We will discuss how to develop these functions in class.

Another Example :

- Here is another example of a generic data structure representing a doubly linked list.

typedefstructDLL_NODE{

    void*key;   /*Key for node*/

    void*value;

                                     /*The value for the node*/struct

    DLL_NODE*next;

                                     /*pointer to next node*/structD

    LL_NODE*prev;   /*pointer to previous node*/

}dll_node;

    typedefstructDLL{

    dll_node*head;

                                       /*head node of the list*/int(*cm

    p) (void*,void*);   /*Compare function pointer*/

    }dll_l;

```
intdll_init_list (dll_l*list);
intdll_set_cmp
(dll_l*list,int(*cmp)(void*,void*));intdll_insert(dll
_l*list,void*key,void*value);intdll_retrieve(dll_l*li
st,void*key,void**value);
```

3.13 GENERIC ALGORITHMS

- Templates may also be used to define generic algorithms. C++ uses templates to enable generic programming techniques. The C++ Standard Library includes the Standard Template Library or STL that provides a framework of templates for common data structures and algorithms. Templates in C++ may also be used for template meta programming, which is a way of pre-evaluating some of the code at compile-time rather than run-time. Using template specialization, C++ Templates are considered Turing complete.

- We saw the following generic function swap which interchanges the values of its two parameters :

```
template <class T>
void swap(T& x, T& y)
{
T temp = x;
x = y;
y = temp;
}
```

- This function may be used for any two parameters of the same type that support the "=" operation. Therefore, we can use it to swap integers, reals, and even user-defined types such as pairs. This is quite a useful capability because it gives us the possibility to write higher-level generic functions such as sort if they only use generic functions. The ability to write such generic functions is helped in C++ by the fact that generic functions do not have to be instantiated to be used.

- To use a template data structure, C++ requires explicit instantiation of the structure, as we saw, for example, in pair<int,int>. For functions, on the other hand, explicit instantiation is not necessary. The compiler will infer the instance required and generate it automatically. For example, the following program fragment is valid :

```
int a, b;
char p, q;
pair<int,string> p1, p2;
...
swap(a, b); //swap integers
swap(p, q); //swap strings
swap(p1, p2); //swap pairs
```

- The compiler will generate three different swap functions, for integers, strings and pairs of (int, string). To generate an appropriate function, the compiler checks at generation time that the parameters meet the expected requirements. Examination of the body of swap shows that the parameters passed must support assignment, that is, to be able to be passed and to be able to be assigned.

- The implicit parameter requirements in C++ are made explicit in Ada generic functions. The same swap function is defined in Ada as :

```
generic
type T is private;
procedureswap (a, b : T) is
begin
temp : T = a;
a = b;
b = temp;
end swap;
```

- The generic is explicitly stated to be based on a type T which is private. The private indication means that the type supports assignment and equality. In general, if other operations are required of the type, they have to be stated. For example, a generic max function will require its operands to support an order operations such as ">" :

```
generic
type T is private;
with function "<" (a, b : T) return BOOLEAN is <>;
function max (a, b : T) return BOOLEAN is
begin
ifa<b
then return a;
else return b;
end if;
end max;
```

- To use the function, we have to first instantiate an instance of it :

```
function int_max is new max (INTEGER);
```

- The type parameters passed at instantiation time are checked to ensure that they support the required operations. After instantiation, we have a new function that we may call :

```
m := int_max (3, 6);
```

- The Ada view is that different functions are generated and used while the C++ view is that there is just one function max which is generic. It is the compiler's job to generate as many instances as it wants to satisfy all the calls to the function. The C++ approach is more flexible and is more supportive of generic programming because generic functions are not treated any differently from non-generic functions : you simply call them. Ada treats generic functions as a special type of function that you must instantiate before you can call.

3.14 GENERIC MODULES

- Generic programming is a style of computer programming in which algorithms are written in terms of types to-be-specified-later that are then instantiated when needed for specific types provided as parameters.

- This approach, pioneered by ML in 1973, permits writing common functions or types that differ only in the set of types on which they operate when used, thus reducing duplication. Such software entities are known as generics in Ada, Delphi, Eiffel, Java, C#, F#, Objective-C, Swift, and Visual Basic .NET; parametric polymorphism in ML, Scala, Haskell (the Haskell community also uses the term "generic" for a related but somewhat different concept) and Julia; templates in C++ and D; and parameterized types in the influential 1994 book Design Patterns. The authors of Design Patterns note that this technique, especially when combined with delegation, is very powerful but also quote the following

- Dynamic, highly parameterized software is harder to understand than more static software.

- When a plain module contains a set of sub-modules, one way of looking at what the module performs is by seeing it as a combination of the results of the different sub-modules.

- The definition of generic modules opens to the user the possibility of defining specific, and reusable, operations of composition of modules. A generic module is indeed an abstraction of a combination by means of giving names to the submodules that will be obtained only at application time.

- Generic modules are then operations (or functions) on modules. The technique to define generic modules is the same as to define functions, that is, it consists of the isolation of a piece of program, or module, from its context and its abstraction by specifying :

  ➢ Those modules upon which the abstracted module may depend (requirements or parameters of the generic module).

  ➢ The contribution of the abstracted module to the rest of the program (results or export interface of the generic module).

- The obvious referent of this technique is functional programming, where such abstractions (functions) form the basic program units. The functional body defines how to compute the output (results) in terms of the input (requirements).

PROGRAM	: := moddecl$^+$
moddecl	: := Module amodid [([paramlist])] [= bodyexpr]
bodyexpr	: := begin decl end | pathid [([iparamlist])]
paramlist	: := amodid ; paramlis | amodid
iparamlist	: := bodyexpr ; iparamlist | bodyexpr

Syntax of Generic Module Definition

- A method for building large KB systems consists of applying generic modules to previously built plain modules. Keeping the common parts in a generic module we can save code and time, and make the code much more understandable. The instantiation of a generic module over a set of arguments generates a plain module, and hence it can appear in the code in the same places as a module declaration does.

3.15 HIGHER LEVELS OF GENERICITY

- One of the goals of Object Oriented Programming is genericity.

- Ideally, generic programs can be written once, compiled once and used for different data types.

- C++ achieves genericity two ways :

  ➢ Using virtual functions and derived classes to achieve polymorphism.

  ➢ Using templates to mimic polymorphism.

- Templated classes must be re-compiled for each data type. Some do not consider this OOP.

Genericity in C++

- void * and function pointers work in C++.

Generic list example :

Program 3.8 : Destructor doesn't know how to put away the objects that data points to.

```
class Node{
private :
void *data ;  // points to real data
Node *next ;  // points to next Node on the queue
Node() { data = NULL ; next = NULL ; }
  ~Node() { /* ??? */ }
};
```

Genericity in C++ : Class Derivation

- Class derivation allows us to specify how classes are related.
- An inheritance hierarchy has a base class that has all the common properties and methods that a generic algorithm needs.
- The derived classes inherit the properties of the base class.

Example :

> We can have a NumberArray class with a SelectionSort() member function.

> We can derive IntArray, FloatArray, DoubleArray from NumberArray and inherit the SelectionSort() member function.

- We have seen that we may define a generic algorithm that works on any type of object passed to it. For example, the max algorithm may be applied to any ordered type. This facility allows us to write one algorithm for n different data types rather than n different algorithms. It leads to great savings for writers of libraries. But consider a higher level of generality. Suppose we want to write an algorithm that works on different types of data structures, not just different data types.

- For example, we may want to write one algorithm to do a linear search in any "linear" data structure. Of course, we have to capture the notion of linearity somehow but intuitively, we want to be able to find an element in a collection regardless of whether the collection is implemented as an array, a list. The goal of the generic programming paradigm is to develop exactly these kinds of units.

- A high level of genericity is usually associated with functional languages and we will see it in the context of ML. There are no particular language facilities in Ada or C++ for this kind of programming. However, the flexibility of C++ templates, combined with overloading of operators supports a high degree of generic programming.

- For example, consider the following function find :

```
template<class Iter, class T>
Iter find ( Iter f, Iter l, T x)
{
while (*f != last && *f != x)
++f;
return f;
}
```

- We might think of this function as accepting two pointers into a sequence of elements. It sequences through the elements by using the ++ on the first pointer until either the value x is found or the sequence is exhausted. So, the following code fragment looks through the first half of an integer array :

```
int a[100];
int x;
int *r;
...
r= find(x, &a[0], &a[50]);
if (r == &a[5])
// not found
...
```

- We have used an integer pointer as the template parameter. However, the function is somewhat abstract : nothing in its explanation constrains us to use it with pointers and arrays! It is based on an abstract object which we have called Iter (for iterator). We can think of an iterator as a generalization of a C++ pointer.

- It must support the operations : *, to return a value, ++ to step to the next position, == and! = for comparison with another Iter. Certainly pointers meet these requirements. But we might imagine writing a list object that also provides an Iter type object which supports ++, *, ==, and!= operations with the same semantics as those of pointers into arrays. More importantly, any time a library writer provides a new linear structure, he can also provide it with such iterators.

- In this way, any generic operations will be immediately usable with the library's new data structures. What we are doing is to treat operations such as! =, *, and ++ as generic operations and writing a higher level operation find in terms of them.

- This style of generic programming is possible in C++ and likely will be the way standard libraries are provided. The advantage of such an approach for programming in the large is the reduction of the amount of code that wants to be written because one generic unit may be customized automatically depending on the context of its use. It is a form of modularity in which we modularize based on common properties and specific properties. Object-oriented programming is another approach to achieving this similar kind of modularity.

3.16 INTRODUCTION TO PROGRAMMING PARADIGMS

- A **programming paradigm** is a style or "way" of programming. Programming paradigms are a way to classify programming languages according to the style of computer programming. Features of various programming languages determine which programming paradigms they belong to; as a result, some languages fall into only one paradigm, while others fall into multiple paradigms. Some paradigms are concerned mainly with implications for the execution model of the language, such as allowing side effects, or whether the sequence of operations is defined by the execution model. Other paradigms are concerned mainly with the way that code is organized, such as grouping code into units along with the state that is modified by the code. Yet others are concerned mainly with the style of syntax and grammar.

- Common programming paradigms include imperative which allows side effects, functional which disallows side effects, declarative which does not state the order in which operations execute, object-oriented which groups code together with the state the code modifies, procedural which groups code into functions, logic which has a particular style of execution model coupled to a particular style of syntax and grammar, and symbolic programming which has a particular style of syntax and grammar.

- For example, languages that fall into the imperative paradigm have two main features : they state the order in which operations occur, with constructs that explicitly control that order, and they allow side effects, in which state can be modified at one point in time, within one unit of code, and then later read at a different point in time inside a different unit of code.

- The communication between the units of code is not explicit. Meanwhile, in object-oriented programming, code is organized into objects that contain state that is only modified by the code that is part of the object. Most object-oriented languages are also imperative languages. In contrast, languages that fit the declarative paradigm do not state the order in which to execute operations. Instead, they supply a number of operations that are available in the system, along with the conditions under which each is allowed to execute. The implementation of the language's execution model tracks which operations are free to execute and chooses the order on its own.

3.16.1 Procedural Paradigms

- Procedural programming can be defined as a subtype of imperative programming as a programming paradigm based upon the concept of procedure calls, in which statements are structured into procedures (also known as subroutines or functions). Procedure calls are modular and are bound by scope. A procedural program is composed of one or more modules. Each module is composed of one or more subprograms. Modules may consist of procedures, functions, subroutines or methods, depending on the programming language. Procedural programs may possibly have multiple levels or scopes, with subprograms defined inside other subprograms. Each scope can contain names which cannot be seen in outer scopes.

- Procedural programming offers many benefits over simple sequential programming since procedural code :

  ➢ Is easier to read and more maintainable

  ➢ Is more flexible

  ➢ Facilitates the practice of good program design

  ➢ Allows modules to be used again in the form of code libraries.

- Procedural programming is a programming paradigm, derived from structured programming, based upon the concept of the procedure call. Procedures, also known as routines, subroutines, or functions (not to be confused with mathematical functions, but similar to those used in functional programming), simply contain a series of computational steps to be carried out. Any given procedure might be called at any point during a program's execution, including by other procedures or itself. Procedural programming languages include C, Go, Fortran, Pascal, Ada, and BASIC.

- Computer processors provide hardware support for procedural programming through a stack register and instructions for calling procedures and returning from them. Hardware support for other types of programming is possible, but no attempt was commercially successful (for example Lisp machines or Java processors).

3.16.2 Object Oriented Paradigm

- Object-oriented programming (OOP) is a programming paradigm based upon objects (having both data and methods) that aims to incorporate the advantages of modularity and reusability. Objects, which are usually instances of classes, are used to interact with one another to design applications and computer programs.

- In the object-oriented paradigm the focus is on objects that represent either data or computational entities used in a program. One of the key features is a mechanism for encapsulating data values representing the value of an object with the operations that can be applied to the object. This is an extension of the usual notion of type, and in an object-oriented language such an encapsulation is called a class. Another key feature is the ability to add additional component data values and operations to an existing class of objects in order to obtain a new class of objects.

- The object-oriented paradigm took its shape from the initial concept of a new programming approach, while the interest in design and analysis methods came much later.

  ➢ The first object–oriented language was Simula (Simulation of real systems) that was developed in 1960 by researchers at the Norwegian Computing Center.

  ➢ In 1970, Alan Kay and his research group at Xerox PARK created a personal computer named Dynabook and the first pure object-oriented programming language (OOPL) - Smalltalk, for programming the Dynabook.

  ➢ In the 1980s, Grady Booch published a paper titled Object Oriented Design that mainly presented a design for the programming language, Ada. In the ensuing editions, he extended his ideas to a complete object–oriented design method.

  ➢ In the 1990s, Coad incorporated behavioral ideas to object-oriented methods.

- The other significant innovations were Object Modeling Techniques (OMT) by James Rumbaugh and Object-Oriented Software Engineering (OOSE) by Ivar Jacobson.

Object-Oriented Analysis

- Object–Oriented Analysis (OOA) is the procedure of identifying software engineering requirements and developing software specifications in terms of a software system's object model, which comprises of interacting objects.

- The main difference between object-oriented analysis and other forms of analysis is that in object-oriented approach, requirements are organized around objects, which integrate both data and functions. They are modeled after real-world objects that the system interacts with. In traditional analysis methodologies, the two aspects - functions and data - are considered separately.

- Grady Booch has defined OOA as, "Object-oriented analysis is a method of analysis that examines requirements from the perspective of the classes and objects found in the vocabulary of the problem domain".

- The primary tasks in object-oriented analysis (OOA) are :

  ➢ Identifying objects

  ➢ Organizing the objects by creating object model diagram

  ➢ Defining the internals of the objects, or object attributes

  ➢ Defining the behavior of the objects, i.e., object actions

  ➢ Describing how the objects interact

- The common models used in OOA are use cases and object models.

Object-Oriented Design

- Object–Oriented Design (OOD) involves implementation of the conceptual model produced during object-oriented analysis. In OOD, concepts in the analysis model, which are technology–independent, are mapped onto implementing classes, constraints are identified and interfaces are designed, resulting in a model for the solution domain, i.e., a detailed description of how the system is to be built on concrete technologies.

- The implementation details generally include :
  - ➤ Restructuring the class data (if necessary),
  - ➤ Implementation of methods, i.e., internal data structures and algorithms,
  - ➤ Implementation of control, and
  - ➤ Implementation of associations.

- Grady Booch has defined object-oriented design as "a method of design encompassing the process of object-oriented decomposition and a notation for depicting logical and physical as well as static and dynamic models of the system under design".

Object-Oriented Programming

- Object-oriented programming (OOP) is a programming paradigm based upon objects (having both data and methods) that aims to incorporate the advantages of modularity and reusability. Objects, which are usually instances of classes, are used to interact with one another to design applications and computer programs.

- The important features of object–oriented programming are :
  - ➤ Bottom–up approach in program design
  - ➤ Programs organized around objects, grouped in classes
  - ➤ Focus on data with methods to operate upon object's data
  - ➤ Interaction between objects through functions
  - ➤ Reusability of design through creation of new classes by adding features to existing classes

- Some examples of object-oriented programming languages are C++, Java, Smalltalk, Delphi, C#, Perl, Python, Ruby, and PHP.

- Grady Booch has defined object–oriented programming as "a method of implementation in which programs are organized as cooperative collections of objects, each of which represents an instance of some class, and whose classes are all members of a hierarchy of classes united via inheritance relationships".

3.16.3 Functional Paradigm

- In functional programming, programs are executed by evaluating expressions, in contrast with imperative programming where programs are composed of statements which change global state when executed. Functional programming typically avoids using mutable state.

- Functional programming requires that functions are first-class, which means that they are treated like any other values and can be passed as arguments to other functions or be returned as a result of a function. Being first-class also means that it is possible to define and manipulate functions from within other functions.

- Special attention needs to be given to functions that reference local variables from their scope. If such a function escapes their block after being returned from it, the local variables must be retained in memory, as they might be needed later when the function is called. Often it is difficult to determine statically when those resources can be released, so it is necessary to use automatic memory management.

- In computer science, functional programming is a programming paradigm—a style of building the structure and elements of computer programs—that treats computation as the evaluation of mathematical functions and avoids changing-state and mutable data.

- It is a declarative programming paradigm, which means programming is done with expressions or declarations instead of statements. In functional code, the output value of a function depends only on the arguments that are input to the function, so calling a function f twice with the same value for an argument x will produce the same result $f(x)$ each time. Eliminating side effects, i.e. changes in state that do not depend on the function inputs, can make it much easier to understand and predict the behavior of a program, which is one of the key motivations for the development of functional programming.

- Functional programming has its roots in lambda calculus, a formal system developed in the 1930s to investigate computability, function definition, function application, and recursion. Many functional programming languages can be viewed as elaborations on the lambda calculus. Another well-known declarative programming paradigm, logic programming, is based on relations.

- In contrast, imperative programming changes state with commands in the source language, the most simple example being assignment. Imperative programming does have functions—not in the mathematical sense—but in the sense of subroutines. They can have side effects that may change the value of program state. Functions without return values therefore make sense. Because of this, they lack referential transparency, i.e. the same language expression can result in different values at different times depending on the state of the executing program.

- Functional programming languages, especially purely functional ones such as Hope, have largely been emphasized in academia rather than in commercial software development. However, prominent programming languages which support functional programming such as Common Lisp, Scheme, Clojure, Wolfram Language (also known as Mathematica), Racket, Erlang, OCaml, Haskell, and F# have been used in industrial and commercial applications by a wide variety of organizations. Functional programming is also supported in some domain-specific programming languages like R (statistics), J, K and Q from Kx Systems (financial analysis), XQuery/XSLT (XML), and Opal. Widespread domain-specific declarative languages like SQL and Lex/Yacc use some elements of functional programming, especially in eschewing mutable values.

- Programming in a functional style can also be accomplished in languages that are not specifically designed for functional programming. For example, the imperative Perl programming language has been the subject of a book describing how to apply functional programming concepts. This is also true of the PHP programming language.C++11, Java 8, and C# 3.0 all added constructs to facilitate the functional style. The Julia language also offers functional programming abilities.

- An interesting case is that of Scala– it is frequently written in a functional style, but the presence of side effects and mutable states place it in a grey area between imperative and functional languages.

3.16.4 Logical Paradigm

- Logical programming is a programming paradigm based on formal logic. A program written in a logic programming language is a set of sentences in logical form, expressing facts and rules about some problem domain. Major logic programming language families include Prolog, Answer set programming (ASP) and Datalog.

- A Programming Paradigm based on *logic* (more accurately, the Predicate Calculus). A program is represented by a set of facts (statements/relationships which are held to be true), and a set of axioms (i.e. if A is true, then B is true). The axioms and clauses may have arguments.

  ➢ For example, one could define the relation child(A,B), meaning that A is a child of B. One then could establish a set of facts (stored in a database--see below) :

child(Pebbles,Fred)

child(Pebbles,Wilma)

child(Wilma,Freds-mother-in-law) (what's her name?)

child(Bam-bam,Barney)

child(Bam-bam,Betty)

- One can query the database :

child? (Pebbles,Fred) -> True

child? (Pebbles,Barney) -> False (at least Fred hopes not!)

- One then can define a descendent relationship, the transitive closure of the child relationship (this is pseudocode, obviously)

descendent(A,B) := child(A,B)

descendent(A,B) := exists(x : child(A,x) && descendent(x,B))

- One can query these relationships as well.

descendent? (Pebbles,Fred) -> True

descendent? (Pebbles,Freds-mother-in-law)? True

descendent? (Pebbles,Barney) -> False

- The Logical Paradigm takes a declarative approach to problem-solving. Various logical assertions about a situation are made, establishing all known facts. Then queries are made. The role of the computer becomes maintaining data and logical deduction.

3.16.4.1 Logical Paradigm Programming

- A logical program is divided into three sections :

  ➢ A series of definitions/declarations that define the problem domain

  ➢ Statements of relevant facts

  ➢ Statement of goals in the form of a query

- Any deducible solution to a query is returned. The definitions and declarations are constructed entirely from relations. i.e. X is a member of Y or X is in the internal between a and b etc.

Advantages :

The advantages of logic oriented programming are :

- The system solves the problem, so the programming steps themselves are kept to a minimum;

- Proving the validity of a given program is simple.

domains

  being = symbol

predicates

  animal(being) % all animals are beings

dog(being) % all dogs are beings

die(being) % all beings die

clauses

  animal(X) :- dog(X) % all dogs are animals

dog(fido). % fido is a dog

die(X) :- animal(X) % all animals die

3.16.5 The Rule-Based (or Logic) Paradigm

- In a rule-based language, programs are constructed by defining a set of rules for various goals. These rules essentially define logical expressions whose value is true. A "program" is a search for some combination of rule applications that results in a valid logical expression (an expression that is true).

- For example, in a language like Prolog we could define function max(X, Y, R) that determines the maximum of two values X and Y by

  max (X, Y, R) -> pre_max(X, Y) , post_max (X, Y, R).

  pre_max (X, Y) -> integer(X), integer(Y).

  post_max(X, Y, R) -> (R=X ; R=Y), R>=X, R>=Y.

- In Prolog, the comma (,) is an operator that denotes logical AND, and the semicolon (;) is an operator that denotes logical OR. So the above definition for max says that the value of max(X, Y, R) is true if pre_max(X, Y) is true and post_max(X, Y, R) is true. The rule for pre_max(X, Y) says that pre_max(X, Y) is true if integer(X) and integer(Y) are both true, where integer is a predefined predicate function that is true if its operand is of type integer and is false otherwise. Thus for max(X, Y, R) to be true, X and Y must be integers and post_max(X, Y, R) must be true.

- The last rule says that for post_max(X, Y, R) to be true, R is equal to X or equal to Y, and R is greater than or equal to both X and Y. Note that the definition of max would not be valid if post_max were defined as

  post_max(X, Y, R) -> R>=X, R>=Y.

  (Why?)

- Having made these definitions, we can then interact with the Prolog system in a manner similar to interacting with sml. An example of some interactions, where the prompt is a question mark (?), is shown below.

  ? max (3, 5, 7).

  no

  ? max (3, 5, 3).

  no

  ? max (3, 5, 5).

  yes

  ? max (8, 5, X).

  yes, X=8

- When we entered the expression max(3, 5, 7)., the system responded "no", indicating that max(3, 5, 7) is false. The first three expressions illustrate that if we enter an expression that can be evaluated (i.e., if the values of the parameters are known), then the expression is evaluated and a result of true (yes) or false (no) is obtained. The last expression (max (8, 5, X)), illustrates that if there is a variable for one of the parameters, then Prolog tries to find a value that makes the expression true, and if it can then it reports that value (or values).

- A "program" in Prolog is just a sequence of expressions that are ANDed together. For example, the following is a program to read two integers and print their maximum :

```
write('Enter first number : '), read(X),
write('Enter second number : '), read(Y),
write('The max of '), write(X),
write(' and '), write(Y),
write(' is '),
max(X, Y, R),
write(R).
```

- This illustrates that read is a predefined predicate function that assigns the next input value as the value of its argument and returns true if the operation is successful, and write works in a similar manner. Thus the program reads a value for X and a value for Y, finds the max of X and Y, and prints out X, Y, and their max. Note that the "program" terminates if any of the terms (separated by commas) evaluates to false, because then the entire expression would be known to be false and the only objective is to find a way to produce a true result.

- Rule-based languages enjoyed a surge of popularity during the 1980s, but recently their usage has declined. They are well-suited to knowledge-oriented applications such as medical or other problem diagnosis systems.

3.17 STUDY OF JAVA AS OBJECT ORIENTED PROGRAMMING LANGUAGE

- Java is an object-oriented language similar to C++, but simplified to eliminate language features that cause common programming errors. Java source code files (files with a .java extension) are compiled into a format called byte code (files with a .class extension), which can then be executed by a Java interpreter.

- Object means a real word entity such as pen, chair, table etc. Object-Oriented Programming is a methodology or paradigm to design a program using classes and objects. It simplifies the software development and maintenance by providing some concepts :

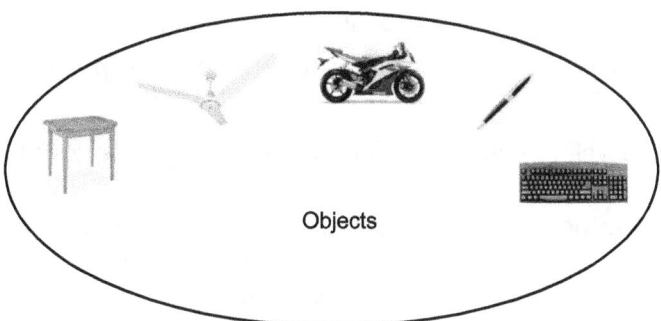

Fig. 3.2 : Real world objects

- ➢ Object
- ➢ Class
- ➢ Inheritance
- ➢ Polymorphism
- ➢ Abstraction
- ➢ Encapsulation

- Java is known as an Object Oriented language. So, what does Object Oriented mean? It means that the foundations of any kind of program constructed in Java might be imagined in terms of Objects. A good example of this idea should be to have a look at a handful of sample business requirements for a product. Imagine that we are tasked with constructing a software program intended to keep track of an actual public library system. This system must keep track of each of the branches associated with the libraries, the whole set of materials that can be contained in the branches, and additionally all of the people that may need to access books from the library's branch.

- The first thing we're able to do is examine those specs and pinpoint all of the keywords which happen to be nouns. For the record, a noun is actually a person, place or thing. Which means, if we analyze our requirements we distinguish these particular nouns :

- ➢ Library
- ➢ Book
- ➢ Branch
- ➢ Customer

- All these words represent Objects in Java. This really is, in essence, Object Oriented programming (generally known as O-O programming). What we can now go about doing, is in fact arrange these four Objects on to some sort of piece of paper, and begin to distinguish what sort of attributes each one of these Objects contains. What do I mean by the attributes? Well, in O-O development this is known as identifying the "has a" relationships. To provide an example, a Branch "has an" address, a Book "has a" title, a

Customer "has a" name. We will map out the most important attributes that each one of these Objects contain, and build ourselves a terrific starting point for the design of our Java application.

- Object oriented development allows developers to think in terms of real life "things" or Objects, and simply solve issues with all those Objects. It's important to remember that Java is actually not the only O-O programming language in existence, as it was initially started nearly five decades ago and plenty of modern programming languages utilize Object Oriented principles. Some of these languages include C++, C#, Objective-C, Python, Ruby and Visual Basic.

- So what would the Objects from our example look like in code? Let's take a look at the BookObject :

```java
public class Book
{
private String author;
private String title;
private Integer isbn;
private Integer numberOfPages;

public String getAuthor()
    {
return author;
    }
public void setAuthor(String author)
    {
this.author = author;
    }
public String getTitle()
    {
return title;
    }
```

```
public void setTitle(String title)
   {
this.title = title;
   }
public Integer getIsbn()
   {
returnisbn;
   }
public void setIsbn(Integer isbn)
   {
this.isbn = isbn;
   }
public Integer getNumberOfPages()
   {
returnnumberOfPages;
   }
public void setNumberOfPages(Integer numberOfPages)
   {
this.numberOfPages = numberOfPages;
   }
}
```

- Okay, so what can we identify in this code that we are already familiar with? Well, we certainly see the word public a lot sprinkled around here. To refresh your memory, the word public is a modifier that allows for any Java Class to have access to the code within the scope of what it's modifying. So, you see that the first public keyword is placed on the Class name, which in this case is Book. This means that our Book Class will be accessible by all other Classes in our project.

- **Note :** You may have noticed I used the terms Class and Object to describe the same thing. In actual fact, they are very similar; the only difference is that the Class can be considered the blueprint for an Object. An Object is what is physically created when the Java program is running. So if I want to "create" a Book, let's say a "Harry Potter" Book, I would "instantiate" (or "create") a Book Object based on its Class blueprint.

- Let's move on to the private modifier that you see on the first four variables (or attributes) of our Book Class. This is kind of strange you might think. If a Book has attributes like a title, an author etc. then why are these marked as private? Wouldn't we want other Classes to have access to a Books title for instance? Yes and no, this approach used here is called encapsulation, and it's one of the fundamental principles in Object Oriented programming. Let's flip over to Wiki for a definition of encapsulation :

- In a programming language, encapsulation is used to refer to one of two related but distinct notions, and sometimes to the combination thereof :

  ➤ A language mechanism for restricting access to some of the object's components.

  ➤ A language construct that facilitates the bundling of data with the methods (or other functions) operating on that data.

- In our example, we are touching on the first part of this definition, which is restricting access. We don't want just anyone to be able to come in and say, change the title of our Book Object. We want to be able to "screen" or "moderate" what changes are allowed and which are not. So we accomplish this by setting the attributes of our Book to be private and introduce public methods where you'll be able to retrieve and/or change the value of our Book's attributes. So, if you want to know what a Book's particular title is, you would have to "ask" like this :

```
String aBooksTitle = book.getTitle();
```

- And just the same, if you wanted to change a particular Book's title, you would do this :

```
book.setTitle("Harry Potter Vol. 2");
```

EXERCISE

1. Explain Software design method.
2. Explain the Concepts in support of modularity.
3. What is Encapsulation? Explain with example.
4. Explain the Interface and implementation.
5. What is Separate and independent compilation?
6. What is Abstract data types?
7. Explain the classes, and modules?
8. Explain Generic units and Generic data structures.
9. Explain four main Programming paradigms?
10. Differentiate between procedural, object oriented, functional, and logic & rule based Programming paradigms.

✠ ✠ ✠

JAVA AS OBJECT ORIENTED PROGRAMMING LANGUAGE – OVERVIEW

4.1 JAVA

- Java is a programming language and a platform. Java is a high level, robust, secured and object-oriented programming language.

- Platform : Any hardware or software environment in which a program runs, is known as a platform. Since Java has its own runtime environment (JRE) and API, it is called platform.

4.1.1 Where it is used?

There are many devices where Java is currently used. Some of them are as follows:

- Desktop Applications such as acrobat reader, media player, antivirus etc.
- Web Applications such as irctc.co.in, Javatpoint.com etc.
- Enterprise Applications such as banking applications
- Mobile
- Embedded System
- Smart Card
- Robotics
- Games etc.

4.1.2 Types of Java Applications

There are mainly four types of applications that can be created using Java programming :

- **Standalone Application :**

It is also known as desktop application or window-based application. An application that we need to install on every machine such as media player, antivirus etc. AWT and Swing are used in Java for creating standalone applications.

- **Web Application :**

An application that runs on the server side and creates dynamic page, is called web application. Currently, servlet, jsp, struts, jsf etc. technologies are used for creating web applications in Java.

- **Enterprise Application :**

An application that is distributed in nature, such as banking applications etc. It has the advantage of high level security, load balancing and clustering. In Java, EJB is used for creating enterprise applications.

- **Mobile Application :**

An application that is created for mobile devices. Currently Android and Java ME are used for creating mobile applications.

4.2 HISTORY OF JAVA

- The history of Java starts from Green Team. Java team members also known as Green Team, initiated a revolutionary task to develop a language for digital devices such as set-top boxes, televisions etc.

- For the green team members, it was an advance concept at that time. But, it was suited for internet programming. Later, Java technology as incorporated by Netscape.

- Currently, Java is used in internet programming, mobile devices, games, e-business solutions etc. Following are the major points that describes the history of Java.

- James Gosling, Mike Sheridan, and Patrick Naughton initiated the Java language project in June 1991. The small team of sun engineers called Green Team.

- Originally designed for small, embedded systems in electronic appliances like set-top boxes.

- Firstly, it was called "Greentalk" by James Gosling and file extension was .gt. After that, it was called Oak and was developed as a part of the Green project.

- Why Oak? Oak is a symbol of strength and chosen as a national tree of many countries like U.S.A., France, Germany, Romania etc.

- In 1995, Oak was renamed as "Java" because it was already a trademark by Oak Technologies.

- Why did they choose Java name for Java language? The team gathered to choose a new name. The suggested words were "dynamic", "revolutionary", "Silk", "jolt", "DNA" etc. They wanted something that reflected the essence of the technology : revolutionary, dynamic, lively, cool, unique, and easy to spell and fun to say.

- According to James Gosling, "Java was one of the top choices along with Silk". Since Java was so unique, most of the team members preferred Java.

- Java is an island of Indonesia, where coffee was first produced, called Java coffee.

- Originally developed by James Gosling at Sun Microsystems which is now a subsidiary of Oracle Corporation and released in 1995.

- In 1995, Time magazine called Java one of the Ten Best Products of 1995.

- JDK 1.0 released in (January 23, 1996).

4.2.1 Java Version History

There are many Java versions that have been released. Current stable release of Java is Java SE 8. DEEPA

- JDK Alpha and Beta (1995)
- JDK 1.0 (23rd Jan, 1996)
- JDK 1.1 (19th Feb, 1997)
- J2SE 1.2 (8th Dec, 1998)
- J2SE 1.3 (8th May, 2000)
- J2SE 1.4 (6th Feb, 2002)
- J2SE 5.0 (30th Sep, 2004)
- Java SE 6 (11th Dec, 2006)
- Java SE 7 (28th July, 2011)
- Java SE 8 (18th March, 2014)
- Java SE 8-31 CPU (20th Jan, 2015)
- Java SE 8-71 CPU (19th Jan, 2016)
- Java SE 8-111 CPU (18th Oct, 2016)

4.3 JAVA FEATURES

There are many features of Java. The Java Features given below are simple and easy to understand.

- Simple and Small
- Object-Oriented
- Platform independent
- Secured
- Robust
- Architecture neutral
- Portable
- High Performance
- Distributed
- Multithreaded
- **Simple and Small :**
  - ➢ Java language is simple because syntax is based on C++ so easier for programmers to learn it after C++.
  - ➢ Java is easily programmable, with a minimum of training, since it is based on C++.
  - ➢ It enables construction of compact software that can run 'stand-alone' even on small machines.

- **Object – Oriented :**
  - ➢ An object-oriented design enables the development of small, modular, self contained units, each of which could later be used as building block for any specific application.
  - ➢ It also facilitates a clean definition of interfaces and allows 'plug-and-play' features, where in reusable software components can be distributed easily across diverse hardware platforms.
  - ➢ Programmers can even attach their applications and data together, and bundle the combination as a single entity.
  - ➢ To be truly considered as 'object oriented' a programming language should support a minimum of four characteristics.

    1. **Encapsulation :** Implements information hiding and modularity that is abstraction.

    2. **Polymorphism :** The same message sent to different objects results in behavior that is dependent on the nature of the object receiving the message.

    3. **Inheritance :** You define new classes and behavior based on existing classes to obtain code re-use and code organization.

    4. **Dynamic Binding :** Objects could come from anywhere possibly across the network. You need to be able to send messages to objects without having to know their specific type at the time you write your code. Dynamic binding provides maximum flexibility while a program is executing.

- **Platform Independent :**

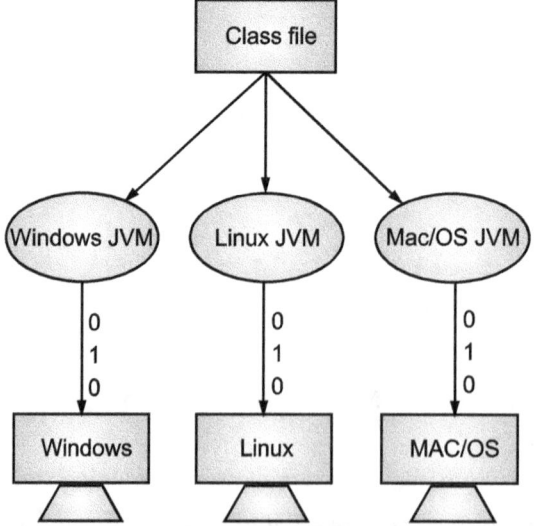

Fig. 4.1 : Platform indepdendency

➢ A platform is the hardware or software environment in which a program runs.

➢ There are two types of platforms software-based and hardware-based. Java provides software-based platform.

➢ The Java platform differs from most other platforms in the sense that it is a software-based platform that runs on the top of other hardware-based platforms. It has two components :

    1. Runtime Environment

    2. API (Application Programming Interface)

➢ Java code can be run on multiple platforms e.g. Windows, Linux, Sun Solaris, Mac/OS etc.

➢ Java code is compiled by the compiler and converted into bytecode. This bytecode is a platform-independent code because it can be run on multiple platforms i.e. Write Once and Run Anywhere.

- **Secured :**

Java is secure because :

(a) No explicit pointer

(b) Java Programs run inside virtual machine sandbox

➢ Classloader : Adds security by separating the package for the classes of the local file system from those that are imported from network sources.

➢ Bytecode Verifier : Checks the code fragments for illegal code that can violate access right to objects.

➢ Security Manager : Determines what resources a class can access such as reading and writing to the local disk.

➢ These security features are provided by Java language. Some security can also be provided by application developer through SSL, JAAS, Cryptography etc.

- **Robust :**

➢ Robust simply means strong. Java uses strong memory management. There is a lack of pointers that avoids security problem. There is automatic garbage collection in Java.

➢ There is exception handling and type checking mechanism in Java. All these points make Java robust.

➢ Java programs are robust because explicit memory manipulations by the programmer are prevented.

- **Architecture-Neutral :**
  - ➢ There are no implementation dependent features e.g. size of primitive types is fixed.
  - ➢ In C programming, int data type occupies 2 bytes of memory for 32-bit architecture and 4 bytes of memory for 64-bit architecture. But in Java, it occupies 4 bytes of memory for both 32 and 64 bit architectures.
  - ➢ The Java Compiler generates an architecture-neutral object file, 'generic', Byte Code instructions, which have nothing to do with a particular computer architecture. This compiled code is executable on any processor, given the presence of the Java run-time system, which will translate it into native machine code on the fly.
  - ➢ The same version of the software runs on all platforms, independent of any CPU or hardware architecture, across networks.
- **Portable**
  - ➢ We may carry the Java bytecode to any platform.
- **High-Performance :**
  - ➢ Java is faster than traditional interpretation since byte code is "close" to native code still somewhat slower than a compiled language (e.g., C++)
- **Distributed :**
  - ➢ We can create distributed applications in Java. RMI and EJB are used for creating distributed applications.
  - ➢ We may access files by calling the methods from any machine on the internet.
- **Multi-Threaded :**
  - ➢ A thread is like a separate program, executing concurrently. We can write Java programs that deal with many tasks at once by defining multiple threads.
  - ➢ The main advantage of multi-threading is that it doesn't occupy memory for each thread. It shares a common memory area. Threads are important for multi-media, Web applications etc.

4.4 C++ Vs JAVA

There are many differences and similarities between C++ programming language and Java. A list of top differences between C++ and Java are given below :

Content	C++	Java
Platform-independent	C++ is platform-dependent.	Java is platform-independent.
Mainly used for	C++ is mainly used for system programming.	Java is mainly used for application programming. It is widely used in window, web-based, enterprise and mobile applications.

Contd...

Goto statement	C++ supports goto statement.	Java doesn't support goto statement.
Multiple inheritance	C++ supports multiple inheritance.	Java doesn't support multiple inheritance through class. It can be achieved by interfaces in Java.
Operator Overloading	C++ supports operator overloading.	Java doesn't support operator overloading.
Pointers	C++ supports pointers. You can write pointer program in C++.	Java supports pointer internally. But you can't write the pointer program in Java. It means Java has restricted pointer support in Java.
Compiler and Interpreter	C++ uses compiler only.	Java uses compiler and interpreter both.
Call by Value and Call by reference	C++ supports both call by value and call by reference.	Java supports call by value only. There is no call by reference in Java.
Structure and Union	C++ supports structures and unions.	Java doesn't support structures and unions.
Thread Support	C++ doesn't have built-in support for threads. It relies on third-party libraries for thread support.	Java has built-in thread support.
Virtual Keyword	C++ supports virtual keyword so that we can decide whether or not to override a function.	Java has no virtual keyword. We can override all non-static methods by default. In other words, non-static methods are virtual by default.
unsigned right shift >>>	C++ doesn't support >>> operator.	Java supports unsigned right shift >>> operator that fills zero at the top for the negative numbers. For positive numbers, it works same like >> operator.

4.5 JAVA AND INTERNET

- Java is strongly associated with the Internet. Internet users can use Java to create applet programs and run them locally using a "Java-enabled browser" such as HotJava. They can also use a Java-enabled browser to download an applet located on a computer anywhere in the Internet and run it on his local computer.

- In fact, Java applets have made the Internet a true extension of the storage system of the local computer.

- Internet users can also setup their websites containing Java applets that could be used by other remote users of Internet. This feature made Java most popular programming language for Internet.

- The Java programming language enables the Web documents authors to deliver small application programs to anyone browsing the pages of the html documents.

- The page becomes alive because it can create game score boards, execute animated cartoons, audio files and video clippings.

- In addition, it changed the way Internet and WWW worked by allowing architecturally neutral compiled code to be dynamically loaded from anywhere in the network of heterogeneous systems and executed transparently. The Internet usage before and after Java is shown in following Fig. 4.2 and 4.3.

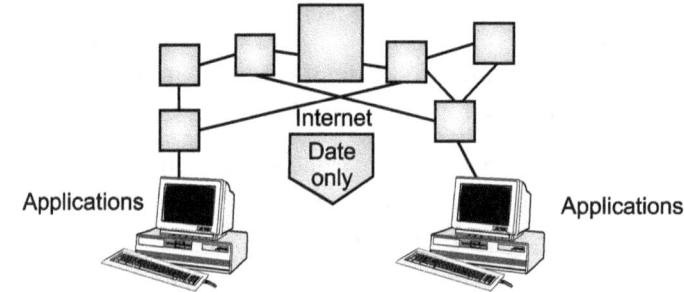

Fig. 4.2 : Internet usage Pre-Java

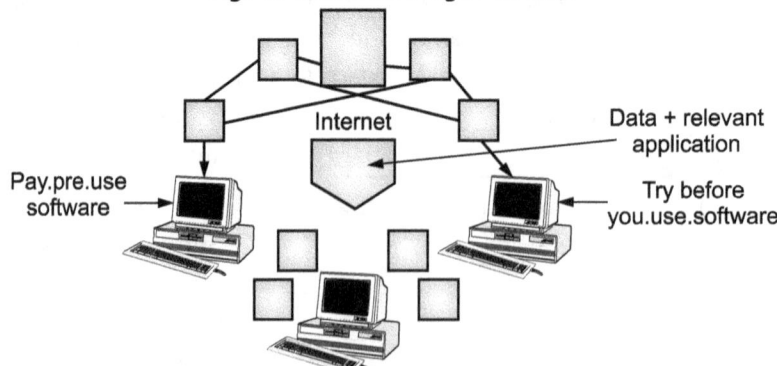

Fig. 4.3 : Internet usage Post-Java

- An applet is a special Java program that is designed to be transmitted over the Internet and automatically executed by a Java-compatible web browser. Furthermore, an applet is downloaded on demand, without further interaction with the user.
- If the user clicks a link that contains an applet, the applet will be automatically downloaded and run in the browser.
- Applets are intended to be small programs. They are typically used to display data provided by the server, handle user input, or provide simple functions, such as a loan calculator, that execute locally, rather than on the server.
- In essence, the applet allows some functionality to be moved from the server to the client.
- The creation of the applet changed Internet programming because it expanded the universe of objects that can move about freely in cyberspace.

4.6 JAVA AND WORLD WIDE WEB

- World Wide Web (WWW) is an open-ended information retrieval system designed to be used in the Internet's distributed environment. This system contains web pages that provide both information and controls.
- Web system is open-ended and we can navigate to a new document in any direction. This is made possible with the help of a language called Hypertext Markup Language (HTML).
- Web pages contain HTML tags that enable us to find, retrieve, manipulate and display documents worldwide.
- Java was meant to be used in distributed environments such as Internet. Since, both the Web and Java share the same philosophy, Java could be easily incorporated into the Web system.
- Before Java, the World Wide Web was limited to the display of still images and texts. However, the incorporation of Java into Web pages has made it capable of supporting animation, graphics, games, and a wide range of special effects.

4.7 WEB BROWSER

- A web browser is a software application for retrieving, presenting, and traversing information resources on the World Wide Web.
- An information resource is identified by a Uniform Resource Identifier (URI/URL) and may be a web page, image, video or other piece of content.
- Hyperlinks present in resources enable users easily to navigate their browsers to related resources.
- Although browsers are primarily intended to use the World Wide Web, they can also be used to access information provided by web servers in private networks or files in file systems.
- The major web browsers are Firefox, Google Chrome, Internet Explorer/Microsoft Edge, Opera, and Safari.

4.8 SIMPLE JAVA PROGRAM

- In this topic, we will learn how to write the simple program of Java. We can write a simple hello Java program easily after installing the JDK.

- To create a simple Java program, you need to create a class that contains main method. Let's understand the requirement first.

4.8.1 Requirement for Hello Java Example

- For executing any Java program, you need to
  - ➤ Install the JDK if you don't have installed it, download the JDK and install it.
  - ➤ Set path of the jdk/bin directory. http ://www.Javatpoint.com/how-to-set-path-in-Java.
  - ➤ Create the Java program compile and run the Java program.

4.8.2 Creating Hello Java Example

Let's create the hello Java program :

```
class Simple
{
public static void main(String args[])
  {
     System.out.println("Hello Java");
  }
}
```

save this file as Simple.Java

To Compile :   Javac Simple.Java

To Execute :   Java Simple

Output : Hello Java

4.8.3 Explanation of First Java Program

- **class** keyword is used to declare a class in Java.

- **public** keyword is an access modifier which represents visibility, it means it is visible to all.

- **static** is a keyword, if we declare any method as static, it is known as static method. The core advantage of static method is that there is no need to create object to invoke the static method. The main method is executed by the JVM, so it doesn't require to create object to invoke the main method. So, it saves memory.

- **void** is the return type of the method, it means it doesn't return any value.
- **main** represents startup of the program.
- **String[] args** is used for command line argument..
- **System.out.println()** is used print statement. here System is the class, out is the object of class System and println() is the function which is used to print the text.

There are many ways to write a Java program. The modifications that can be done in a Java program are given below :

(1) By changing sequence of the modifiers, method prototype is not changed.

Let's see the simple code of main method.

- Static public void main(String args[])

(2) Subscript notation in Java array can be used after type, before variable or after variable.

Let's see the different codes to write the main method.

- Public static void main(String[] args)
- Public static void main(String []args)
- Public static void main(String args[])

(3) You can provide var-args support to main method by passing 3 ellipses (dots)

Let's see the simple code of using var-args in main method. Public static void main (String... args)

(4) Having semicolon at the end of class in Java is optional.

Let's see the simple code.

```
class A
{
    static public void main(String... args)
    {
    System.out.println("hello Java4");
    }
};
```

4.8.4 Internal Details of Hello Java Program

- In the previous topic, we have learned about the first program, how to compile and how to run the first Java program. Here, we are going to learn, what happens while compiling and running the Java program. Moreover, we will see some question based on the first program.

What Happens at Compile Time?

- At compile time, Java file is compiled by Java Compiler and converts the Java code into bytecode.

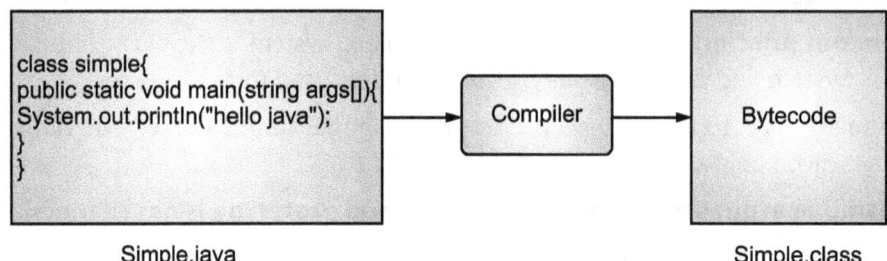

Simple.java   Simple.class

Fig. 4.4 : Java program complication process

What Happens at Runtime?

- At runtime, following steps are performed :

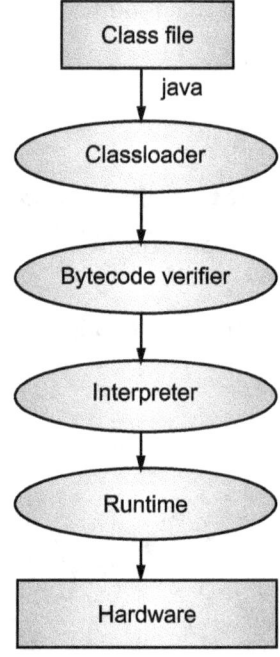

Fig. 4.5 : Java program runtime process

Classloader :

Classloader is the subsystem of JVM that is used to load class files.

Bytecode Verifier :

Bytecode Verifier checks the code fragments for illegal code that can violate access right to objects.

Interpreter :

Interpreter read bytecode stream then execute the instructions.

Can you save a Java source file by other name than the class name?

Yes, if the class is not public. It is explained in the Fig. 4.6 given below :

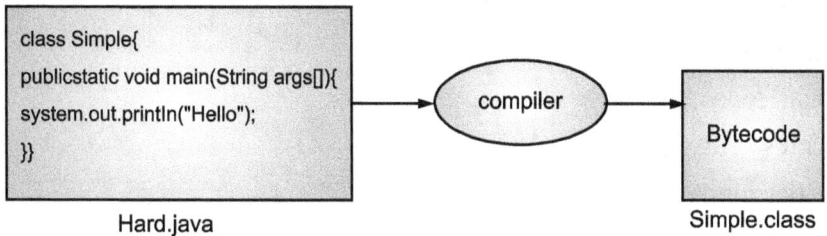

Hard.java   Simple.class

Fig. 4.6 : Example of Java program complication

To Compile :   Javac Hard.Java

To Execute :   Java Simple

Can you have multiple classes in a Java source file?

Yes, like the Fig. 4.7 given below illustrates :

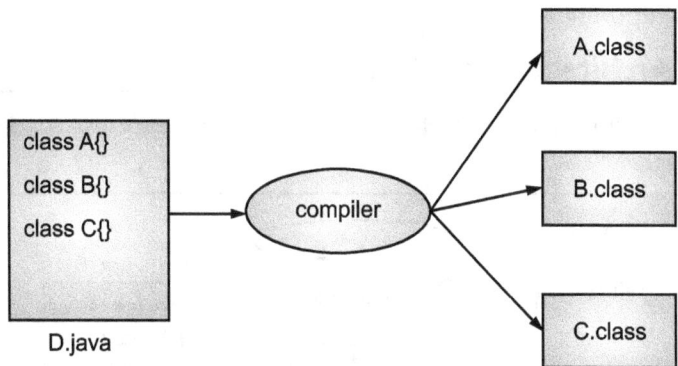

Fig. 4.7 : Example of multiple classes in Java source file

4.9 JVM (JAVA VIRTUAL MACHINE)

- JVM (Java Virtual Machine) is an abstract machine. It is a specification that provides runtime environment in which Java bytecode can be executed.

- JVMs are available for many hardware and software platforms i.e. JVM is platform dependent.

- JVM is :

  ➢ **A Specification :** Where working of Java Virtual Machine is specified. But implementation provider is independent to choose the algorithm. Its implementation has been provided by Sun and other companies.

- ➢ **An Implementation :** Its implementation is known as JRE (Java Runtime Environment).
- ➢ **Runtime Instance :** Whenever you write Java command on the command prompt to run the Java class, an instance of JVM is created.
- The JVM performs following operation :
  - ➢ Loads code
  - ➢ Verifies code
  - ➢ Executes code
  - ➢ Provides runtime environment
- JVM provides definitions for the :
  - ➢ Memory area
  - ➢ Class file format
  - ➢ Register set
  - ➢ Garbage-collected heap
  - ➢ Fatal error reporting etc.

4.9.1 Internal Architecture of JVM

Let's understand the internal architecture of JVM. It contains class loader, memory area, execution engine etc.

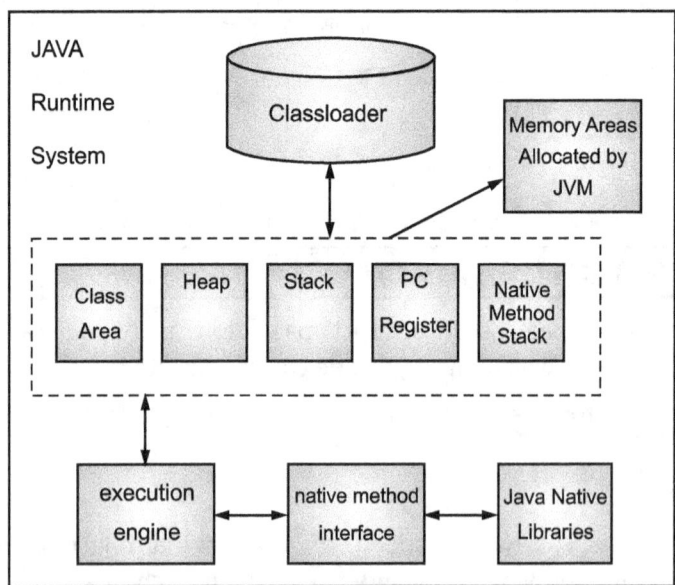

Fig. 4.8 : Internal architecture of JVM

- **Classloader :**

  Classloader is a subsystem of JVM that is used to load class files.

- **Class(Method) Area :**

  Class(Method) Area stores per-class structures such as the runtime constant pool, field and method data, the code for methods.

- **Heap :**

  It is the runtime data area in which objects are allocated.

- **Stack :**

  Java Stack stores frames. It holds local variables and partial results, and plays a part in method invocation and return. Each thread has a private JVM stack, created at the same time as thread. A new frame is created each time a method is invoked. A frame is destroyed when its method invocation completes.

- **Program Counter Register :**

  It contains the address of the Java virtual machine instruction currently being executed.

- **Native Method Stack :**

  It contains all the native methods used in the application.

- **Execution Engine :**

  It contains :

  - ➢ **A Virtual Processor**
  - ➢ **Interpreter :** Read bytecode stream then execute the instructions.
  - ➢ **Just-In-Time(JIT) Compiler :** It is used to improve the performance.JIT compiles parts of the byte code that have similar functionality at the same time, and hence reduces the amount of time needed for compilation.

4.9.2 Difference between JDK, JRE and JVM

JVM

- JVM (Java Virtual Machine) is an abstract machine. It is a specification that provides runtime environment in which Java bytecode can be executed.

- JVMs are available for many hardware and software platforms. JVM, JRE and JDK are platform dependent because configuration of each OS differs. But, Java is platform independent.

- The JVM performs following main tasks :

  - ➢ Loads code
  - ➢ Verifies code
  - ➢ Executes code
  - ➢ Provides runtime environment

JRE

- JRE is an acronym for Java Runtime Environment. It is used to provide runtime environment. It is the implementation of JVM. It physically exists.

- It contains set of libraries + other files that JVM uses at runtime. Implementation of JVMs are also actively released by other companies besides Sun Micro Systems.

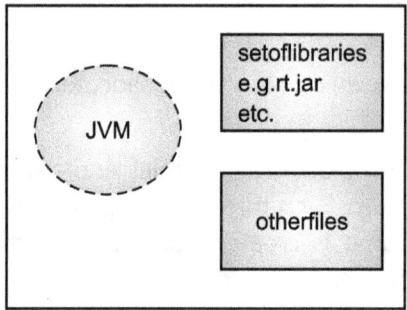

Fig. 4.9 : Java runtime enviornment

JDK

- JDK is an acronym for Java Development Kit. It physically exists. It contains JRE + development tools.

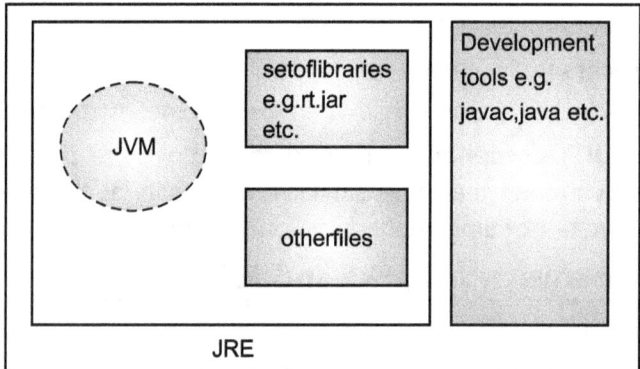

Fig. 4.10 : Java development kit

4.10 JAVA OOPS CONCEPTS

- Object Oriented Programming is a paradigm that provides many concepts such as **inheritance**, **data binding**, **polymorphism** etc.

- **Simula** is considered as the first object-oriented programming language. The programming paradigm where everything is represented as an object, is known as truly object-oriented programming language.

- **Smalltalk** is considered as the first truly object-oriented programming language.

- **Object-Oriented Programming** is a methodology or paradigm to design a program using classes and objects. It simplifies the software development and maintenance by providing some concepts :
  - ➤ Object
  - ➤ Class
  - ➤ Inheritance
  - ➤ Polymorphism
  - ➤ Abstraction
  - ➤ Encapsulation

Object :
- Object is a real word entity such as pen, chair, table etc. Any entity that has state and behavior is known as an object.
- For example : chair, pen, table, keyboard, bike etc. It can be physical and logical.

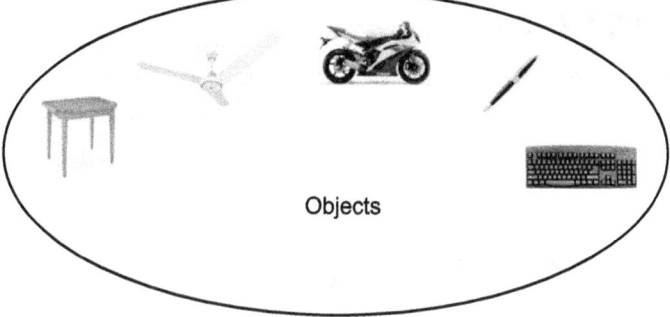

Fig. 4.11 : Object

Class :
- It is a User defined entity.
- Collection of objects is called class. It is a logical entity.

Inheritance :
- When one object acquires all the properties and behaviours of parent object, it is called as inheritance.
- It provides code reusability. It is used to achieve runtime polymorphism.

Polymorphism :
- When one task is performed by different ways i.e. known as polymorphism.
- For example, to convince the customer differently, to draw something e.g. shape or rectangle etc.
- In Java, we use method overloading and method overriding to achieve polymorphism.
- Another example can be to speak something e.g. cat speaks meaw, dog barks woof etc.

Abstraction :

- Hiding internal details and showing functionality is known as abstraction.
- For example, phone call, we don't know the internal processing.
- In Java, we use abstract class and interface to achieve abstraction.

Encapsulation :

- Binding or wrapping code and data together into a single unit is known as encapsulation.
- For example, capsule, it is wrapped with different medicines.

Fig. 4.12 : Capsule

- A Java class is the example of encapsulation. Java bean is the fully encapsulated class because all the data members are private here.

4.11 VARIABLES IN JAVA

- **Variable** is name of reserved area allocated in memory. In other words, it is a name of memory location. It is a combination of "vary + able" that means its value can be changed.
- int data=50;   //Here data is variable

Types of Variable

There are three types of variables in Java :

- Local variable
- Instance variable
- Static variable

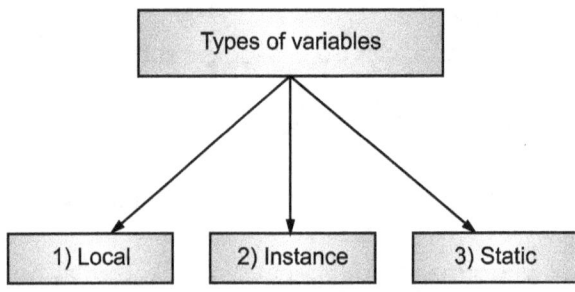

Fig. 4.13 : Types of variable

- **Local Variable**

A variable which is declared inside the method is called local variable.

- **Instance Variable**

A variable which is declared inside the class but outside the method, is called instance variable. It is not declared as static.

- **Static Variable**

A variable that is declared as static is called static variable. It cannot be local.

Example : Understand the Types of Variables in Java

```
class A
{
    int data=50;              //instance variable
    static int m=100;         //static variable
    void method()
    {
        int n=90;             //local variable
    }
}                             //end of class
```

4.12 DATA TYPES IN JAVA

Data types represent the different values to be stored in the variable. In Java, there are two types of data types :

- Primitive data types
- Non-primitive data types

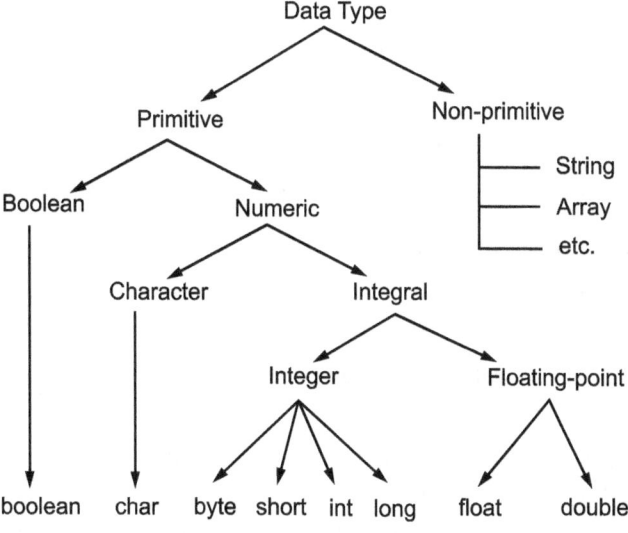

Fig. 4.14 : Data types in Java

Data Type	Default Value	Default Size
boolean	false	1 bit
char	'\u0000'	2 byte
byte	0	1 byte
short	0	2 byte
int	0	4 byte
long	0L	8 byte
float	0.0f	4 byte
double	0.0d	8 byte

Why character uses 2 byte in Java and what is \u0000?

- It is because Java uses Unicode system than ASCII code system. The \u0000 is the lowest range of Unicode system.

Unicode System :

- Unicode is a universal international standard character encoding that can represent most of the world's written languages.

4.12.1 Primitive Data Types

- **Primitive** data types are those whose variables allows us to store only one value but they never allow us to store multiple values of same type.
- This is a data type whose variable can hold maximum one value at a time.

Example :

```
int a;  // valid
a=10;  // valid
a=10, 20, 30;  // invalid
```

Here "a" store only one value at a time because it is primitive type variable.

4.12.2 User Defined Data Types

- User defined data types are those which are developed by programmers by making use of appropriate features of the language.
- User defined data types related variables allows us to store multiple values either of same type or different type or both.
- This is a data type whose variable can hold more than one value of dissimilar type, in Java it is achieved using class concept.
- In Java, both derived and user defined data type is combinedly named as reference data type.

- In C language, user defined data types can be developed by using struct, union, enum etc.
- In Java programming, user defined datatype can be developed by using the features of classes and interfaces.

Example :

```
Student  s = new  Student();
```

- In Java, we have eight data types which are organized in four groups. They are
  - (1) Integer category data types
  - (2) Character category data types
  - (3) Float category data types
  - (4) Boolean category data types

(1) Integer Category Data Types :

- These category data types are used for storing integer data in the main memory of computer by allocating sufficient amount of memory space.
- Integer category data types are divided into four types which are given in following table

Data Type	Size	Range	
1	Byte	1	+ 127 to -128
2	Short	2	+ 32767 to -22768
3	Int	4	+ x to - (x+1)
4	Long	8	+ y to - (y+1)

(2) Character Category Data Types :

- A character is an identifier which is enclosed within single quotes.
- In Java to represent character data, we use a data type called char. This data type takes two bytes since it follows Unicode character set.

Data Type	Size(Byte)	Range
Char	2	232767 to -32768

- Java supports more than 18 international languages so Java takes 2 byte for characters, because for 18 international language 1 byte of memory is not sufficient for storing all characters and symbols present in 18 languages.
- Java supports Unicode but C supports ASCII code. In ASCII code, only English language is present, so for storing all English letters and symbols 1 byte is sufficient.
- Unicode character set is one which contains all the characters which are available in 18 international languages and it contains 65536 characters.

(3) Float Category Data Types :

- Float category data types are used for representing float values. This category contains two data types, they are in the given table

Data Type	Size	Range	Number of Decimal Places
Float	4	+2147483647 to -2147483648	8
Double	8	+ 9.223*1018	16

(4) Boolean Category Data Types :

- Boolean category data type is used for representing or storing logical values : true or false.

- In Java programming, to represent Boolean values or logical values, we use a data type called Boolean.

- Boolean data type takes zero bytes of main memory space because Boolean data type of Java is implemented by Sun Micro System with a concept of flip - flop.

- A flip - flop is a general purpose register which stores one bit of information (one true and zero false).

Data Type	Default Value	Default size
boolean	false	1 bit

4.12.3 Differences between Primitive Data Types and User Defined Data Types

- Primitive data types are also known as basic data types. Those data types are not derived from others. for eg. int , float, double etc are known as primitive data types .

- User defined datatypes are data types whose names can be defined by users. for eg. struct(structure), pointers, enums etc .

- Primitive data types include integer, character, float etc. which are defined already inside the language i.e, user can use these data types without defining them inside the language.

- User defined data types are the data types which users have to define while or before using them. For eg. - in C language, structure and union are used as user-defined data types.

4.12.4 Signed Vs. Unsigned Data Type

- Java does not support unsigned data types.
- The byte, short, int, and long are all signed data types.
- For a signed data type, half of the range of values stores positive number and half for negative numbers, as one bit, is used to store the sign of the value.

- For example, a byte takes 8 bits; its range is -128 to 127. If you were to store only positive numbers in a byte, its range would have been 0 to 255.

- Java has some static methods in wrapper classes to support operations treating the bits in the signed values as if they are unsigned integers.

Example :

- The following code shows how to get the value stored in a byte as an unsigned integer :

```java
public class Main
{
  public static void main(String[] args)
    {
        byte b = -10;
        int x = Byte.toUnsignedInt(b);
        System.out.println("Signed value in byte  = " + b);
        System.out.println("Unsigned value in  byte  = " + x);
    }
}
```

Output :

Signed value in byte =-10

Unsigned value in byte = 246

4.12.5 Explicit Pointers Type

- An explicit pointer is a variable which contains number referring to an address in memory.

- An implicit one allows you to use that address in memory, but doesn't allow you to refer to it by a number.

- In the following C code, implicit is a variable of type char and contains 'a', explicit is a variable which stores a number representing the address of 'a'.

- Normal numeric operations can be done on it which can be very useful when dealing with arrays.

- char implicit = 'a';

- void* explicit = &implicit;

- Explicit pointers can often lead to bad code. That is not to say that they are a bad thing, but they are very easy to misuse. Allowing them in Java would certainly cause problems when changing between different virtual machines, and perhaps when using different architectures or operating systems.

4.13 JAVA ARRAY

- Array is a collection of similar type of elements that have contiguous memory locations.

- Java array is an object that contains elements of similar data type. It is a data structure where we store similar elements. We can store only fixed set of elements in a Java array.

- Array in Java is index based, first element of the array is stored at 0 index.

- Instead of declaring individual variables, such as number0, number1, ..., and number99, you declare one array variable such as numbers and use numbers[0], numbers[1], and ..., numbers[99] to represent individual variables.

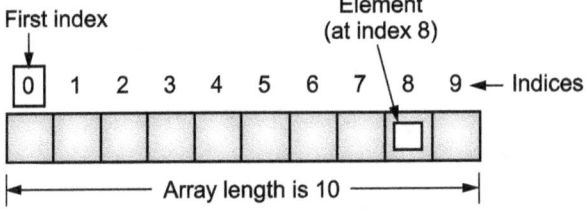

Fig. 4.15 : Array

Advantage of Java Array :

- **Random access :** We can get any data located at any index position.

- **Code Optimization :** It makes the code optimized, we can retrieve or sort the data easily.

Disadvantage of Java Array :

- **Size Limit :** We can store only fixed size of elements in the array. It doesn't grow its size at runtime. To solve this problem, collection framework is used in Java.

Declaring Array Variables :

- To use an array in a program, you must declare a variable to reference the array, and you must specify the type of array the variable can reference. Here is the syntax for declaring an array variable

Syntax :

```
dataType[] arrayRefVar;   // preferred way.
    or
dataType arrayRefVar[];  // works but not preferred way.
```

- **Note :** The style **dataType[] arrayRefVar** is preferred. The style **dataType arrayRefVar[]** comes from the C/C++ language and was adopted in Java to accommodate C/C++ programmers.

Example :

- The following code snippets are examples of this syntax :

  double[] myList; // preferred way.

      or

  double myList[]; // works but not preferred way.

Creating Arrays :

- You can create an array by using the new operator with the following syntax :

Syntax :

  arrayRefVar = new dataType[arraySize];

The above statement does two things :

- It creates an array using new dataType[arraySize].
- It assigns the reference of the newly created array to the variable arrayRefVar.
- Declaring an array variable, creating an array, and assigning the reference of the array to the variable can be combined in one statement, as shown below –

  dataType[] arrayRefVar = new dataType[arraySize];

- Alternatively you can create arrays as follows :

  dataType[] arrayRefVar = {value0, value1, ..., valuek};

- The array elements are accessed through the **index**. Array indices are 0-based; that is, they start from 0 to **arrayRefVar.length-1**.

Example :

- Following statement declares an array variable, myList, creates an array of 10 elements of double type and assigns its reference to myList –

  double[] myList = new double[10];

- Following Fig. 4.16 represents array myList. Here, myList holds ten double values and the indices are from 0 to 9.

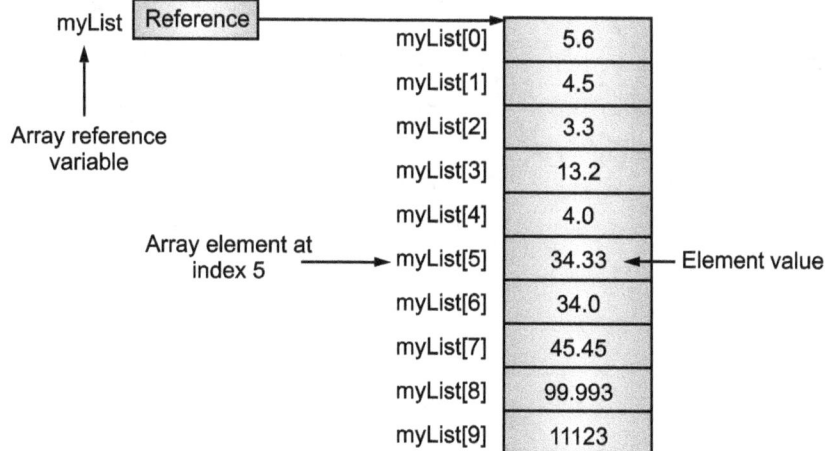

Fig. 4.16 : Array example

Types of Array in Java :

There are two types of array.

1. Single Dimensional Array
2. Multidimensional Array

4.13.1 Single Dimensional Array in Java

Syntax to Declare an Array in Java :

*   dataType[] arr; (or)
*   dataType []arr; (or)
*   dataType arr[];

Instantiation of an Array in Java

arrayRefVar=new datatype[size];

Example of Single Dimensional Java Array :

*   Let's see the simple example of Java array, where we are going to declare, instantiate, initialize and traverse an array.

```
class Testarray
{
    public static void main(String args[])
    {
        int a[]=new int[5];          //declaration and instantiation
        a[0]=10;//initialization
        a[1]=20;
        a[2]=70;
        a[3]=40;
        a[4]=50;
        //printing array
        for(int i=0;i<a.length;i++)   //length is the property of array
        System.out.println(a[i]);
    }
}
```

Output :

10
20
70
40
50

Declaration, Instantiation and Initialization of Java Array

- We can declare, instantiate and initialize the Java array together by :

  int a[]={33,3,4,5};//declaration, instantiation and initialization

- Let's see the simple example to print this array.

```
class Testarray1
{
    public static void main(String args[])
    {
        int a[]={33,3,4,5};            //declaration, instantiation and initialization
        //printing array
        for(int i=0;i<a.length;i++)    //length is the property of array
        System.out.println(a[i]);
    }
}
```

Output :

33

3

4

5

Passing Array to Method in Java :

- We can pass the Java array to method so that we can reuse the same logic on any array.
- Let's see the simple example to get minimum number of an array using method.

```
class Testarray2
{
    static void min(int arr[])
    {
        int min=arr[0];
        for(int i=1;i<arr.length;i++)
        if(min>arr[i])
         min=arr[i];
        System.out.println(min);
```

```
    }
    public static void main(String args[])
    {
        int a[]={33,3,4,5};
        min(a);                        //passing array to method
    }
}
```

Output :

3

4.13.2 Multidimensional Array in Java

- In such case, data is stored in row and column based index. It is also known as matrix form.

Syntax to Declare Multidimensional Array in Java

```
dataType[][] arrayRefVar; (or)
dataType [][]arrayRefVar; (or)
dataType arrayRefVar[][]; (or)
dataType []arrayRefVar[];
```

Example to Instantiate Multidimensional Array in Java :

```
int[][] arr=new int[3][3];        //3 row and 3 column
```

Example to Initialize Multidimensional Array in Java :

```
arr[0][0]=1;
arr[0][1]=2;
arr[0][2]=3;
arr[1][0]=4;
arr[1][1]=5;
arr[1][2]=6;
arr[2][0]=7;
arr[2][1]=8;
arr[2][2]=9;
```

Example of Multidimensional Java Array :

- Let's see the simple example to declare, instantiate, initialize and print the 2Dimensional array.

```
class Testarray3
{
    public static void main(String args[])
    {
        //declaring and initializing 2D array
        int arr[][]={{1,2,3},{2,4,5},{4,4,5}};
        //printing 2D array
        for(int i=0;i<3;i++)
        {
            for(int j=0;j<3;j++)
            {
                System.out.print(arr[i][j]+" ");
            }
            System.out.println();
        }
    }
}
```

Output :

1 2 3

2 4 5

4 4 5

4.13.3 Alternative Array Declaration Syntax

- Here, the square brackets follow the type specifier, not the name of the array variable. For example, the following two declarations are equivalent :

```
int a1[] = new int[3];
int[] a2 = new int[3];
```

- The following declarations are also equivalent :

```
char twod1[][] = new char[3][4];
char[][] twod2 = new char[3][4];
```

- This alternative declaration form offers convenience when declaring several arrays at the same time :

```
int[] nums, nums2, nums3;   // create three arrays
```

4.14 CONTROL STATEMENT

- A program executes from top to bottom except when we use control statements, we can control the order of execution of the program, based on logic and values.

- In Java, control statements can be divided into the following three categories :

  (1) Selection Statements

  (2) Iteration Statements

  (3) Jump Statements

4.14.1 Selection Statements

Selection statements allow you to control the flow of program execution on the basis of the outcome of an expression or state of a variable known during runtime.

Selection statements can be divided into the following categories :

- The if and if-else statements

- The if-else statements

- The if-else-if statements

- The switch statements

- The Nested switch statements

1. The if Statements :

- The first contained statement that can be a block of an if statement only executes when the specified condition is true.

- If the condition is false and there is not else keyword, then the first contained statement will be skipped and execution continues with the rest of the program.

- The condition is an expression that returns a Boolean value.

Example :

```
import Java.util.Scanner;
public class IfDemo
{
    public static void main(String[] args)
    {
        int age;
```

```
    Scanner inputDevice = new Scanner(System.in);
    System.out.print("Please enter Age : ");
    age = inputDevice.nextInt();
    if(age > 18)
        System.out.println("above 18 ");
    }
}
```

Output :

Please enter Age : 19

above 18

2. The if-else Statements :

- In if-else statements, if the specified condition in the if statement is false, then the statement after the else keyword that can be a block will execute.

Example :

```
import Java.util.Scanner;
public class IfElseDemo
{
    public static void main( String[] args )
    {
        int age;
        Scanner inputDevice = new Scanner( System.in );
        System.out.print( "Please enter Age : " );
        age = inputDevice.nextInt();
        if ( age >= 18 )
            System.out.println( "above 18 " );
        else
            System.out.println( "below 18" );
    }
}
```

Output :

Please enter Age : 11

below 18

3. The if-else-if Statements :

- if-else-if statements is also called as nested if else.
- This statement following the else keyword can be another if or if-else statement.

Syntax :

```
if(condition)
   statements;
else if (condition)
   statements;
else if(condition)
   statement;
else
   statements;
```

- Whenever the condition is true, the associated statement will be executed and the remaining conditions will be bypassed. If none of the conditions are true, then the else block will execute.

Example :

```
import Java.util.Scanner;
public class IfElseIfDemo
{
   public static void main( String[] args )
   {
      int age;
      Scanner inputDevice = new Scanner( System.in );
      System.out.print( "Please enter Age : " );
      age = inputDevice.nextInt();
      if ( age >= 18 && age <=35 )
         System.out.println( "between 18-35 " );
      else if(age >35 && age <=60)
         System.out.println("between 36-60");
      else
         System.out.println( "not matched" );
   }
}
```

Output :

Please enter Age : 55

between 36-60

4. The Switch Statements :

- The switch statement is a multi-way branch statement.

- The switch statement of Java is another selection statement that defines multiple paths of execution of a program.

- It provides a better alternative than a large series of if-else-if statements.

Example :

```java
import Java.util.Scanner;
public class SwitchDemo
{
    public static void main( String[] args )
    {
        int age;
        Scanner inputDevice = new Scanner( System.in );
        System.out.print( "Please enter Age : " );
        age = inputDevice.nextInt();
        switch ( age )
        {
            case 18 :
                System.out.println( "age 18" );
                break;
            case 19 :
                System.out.println( "age 19" );
                break;
            default :
                System.out.println( "not matched" );
                break;
        }
    }
}
```

Output :

Please enter Age : 19

age 19

- An expression must be of a type of byte, short, int or char. Each of the values specified in the case statement must be of a type compatible with the expression. Duplicate case values are not allowed.

- The break statement is used inside the switch to terminate a statement sequence. The break statement is optional in the switch statement.

5. The Nested Switch Statements

- We can use a switch as part of the statement sequence of an outer switch. This is called a nested switch. Since a switch statement defines its own block, no conflicts arise between the case constants in the inner switch and those in the outer switch.

- For example, the following

```
switch(count)
{
case 1 :
switch(target)
{ // nested switch
    case 0 :
        System.out.println("target is zero");
        break;
    case 1 : // no conflicts with outer switch
        System.out.println("target is one");
        break;
}
break;
case 2 : // ...
}
```

- Here, the case 1 : statement in the inner switch does not conflict with the case 1 : statement in the outer switch. The count variable is compared only with the list of cases at the outer level.

- If count is 1, then target is compared with the inner list cases.

- The switch looks only for a match between the value of the expression and one of its case constants.

- No two case constants in the same switch can have identical values. Of course, a switch statement and an enclosing outer switch can have case constants in common.
- A switch statement is usually more efficient than a set of nested ifs. The last point is particularly interesting because it gives insight into how the Java compiler works.
- When it compiles a switch statement, the Java compiler will inspect each of the case constants and create a "jump table" that it will use for selecting the path of execution depending on the value of the expression.
- Therefore, if you need to select among a large group of values, a switch statement will run much faster than the equivalent logic code using a sequence of if-elses. The compiler can do this because it knows that the case constants are all the same type and simply must be compared for equality with the switch expression.

4.14.2 Iteration Statements

Repeating the same code fragment several times until a specified condition is satisfied is called iteration statement. Iteration statements execute the same set of instructions until a termination condition is met. Java provides the following loop for iteration statements :

- The while loop
- The for loop
- The do-while loop
- The for each loop
- Declaring Loop Control Variables Inside the for Loop
- Using the Comma

1. The while Loop :

- It continually executes a statement that is usually to be block while a condition is true. The condition must return a Boolean value.

Example :

```
public class WhileDemo
{
    public static void main( String[] args )
    {
        int i = 0;
        while ( i < 5 )
        {
            System.out.println( "Value :: " + i );
            i++;
        }
    }
}
```

Output :

Value ::0

Value ::1

Value ::2

Value ::3

Value ::4

2. The do-While Loop :

- The do-while loop executes at least one time then it will check the expression prior to the next iteration.

- The only difference between a while and a do-while loop is that do-while evaluates its expression at the bottom of the loop instead of the top.

Example :

```java
public class DoWhileDemo
{
    public static void main( String[] args )
    {
        int i = 0;
        do
        {
            System.out.println( "value :: " + i );
            i++;
        }
        while ( i < 5);
    }
}
```

Output :

value ::0

value ::1

value ::2

value ::3

value ::4

3. The for Loop :

- A for loop executes a statement that is usually a block as long as the Boolean condition evaluates to true.
- A for loop is a combination of the three elements initialization statement, Boolean expression and increment or decrement statement.

Syntax :

```
for(<initialization>;   <condition>;   <increment or decrement statement>)
    {
        <block of code>
    }
```

- The initialization block executes first before the loop starts. It is used to initialize the loop variable.
- The condition statement evaluates every time prior to when the statement that is usually a block executes, if the condition is true then only the statement that is usually a block will execute.
- The increment or decrement statement executes every time after the statement that is usually a block.

Example :

```
public class WhileDemo
{
    public static void main( String[] args )
    {
        int i = 0;
        while ( i < 5 )
        {
            System.out.println( "value :: " + i );
            i++;
        }
    }
}
```

Output :

value ::0

value ::1

value ::2

value ::3

value ::4

4. The for Each Loop :

- This was introduced in Java 5. This loop is basically used to traverse the array or collection elements.

Example :

```java
public class ForEachDemo
{
    public static void main( String[] args )
    {
        int[] i = { 1, 2, 3, 4, 5 };
        for ( int j : i )
        {
            System.out.println( "value :: " + j );
        }
    }
}
```

Output :

value ::1

value ::2

value ::3

value ::4

value ::5

5. Declaring Loop Control Variables Inside the for Loop

- Variable that controls a for loop is needed only for the purposes of the loop and is not used in another place. When this is the case, it is possible to declare the variable inside the initialization portion of the for.

- For example, here is the preceding program recoded so that the loop control variable n is declared as an int inside the for :

```java
// Declare a loop control variable inside the for.
class ForTick
{
    public static void main(String args[])
    {
        // here, n is declared inside of the for loop
```

```
        for(int n=10; n>0; n--)
            System.out.println("tick " + n);
    }
}
```

- When you declare a variable inside a for loop, there is one important point to remember: the scope of that variable ends when the for statement does.

- If you need to use the loop control variable elsewhere in your program, you will not be able to declare it inside the for loop. When the loop control variable will not be needed elsewhere, most Java programmers declare it inside the for.

- For example, here is a simple program that tests for prime numbers. Notice that the loop control variable i is declared inside the for since it is not needed elsewhere.

```
// Test for primes.
class FindPrime
{
public static void main(String args[])
{
    int num;
    boolean is Prime;
    num = 14;
    if(num < 2)
        isPrime = false;
    else
        isPrime = true;
    for(int i=2; i <= num/i; i++)
    {
        if((num % i) == 0)
        {
            isPrime = false;
            break;
        }
    }
}
```

```
    if(isPrime)
        System.out.println("Prime");
    else
        System.out.println("Not Prime");
  }
}
```

6. Using the Comma :

- There will be times when you will want to include more than one statement in the initialization and iteration portions of the for loop.

- For example, consider the loop in the following program :

```
class Sample
{
    public static void main(String args[])
    {
        int x, y;
        y = 4;
        for(x=1; x<y; x++)
        {
            System.out.println("x = " + x);
            System.out.println("y = " + y);
            y--;
        }
    }
}
```

- The loop is controlled by the interaction of two variables. Since the loop is governed by two variables, it would be useful if both could be included in the for statement, itself, instead of y being handled manually.

- Java provides a way to accomplish this to allow two or more variables to control x for loop, Java permits you to include multiple statements in both the initialization and iteration portions of the for. Each statement is separated from the next by a comma.

- Using the comma, the preceding **for** loop can be more efficiently coded, as shown in following example :

```
// Using the comma.
class Comma
{
    public static void main(String args[])
    {
        int a, b;
        for(a=1, b=4; a<b; a++, b--)
        {
            System.out.println("a = " + a);
            System.out.println("b = " + b);
        }
    }
}
```

- In this example, the initialization portion sets the values of both **a** and **b**. The two comma separated statements in the iteration portion are executed each time the loop repeats.

Output :

a = 1

b = 4

a = 2

b = 3

4.14.3 Jump Statements

Jump statements are used to unconditionally transfer the program control to another part of the program.

Java provides the following jump statements :

- Break statement
- Continue statement
- Return statement

Break Statement :

- The break statement immediately quits the current iteration and goes to the first statement following the loop. Another form of break is used in the switch statement.

- The break statement has the following two forms :
  1. Unlabeled Break Statement
  2. Labeled Break Statement

1. Unlabeled Break Statement :

This is used to jump program control out of the specific loop on the specific condition.

Example :

```java
public class UnLabeledBreakDemo
{
    public static void main( String[] args )
    {
        for ( int var = 0; var < 5; var++ )
        {
            System.out.println( "Var is : " + var );
            if ( var == 3 )
                break;
        }
    }
}
```

Output :

var is ::0

var is ::1

var is ::2

var is ::3

2. Labeled Break Statement :

This is used for when we want to jump the program control out of nested loops or multiple loops.

Example :

```java
public class LabeledBreakDemo
{
    public static void main( String[] args )
    {
```

```
Outer : for ( int var1 = 0; var1 < 5; var1++ )
{
    for ( int var2 = 1; var2 < 5; var2++ )
    {
        System.out.println( "var1 :" + var1 + ", var2 :" + var2 );
        if ( var1 == 3 )
            break Outer;
    }
}
}
}
```

Output :

var1:0,var2:1

var1:0,var2:2

var1:0,var2:3

var1:0,var2:4

var1:1,var2:1

var1:1,var2:2

var1:1,var2:3

var1:1,var2:4

var1:2,var2:1

var1:2,var2:2

var1:2,var2:3

var1:2,var2:4

var1:3,var2:1

Continue Statement :

The continue statement is used when you want to continue running the loop with the next iteration and want to skip the rest of the statements of the body for the current iteration.

The continue statement has the following two forms :

1. Unlabeled Continue Statement
2. Labeled Continue Statement

1. Unlabeled Continue Statement :

This statement skips the current iteration of the innermost for, while and do-while loop.

Example :

```
public class UnlabeledContinueDemo
{
   public static void main( String[] args )
   {
      for ( int var1 = 0; var1 < 4; var1++ )
      {
         for ( int var2 = 0; var2 < 4; var2++ )
         {
            if ( var2 == 2 )
               continue;
            System.out.println( "var1 :" + var1 + ", var2 :" + var2 );
         }
      }
   }
}
```

Output :

var1:0,var2:0

var1:0,var2:1

var1:0,var2:3

var1:1,var2:0

var1:1,var2:1

var1:1,var2:3

var1:2,var2:0

var1:2,var2:1

var1:2,var2:3

var1:3,var2:0

var1:3,var2:1

var1:3,var2:3

2. Labeled Continue Statement :

This statement skips the current iteration of the loop with the specified label.

Example :

```
public class LabeledContinueDemo
{
    public static void main( String[] args )
    {
        Outer : for ( int var1 = 0; var1 < 5; var1++ )
        {
            for ( int var2 = 0; var2 < 5; var2++ )
            {
                if ( var2 == 2 )
                    continue Outer;
                System.out.println( "var1 :" + var1 + ", var2 :" + var2 );
            }
        }
    }
}
```

Output :

var1:0,var2:0

var1:0,var2:1

var1:1,var2:0

var1:1,var2:1

var1:2,var2:0

var1:2,var2:1

var1:3,var2:0

var1:3,var2:1

var1:4,var2:0

var1:4,var2:1

Return Statement :

- The return statement is used to immediately quit the current method and return to the calling method.

- It is mandatory to use a return statement for non-void methods to return a value.

Example :

```
public class ReturnDemo
{
    public static void main( String[] args )
    {
        ReturnDemo returnDemo = new ReturnDemo();
        System.out.println( "No : " + returnDemo.returnCall() );
    }


    int returnCall()
    {
        return 5;
    }
}
```

Output :

No : 5

4.15 STRING HANDLING : STRING CLASS METHODS

- Strings are a sequence of characters. In Java programming language, strings are treated as objects.

- The Java.lang.String class provides a lot of methods to work on a string. By the help of these methods, we can perform operations on string such as trimming, concatenating, converting, comparing, replacing strings etc.

- Java String is a powerful concept because everything is treated as a string if you submit any form in window based, web based or mobile application.

- The Java platform provides the String class to create and manipulate strings.

Creating Strings

- Creation of string is as follows :

```
String greeting = "Hello world!";
```

Example :

public class StringDemo

```
{
  public static void main(String args[])
    {
            char[] helloArray = { 'h', 'e', 'l', 'l', 'o', '.' };
            String helloString = new String(helloArray);
            System.out.println( helloString );
    }
}
```

Output :

hello

4.15.1 String Methods

List of methods supported by String class is as follows :

Sr. No.	Method	Description
1.	char charAt(int index)	Returns the character at the specified index.
2.	int compareTo(Object o)	Compares this String to another Object.
3.	int compareTo(String anotherString)	Compares two strings lexicographically.
4.	int compareToIgnoreCase(String str)	Compares two strings lexicographically, ignoring case differences.
5.	String concat(String str)	Concatenates the specified string to the end of this string.
6.	boolean contentEquals(StringBuffer sb)	Returns true if and only if this String represents the same sequence of characters as the specified StringBuffer.
7.	static String copyValueOf(char[] data)	Returns a String that represents the character sequence in the array specified.
8.	static String copyValueOf(char[] data, int offset, int count)	Returns a String that represents the character sequence in the array specified.
9.	boolean endsWith(String suffix)	Tests if this string ends with the specified suffix.

Contd...

10.	boolean equals(Object anObject)	Compares this string to the specified object.
11.	boolean equalsIgnoreCase(String anotherString)	Compares this String to another String, ignoring case considerations.
12.	byte getBytes()	Encodes this String into a sequence of bytes using the platform's default charset, storing the result into a new byte array.
13.	byte[] getBytes(String charsetName)	Encodes this String into a sequence of bytes using the named charset, storing the result into a new byte array.
14.	void getChars(int srcBegin, int srcEnd, char[] dst, int dstBegin)	Copies characters from this string into the destination character array.
15.	int hashCode()	Returns a hash code for this string.
16.	int indexOf(int ch)	Returns the index within this string of the first occurrence of the specified character.
17.	int indexOf(int ch, int fromIndex)	Returns the index within this string of the first occurrence of the specified character, starting the search at the specified index.
18.	int indexOf(String str)	Returns the index within this string of the first occurrence of the specified substring.
19.	int indexOf(String str, int fromIndex)	Returns the index within this string of the first occurrence of the specified substring, starting at the specified index.
20.	String intern()	Returns a canonical representation for the string object.
21.	int lastIndexOf(int ch)	Returns the index within this string of the last occurrence of the specified character.
22.	int lastIndexOf(int ch, int fromIndex)	Returns the index within this string of the last occurrence of the specified character, searching backward starting at the specified index.
23.	int lastIndexOf(String str)	Returns the index within this string of the rightmost occurrence of the specified substring.
24.	int lastIndexOf(String str, int fromIndex)	Returns the index within this string of the last occurrence of the specified substring, searching backward starting at the specified index.

Contd...

25.	int length()	Returns the length of this string.
26.	boolean matches(String regex)	Tells whether or not this string matches the given regular expression.
27.	boolean regionMatches(boolean ignoreCase, int toffset, String other, int ooffset, int len)	Tests if two string regions are equal.
28.	boolean regionMatches(int toffset, String other, int ooffset, int len)	Tests if two string regions are equal.
29.	String replace(char oldChar, char newChar)	Returns a new string resulting from replacing all occurrences of oldChar in this string with newChar.
30.	String replaceAll(String regex, String replacement	Replaces each substring of this string that matches the given regular expression with the given replacement.
31.	String replaceFirst(String regex, String replacement)	Replaces the first substring of this string that matches the given regular expression with the given replacement.
32.	String[] split(String regex)	Splits this string around matches of the given regular expression.
33.	String[] split(String regex, int limit)	Splits this string around matches of the given regular expression.
34.	boolean startsWith(String prefix)	Tests if this string starts with the specified prefix.
35.	boolean startsWith(String prefix, int toffset)	Tests if this string starts with the specified prefix beginning a specified index.
36.	CharSequence subSequence(int beginIndex, int endIndex)	Returns a new character sequence that is a subsequence of this sequence.
37.	String substring(int beginIndex)	Returns a new string that is a substring of this string.
38.	String substring(int beginIndex, int endIndex)	Returns a new string that is a substring of this string.
39.	char[] toCharArray()	Converts this string to a new character array.
40.	String toLowerCase()	Converts all of the characters in this String to lower case using the rules of the default locale.

Contd...

41.	String toLowerCase(Locale locale)	Converts all of the characters in this String to lower case using the rules of the given Locale.
42.	String toString()	This object (which is already a string!) is itself returned.
43.	String toUpperCase()	Converts all of the characters in this String to upper case using the rules of the default locale.
44.	String toUpperCase(Locale locale)	Converts all of the characters in this String to upper case using the rules of the given Locale.
45.	String trim()	Returns a copy of the string, with leading and trailing whitespace omitted.

EXERCISE

1. Explain the different features of JAVA.
2. What is JVM? Explain in brief.
3. Explain the different Data types in JAVA.
4. Differentiate between Primitive data types and User defined data types.
5. What is Array? Explain Single and Multi dimensional array.
6. Explain Selection Control Statements?
7. Explain Iterative Control Statements?
8. Explain Jump Control Statements?
9. Explain String class methods?
10. Explain OOP concepts of JAVA.

INHERITANCE, POLYMORPHISM, ENCAPSULATION USING JAVA

5.1 CLASS FUNDAMENTALS

- A class is a template that defines the form of an object. It specifies both the data and the code that will operate on that data.
- A class is declared by using class keyword.
- General form of a class definition is shown here:

```
class classname
{
    datatype instance-variable1;
    datatype instance-variable2;
    // ...
    datatype instance-variableN;
    returntype methodname1(parameter-list)
    {
        // body of method
    }
    returntype methodname2(parameter-list)
    {
        // body of method
    }
    // ...
    returntype methodnameN(parameter-list)
    {
        // body of method
    }
}
```

- The data, or variables, defined within a class are called instance variables.
- The code is contained within methods.
- The methods and variables defined within a class are called members of the class.
- Everything in Java is defined in a class.

For example:

```
class Employee
{
    String name;
    int empid;
    String emailAddress;
    int yearOfBirth;
        void read()
    {
                // ...
    }
    void disp()
    {
                // ...
    }
}
```

- The order of data fields and methods in a class is not significant.
- If you recall, each class must be saved in a file that matches its name, for example: Employee.Java

5.2 DECLARING OBJECTS

- An object is an instance of a particular class.
- To create an object of a particular class, use the new operator, followed by an invocation of a constructor for that class, such as:

new MyClass()

➢ The constructor method initializes the state of the new object.

➢ The new operator returns a *reference* to the newly created object.

- As with primitives, the variable type must be compatible with the value type when using object references as follows :

  Employee e = new Employee();

- To access member data or methods of an object, use the dot (.) notation: variable.method()

- Consider this simple example of creating and using instances of the Employee class:

```java
public class EmployeeDemo
{
  public static void main(String[] args)
  {
      Employee e1 = new Employee();
    e1.name = "John";
      e1.empid = "555";
    e1.emailAddress = "john@company.com";
    Employee e2 = new Employee();
    e2.name = "Tom";
    e2.empid = "456";
    e2.yearOfBirth = 1974;
    System.out.println("Name : " + e1.name);
    System.out.println("Empid : " + e1.empid);
    System.out.println("Email Address : " +  e1.emailAddress);
    System.out.println("Year Of Birth : " + e1.yearOfBirth);
    System.out.println("Name : " + e2.name);
    System.out.println("Empid : " + e2.empid);
    System.out.println("Email Address : " + e2.emailAddress);
    System.out.println("Year Of Birth : " + e2.yearOfBirth);
  }
}
```

Output :

Name : John

SSN : 555

Email Address : john@company.com

Year Of Birth : 0

Name : Tom

SSN : 456

Email Address : null

Year Of Birth : 1974

5.3 CLASS V/s OBJECT

- A *class* is a template for how to build an object.
  - ➢ A class is a prototype that defines state placeholders and behaviour common to all objects of its kind.
  - ➢ Each object is a member of a single class — there is no multiple inheritance in Java.
- An *object* is an instance of a particular class.
  - ➢ There are typically many object instances for any one given class.
  - ➢ Each object of a given class has the same built-in behaviour but possibly a different data.
  - ➢ Objects are *instantiated*.
- For example, each car starts of with a design that defines its features and properties.
- It is the design that is used to build a car of a particular type or class.
- When the physical cars roll off the assembly line, those cars are *instances* of that class.
- Many people can have an BMW, but there is typically only one design for that particular class of cars.

5.4 ASSIGNING OBJECT REFERENCE VARIABLES

- Object reference variables act differently than do variables of a primitive type, such as int.
- When you assign one primitive-type variable to another, the situation is straightforward. The variable on the left receives a *copy* of the *value* of the variable on the right.
- When you assign one object reference variable to another, the situation is a bit more complicated because you are changing the object that the reference variable refers to.
- The effect of this difference can cause some results. For example, consider the following example :

      Vehicle car1=new Vehicle();

      Vehicle car2=car1;

- car2 is being assigned a reference to a copy of the object referred to by car1. That is, you might think that car1 and car2 refer to separate and distinct objects. However, this would be wrong. Instead, after this fragment executes, car1 and car2 will both refer to the same object.

- The assignment of car1 to car2 did not allocate any memory or copy any part of the original object. It simply makes car2 refer to the same object as does car1. Thus, any changes made to the object through car2 will affect the object to which car1 is referring, since they are the same object.

5.5 ADDING METHODS TO A CLASS

- Methods are subroutines that manipulate the data defined by the class and, in many cases, provide access to that data.

- General form of a method is as follows :

```
return_type name(parameter-list)
{
    // body of method
}
```

- Here, return_type specifies the type of data returned by the method. This can be any valid type, including class types that you create. If the method does not return a value, its return type must be void.

- The name of the method is specified by name. This can be any identifier other than those already used by other items within the current scope.

- The parameter-list is a sequence of type and identifier pairs separated by commas. Parameters are essentially variables that receive the value of the arguments passed to the method when it is called. If the method has no parameters, then the parameter list will be empty.

- Methods that have a return type other than void return a value to the calling routine using the following form of the return statement:

    return value;

    Here, value is the value returned.

- Let's begin by adding a method to the Box class as shown following:

```
class Box
{
    double width;
    double height;
```

```
    double depth;
    void volume() //Method definition
    {
        System.out.print("Volume is ");
        System.out.println(width * height * depth);
    }
}
class BoxDemo
{
    public static void main(String args[])
    {
        Box mybox1 = new Box();
        mybox1.width = 10;
        mybox1.height = 10;
        mybox1.depth = 10;

        mybox1.volume();//Method invoking
    }
}
```

Output :

Volume is 1000.0

5.6 RETURNING A VALUE

- There are two forms of return—one for use in void methods that do not return a value and one for returning values.

- In a void method, you can cause the immediate termination of a method by using this form of return :

    return;

- When this statement executes, program control returns to the caller, skipping any remaining code in the method.

- Example shows volume() returns the volume of a box.

```
class Box
{
    double width;
```

```
        double height;
        double depth;
        double volume()
        {
        return width * height * depth;
        }
    }
    class BoxDemo4
    {
        public static void main(String args[])
        {
        Box mybox1 = new Box();
            double vol;
        mybox1.width = 10;
        mybox1.height = 10;
        mybox1.depth = 10;
        vol = mybox1.volume();
        System.out.println("Volume is " + vol);
        }
    }
```

Output :

Volume is 1000

- In above program, when volume( ) is called, it is put on the right side of an assignment statement.

- On the left is a variable, in this case vol, that will receive the value returned by volume( ).

- Thus, after vol = mybox1.volume(); executes, the value of mybox1.volume( ) is 1,000 and this value then is stored in vol.

5.7 CONSTRUCTORS

- Constructor in Java is a special type of method that is used to initialize the object.

- Java constructor is invoked at the time of object creation. It constructs the values that provides data for the object, that is why it is known as Constructor.

5.7.1 Rules for Creating Constructor

- Constructor name must be same as its class name.

- Constructor must have no explicit return type.

- Every class has a constructor whether it's normal one or an abstract class.

- Constructors are not methods and they don't have any return type.

- Constructors can use any access specifier, they can be declared as private also. Private constructors are possible in Java but their scope is within the class only.

- If you don't define any constructor within the class, compiler will do it for you and it will create a constructor for you.

- this() and super() should be the first statement in the constructor code. If you don't mention them, compiler does it for you accordingly.

- Constructor overloading is possible but overriding is not possible. Which means we can have overloaded constructor in our class but we can't override a constructor.

- Constructors can not be inherited.

- Interfaces do not have constructors.

- Abstract can have constructors and these will get invoked when a class, which implements interface, gets instantiated i.e. object creation of concrete class.

- A constructor can also invoke another constructor of the same class – By using this().

5.7.2 Types of Java Constructors

There are three types of constructors :

1. Default constructor

2. Parameterized constructor

3. Copy constructor

1. **Default Constructor**

- A constructor that have no parameter is known as default constructor.

- Syntax of default constructor :

```
<class_name>()
{
}
```

Example of default constructor

In this example, we are creating the no-argument constructor in the Bike class. It will be invoked at the time of object creation.

```
class Bike1
{
    Bike1()
    {
        System.out.println("Bike is created");
    }
    public static void main(String args[])
    {
        Bike1 b=new Bike1();
    }
}
```

Output :

Bike is created

Rule : If there is no constructor in a class, compiler automatically creates a default constructor.

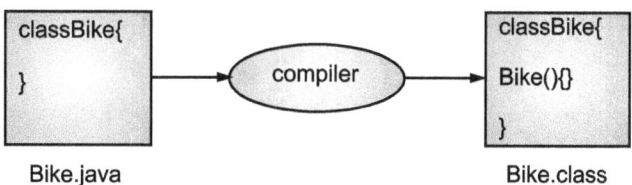

Bike.java   Bike.class

Fig. 5.1 : Example of default constructor

Example of default constructor that displays the default values

```
class Student
    {
        int id;
        String name;
        void display()
        {
        System.out.println(id+" "+name);
        }
    public static void main(String args[])
        {
```

```
        Student s1=new Student();
        Student s2=new Student();
        s1.display();
        s2.display();
    }
}
```

Output :

0 null

0 null

Explanation : In the above class, you are not creating any constructor so compiler provides you a default constructor. Here 0 and null values are provided by default constructor.

2. **Parameterized Constructor**

- A constructor that has parameters is known as parameterized constructor.

- Parameterized constructor is used to provide different values to the distinct objects.

Example of parameterized constructor:

Here, we have created the constructor of Student class that has two parameters. We can have any number of parameters in the constructor.

```
class Student
{
    int id;
    String name;
    Student(int i, String n)
    {
        id = i;
        name = n;
    }
    void display()
    {
        System.out.println(id+" "+name);
    }
    public static void main(String args[])
```

```
    {
        Student s1 = new Student4(111,"abc");
        Student s2 = new Student4(222,"pqr");
        s1.display();
        s2.display();
    }
}
```

Output :

111 abc

222 pqr

3. Copy Constructor

- There is no copy constructor in Java. But, we can copy the values of one object to another like copy constructor in C++.

- There are many ways to copy the values of one object into another in Java. They are :

  ➢ By constructor

  ➢ By assigning the values of one object into another

  ➢ By clone() method of Object class

Example : In this example, we are going to copy the values of one object into another using Java constructor.

```
class Student
{
        int id;
        String name;
        Student(int i,String n)
        {
                id = i;
            name = n;
        }
         Student(Student s)
         {
                id = s.id;
            name =s.name;
        }
```

```
    void display()
    {
    System.out.println(id+" "+name);
    }
    public static void main(String args[])
    {
    Student s1 = new Student(111,"abc");
    Student s2 = new Student(s1);
        s1.display();
        s2.display();
    }
}
```

Output :

111 abc

111 abc

5.7.3 Difference between Constructor and Method in Java

Sr. No.	Java Constructor	Java Method
1.	Constructor is used to initialize the state of an object.	Method is used to expose behaviour of an object.
2.	Constructor must not have return type.	Method must have return type.
3.	Constructor is invoked implicitly.	Method is invoked explicitly.
4.	The Java compiler provides a default constructor if you don't have any constructor.	Method is not provided by compiler in any case.
5.	Constructor name must be same as the class name.	Method name may or may not be same as class name.

5.8 this KEYWORD

- There can be a lot of usage of **Java this keyword**. In Java, this is a **reference variable** that refers to the current object.
- Here is given the 6 usage of Java this keyword.
  - ➤ this keyword can be used to refer current class instance variable.
  - ➤ this() can be used to invoke current class constructor.
  - ➤ this keyword can be used to invoke current class method.
  - ➤ this can be passed as an argument in the method call.

> ➢ this can be passed as argument in the constructor call.
> ➢ this keyword can also be used to return the current class instance.

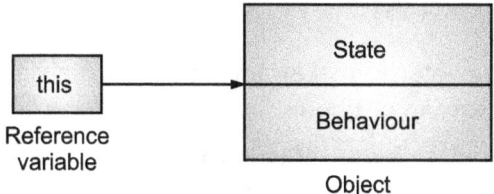

Fig. 5.2 : this Keyword

The 'this' Keyword can be used to refer Current Class Instance Variable. If there is ambiguity between the instance variable and parameter, this keyword resolves the problem of ambiguity.

Let's understand the problem if we don't use this keyword by the example given below :

```
class Student10
{
    int id;
    String name;
    Student10(int id,String name)
    {
        id = id;
        name = name;
    }
    void display()
    {
        System.out.println(id+" "+name);
    }
    public static void main(String args[])
    {
        Student10 s1 = new Student10(111,"abc");
        Student10 s2 = new Student10(321,"pqr");
        s1.display();
        s2.display();
    }
}
```

Output :

0 null

0 null

In the above example, parameter formal arguments and instance variables are same that is why we are using this keyword to distinguish between local variable and instance variable

Solution of the above Problem by this Keyword

```
class Student
{
   int id;
   String name;
   Student(int id,String name)
  {
  this.id = id;
  this.name = name;
  }
  void display()
  {
      System.out.println(id+" "+name);
  }
  public static void main(String args[])
  {
  Student s1 = new Student (111,"Karan");
  Student s2 = new Student(222,"Aryan");
  s1.display();
  s2.display();
 }
}
```

Output :

    111 Karan

    222 Aryan

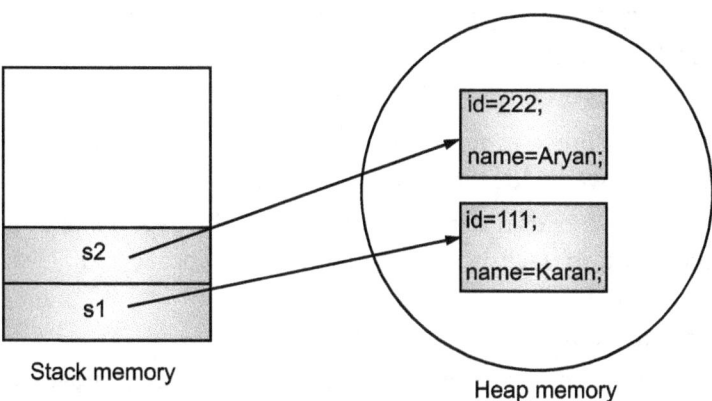

Fig. 5.3 : Example of this keyword

Where this keyword is not required

If local variables (formal arguments) and instance variables are different, there is no need to use this keyword like in the following program :

```
class Student
{
    int id;
    String name;
    Student(int i,String n)
    {
        id = i;
        name = n;
    }
    void display()
    {
        System.out.println(id+" "+name);
    }
    public static void main(String args[])
    {
        Student e1 = new Student(111,"abc");
        Student e2 = new Student(222,"pqr");
        e1.display();
        e2.display();
    }
}
```

Output :

111 abc

222 pqr

5.9 GARBAGE COLLECTION

- In Java, garbage means unreferenced objects.
- Garbage Collection is process of reclaiming the runtime unused memory automatically. In other words, it is a way to destroy the unused objects.
- In C language, we were using free() function and in C++ language we were using delete() function But, in Java it is performed automatically. So, Java provides better memory management.

Advantages of Garbage Collection:

- It makes Java memory efficient because garbage collector removes the unreferenced objects from heap memory.
- It is automatically done by the garbage collector, so we don't need to make extra efforts.

There are many ways of making an object unreferenced :

1. By nulling the reference
2. By assigning a reference to another
3. By anonymous object etc.

1. **By Nulling a Reference :**
   - Employee e=new Employee();
   - e=null;

2. **By Assigning a Reference to Another :**
   - Employee e1=new Employee();
   - Employee e2=new Employee();
   - e1=e2;//now the first object referred by e1 is available for garbage collection

3. **By Anonymous Object :**
   - new Employee();

5.10 FINALIZE() METHOD

- The finalize() method is invoked each time before the object is garbage collected.
- The finalize() method can be used to perform cleanup processing. This method is defined in Object class as follows :

```
protected void finalize()
{
}
```

- The Garbage collector of JVM collects only those objects that are created by new keyword. So, if you have created any object without new, you can use finalize method to perform cleanup processing that is destroying remaining objects.

- The gc() method is used to invoke the garbage collector to perform cleanup processing. The gc() is found in System and Runtime classes.

```
public static void gc()
{
}
```

- Garbage collection is performed by a daemon thread called Garbage Collector(GC). This thread calls the finalize() method before object is garbage collected.

Simple Example of garbage collection and finalize() in Java

```
public class TestGarbage
{
    public void finalize()
    {
        System.out.println("object is garbage collected");
    }
    public static void main(String args[])
    {
        TestGarbage s1=new TestGarbage();
        TestGarbage s2=new TestGarbage();
        s1=null;
        s2=null;
        System.gc();
    }
}
```

Output :

object is garbage collected

object is garbage collected

5.11 OVERLOADING METHODS

- If a class have multiple methods by same name but different parameters, it is known as **Method Overloading**.

- If we have to perform only one operation, having same name of the methods increases the readability of the program.

- Suppose you have to perform addition of the given numbers but there can be any number of arguments, if you write the method such as a(int,int) for two parameters, and b (int,int,int) for three parameters then it may be difficult for you as well as other programmers to understand the behavior of the method because its name differs. So, we perform method overloading to figure out the program quickly.

Advantage of Method Overloading

- Method overloading increases the readability of the program.

Different Ways to Overload the Method

There are two ways to overload the method in Java

1. By changing number of arguments

2. By changing the data type

1. Example of Method Overloading by Changing the No. of Arguments

In this example, we have created two overloaded methods, first sum method performs addition of two numbers and second sum method performs addition of three numbers.

```
class Calculation
{
    void sum(int a,int b)
    {
    System.out.println(a+b);
    }
    void sum(int a,int b,int c)
    {
    System.out.println(a+b+c);
    }
    public static void main(String args[])
    {
    Calculation obj=new Calculation();
    obj.sum(10,10,10);
     obj.sum(20,20);
    }
}
```

Output :

30

40

2. Example of Method Overloading by Changing Data Type of Argument

In this example, we have created two overloaded methods that differ in data type. The first sum method receives two integer arguments and second sum method receives two double arguments.

```
class Calculation
{
    void sum(int a,int b)
    {
        System.out.println(a+b);
    }
    void sum(double a,double b)
    {
        System.out.println(a+b);
    }
    public static void main(String args[])
    {
        Calculation obj=new Calculation();
        obj.sum(10.5,10.5);
        obj.sum(20,20);
    }
}
```

Output :

21.0

40

5.12 ARGUMENT PASSING

There are two ways that a computer language can pass an argument to a subroutine.

1. Call-by-Value :

- This approach copies the *value* of an argument into the formal parameter of the subroutine. Therefore, changes made to the parameter of the subroutine have no effect on the argument.

- When you pass a primitive type to a method, it is passed by value. Thus, a copy of the argument is made and what occurs to the parameter that receives the argument has no effect outside the method.

For example, consider the following program :

```
class Test
   {
   void fun(int i, int j)
     {
        i *= 2;
        j /= 2;
     }
   }
   lass CallByValue
{
   public static void main(String args[])
     {
        Test ob = new Test();
        int a = 15, b = 20;
        System.out.println("a and b before call : " +a + " " + b);
        ob.fun(a, b);
        System.out.println("a and b after call : " +a + " " + b);
     }
}
```

Output :

    a and b before call : 15 20

    a and b after call : 15 20

As you can see, the operations that occur inside **fun( )** have no effect on the values of **a** and **b** used in the call , their values here did not change to 30 and 10.

2. **Call-by-Reference :**

- In this approach, a reference to an argument not the value of the argument is passed to the parameter. Inside the subroutine, this reference is used to access the actual argument specified in the call. This means that changes made to the parameter will affect the argument used to call the subroutine.

- When you create a variable of a class type, you are only creating a reference to an object. Thus, when you pass this reference to a method, the parameter that receives it will refer to the same object as that referred to by the argument. This effectively means that objects act as if they are passed to methods by use of call-by-reference.

- Changes to the object inside the method *do* affect the object used as an argument.

For example, consider the following program :

```
class Test
{
    int a, b;
    Test(int i, int j)
    {
        a = i;
        b = j;
    }
    // pass an object
    void fun(Test obj)
    {
        obj.a *= 2;
        obj.b /= 2;
    }
}
class PassObjRef
{
    public static void main(String args[])
    {
        Test ob = new Test(15, 20);
        System.out.println("ob.a and ob.b before call : " +ob.a + " " + ob.b);
            ob.fun(ob);
        System.out.println("ob.a and ob.b after call : " +ob.a + " " + ob.b);
    }
}
```

Output :

ob.a and ob.b before call : 15 20

ob.a and ob.b after call : 30 10

5.13 OBJECTS AS PARAMETERS

- We can pass Object as a parameter to methods.

Example :

```
// Objects may be passed to methods.
class Test
{
    int a, b;
    Test(int i, int j)
    {
        a = i;
        b = j;
    }
    // return true if o is equal to the invoking object
    boolean equalTo(Test obj)
    {
        if(obj.a == a && obj.b == b)
            return true;
        else
            return false;
    }
}
class PassOb
{
    public static void main(String args[])
    {
        Test ob1 = new Test(100, 22);
        Test ob2 = new Test(100, 22);
```

```
            Test ob3 = new Test(50, 60);
            System.out.println("ob1 == ob2 : " + ob1.equalTo(ob2));
            System.out.println("ob1 == ob3 : " + ob1.equalTo(ob3));
      }
}
```

Output :

ob1 == ob2 : true

ob1 == ob3 : false

• In above program, The equalTo( ) method inside Test compares two objects for equality and returns the result. That is, it compares the invoking object with the one that it is passed.

• If they contain the same values, then the method returns true. Otherwise, it returns false.

5.14 RETURNING OBJECTS

• A method can return any type of data, including class types that you create.

For example, in the following program, the **fun( )** method returns an object in which the value of **a** is ten greater than it is in the invoking object.

```
      // Returning an object.
      class Test
      {
            int a;
            Test(int i)
            {
                        a = i;
            }
            Test fun()
            {
            Test temp = new Test(a+10);
                  return temp;
            }
      }
```

```
class Demo
{
    public static void main(String args[])
    {
    Test ob1 = new Test(2);
    Test ob2;
    ob2 = ob1.fun();
    System.out.println("ob1.a : " + ob1.a);
    System.out.println("ob2.a : " + ob2.a);
     ob2 = ob2.fun();
    System.out.println("ob2.a after second increase : "+ ob2.a);
    }
}
```

Output :

ob1.a : 2

ob2.a : 12

ob2.a after second increase : 22

- As you can see, each time fun( ) is invoked, a new object is created, and a reference to it is returned to the calling routine.

5.15 ACCESS CONTROL

- Java supplies a rich set of access modifiers.

- Java's access modifiers are public, private, and protected. Java also defines a default access level. protected applies only when inheritance is involved.

- When a member of a class is modified by public, then that member can be accessed by any other code.

- When a member of a class is specified as private, then that member can only be accessed by other members of its class.

- Now you can understand why main( ) has always been preceded by the public modifier. It is called by code that is outside the program that is, by the Java run-time system.

- When no access modifier is used, then by default the member of a class is public within its own package, but cannot be accessed outside of its package.

To understand the effects of public and private access, consider the following program :

```java
class Test
{
        int a; // default access
        public int b; // public access
        private int c; // private access
        // methods to access c
        void setc(int i)
            {
                        c = i;
            }
        int getc()
            {
                    return c;
            }
}
class AccessTest
{
    public static void main(String args[])
    {
        Test ob = new Test();
        // These are OK, a and b may be accessed directly
        ob.a = 10;
        ob.b = 20;
        // This is not OK and will cause an error
        // ob.c = 100; // Error!
        // You must access c through its methods
        ob.setc(100); // OK
        System.out.println("a, b, and c : " + ob.a + " " +ob.b + " " + ob.getc());
    }
}
```

- As you can see, inside the Test class, a uses default access, which for this example is the same as specifying public. b is explicitly specified as public. Member c is given private access. This means that it cannot be accessed by code outside of its class. So, inside the AccessTest class, c cannot be used directly.

- It must be accessed through its public methods : setc( ) and getc( ). If you were to remove the comment symbol from the beginning of the following line, // ob.c = 100; // Error! then you would not be able to compile this program because of the access violation.

5.16 STATIC

- In JAVA, It is possible to create a member that can be used by itself, without reference to a specific instance. To create such a member, follow its declaration with the keyword static.

- When a member is declared static, it can be accessed before any objects of its class are created, and without reference to any object.

- You can declare methods and variables to be static.

- The most common example of a static member is main( ).

- main( ) is declared as static because it must be called before any objects exist.

- Instance variables declared as static are basically global variables. When objects of its class are declared, no copy of a static variable is made. Instead, all instances of the class share the same static variable.

- Methods declared as static have several limitations :

  ➢ They can only directly call other static methods.

  ➢ They can only directly access static data.

  ➢ They cannot refer to this or super keywords.

- If you need to do computation in order to initialize your static variables, you can declare a static block that gets executed exactly once, when the class is first loaded.

The following example shows a class that has a static method, some static variables, and a static initialization block :

```
class UseStaticEg
{
    static int a = 3;
    static int b;
    static void fun(int x)
```

```
        {
        System.out.println("x = " + x);
        System.out.println("a = " + a);
        System.out.println("b = " + b);
        }
        static
        {
        System.out.println("Static block initialized.");
                b = a * 4;
        }
        public static void main(String args[])
    {
                fun(42);
    }
}
```

- In above program UseStaticEg class is loaded, all of the static statements are run. First, a is set to 3, then the static block executes, which prints a message and then initializes b to a*4 or 12. Then main( ) is called, which calls fun( ), passing 42 to x. The three println( ) statements refer to the two static variables a and b, as well as to the local variable x.

Output :

Static block initialized.

        x = 42

        a = 3

        b = 12

5.17 FINAL

- A field can be declared as final. Its contents from being modified, making it, essentially, a constant. This means that you must initialize a final field when it is declared.

- You can do this in one of two ways :

  ➢ You can give it a value when it is declared.

  ➢ You can assign it a value within a constructor.

- Example :

      final int FILE_NEW = 1;

      final int FILE_OPEN = 2;

      final int FILE_SAVE = 3;

      final int FILE_QUIT = 4;

- Subsequent parts of your program can now use FILE_OPEN as if they were constants, without apprehension that a value has been changed. It is a common coding convention to choose all uppercase identifiers for final fields, as this example shows.
- In addition to fields, both method parameters and local variables can be declared final.
- Declaring a parameter final prevents it from being changed within the method. Declaring a local variable final prevents it from being assigned a value more than once.
- The keyword final can also be applied to methods, but its meaning is substantially different than when it is applied to variables.

5.18 NESTED AND INNER CLASSES

- A class within another class is known as nested classes.
- The scope of a nested class is bounded by the scope of its enclosing class. Thus, if class B is defined within class A, then B does not exist independently of A.
- A nested class has access to the members, including private members, of the class in which it is nested. However, the enclosing class does not have access to the members of the nested class.
- A nested class that is declared directly within its enclosing class scope is a member of its enclosing class.
- It is also possible to declare a nested class that is local to a block.
- There are two types of nested classes : static and non-static.

    1. **A Static Nested Class :** A static nested class is one that has the static modifier applied. Because it is static, it must access the non-static members of its enclosing class through an object. That is, it cannot refer to non-static members of its enclosing class directly. Because of this restriction, static nested classes are rarely used.

    2. **A Non-Static Nested Class :** The important type of nested class is the inner class. An inner class is a non-static nested class. It has access to all the variables and methods of its outer class and may refer to them directly in the same way that other non-static members of the outer class do.

The following program illustrates how to define and use an inner class. The class named Outer has one instance variable named outer_x, one instance method named test( ), and defines one inner class called Inner.

```java
class Outer
{
    int outer_x = 100;
    void test()
    {
        Inner inner = new Inner();
        inner.display();
    }
    // this is an inner class
    class Inner
    {
        void display()
        {
            System.out.println("display : outer_x = " + outer_x);
        }
    }
}
class InnerClassDemo
{
    public static void main(String args[])
    {
        Outer outer = new Outer();
        outer.test();
    }
}
```

Output :

display : outer_x = 100

- In the program, an inner class named Inner is defined within the scope of class Outer. Therefore, any code in class Inner can directly access the variable outer_x.

- An instance method named display( ) is defined inside Inner. This method displays outer_x on the standard output stream.

- The main( ) method of InnerClassDemo creates an instance of class Outer and invokes its test( ) method. That method creates an instance of class Inner and the display( ) method is called.

5.19 COMMAND-LINE ARGUMENTS

- We can pass information into a program at the time of execution of program. This is accomplished by passing command-line arguments to main( ).

- A command-line argument is the information that directly follows the program's name on the command line when it is executed.

- To access the command-line arguments inside a Java program is quite easy, they are stored as strings in a string array passed to the args parameter of main( ).

- The first command-line argument is stored at args[0], the second at args[1], and so on.

For example, the following program displays all of the command-line arguments that it is called with :

```
// Display all command-line arguments.
class CommandLine
{
    public static void main(String args[])
    {
    for(int i=0; i<args.length; i++)
    System.out.println("args[" + i + "] : " +args[i]);
    }
}
```

- To execute above program use following statement

    Javac CommandLine.Java

    Java CommandLine this is Java program 100 200

Output :

    args[0] : this

    args[1] : is

    args[2] : Java

    args[3] : program

    args[4] : 100

    args[5] : 200

5.20 VARIABLE-LENGTH ARGUMENTS

- Java has included a feature that simplifies the creation of methods that need to take a variable number of arguments. This feature is called varargs and it is short for variable-length arguments.

- A method that takes a variable number of arguments is called a varargs method.

- Variable-length arguments could be handled two ways

  ➢ First, if the maximum number of arguments was small and known, then you could create overloaded versions of the method, one for each way the method could be called. Although this works and is suitable for some cases, it applies to only a narrow class of situations. In cases where the maximum number of potential arguments was larger, or unknowable,

  ➢ a second approach was used in which the arguments were put into an array, and then the array was passed to the method.

Example :

```
class PassArray
{
    static void vaTest(int v[])
    {
    System.out.print("Number of args : " + v.length +" Contents : ");
        for(int x : v)
    System.out.print(x + " ");
    System.out.println();
    }
    public static void main(String args[])
    {
    int n1[] = { 10 };
    int n2[] = { 1, 2, 3 };
    int n3[] = { };
    vaTest(n1); // 1 arg
    vaTest(n2); // 3 args
    vaTest(n3); // no args
    }
}
```

Output :

Number of args : 1 Contents : 10

Number of args : 3 Contents : 1 2 3

Number of args : 0 Contents :

- In the above program, the method vaTest( ) is passed its arguments through the array v. This old-style approach to variable-length arguments does enable vaTest( ) to take an arbitrary number of arguments.

- However, it requires that these arguments be manually packaged into an array prior to calling vaTest( ). Not only is it tedious to construct an array each time vaTest( ) is called, it is potentially error-prone.

5.21 INHERITANCE

- Inheritance is one of the feature of Object-Oriented Programming.

- Inheritance allows a class to use the properties and methods of another class. In other words, the derived class inherits the states and behaviors from the base class.

- The class which inherits the properties of other is known as subclass (derived class, child class) and the class whose properties are inherited is known as superclass (base class, parent class).

- The derived class is also called subclass and the base class is also known as super-class.

- The derived class can add its own additional variables and methods. These additional variable and methods differentiate the derived class from the base class.

- Inheritance is a compile-time mechanism. A super-class can have any number of subclasses. But a subclass can have only one superclass.

- The superclass and subclass have "is-a" relationship between them.

- Inheritance can be defined as the process where one class acquires the properties (methods and fields) of another. With the use of inheritance, the information is made manageable in a hierarchical order.

5.21.1 extends Keyword

- **extends** is the keyword used to inherit the properties of a class. Following is the syntax of extends keyword.

Syntax

```
class Super
{
    .....
    .....
}
```

```
    class Sub extends Super
    {
        .....
        .....
    }
```

Example :

```
class Calculation
{
  int z;
  public void addition(int x, int y)
    {
            z = x + y;
            System.out.println("The sum of the given numbers :"+z);
    }
  public void Subtraction(int x, int y)
    {
      z = x - y;
      System.out.println("The difference between the given numbers :"+z);
    }
}
public class My_Calculation extends Calculation
{
  public void multiplication(int x, int y)
    {
      z = x * y;
        System.out.println("The product of the given numbers :"+z);
    }
  public static void main(String args[])
    {
            int a = 20, b = 10;
            My_Calculation demo = new My_Calculation();
            demo.addition(a, b);
            demo.Subtraction(a, b);
            demo.multiplication(a, b);
    }
}
```

Output :

The sum of the given numbers: 30

The difference between the given numbers: 10

The product of the given numbers: 200

- In the given program, when an object to **My_Calculation** class is created, a copy of the contents of the superclass is made within it. That is why, using the object of the subclass you can access the members of a superclass.

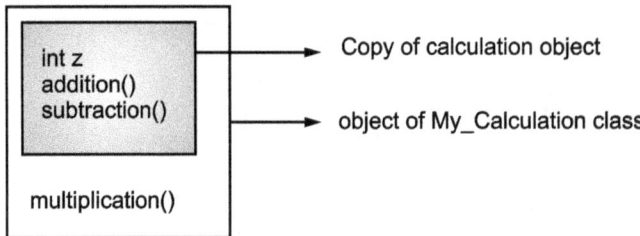

Fig. 5.4 : Example of extend keyword

- The Superclass reference variable can hold the subclass object, but using that variable you can access only the members of the superclass, so to access the members of both classes it is recommended to always create reference variable to the subclass.

5.21.2 Types of Inheritance

There are various types of inheritance

1. Single Inheritance
2. Multilevel Inheritance
3. Hierarchical inheritance
4. Multiple Inheritance
5. Hybrid inheritance

The above types if inheritances are explained one by one.

1. Single Inheritance :

- Single inheritance is a type of inheritance in which single derived class is inheriting the properties from single base class.

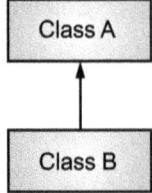

Fig. 5.5 : Single inheritance

Syntax :

```
public class A
{
    .............
}
public class B extends  A
{
    .................
}
```

Example :

```
class Vehicle
{
  String color;
  int speed;
  int size;
  void attributes()
    {
            System.out.println("Color : " + color);
            System.out.println("Speed : " + speed);
            System.out.println("Size : " + size);
    }
}
// A subclass which extends for vehicle
class Car extends Vehicle
{
  int CC;
  int gears;
  void attributescar()
    {
      // The subclass refers to the members of the superclass
        System.out.println("Color of Car : " + color);
        System.out.println("Speed of Car : " + speed);
```

```
            System.out.println("Size of Car : " + size);
            System.out.println("CC of Car : " + CC);
            System.out.println("No of gears of Car : " + gears);
    }
}
public class Test
{
    public static void main(String args[])
    {
            Car b1 = new Car();
            b1.color = "Blue";
            b1.speed = 200 ;
            b1.size = 22;
            b1.CC = 1000;
            b1.gears = 5;
            b1.attributescar();
    }
}
```

Output :

Color of Car : Blue

Speed of Car : 200

Size of Car : 22

CC of Car : 1000

No of gears of Car : 5

- The derived class inherits all the members and methods that are declared as public or protected.

- If declared as private it can not be inherited by the derived classes. The private members can be accessed only in its own class.

- The derived class cannot inherit a member of the base class if the derived class declares another member with the same name.

2. Multilevel Inheritance

- Class C inherits class B and class B inherits class A which means B is a parent class of C and A is a parent class of B. So, in this case class C is implicitly inheriting the properties and method of class A along with B that's what is called multilevel inheritance.

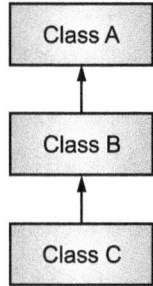

Fig. 5.6 : Multilevel inheritance

Syntax :

```
public class A
{
            ............
}
public class B extends  A
{
            .................
}
public class C extends B
{
            ..........
}
```

Example :

In this example, we have three classes – Car, Maruti and Maruti800. We have done a setup – class Maruti extends Car and class Maurit800 extends Maruti. With the help of this Multilevel hierarchy setup, our Maurti800 class is able to use the methods of both the classes Car and Maruti.

```
class Car
{
    public Car()
    {
        System.out.println("Class Car");
    }
```

```java
    public void vehicleType()
    {
        System.out.println("Vehicle Type : Car");
    }
}
class Maruti extends Car
{
    public Maruti()
    {
        System.out.println("Class Maruti");
    }
    public void brand()
    {
        System.out.println("Brand : Maruti");
    }
    public void speed()
    {
        System.out.println("Max : 90Kmph");
    }
}
public class Maruti800 extends Maruti
{
    public Maruti800()
    {
        System.out.println("Maruti Model : 800");
    }
    public void speed()
    {
        System.out.println("Max : 80Kmph");
    }
```

```
    public static void main(String args[])
    {
        Maruti800 obj=new Maruti800();
        obj.vehicleType();
        obj.brand();
        obj.speed();
    }
}
```

Output :

Class Car

Class Maruti

Maruti Model : 800

Vehicle Type : Car

Brand : Maruti

Max : 80Kmph

3. **Hierarchical Inheritance**

    *   When a class has more than one child class (sub classes) or in other words more than one child class has the same parent class, then such kind of inheritance is known as Hierarchical Inheritance.

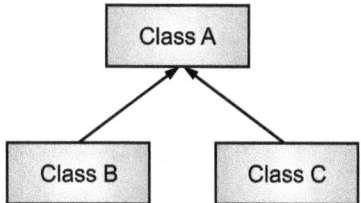

Fig. 5.7 : Hierarchical inheritance

Example :

```
Class A
{
 public void methodA()
 {
    System.out.println("method of Class A");
 }
}
Class B extends A
```

```
{
 public void methodB()
 {
    System.out.println("method of Class B");
 }
}
Class C extends A
{
 public void methodC()
 {
 System.out.println("method of Class C");
 }
}
Class D extends A
{
 public void methodD()
 {
    System.out.println("method of Class D");
 }
}
Class MyClass
{
 public void methodB()
 {
    System.out.println("method of Class B");
 }
 public static void main(String args[])
 {
    B obj1 = new B();
    C obj2 = new C();
    D obj3 = new D();
    obj1.methodA();
    obj2.methodA();
    obj3.methodA();
 }
}
```

Output :

method of Class A

method of Class A

method of Class A

4. Multiple Inheritance :

- C++, Common lisp and few other languages supports multiple inheritance while Java doesn't support it. It is just to remove ambiguity, because multiple inheritance can cause ambiguity in few scenarios. One of the most common scenario is Diamond problem.

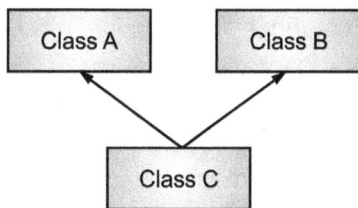

Fig. 5.8 : Multiple inheritance

- What is diamond problem?

Consider the below diagram which shows multiple inheritance as Class D extends both Class B and C. Now let's assume we have a method in class A and class B and C overrides that method in their own way. Because D is extending both B and C so if D wants to use the same method which method would be called (the overridden method of B or the overridden method of C). Ambiguity. That's the main reason why Java doesn't support multiple inheritance.

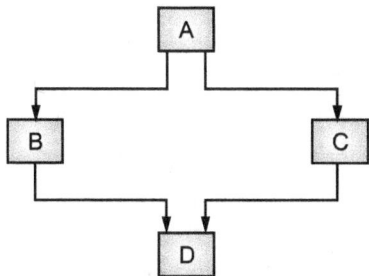

Fig. 5.9 : Hybrid inheritance

Example : How to achieve multiple inheritance in Java using interfaces?

```
interface X
{
  public void myMethod();
}
```

```
interface Y
{
  public void myMethod();
}
class Demo implements X, Y
{
  public void myMethod()
  {
    System.out.println(" Multiple inheritance using interfaces");
  }
}
```

- As you can see that the class implemented two interfaces. A class can implement any number of interfaces. In this case, there is no ambiguity even though both the interfaces are having same method. Because methods in an interface are always abstract by default, which doesn't let them to give their implementation (or method definition) in interface itself.

5. **Hybrid Inheritance**

- If you are using only classes to implement hybrid inheritance, then this is not allowed in Java, however using interfaces it's possible to have Hybrid inheritance in Java.

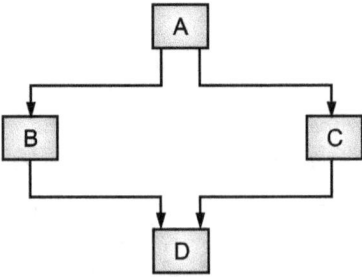

Fig. 5.10 : Hybrid inheritance

- Java doesn't support multiple inheritance, the hybrid inheritance is also not possible.

Case 1 : Using classes : If in above figure B and C are classes then this inheritance is not allowed as a single class cannot extend more than one class (Class D is extending both B and C).

Case 2 : Using Interfaces : If B and C are interfaces then the above hybrid inheritance is allowed as a single class can implement any number of interfaces in Java.

- Let's understand the above concept with the help of examples :

Using Classes to form Hybrid

```java
public class A
{
    public void methodA()
    {
        System.out.println("Class A methodA");
    }
}
public class B extends A
{
  public void methodA()
  {
   System.out.println("Childclass B is overriding inherited method A");
  }
    public void methodB()
    {
        System.out.println("Class B methodB");
    }
}
public class C extends A
{
    public void methodA()
    {
        System.out.println("Child class C is overriding the methodA");
    }
    public void methodC()
    {
        System.out.println("Class C methodC");
    }
}
```

```
public class D extends B, C
{
    public void methodD()
    {
        System.out.println("Class D methodD");
    }
    public static void main(String args[])
    {
        D obj1= new D();
        obj1.methodD();
        obj1.methodA();
    }
}
```

Output :

Error!!

- Above code shows an error, because Multiple inheritance is not allowed in Java so class D cannot extend two classes (B and C).

- In the above program class B and C both are extending class A and they both have overridden the methodA(), which they can do as they have extended the class A. But since both have different version of methodA(), compiler is confused which one to call when there has been a call made to methodA() in child class D (child of both B and C, it's object is allowed to call their methods), this is a ambiguous situation and to avoid it, such kind of scenarios are not allowed in Java.

Using Interfaces to form Hybrid

```
interface A
{
    public void methodA();
}
interface B extends A
{
    public void methodB();
}
interface C extends A
```

```
{
   public void methodC();
}
class D implements B, C
{
   public void methodA()
   {
       System.out.println("MethodA");
   }
   public void methodB()
   {
       System.out.println("MethodB");
   }
   public void methodC()
   {
       System.out.println("MethodC");
   }
   public static void main(String args[])
   {
       D obj1= new D();
       obj1.methodA();
       obj1.methodB();
       obj1.methodC();
   }
}
```

Output :

MethodA

MethodB

MethodC

- Even though class D didn't implement interface "A" still we have to define the methodA() in it. It is because interface B and C extends the interface A.

- The above code would work without any issues and that's how we implemented hybrid inheritance in Java using interfaces.

5.22 MEMBER ACCESS AND INHERITANCE

- A subclass cannot access the private members of the superclass.
- For example, consider the following simple class hierarchy: If you try to compile the following program, you will get the error message.

```
class A
{
    private int j; // private to A
}
class B extends A
{
    int total;
    void sum()
    {
        total = j; // ERROR, j is not accessible here
    }
}
```

Output :

The field A.j is not visible

- Java's access specifiers are public, private, protected and a default access level.A public class member can be accessed by any other code. A private class member can only be accessed within its class.

5.22.1 Default (without an Access Modifier)

- A class's fields, methods and the class itself may be default.
- A class's default features are accessible to any class in the same package.
- A default method may be overridden by any subclass that is in the same package as the superclass.

5.22.2 Protected

- Protected features are more accessible than default features.
- Only variables and methods may be declared protected.
- A protected feature of a class is available to all classes in the same package (like a default).

- Moreover, a protected feature of a class can be available to its subclasses.

Example : Here is an example for a public member variable

     public int i;

- The following code defines a private member variable and a private member method :

```
private double j;
private int myMethod(int a, char b)
{ // ...}
class Test
{
    int a;      // default access
    public int b; // public access
    private int c; // private access
    // methods to access c
    void setc(int i)
    {
        c = i;
    }
    int getc()
    {
        return c;
    }
}
public class Main
{
    public static void main(String args[])
    {
        Test ob = new Test();
        ob.a = 1;
        ob.b = 2;
        // This is not OK and will cause an error
```

```
    // ob.c = 100; // Error!
     // You must access c through its methods
    ob.setc(100); // OK
    System.out.println("a, b, and c : " + ob.a + " " + ob.b + " " +          ob.getc());
    }
}
```

Output :

a, b, and c : 1 2 100

5.23 SUPER CLASS REFERENCE

• A reference variable of a superclass can be assigned a reference to any subclass derived from that superclass.

For example, consider the following :

```
class RefDemo
{
    public static void main(String args[])
    {
        BoxWeight weightbox = new BoxWeight(3, 5, 7, 8.37);
        Box plainbox = new Box();
        double vol;
        vol = weightbox.volume();
        System.out.println("Volume of weightbox is " + vol);
        System.out.println("Weight of weightbox is " +weightbox.weight);
        System.out.println();
        // assign BoxWeight reference to Box reference
        plainbox = weightbox;
        vol = plainbox.volume(); // OK, volume() defined in Box
        System.out.println("Volume of plainbox is " + vol);
    }
}
```

- Here, weightbox is a reference to BoxWeight objects, and plainbox is a reference to Box objects. Since BoxWeight is a subclass of Box, it is permissible to assign plainbox a reference to the weightbox object.

- It is important to understand that it is the type of the reference variable not the type of the object that it refers to that determines what members can be accessed. That is, when a reference to a subclass object is assigned to a superclass reference variable, you will have access only to those parts of the object defined by the superclass. This is why plainbox can't access weight even when it refers to a BoxWeight object.

5.24 USING SUPER

- Whenever a subclass needs to refer to its immediate superclass, it can do so by use of the keyword super.

- Super has two general forms. The first calls the superclass' constructor. The second is used to access a member of the superclass that has been hidden by a member of a subclass.

(a) Using Super to Call Superclass Constructors

- A subclass can call a constructor defined by its superclass by use of the following form of super :

```
super(arg-list);
```

- Here, arg-list specifies any arguments needed by the constructor in the superclass. Super( )

- There must always be the first statement executed inside a subclass' constructor.

- If a class is inheriting the properties of another class, the subclass automatically acquires the default constructor of the superclass. But if you want to call a parameterized constructor of the superclass, you need to use the super keyword as shown below.
  super(values);

- Example demonstrates how to use the super keyword to invoke the parametrized constructor of the superclass. This program contains a superclass and a subclass, where the superclass contains a parameterized constructor which accepts a string value, and we used the super keyword to invoke the parameterized constructor of the superclass.

```
class Superclass
{
  int age;
  Superclass(int age)
  {
    this.age = age;
  }
}
```

```
  public void getAge()
{
    System.out.println("The value of the variable named age in super class is : " +age);
  }
}
public class Subclass extends Superclass
{
  Subclass(int age)
   {
      super(age);
   }
  public static void main(String argd[])
   {
     Subclass s = new Subclass(24);
     s.getAge();
   }
}
```

Compile and execute the above code using the following syntax.

Javac Subclass

Java Subclass

Output :

The value of the variable named age in super class is : 24

(b) Using Super to Access a Member of the Superclass that has been Hidden by a Member of a Subclass

- The second form of super acts somewhat like this, except that it always refers to the superclass of the subclass in which it is used. This usage has the following general form :

        super.member

    Here, member can be either a method or an instance variable.

- This second form of super is most applicable to situations in which member names of a subclass hide members by the same name in the superclass.

Consider this simple class hierarchy :

```
// Using super to overcome name hiding.
class A
    {
        int i;
    }
// Create a subclass by extending class A.
class B extends A
    {
        int i; // this i hides the i in A
        B(int a, int b)
        {
            super.i = a; // i in A
            i = b; // i in B
        }
        void show
        {
            System.out.println("i in superclass : " + super.i);
            System.out.println("i in subclass : " + i);
        }
    }
class UseSuper
    {
        public static void main(String args[])
            {
            B subOb = new B(1, 2);
                subOb.show();
            }
    }
```

Output :

i in superclass : 1

i in subclass : 2

- Although the instance variable i in B hides the i in A, super allows access to the i defined in the superclass. As you will see, super can also be used to call methods that are hidden by a subclass.

5.25 CONSTRUCTOR CALL SEQUENCE

- When a class hierarchy is created, in what order are the constructors for the classes that make up the hierarchy executed?

- For example, given a subclass called B and a superclass called A, is A's constructor executed before B's, or vice versa? The answer is that in a class hierarchy, constructors complete their execution in order of derivation, from superclass to subclass. Further, since super( ) must be the first statement executed in a subclass' constructor, this order is the same whether or not super( ) is used.

- If super( ) is not used, then the default or parameter less constructor of each superclass will be executed.

The following program illustrates when constructors are executed :

```
class A
{
    A()
    {
        System.out.println("Inside A's constructor.");
    }
}
// Create a subclass by extending class A.
class B extends A
{
    B()
    {
        System.out.println("Inside B's constructor.");
    }
}
// Create another subclass by extending B.
class C extends B
{
    C()
    {
        System.out.println("Inside C's constructor.");
    }
}
```

```
class CallingCons
{
    public static void main(String args[])
    {
        C c = new C();
    }
}
```

Output :

Inside A's constructor

Inside B's constructor

Inside C's constructor

- As you can see, the constructors are executed in order of derivation.
- If you think about it, it makes sense that constructors complete their execution in order of derivation. Because a superclass has no knowledge of any subclass, any initialization it needs to perform is separate from and possibly prerequisite to any initialization performed by the subclass. Therefore, it must complete its execution first.

5.26 METHOD OVERRIDING

- Method overriding means to override the functionality of an existing method.
- If a class inherits a method from its superclass, then there is a chance to override the method, if it is not marked final.
- The benefit of overriding is the ability to define a behavior that's specific to the subclass type, which means a subclass can implement a parent class method based on its requirement.

Rules for Method Overriding

- The argument list should be the same as that of the overridden method.
- The return type should be the same or a subtype of the return type declared in the original overridden method in the superclass.
- The access level cannot be more restrictive than the overridden method's access level. For example : If the superclass method is declared public then the overridding method in the sub class cannot be either private or protected.
- Instance methods can be overridden only if they are inherited by the subclass.
- A method declared final cannot be overridden.
- A method declared static cannot be overridden but can be re-declared.

- If a method cannot be inherited, then it cannot be overridden.
- A subclass within the same package as the instance's superclass can override any superclass method that is not declared private or final.
- A subclass in a different package can only override the non-final methods declared public or protected.
- An overriding method can throw any uncheck exceptions, regardless of whether the overridden method throws exceptions or not. However, the overriding method should not throw checked exceptions that are new or broader than the ones declared by the overridden method. The overriding method can throw narrower or fewer exceptions than the overridden method.
- Constructors cannot be overridden.

Example :

```
    class Animal
    {
        public void move()
        {
            System.out.println("Animals can move");
        }
    }
    class Dog extends Animal
    {
        public void move()
        {
            System.out.println("Dogs can walk and run");
        }
    }
public class TestDog
{
  public static void main(String args[])
    {
        Animal a = new Animal();   // Animal reference and object
        Animal b = new Dog();   // Animal reference but Dog object
        a.move();   // runs the method in Animal class
        b.move();   // runs the method in Dog class
    }
}
```

Output :

Animals can move

Dogs can walk and run

In the above example, you can see that even though **b** is a type of Animal it runs the move method in the Dog class. The reason for this is, in compile time, the check is made on the reference type.

- However, in the runtime, JVM figures out the object type and would run the method that belongs to that particular object.
- Therefore, in the above example, the program will compile properly since Animal class has the method move. Then, at the runtime, it runs the method specific for that object.

Example :

```
class Animal
{
  public void move()
    {
            System.out.println("Animals can move");
    }
}
class Dog extends Animal
{
  public void move()
    {
      System.out.println("Dogs can walk and run");
    }
  public void bark()
    {
            System.out.println("Dogs can bark");
    }
}
public class TestDog
{
  public static void main(String args[])
    {
      Animal a = new Animal();   // Animal reference and object
      Animal b = new Dog();   // Animal reference but Dog object
```

```
    a.move();   // runs the method in Animal class
       b.move();   // runs the method in Dog class
    b.bark();

  }

}
```

Output :

TestDog.Java :26 : error : cannot find symbol

    b.bark();

     ∧

 symbol :   method bark()

 location : variable b of type Animal

1 error

This program will throw a compile time error since b's reference type Animal doesn't have a method by the name of bark.

5.27 DYNAMIC METHOD DISPATCH

- Dynamic method dispatch is the mechanism by which a call to an overridden method is resolved at run time, rather than compile time.

- Dynamic Method Dispatch is related to a principle that states that a super class reference can store the reference of subclass object. However, it can't call any of the newly added methods by the subclass but a call to an overridden method results in calling a method of that object whose reference is stored in the super class reference.

- It simply means that which method would be executed, simply depends on the object reference stored in super class object.

- upcasting : When parent class reference variable refers to child class object ,it is called upcasting

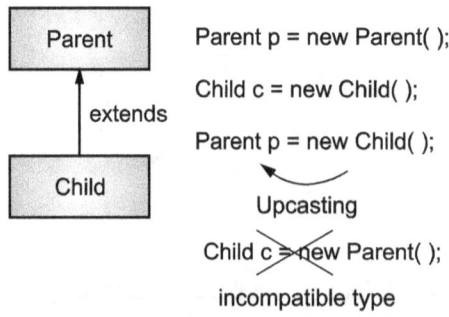

Fig. 5.11 : Dynamic method dispatch

Example for Dynamic Method Dispatch

```java
class A
{
    void callme()
    {
        System.out.println("Inside A's callme method");
    }
}
class B extends A
{
    void callme()   // override callme()
    {
        System.out.println("Inside B's callme method");
    }
}
class C extends A
{
    void callme() // override callme()
    {
        System.out.println("Inside C's callme method");
    }
}
public class Dynamic_disp
{
    public static void main(String args[])
    {
        A a = new A(); // object of type A
        B b = new B(); // object of type B
        C c = new C(); // object of type C
        A r; // obtain a reference of type A
```

```
        r = a; // r refers to an A object
        r.callme(); // calls A's version of callme
        r = b; // r refers to a B object
        r.callme(); // calls B's version of callme
        r = c; // r refers to a C object
        r.callme(); // calls C's version of callme
    }
}
```

Output :

Inside A's callme method

Inside B's callme method

Inside C's callme method

- Here reference of type A, called r, is declared. The program then assigns a reference to each type of object to r and uses that reference to invoke callme( ).

- As the output shows, the version of callme( ) executed is determined by the type of object being referred to at the time of the call.

5.28 ABSTRACT CLASS

- A class that is declared with abstract keyword, is known as abstract class in Java. It can have abstract and non-abstract methods (method with body).

- **Abstraction** is a process of hiding the implementation details and showing only functionality to the user.

- Another way, it shows only important things to the user and hides the internal details for example sending sms, you just type the text and send the message. You don't know the internal processing about the message delivery.

- One of the classes to achieve Abstaction is Abstract class

- A class that is declared as abstract is known as **abstract class**. It needs to be extended and its method implemented. It cannot be instantiated.

Syntax :

```
abstract class A
{

}
```

Example :

```
abstract class Shape
{
    abstract void draw();
}
//In real scenario, implementation is provided by others i.e. unknown by end user
class Rectangle extends Shape
{
    void draw()
    {
        System.out.println("drawing rectangle");
    }
}
    class Circle1 extends Shape
    {
        void draw()
        {
            System.out.println("drawing circle");
        }
    }
    //In real scenario, method is called by programmer or user
    class TestAbstraction1
    {
        public static void main(String args[])
        {
            Shape s=new Circle1();

    //In real scenario, object is provided through method e.g. getShape() method
            s.draw();
        }
    }
```

Output :

drawing circle

5.29 THE OBJECT CLASS

- There is one special class Object, defined by Java.
- All other classes are subclasses of Object. That is, Object is a superclass of all other classes.
- Reference variable of type Object can refer to an object of any other class. Also, since arrays are implemented as classes, a variable of type Object can also refer to any array.
- Object defines the following methods, which means that they are available in every object.

Method	Purpose
Object clone( )	Creates a new object that is the same as the object being cloned.
boolean equals(Object *object*)	Determines whether one object is equal to another.
void finalize( )	Called before an unused object is recycled.
Class<?> getClass( )	Obtains the class of an object at run time.
int hashCode( )	Returns the hash code associated with the invoking object.
void notify( )	Resumes execution of a thread waiting on the invoking object.
void notifyAll( )	Resumes execution of all threads waiting on the invoking object.
String toString( ).	Returns a string that describes the object

5.30 PACKAGES

- Packages are used in Java to prevent naming conflicts, to control access, to make searching/locating and usage of classes, interfaces, enumerations and annotations easier, etc.
- A Package can be defined as a grouping of related types classes, interfaces, enumerations and annotations providing access protection and namespace management.
- Some of the existing packages in Java are:
  A. Java.lang – bundles the fundamental classes
  B. Java.io – classes for input, output functions are bundled in this package
- Package in Java can be categorized in two form, built-in package and user-defined package.

Built-in Package : Existing Java package for example Java.lang, Java.util etc.

User-defined-Package : Java package created by user to categorized classes and interface

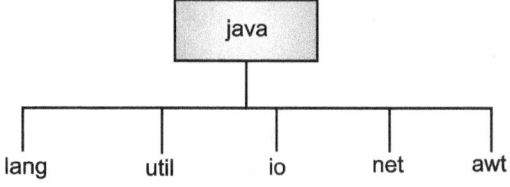

Fig. 5.12 : Packages

5.30.1 Advantages of Java Package

- Java package is used to categorize the classes and interfaces so that they can be easily maintained.

- Java package provides access protection.

- Java package removes naming collision.

5.30.2 Defining a Package

- In Java, any classes declared within that file will belong to the specified package.

- The package statement defines a name space in which classes are stored. If you skip the package statement, the class names are put into the default package, which has no name.

- Most of the time, you will define a package for your code.

- This is the general form of the package statement :

    package *pkg*;

    Here, *pkg* is the name of the package.

- For example, the following statement creates a package called MyPackage :

    package MyPackage;

- Java uses file system directories to store packages. For example, the .class files for any classes you declare to be part of MyPackage must be stored in a directory called MyPackage.

- Remember that case is significant, and the directory name must match the package name exactly.

- The package statement simply specifies to which package the classes defined in a file belong. It does not exclude other classes in other files from being part of that same package.

- Most real-world packages are spread across many files. You can create a hierarchy of packages. To do so, simply separate each package name from the one above it by use of a period.

- The general form of a multileveled package statement is shown here :

  package *pkg1*[.*pkg2*[.*pkg3*]];

- A package hierarchy must be reflected in the file system of your Java development system.

- Example, a package declared as package Java.awt.image; needs to be stored in **Java\awt\image** in a Windows environment. Be sure to choose your package names carefully. You cannot rename a package without renaming the directory in which the classes are stored.

5.30.3 Finding Packages and CLASSPATH

- Packages are mirrored by directories.

- Java run-time system uses the current working directory as its starting point. Thus, if your package is in a subdirectory of the current directory, it will be found.

- You can specify a directory path or paths by setting the CLASSPATH environmental variable.

- You can use the -classpath option with Java and Javac to specify the path to your classes.

- For example, consider the following package specification:

  package MyPack

- For a program to find MyPack, one of three things must be true. Either the program can be executed from a directory immediately above MyPack, or the CLASSPATH must be set to include the path to MyPack, or the -classpath option must specify the path to MyPack when the program is run via Java.

- When the second two options are used, the class path must not include MyPack, itself. It must simply specify the path to MyPack.

- For example, in a Windows environment, if the path to MyPack is

  C :\MyPrograms\Java\MyPack

  then the class path to MyPack is

  C :\MyPrograms\Java

5.30.4 Access Protection

- Java provides many levels of protection to allow fine-grained control over the visibility of variables and methods within classes, subclasses, and packages.

- Classes and packages are both means of encapsulating and containing the name space and scope of variables and methods.

- Packages act as containers for classes and other subordinate packages. Classes act as containers for data and code.

- The class is Java's smallest unit of abstraction. Because of the interplay between classes and packages.
- Java addresses four categories of visibility for class members:
  - ➢ Subclasses in the same package
  - ➢ Non-subclasses in the same package
  - ➢ Subclasses in different packages
  - ➢ Classes that are neither in the same package nor subclasses
- The three access modifiers, private, public, and protected, provide a variety of ways to produce the many levels of access required by these categories.
- Anything declared public can be accessed from anywhere. Anything declared private cannot be seen outside of its class. When a member does not have an explicit access specification, it is visible to subclasses as well as to other classes in the same package. This is the default access.
- If you want to allow an element to be seen outside your current package, but only to classes that subclass your class directly, then declare that element protected.
- Following Table applies only to members of classes. A non-nested class has only two possible access levels: default and public.
- When a class is declared as public, it is accessible by any other code. If a class has default access, then it can only be accessed by other code within its same package.
- When a class is public, it must be the only public class declared in the file, and the file must have the same name as the class.

	Private	No Modifier	Protected	Public
Same class	Yes	Yes	Yes	Yes
Same package subclass	No	Yes	Yes	Yes
Same package non-subclass	No	Yes	Yes	Yes
Different package subclass	No	No	Yes	Yes
Different package non-subclass	No	No	No	Yes

5.30.5 Importing Packages

- **import** keyword is used to import built-in and user-defined packages into your Java source file. So, that your class can refer to a class that is in another package by directly using its name.

There are 3 different ways to refer to class that is present in different package

1. Using Fully Qualified Name

Example :

```
class MyDate extends Java.util.Date
{
//statement;
}
```

2. Import the Only Class you Want to Use.

Example :

```
import Java.util.Date;
class MyDate extends Date
{
//statement.
}
```

3. Import all the Classes from the Particular Package

Example :

```
import Java.util.*;
class MyDate extends Date
{
//statement;
}
```

5.31 INTERFACES

- An interface is a reference type in Java. It is similar to class. It is a collection of abstract methods.
- A class implements an interface, thereby inheriting the abstract methods of the interface.
- Along with abstract methods, an interface may also contain constants, default methods, static methods, and nested types. Method bodies exist only for default methods and static methods.
- Writing an interface is similar to writing a class. But a class describes the attributes and behaviors of an object and an interface contains behaviors that a class implements.

Interfaces have the Following Properties :

- An interface is implicitly abstract. You do not need to use the abstract keyword while declaring an interface.
- Each method in an interface is also implicitly abstract, so the abstract keyword is not needed.
- Methods in an interface are implicitly public.

An Interface is Similar to a Class in the Following Ways :

- An interface can contain any number of methods.
- An interface is written in a file with a **.Java** extension, with the name of the interface matching the name of the file.
- The byte code of an interface appears in a **.class** file.

- Interfaces appear in packages, and their corresponding bytecode file must be in a directory structure that matches the package name.

An Interface is Different from a Class in Several Ways, Including :

- You cannot instantiate an interface.

- An interface does not contain any constructors.

- All the methods in an interface are abstract.

- An interface cannot contain instance fields. The only fields that can appear in an interface must be declared both static and final.

- An interface is not extended by a class; it is implemented by a class.

- An interface can extend multiple interfaces.

5.31.1 Defining an Interface

- An interface is defined much like a class. This is a simplified general form of an interface:

```
access interface name
{
    return-type method-name1(parameter-list);
    return-type method-name2(parameter-list);
    type final-varname1 = value;
    type final-varname2 = value;
    //...
    return-type method-nameN(parameter-list);
    type final-varnameN = value;
}
```

- The interface keyword is used to declare an interface. Here is a simple example to declare an interface:

```
import Java.lang.*;
// Any number of import statements
public interface NameOfInterface
{
  // Any number of final, static fields
  // Any number of abstract method declarations\
}
```

5.31.2 Implementing Interfaces

- Once an interface has been defined, one or more classes can implement that interface.

- To implement an interface, include the implements clause in a class definition, and then create the methods required by the interface.

- The general form of a class that includes the implements clause looks like this:

```
class classname [extends superclass] [implements interface [,interface...]]
{
    // class-body
}
```

- If a class implements more than one interface, the interfaces are separated with a comma.

- If a class implements two interfaces that declare the same method, then the same method will be used by clients of either interface.

- The methods that implement an interface must be declared public. Also, the type signature of the implementing method must match exactly the type signature specified in the interface definition.

- Here is a small example class that implements the Callback interface shown earlier:

```
class Client implements Callback
{
// Implement Callback's interface
    public void callback(int p)
    {
    System.out.println("callback called with " + p);
    }
}
```

- Here, callback( ) is declared using the public access modifier.

- When you implement an interface method, it must be declared as public. It is both permissible and common for classes that implement interfaces to define additional members of their own.

For example, the following version of Client implements callback() and adds the method nonIfaceMeth() :

```
class Client implements Callback
{
    // Implement Callback's interface
    public void callback(int p)
    {
    System.out.println("callback called with " + p);
    }
    void nonIfaceMeth()
    {
    System.out.println("Classes that implement interfaces " + "may also define other members, too.");
    }
}
```

5.31.3 Nested Interfaces

- An interface can be declared a member of a class or another interface. Such an interface is called a member interface or a nested interface.

- A nested interface can be declared as public, private, or protected. This differs from a top-level interface, which must either be declared as public or use the default access level, as previously described.

- When a nested interface is used outside of its enclosing scope, it must be qualified by the name of the class or interface of which it is a member. Thus, outside of the class or interface in which a nested interface is declared, its name must be fully qualified.

Here is an example that demonstrates a nested interface:

```
// A nested interface example.
// This class contains a member interface.
class A
{
    // this is a nested interface
    public interface NestedIF
```

```
    {
        boolean isNotNegative(int x);
    }
}
// B implements the nested interface.
class B implements A.NestedIF
{
    public boolean isNotNegative(int x)
    {
        return x < 0 ? false : true;
    }
}
class NestedIFDemo
{
    public static void main(String args[])
    {
        // use a nested interface reference
        A.NestedIF nif = new B();
        if(nif.isNotNegative(10))
        System.out.println("10 is not negative");
        if(nif.isNotNegative(-12))
        System.out.println("this won't be displayed");
    }
}
```

- Notice that A defines a member interface called NestedIF and that it is declared public. Next, B implements the nested interface by specifying implements A.NestedIF Notice that the name is fully qualified by the enclosing class' name. Inside the main() method, an A.NestedIF reference called nif is created, and it is assigned a reference to a B object. Because B implements A.NestedIF, this is legal.

5.31.4 Extending Interfaces

- One interface can inherit another by use of the keyword extends.
- An interface can extend another interface in the same way that a class can extend another class.
- The extends keyword is used to extend an interface, and the child interface inherits the methods of the parent interface.

- The syntax is the same as for inheriting classes. When a class implements an interface that inherits another interface, it must provide implementations for all methods required by the interface inheritance chain.

Example :

```
// One interface can extend another.
interface A
{
    void fun1();
    void fun2();
}
// B now includes fun1() and fun2() -- it adds fun3().
interface B extends A
{
    void fun3();
}
// This class must implement all of A and B
class MyClass implements B
{
    public void fun1()
    {
        System.out.println("Implement fun1().");
    }
    public void fun2()
    {
        System.out.println("Implement fun2().");
    }
    public void fun3()
    {
        System.out.println("Implement fun3().");
    }
}
```

```
class IFExtend
{
    public static void main(String arg[])
        {
            MyClass ob = new MyClass();
            ob. fun1();
            ob. fun2();
            ob. fun3();
        }
}
```

- As an experiment, you might want to try removing the implementation for fun1() in MyClass. This will cause a compile-time error.

- Any class that implements an interface must implement all methods required by that interface, including any that are inherited from other interfaces.

5.31.5 Variables in Interfaces

- You can use interfaces to import shared constants into multiple classes by simply declaring an interface that contains variables that are initialized to the desired values.

- When you include that interface in a class that is, when you "implement" the interface, all those variable names will be in scope as constants.

- If an interface contains no methods, then any class that includes such an interface doesn't implement anything.

- It is as if that class were importing the constant fields into the class name space as final variables.

5.32 INSTANCE OF OPERATOR

- In Java, instanceof operator is used to check the type of an object at runtime.

- It is the means by which your program can obtain run-time type information about an object.

- The instanceof operator is also important in case of casting object at runtime.

- The instanceof operator return boolean value, if an object reference is of specified type then it return true otherwise false.

Example of instanceof

```
public class Test
{
    public static void main(String[] args)
    {
        Test t= new Test();
        System.out.println(t instanceof Test);
    }
}
```

Output :

true

More example of instanceof operator

```
class Parent
{}
class Child1 extends Parent
{}
class Child2 extends Parent
{}
class Test
{
    public static void main(String[] args)
    {
        Parent p =new Parent();
        Child1 c1 = new Child1();
        Child2 c2 = new Child2();
        System.out.println(c1 instanceof Parent);      //true
        System.out.println(c2 instanceof Parent);      //true
        System.out.println(p instanceof Child1);      //false
        System.out.println(p instanceof Child2);      //false
        p = c1;
```

```
    System.out.println(p instanceof Child1);        //true
    System.out.println(p instanceof Child2);        //false
    p = c2;
    System.out.println(p instanceof Child1);        //false
    System.out.println(p instanceof Child2);        //true
  }
}
```

Output :

true

true

false

false

true

false

false

true

EXERCISE

1. Explain Class and Object fundamentals
2. What is a Constructor? Explain its Types
4. Write a short note on Garbage collection
5. Explain Finalize() methods
6. Explain the term Method overloading
7. Explain Nested and Inner classes
8. Explain the term Method overriding
9. Differentiate between Method overloading and Method Overriding
10. Explain Dynamic method dispatch
11. Explain Abstract Classes
12. Explain Inheritance in Java
13. Explain the term Packages
14. Explain the term Interfaces
15. Write a short note on instance of operator

✠ ✠ ✠

Unit VI

EXCEPTION HANDLING IN JAVA

6.1 FUNDAMENTAL OF EXCEPTION HANDLING

- Exception is an abnormal condition. In Java, exception is an event that disrupts the normal flow of the program. It is an object which is thrown at runtime.
- An exception is a problem that arises during the execution of a program. When an exception occurs, the normal flow of the program is disrupted and the program/application terminates abnormally.
- An exception can occur for many different reasons. Following are some scenarios where an exception occurs.
  - ➢ A user has entered an invalid data.
  - ➢ A file that needs to be opened cannot be found.
  - ➢ A network connection has been lost in the middle of communication or the JVM has run out of memory.
- Exception handling in Java is one of the powerful mechanisms to handle the runtime errors so that normal flow of the application can be maintained.
- Exception Handling is a mechanism to handle runtime errors such as ClassNotFound, IO, SQL, Remote etc.
- There are five keywords used in Java exception handling.
  - ➢ try
  - ➢ catch
  - ➢ finally
  - ➢ throw
  - ➢ throws

6.1.1 Advantages of Exception Handling

- The core advantage of exception handling is to maintain the normal flow of the application.
- Exception normally disrupts the normal flow of the application, that is why we use exception handling. Let's take a scenario :
  - ➢ statement 1;
  - ➢ statement 2;
  - ➢ statement 3;
  - ➢ statement 4;
  - ➢ statement 5; //exception occurs

- ➤ statement 6;
- ➤ statement 7;
- ➤ statement 8;
- ➤ statement 9;
- ➤ statement 10;

- Suppose there is 10 statements in your program and exception occurs at statement 5, rest of the code will not be executed i.e. statement 6 to 10 will not run. If we perform exception handling, rest of the statement will be executed. That is why we use exception handling in Java.

6.1.2 Hierarchy of Java Exception Classes

- All exception classes are subtypes of the Java.lang.Exception class. The exception class is a subclass of the Throwable class.

- Other than the exception class there is another subclass called Error which is derived from the Throwable class.

- Errors are abnormal conditions that happen in case of severe failures, these are not handled by the Java programs.

- Errors are generated to indicate errors generated by the runtime environment. Example : JVM is out of memory. Normally, programs cannot recover from errors.

- The Exception class has two main subclasses : IOException class and RuntimeException Class.

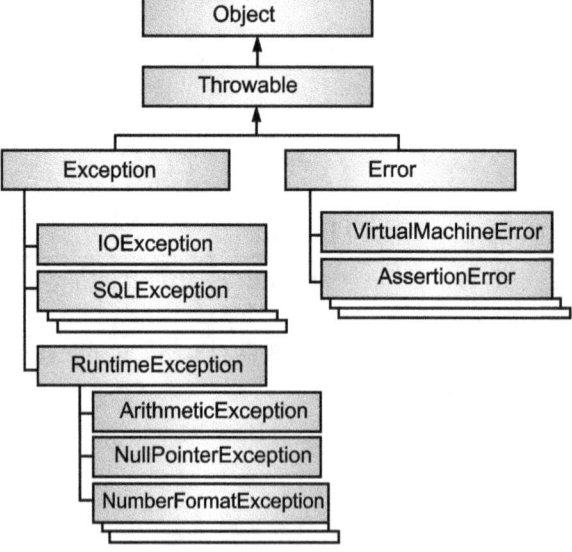

Fig. 6.1 : Hierarchy of Java exception classes

6.2 TYPES OF EXCEPTION

- There are mainly two types of exceptions: checked and unchecked where error is considered as unchecked exception.

- The Sun micro-system says there are three types of exceptions:

  1. Checked Exception

  2. Unchecked Exception

  3. Error

1. Checked Exception

- A checked exception is an exception that occurs at the compile time, these are also called as compile time exceptions. These exceptions cannot simply be ignored at the time of compilation, the programmer should take care of these exceptions.

- The classes that extend Throwable class except RuntimeException and Error are known as checked exceptions e.g. IOException, SQLException etc. Checked exceptions are checked at compile-time.

- For example, if you use FileReader class in your program to read data from a file, if the file specified in its constructor doesn't exist, then a *FileNotFoundException* occurs and the compiler prompts the programmer to handle the exception.

Example :

```
import Java.io.File;
import Java.io.FileReader;
public class FilenotFound_Demo
{
    public static void main (String args[])
      {
          File file = new File ("E ://file.txt");
          FileReader fr = new FileReader(file);
      }
}
```

- If you try to compile the above program, you will get the following exceptions.

Output :

C :\>Javac FilenotFound_Demo.Java

FilenotFound_Demo.Java :8 : error : unreported exception FileNotFoundException; must be caught or declared to be thrown

```
FileReader fr = new FileReader(file);
                   ^
```

1 error

- The methods read() and close() of FileReader class throws IOException, you can observe that the compiler notifies to handle IOException, along with FileNotFoundException.

2. Unchecked Exception

- An unchecked exception is an exception that occurs at the time of execution. These are also called as Runtime Exceptions. These include programming bugs, such as logic errors or improper use of an API.
- Runtime exceptions are ignored at the time of compilation.
- The classes that extend RuntimeException are known as unchecked exceptions e.g. ArithmeticException, NullPointerException, ArrayIndexOutOfBoundsException etc.
- Unchecked exceptions are not checked at compile-time rather they are checked at runtime.
- For example, if you have declared an array of size 5 in your program, and trying to call the 6th element of the array then an *ArrayIndexOutOfBoundsExceptionexception* occurs.

Example :

```
public class Unchecked_Demo
{
  public static void main(String args[])
    {
        int num[] = {1, 2, 3, 4};
            System.out.println(num[5]);
    }
}
```

- If you compile and execute the above program, you will get the following exception.

Output :

Exception in thread "main" Java.lang.ArrayIndexOutOfBoundsException : 5

at Exceptions.Unchecked_Demo.main(Unchecked_Demo.Java :8)

- **There are given some scenarios where unchecked exceptions can occur. They are as follows :**
  - ➢ Scenario where ArithmeticException occurs

    If we divide any number by zero, there occurs an ArithmeticException.

```
        int a=50/0;                        //ArithmeticException
```

➤ Scenario where NullPointerException occurs

If we have null value in any variable, performing any operation by the variable occurs an NullPointerException.

```
String s=null;
System.out.println(s.length());    //NullPointerException
```

➤ Scenario where NumberFormatException occurs

The wrong formatting of any value, may occur

NumberFormat Exception.

Suppose I have a string variable that have characters, converting this variable into digit will occur NumberFormatException.

```
String s="abc";
int i=Integer.parseInt(s);                        //NumberFormatException
```

➤ Scenario where ArrayIndexOutOfBoundsException occurs

If you are inserting any value in the wrong index, it would result ArrayIndexOutOfBoundsException as shown below:

```
int a[]=new int[5];
a[10]=50; //ArrayIndexOutOfBoundsException
```

3. Error

- Error is irrecoverable e.g. OutOfMemoryError, VirtualMachineError, AssertionError etc.
- Errors are not exceptions at all, but problems that arise beyond the control of the user or the programmer.
- Errors are typically ignored in your code because you can rarely do anything about an error.
- For example, if a stack overflow occurs, an error will arise. They are also ignored at the time of compilation.

6.3 UNCAUGHT EXCEPTIONS

- In following program includes an expression that intentionally causes a divide-by-zero error :

```
class Exc
{
    public static void main(String args[])
    {
        int d = 0;
        int a = 42 / d;
    }
}
```

- When the Java run-time system detects the attempt to divide by zero, it constructs a new exception object and then throws this exception. This causes the execution of Exc to stop, because once an exception has been thrown, it must be caught by an exception handler and deal with immediately.

- In this example, we haven't supplied any exception handlers of our own, so the exception is caught by the default handler provided by the Java run-time system.

- Any exception that is not caught by your program will ultimately be processed by the default handler. The default handler displays a string describing the exception, prints a stack trace from the point at which the exception occurred, and terminates the program.

- Here is the exception generated when this example is executed:

  Java.lang.ArithmeticException : / by zero

  at Exc0.main(Exc0.Java :4)

- Java supplies several built-in exception types that match the various sorts of run-time errors that can be generated.

- The stack trace will always show the sequence of method invocations that lead up to the error. For example, here is another version of the preceding program that introduces the same error but in a method separate from main( ) :

```
class Exc1
{
    static void subroutine()
    {
        int d = 0;
        int a = 10 / d;
    }
    public static void main(String args[])
    {
        Exc1.subroutine();
    }
}
```

- The resulting stack trace from the default exception handler shows how the entire call stack is displayed :

  Java.lang.ArithmeticException : / by zero

  at Exc1.subroutine(Exc1.Java :4)

  at Exc1.main(Exc1.Java :7)

6.4 TRY BLOCK

- Try block is used to enclose the code that might throw an exception. It must be used within the method.
- Try block must be followed by either catch or finally block.

Syntax of Try-Catch Block :

```
try
{
    //code that may throw exception
}
catch(Exception_class_Name ref)
{
}
```

Syntax of Try-Finally Block :

```
try
{1
//code that may throw exception
}
finally
{
}
```

6.5 CATCH BLOCK

- Catch block is used to handle the Exception. It must be used after the try block only.
- You can use multiple catch block with a single try.
- A method catches an exception using a combination of the try and catch keywords.
- A try catch block is placed around the code that might generate an exception. Code within a try catch block is referred to as protected code, and the syntax for using try catch looks like the following :

Syntax :

```
try
{
    // Protected code
}
catch(ExceptionName e1)
{
    // Catch block
}
```

- The code which is prone to exceptions is placed in the try block. When an exception occurs, that exception occurred is handled by catch block associated with it.
- Every try block should be immediately followed either by a catch block or finally block.
- A catch statement involves declaring the type of exception you are trying to catch. If an exception occurs in protected code, the catch block (or blocks) that follows the try is checked.
- If the type of exception that occurred is listed in a catch block, the exception is passed to the catch block much as an argument is passed into a method parameter.

Example :

The following is an array declared with 2 elements. Then the code tries to access the 3rd element of the array which throws an exception.

```
import Java.io.*;
public class ExcepTest
{
  public static void main(String args[])
  {
    try
    {
      int a[] = new int[2];
      System.out.println("Access element three :" + a[3]);
    }
    catch(ArrayIndexOutOfBoundsException e)
    {
      System.out.println("Exception thrown :" + e);
    }
    System.out.println("Out of the block");
  }
}
```

This will produce the following result

Output :

Exception thrown :Java.lang.ArrayIndexOutOfBoundsException : 3

Out of the block

Internal Working of Try-Catch Block

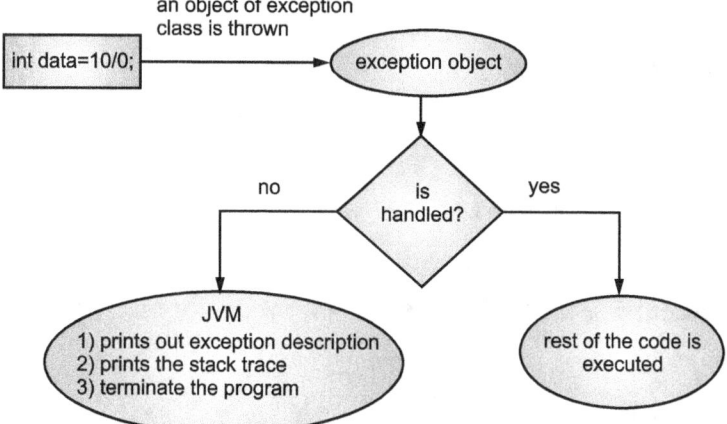

Fig. 6.2 : Internal working of Try-catch block

- The JVM firstly checks whether the exception is handled or not. If exception is not handled, JVM provides a default exception handler that performs the following tasks :

  ➢ Prints out exception description.

  ➢ Prints the stack trace (Hierarchy of methods where the exception occurred).

  ➢ Causes the program to terminate.

- But if exception is handled by the application programmer, normal flow of the application is maintained i.e. rest of the code is executed.

6.6 THROW KEYWORD

- The Java throw keyword is used to explicitly throw an exception.

- You can throw an exception, either a newly instantiated one or an exception that you just caught, by using the throw keyword.

- We can throw either checked or unchecked exception in Java by throw keyword. The throw keyword is mainly used to throw custom exception.

- The syntax of Java throw keyword is given below.

throw exception;

- Example of throw IOException.

throw new IOException("sorry device error);

- In the following example, we have created the validate method that takes integer value as a parameter. If the age is less than 18, we are throwing the ArithmeticException otherwise print a message welcome to vote.

```java
public class TestThrow
{
   static void validate(int age)
   {
       if(age<18)
           throw new ArithmeticException("not valid");
       else
           System.out.println("welcome to vote");
   }
   public static void main(String args[])
   {
           validate(13);
           System.out.println("Rest of the code...");
   }
}
```

Output :

Exception in thread main Java.lang.ArithmeticException : not valid

6.7 THROWS KEYWORD

- The Java throws keyword is used to declare an exception. It gives an information to the programmer that there may occur an exception so it is better for the programmer to provide the exception handling code so that normal flow can be maintained.

- Exception Handling is mainly used to handle the checked exceptions. If there occurs any unchecked exception such as NullPointerException, it is programmers fault that he is not performing check up before the code being used.

- If a method does not handle a checked exception, the method must declare it using the throws keyword. The throws keyword appears at the end of a method's signature.

Syntax of Throws :

```
return_type method_name() throws exception_class_name
{
//method code
}
```

Example :

```java
import Java.io.IOException;
class Testthrows
{
    void m() throws IOException
    {
        throw new IOException("device error"); //checked exception
    }
    void n() throws IOException
    {
        m();
    }
    void p()
    {
        try
        {
            n();
        }
        catch(Exception e)
        {
            System.out.println("exception handled");
        }
    }
    public static void main(String args[])
    {
        Testthrows obj=new Testthrows();
        obj.p();
        System.out.println("normal flow...");
    }
}
```

Output :

exception handled

normal flow ...

Difference between Throw and Throws in Java :

There are many differences between throw and throws keywords

Sr. No.	Throw	Throws
1.	Java throw keyword is used to explicitly throw an exception.	Java throws keyword is used to declare an exception.
2.	Checked exception cannot be propagated using throw only.	Checked exception can be propagated with throws.
3.	Throw is followed by an instance.	Throws is followed by class.
4.	Throw is used within the method.	Throws is used with the method signature.
5.	You cannot throw multiple exceptions.	You can declare multiple exceptions e.g. public void method()throws IOException, SQLException.

6.8 THE FINALLY BLOCK

- The finally block follows a try block or a catch block. A finally block of code always executes, irrespective of occurrence of an Exception.

- Using a finally block allows you to run any cleanup-type statements that you want to execute, no matter what happens in the protected code.

- A finally block appears at the end of the catch blocks and has the following Syntax :

```
try
{
    // Protected code
}
catch(ExceptionType1 e1)
{
    // Catch block
}
catch(ExceptionType2 e2)
```

```
    {
        // Catch block
    }
    catch(ExceptionType3 e3)
    {
        // Catch block
    }
    finally
    {
        // The finally block always executes.
    }
```

Example :

```
public class ExcepTest
{
    public static void main(String args[])
    {
        int a[] = new int[2];
        try
        {
            System.out.println("Access element three :" + a[3]);
        }
        catch(ArrayIndexOutOfBoundsException e)
        {
            System.out.println("Exception thrown :" + e);
        }
        finally
        {
            a[0] = 6;
            System.out.println("First element value : " + a[0]);
            System.out.println("The finally statement is executed");
        }
    }
}
```

Output :

Exception thrown :Java.lang.ArrayIndexOutOfBoundsException : 3

First element value : 6

The finally statement is executed

Note the following :

- A catch clause cannot exist without a try statement.

- It is not compulsory to have finally clauses whenever a try/catch block is present.

- The try block cannot be present without either catch clause or finally clause.

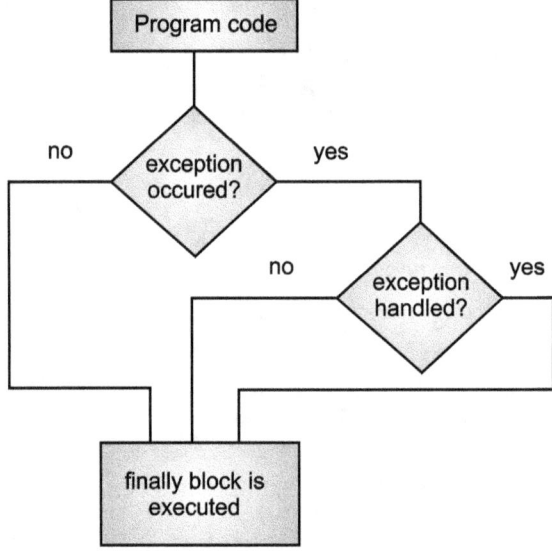

Fig. 6.3 : Finally block

- If you don't handle exception, before terminating the program, JVM executes finally block (if any).

- Finally block in Java can be used to put "cleanup" code such as closing a file, closing connection etc.

Let's see the different cases where finally block can be used.

Case 1

Let's see the Java finally example where exception doesn't occur.

```
class TestFinallyBlock
{
 public static void main(String args[])
```

```
{
    try
        {
            int data=25/5;
            System.out.println(data);
        }
    catch(NullPointerException e)
        {
            System.out.println(e);
        }
    finally
        {
            System.out.println("finally block is always executed");
        }
            System.out.println("rest of the code...");
        }
}
```

Output :

5

finally block is always executed

rest of the code...

Case 2

Let's see the Java finally example where exception occurs and not handled.

```
class TestFinallyBlock1
{
  public static void main(String args[])
    {
    try
        {
            int data=25/0;
            System.out.println(data);
        }
```

```
catch(NullPointerException e)
  {
      System.out.println(e);
  }
   finally
  {
      System.out.println("finally block is always executed");
  }
  System.out.println("rest of the code...");
  }
}
```

Output :

Finally block is always executed

Exception in thread main Java.lang.ArithmeticException :/ by zero

Case 3

Let's see the Java finally example where exception occurs and handled.

```
public class TestFinallyBlock2
{
  public static void main(String args[])
  {
    try
      {
          int data=25/0;
          System.out.println(data);
      }
    catch(ArithmeticException e)
      {
          System.out.println(e);
      }
```

```
    finally
      {
            System.out.println("finally block is always executed");
      }
      System.out.println("rest of the code...");
  }
}
```

Output :

Exception in thread main Java.lang.ArithmeticException :/ by zero

    finally block is always executed

    rest of the code...

6.8.1 Difference between Final, Finally and Finalize

Sr. No.	Final	Finally	Finalize
1.	Final is used to apply restrictions on class, method and variable. Final class can't be inherited, final method can't be overridden and final variable value can't be changed.	Finally is used to place important code, it will be executed whether exception is handled or not.	Finalize is used to perform clean up processing just before object is garbage collected.
2.	Final is a keyword.	Finally is a block.	Finalize is a method.
3.	class FinalExample { public static void main (String[] args) { final int x=100; x=200;//Compile Time Error } }	class FinallyExample { public static void main (String[] args) { Try { int x=300; } catch(Exception e)	class FinalizeExample { public void finalize() { System.out.println("finalize called"); } public static void main(String[] args) {

		{
		System.out.println(e);
		}
		Finally
		{
		System.out.println("finall y block is executed");
		}
		}
		}
			FinalizeExample f1=new FinalizeExample();
			FinalizeExample f2=new FinalizeExample();
			f1=null;
			f2=null;
			System.gc();
			}
			}

6.9 MULTIPLE CATCH BLOCKS

- A try block can be followed by multiple catch blocks.
- The syntax for multiple catch blocks looks like the following :

```
try
{
    // Protected code
}
catch(ExceptionType1 e1)
{
    // Catch block
}
catch(ExceptionType2 e2)
{
    // Catch block
}
catch(ExceptionType3 e3)
{
    // Catch block
}
```

- The previous syntax demonstrates three catch blocks, but you can have any number of them after a single try.

- If an exception occurs in the protected code, the exception is thrown to the first catch block in the list.

- If the data type of the exception thrown matches ExceptionType1, it gets caught there. If not, the exception passes down to the second catch statement. This continues until the exception either is caught or falls through all catches, in which case the current method stops execution and the exception is thrown down to the previous method on the call stack.

Example :

```
try
{
file = new FileInputStream(fileName);
x = (byte) file.read();
    }
    catch(IOException i)
    {
        i.printStackTrace();
return -1;
    }
    catch(FileNotFoundException f) // Not valid!
    {
       f.printStackTrace();
       return -1;
    }
```

- If you have to perform different tasks at the occurrence of different Exceptions, use Java multi catch block.

- Let's see a simple example of Multi-catch block.

```
public class TestMultipleCatchBlock
{
 public static void main(String args[])
 {
  try
```

```
{
 int a[]=new int[5];
 a[5]=30/0;
}
catch(ArithmeticException e)
  {
     System.out.println("task1 is completed");
  }
catch(ArrayIndexOutOfBoundsException e)
  {
     System.out.println("task 2 completed");
  }
catch(Exception e)
  {
    System.out.println("common task completed");
  }
   System.out.println("rest of the code...");
}
```

Output :

    task1 completed

    rest of the code...

- At a time, only one Exception is occured and at a time only one catch block is executed.
- All catch blocks must be ordered from most specific to most general i.e. catch for ArithmeticException must come before catch for Exception.

Example :

```
class TestMultipleCatchBlock1
{
 public static void main(String args[])
  {
  try
  {
```

```
   int a[]=new int[5];
   a[5]=30/0;
  }
  catch(Exception e)
  {
      System.out.println("common task completed");
  }
  catch(ArithmeticException e)
  {
     System.out.println("task1 is completed");
  }
  catch(ArrayIndexOutOfBoundsException e)
  {
     System.out.println("task 2 completed");
}
  System.out.println("rest of the code...");
  }
}
```

Output :

Compile-time error

6.10 NESTED TRY STATEMENTS

- The try block within a try block is known as nested try block in Java.
- Sometimes a situation may arise where a part of a block may cause one error and the entire block itself may cause another error. In such cases, exception handlers have to be nested.

Syntax :

```
try
{
   statement 1;
   statement 2;
   try
```

```
{
    statement 1;
    statement 2;
}
catch(Exception e)
{
}
}
catch(Exception e)
{
}
```

Example :

Let's see a simple example of Java nested try block.

```
class Excep
{
    public static void main(String args[])
    {
    try
        {
        try
            {
                System.out.println("going to divide");
                int b =39/0;
            }
        catch(ArithmeticException e)
            {
                System.out.println(e);
            }
        try
            {
                int a[]=new int[5];
                a[5]=4;
            }
```

```
        catch(ArrayIndexOutOfBoundsException e)
        {
            System.out.println(e);
        }
        System.out.println("other statement);
    }catch(Exception e)
    {
        System.out.println("handeled");
    }
  System.out.println("normal flow..");
}
}
```

6.11 BUILT-IN EXCEPTIONS

* Java defines several exception classes inside the standard package Java.lang.
* The most general of these exceptions are subclasses of the standard type RuntimeException. Since Java.lang is implicitly imported into all Java programs, most exceptions derived from RuntimeException are automatically available.
* Java defines several other types of exceptions that relate to its various class libraries.
* Following is the list of Java Unchecked RuntimeException.

Sr. No.	Exception	Description
1.	ArithmeticException	Arithmetic error, such as divide-by-zero.
2.	ArrayIndexOutOfBoundsException	Array index is out-of-bounds.
3.	ArrayStoreException	Assignment to an array element of an incompatible type.
4.	ClassCastException	Invalid cast.
5.	IllegalArgumentException	Illegal argument used to invoke a method.
6.	IllegalMonitorStateException	Illegal monitor operation, such as waiting on an unlocked thread.
7.	IllegalStateException	Environment or application is in incorrect state.

Contd...

8.	IllegalThreadStateException	Requested operation not compatible with the current thread state.
9.	IndexOutOfBoundsException	Some type of index is out-of-bounds.
10.	NegativeArraySizeException	Array created with a negative size.
11.	NullPointerException	Invalid use of a null reference.
12.	NumberFormatException	Invalid conversion of a string to a numeric format.
13.	SecurityException	Attempt to violate security.
14.	StringIndexOutOfBounds	Attempt to index outside the bounds of a string.
15.	UnsupportedOperationException	An unsupported operation was encountered.

- Following is the list of Java Checked Exceptions Defined in Java.lang.

Sr. No.	Exception	Description
1.	ClassNotFoundException	Class not found.
2.	CloneNotSupportedException	Attempt to clone an object that does not implement the Cloneable interface.
3.	IllegalAccessException	Access to a class is denied.
4.	InstantiationException	Attempt to create an object of an abstract class or interface.
5.	InterruptedException	One thread has been interrupted by another thread.
6.	NoSuchFieldException	A requested field does not exist.
7.	NoSuchMethodException	A requested method does not exist.

6.12 CUSTOM EXCEPTION

- If you are creating your own Exception that is known as custom exception or user-defined exception.

- Java custom exceptions are used to customize the exception according to user need.

- By the help of custom exception, you can have your own exception and message.

- You can create your own exceptions in Java. Keep the following points in mind when writing your own exception classes

- ➢ All exceptions must be a child of Throwable.
- ➢ If you want to write a checked exception that is automatically enforced by the Handle or Declare Rule, you need to extend the Exception class.
- ➢ If you want to write a runtime exception, you need to extend the RuntimeException class.

- We can define our own Exception class as below :

```
class MyException extends Exception
{

}
```

- Example of Java custom exception.

```
class InvalidAgeException extends Exception
{
 InvalidAgeException(String s)
   {
   super(s);
   }
}
class TestCustomException1
{
  static void validate(int age)throws InvalidAgeException
    {
       if(age<18)
           throw new InvalidAgeException("not valid");
         else
           System.out.println("welcome to vote");
    }

  public static void main(String args[])
    {
         try
       {
           validate(13);
         }
```

```
    catch(Exception m)
    {
        System.out.println("Exception occured : "+m);
    }
    System.out.println("rest of the code...");
    }
}
```

Output :

Exception occured : InvalidAgeException : not valid

rest of the code..

6.13 MANAGING I/O : STREAM

- A stream can be defined as a sequence of data.

- There are two kinds of Streams :

1. InputStream

- The InputStream is used to read data from a source.

- This stream is used for reading data from the files. Objects can be created using the keyword **new** and there are several types of constructors available.

- Following constructor takes a file name as a string to create an input stream object to read the file

    InputStream f = new FileInputStream("C :/Java/hello");

- Following constructor takes a file object to create an input stream object to read the file. First we create a file object using File() method as follows :

    File f = new File("C :/Java/hello");

    InputStream f = new FileInputStream(f);

- Once you have InputStream object in hand, then there is a list of helper methods which can be used to read to stream or to do other operations on the stream.

Sr. No.	Method	Description
1.	public void close() throws IOException{}	This method closes the file output stream. Releases any system resources associated with the file. Throws an IOException.

Contd...

2.	protected void finalize()throws IOException {}	This method cleans up the connection to the file. Ensures that the close method of this file output stream is called when there are no more references to this stream. Throws an IOException.
3.	public int read(int r)throws IOException{}	This method reads the specified byte of data from the InputStream. Returns an int. Returns the next byte of data and -1 will be returned if it's the end of the file.
4.	public int read(byte[] r) throws IOException{}	This method reads r.length bytes from the input stream into an array. Returns the total number of bytes read. If it is the end of the file, -1 will be returned.
5.	public int available() throws IOException{}	Gives the number of bytes that can be read from this file input stream. Returns an int.

2. OutputStream :

- The OutputStream is used for writing data to a destination.
- FileOutputStream is used to create a file and write data into it. The stream would create a file, if it doesn't already exist, before opening it for output.
- Here are two constructors which can be used to create a FileOutputStream object.
- Following constructor takes a file name as a string to create an input stream object to write the file –

      OutputStream f = new FileOutputStream("C :/Java/hello")

- Following constructor takes a file object to create an output stream object to write the file. First, we create a file object using File() method as follows :

          File f = new File("C :/Java/hello");
          OutputStream f = new FileOutputStream(f);

- Once you have *OutputStream* object in hand, then there is a list of helper methods, which can be used to write to stream or to do other operations on the stream.

Sr. No.	Method	Description
1.	public void close() throws IOException{}	This method closes the file output stream. Releases any system resources associated with the file. Throws an IOException.

Contd...

2.	protected void finalize()throws IOException {}	This method cleans up the connection to the file. Ensures that the close method of this file output stream is called when there are no more references to this stream. Throws an IOException.
3.	public void write(int w)throws IOException{}	This method writes the specified byte to the output stream.
4.	public void write(byte[] w)	Writes w.length bytes from the mentioned byte array to the OutputStream.

Example :

Following is the example to demonstrate InputStream and OutputStream :

```
import Java.io.*;
public class fileStreamTest
{
  public static void main(String args[])
  {
   try
   {
     byte bWrite [] = {11,21,3,40,5};
     OutputStream os = new FileOutputStream("test.txt");
     for(int x = 0; x < bWrite.length ; x++)
      {
        os.write( bWrite[x] );   // writes the bytes
      }
     os.close();

     InputStream is = new FileInputStream("test.txt");
     int size = is.available();
     for(int i = 0; i < size; i++)
```

```
    {
      System.out.print((char)is.read() + "  ");
    }
    is.close();
  }catch(IOException e)
  {
    System.out.print("Exception");
  }
 }
}
```

The above code would create file test.txt and would write given numbers in binary format. Same would be the output on the stdout screen.

6.14 BYTE STREAMS

* Java byte streams are used to perform input and output of 8-bit bytes.
* There are many classes related to byte streams but the most frequently used classes are, **FileInputStream** and **FileOutputStream**.
* Following is an example which makes use of these two classes to copy an input file into an output file :

Example :

```
import Java.io.*;
public class CopyFile
{
  public static void main(String args[]) throws IOException
   {
      FileInputStream in = null;
      FileOutputStream out = null;
      try
      {
        in = new FileInputStream("input.txt");
        out = new FileOutputStream("output.txt");
```

```
        int c;
        while((c = in.read()) != -1)
        {
                out.write(c);
        }
          }
      finally
    {
      if (in != null)
      {
       in.close();
      }
      if (out != null)
      {
       out.close();
      }
      }
   }
}
```

- Now let's have a file **input.txt** with the following content :

  This is test for copy file.

- As a next step, compile the above program and execute it, which will result in creating output.txt file with the same content as we have in input.txt. So let's put the above code in CopyFile.Java file and do the following :

  $Javac CopyFile.Java

  $Java CopyFile

6.15 CHARACTER STREAMS

- Java **Character** streams are used to perform input and output for 16-bit unicode.

- There are many classes related to character streams but the most frequently used classes are, **FileReader** and **FileWriter**.

- Internally FileReader uses FileInputStream and FileWriter uses FileOutputStream but here the major difference is that FileReader reads two bytes at a time and FileWriter writes two bytes at a time.

- We can re-write the above example, which makes the use of these two classes to copy an input file (having unicode characters) into an output file :

Example :

```java
import Java.io.*;
public class CopyFile
{
  public static void main(String args[]) throws IOException
  {
    FileReader in = null;
    FileWriter out = null;
    try
    {
      in = new FileReader("input.txt");
      out = new FileWriter("output.txt");
      int c;
      while ((c = in.read()) != -1)
      {
        out.write(c);
      }
    }finally
    {
      if (in != null)
      {
        in.close();
      }
      if (out != null)
      {
        out.close();
      }
    }
  }
}
```

- Now let's have a file **input.txt** with the following content :

  This is test for copy file.

- As a next step, compile the above program and execute it, which will result in creating output.txt file with the same content as we have in input.txt. So let's put the above code in CopyFile.Java file and do the following :

  $Javac CopyFile.Java

  $Java CopyFile

6.16 PREDEFINED STREAMS

- All Java programs automatically import the Java.lang package, which defines a class called system, which encapsulates several aspects of the runtime environment.

- System also contains three predefined stream variables : in, out, err. These are declared as public and static within the system.

- System.out refers to the standard OutputStream by default, this is console.

- System.in refers to the standard InputStream which is the keyboard by default.

- System.in is an object of type InputStream, and System.out, and System.err are objects of type OutputStream. These are byte streams and if desired, you can wrap these within character based streams.

6.17 READING CONSOLE INPUT

- The preferred method of reading console input for Java is to use a character-oriented stream, which makes your program easier to internationalize and maintain.

- In Java, input is accomplished by reading from System.in and for that you wrap System.in in a BufferedReader object, to create a character stream.

6.18 WRITING CONSOLE OUTPUT

- Console output is most easily accomplished with print() and println() which are declared inside PrintStream class which is the type of the object referenced by System.out.

A. write()

- PrintStream is an outputStream derived from OutputStream, it also implements the low-level method write(). Thus write() can be used to write to the console.

Syntax :

  void write(int bytevalue)

  here, bytevalue is in integer, only the low-order 8 bits are written.

Example :

```
import Java.io.*;
public class Main
{
    public static void main(String[] args) throws IOException
    {
        BufferedReader br=new BufferedReader(new InputStreamReader(System.in));
        System.out.println("Enter the number");
        int a=Integer.parseInt(br.readLine());
        System.out.println("The number is "+a);
    }
}
```

Output :

Enter the number

10

The number is 10

B. Reading Characters

To read a character from BufferedReader use read().

Syntax :

```
int read() throws IOException
```

Each time that read() is called, it reads a character from the InputStream and returns it as an integer value. It returns -1 when the end of the stream is encountered.

Example :

```
import Java.io.*;
public class Main
{
    public static void main(String[] args) throws IOException
    {
        BufferedReader br=new BufferedReader(new InputStreamReader(System.in));
        System.out.println("Enter the character");
        char a;
        for(int i=0;i<5;i++)
```

```
        {
            a=(char) br.read();
            System.out.println(a);
        }
    }
}
```

Output :

Enter the character

hello

h

e

l

l

o

C. Reading Strings

- To read a string from the keyboard, use the version of readLine() that is a member of BufferedReader class.

Syntax :

```
        String readLine throws IOException
```

It returns a String object.

Example :

```
import Java.io.*;
public class Main
{
public static void main(String[] args) throws IOException
{
BufferedReader br=new BufferedReader(new InputStreamReader(System.in));
System.out.println("Enter the string");
String a=br.readLine();
System.out.println("The character is "+a);
}
}
```

Output :

Enter the string

Hello Streams!

The character is Hello Streams!

6.19 PRINTWRITER CLASS

- The **Java.io.PrintWriter** class prints formatted representations of objects to a text-output stream.
- Following is the declaration for **Java.io.PrintWriter** class :

  public class PrintWriter extends Writer

- Following are the fields for **Java.io.PrintWriter** class :

  ➢ **Protected Writer Out :** This is the character-output stream of this PrintWriter.

  ➢ **Protected Object Lock :** This is the object used to synchronize operations on this stream.

- PrintWriter Class constructors are as follows :

Sr. No.	Constructor	Description
1.	PrintWriter(File file)	This creates a new PrintWriter, without automatic line flushing, with the specified file.
2.	PrintWriter(File file, String csn)	This creates a new PrintWriter, without automatic line flushing, with the specified file and charset.
3.	PrintWriter(OutputStream out)	This creates a new PrintWriter, without automatic line flushing, from an existing OutputStream.
4.	PrintWriter(OutputStream out, boolean autoFlush)	This creates a new PrintWriter from an existing OutputStream.
5.	PrintWriter(String fileName)	This creates a new PrintWriter, without automatic line flushing, with the specified file name.
6.	PrintWriter(String fileName, String csn)	This creates a new PrintWriter, without automatic line flushing, with the specified file name and charset.
7.	PrintWriter(Writer out)	This creates a new PrintWriter, without automatic line flushing.
8.	PrintWriter(Writer out, boolean autoFlush)	This creates a new PrintWriter.

PrintWriter Class methods are as follows :

Sr. No.	Method	Description
1.	PrintWriter append(char c)	This method appends the specified character to this writer.
2.	PrintWriter append(CharSequence csq)	This method appends the specified character sequence to this writer.
3.	PrintWriter append(CharSequence csq, int start, int end)	This method appends a subsequence of the specified character sequence to this writer.
4.	boolean checkError()	This method flushes the stream if it's not closed and checks its error state.
5.	protected void clearError()	This method Clears the error state of this stream.
6.	void close()	This method Closes the stream and releases any system resources associated with it.
7.	void flush()	This method Flushes the stream.
8.	PrintWriter format(Locale 1, String format, Object... args)	This method writes a formatted string to this writer using the specified format string and arguments.
9.	PrintWriter format(String format, Object... args)	This method writes a formatted string to this writer using the specified format string and arguments.
10.	void print(boolean b)	This method prints a boolean value.
11.	void print(char c)	This method prints a character.
12.	void print(char[] s)	This method Prints an array of characters.
13.	void print(double d)	This method Prints a double-precision floating-point number.
14.	void print(float f)	This method prints a floating-point number.
15.	void print(int i)	This method prints an integer.
16.	void print(long l)	This method prints a long integer.
17.	void print(Object obj)	This method prints an object.
18.	void print(String s)	This method prints a string.

Contd...

19.	PrintWriter printf(Locale 1, String format, Object... args)	This is a convenience method to write a formatted string to this writer using the specified format string and arguments.
20.	PrintWriter printf(String format, Object... args)	This is a convenience method to write a formatted string to this writer using the specified format string and arguments.
21.	void println()	This method terminates the current line by writing the line separator string.
22.	void println(boolean x)	This method prints a boolean value and then terminates the line.
23.	void println(char x)	This method prints a character and then terminates the line.
24.	void println(char[] x)	This method prints an array of characters and then terminates the line.
25.	void println(double x)	This method prints a double-precision floating-point number and then terminates the line.
26.	void println(float x)	This method prints a floating-point number and then terminates the line.
27.	void println(int x)	This method prints an integer and then terminates the line.
28.	void println(long x)	This method prints a long integer and then terminates the line.
29.	void println(Object x)	This method prints an Object and then terminates the line.
30.	void println(String x)	This method prints a String and then terminates the line.

6.20 APPLET FUNDAMENTALS

- A Applet is a Java program that runs in a Web browser.
- An applet can be a fully functional Java application because it has the entire Java API at its disposal.
- Applets are small applications that are accessed on an Internet server, transported over the Internet, automatically installed, and run as part of a web document. After an applet arrives on the client, it has limited access to resources so that it can produce a graphical user interface and run various computations without introducing the risk of viruses or breaching data integrity.

6.20.1 The Applet Class

- Every applet is an extension of the *Java.applet.*
- The base Applet class provides methods that a derived Applet class may call to obtain information and services from the browser context.
- These include methods that do the following :
  - ➤ Get applet parameters
  - ➤ Get the network location of the HTML file that contains the applet
  - ➤ Get the network location of the applet class directory
  - ➤ Print a status message in the browser
  - ➤ Fetch an image
  - ➤ Fetch an audio clip
  - ➤ Play an audio clip
  - ➤ Resize the applet
- The Applet class provides an interface by which the viewer or browser obtains information about the applet and controls the applet's execution.
- The Applet class provides default implementations of each of these methods. Those implementations may be overridden as necessary.
- The "Hello World" applet is complete as it stands. The only method overridden is the paint method.
- Example of simple applet named HelloWorldApplet.Java as follows :

```
import Java.applet.*;
import Java.awt.*;
public class HelloWorldApplet extends Applet
{
    public void paint (Graphics g)
    {
      g.drawString ("Hello World", 25, 50);
    }
}
```

These import statements bring the classes into the scope of our applet class :

- Java.applet.Applet
- Java.awt.Graphics

Without those import statements, the Java compiler would not recognize the classes Applet and Graphics, which the applet class refers to.

6.20.2 Invoking an Applet

- An applet may be invoked by embedding directives in an HTML file and viewing the file through an applet viewer or Java-enabled browser.

- The <applet> tag is the basis for embedding an applet in an HTML file.

- Following is an example that invokes the "Hello World" applet –

```
<html>
<title>The Hello, World Applet</title>
<hr>
<applet code = "HelloWorldApplet.class" width = "320" height="120">
    If your browser was Java-enabled, a "Hello, World"
    message would appear here.
</applet>
<hr>
</html>
```

- The code attribute of the <applet> tag is required. It specifies the Applet class to run.

- Width and height are also required to specify the initial size of the panel in which an applet runs.

- The applet directive must be closed with an </applet> tag.

- If an applet takes parameters, values may be passed for the parameters by adding <param> tags between <applet> and </applet>.

- The browser ignores text and other tags between the applet tags.

- Non-Java-enabled browsers do not process <applet> and </applet>. Therefore, anything that appears between the tags, not related to the applet, is visible in non-Java-enabled browsers.

6.21 APPLET ARCHITECTURE

- When Applet is created, it undergoes series of changes in its state. The applet state includes

  ➢ Born or initialize state

  ➢ Running state

  ➢ Idle state

  ➢ Dead or destroyed state

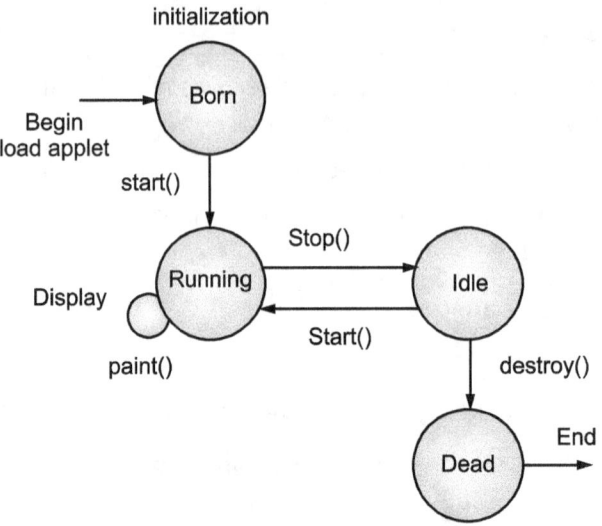

Fig. 6.4 : Applet architecure

Explanation about above Fig. 6.4 is as follows :

1. Initialization State or init()

- Applet enters the initialization state when it is first loaded. This is achieved by overriding init() method.
- This method is intended for whatever initialization is needed for your applet. It is called after the param tags inside the applet tag have been processed.

Syntax :

```
public void init()
{

}
```

- The **init( )** method is the first method to be called.
- This is where you should initialize variables.
- This method is called only once during the run time of applet.
- With init() method following task may do.
    1. Create objects needed by applet
    2. Set up initial values
    3. Load images or fonts
    4. Set up colors

2. Running State or start()

- An applet enters in running state when system calls the start(). This is achieved by overriding start() method.
- This method is automatically called after the browser calls the init method. It is also called whenever the user returns to the page containing the applet after having gone off to other pages.

Syntax :

```
public void start()
{

}
```

- The **start( )** method is called after **init( )**.
- It is also called to restart an applet after it has been stopped. Whereas **init( )** is called once—the first time an applet is loaded
- **start( )** is called each time an applet's HTML document is displayed onscreen. So, if a user leaves a web page and comes back, the applet resumes execution at **start( )**.

3. Idle or Stopped State or stop()

- An applet become idle when it is stopped from running. This is achieved by overriding stop() method.
- This method is automatically called when the user moves off the page on which the applet sits. It can, therefore, be called repeatedly in the same applet.

Syntax :

```
public void stop()
{

}
```

- The **stop( )** method is called when a web browser leaves the HTML document containing the applet—when it goes to another page.
- For example. When **stop( )** is called, the applet is probably running. **stop( )** method is also used to suspend threads that don't need to run.
- When the applet is not visible. It can be restarted when **start( )** is called if the user returns to the page.

4. Dead State or destroy()

- An applet is said to be dead when it is removed from memory. This is achieved by overriding destroy() method.
- This method is only called when the browser shuts down normally. Because applets are meant to live on an HTML page, you should not normally leave resources behind after a user leaves the page that contains the applet.

Syntax :

```
public void destroy()
{

}
```

- The **destroy( )** method is called when the environment determines that applet needs to be removed completely from memory. this point, you should free up any resources the applet may be using stop( ) method is always called before **destroy( )**.

- Like initialization, destroying stage occurs only once in the applet's life cycle.

5. Display State or paint()

- Applet moves to the display state whenever it has to perform some output operations on the screen.

- This happen immediately after the applet enters the running state. The paint method is called to accomplish this task. This is achieved by overriding destroy() method.

- Invoked immediately after the start() method, and also any time the applet needs to repaint itself in the browser. The paint() method is actually inherited from the Java.awt.

Syntax :

```
public void paint(Graphics g)
{
}
```

Example :

```
import Java.applet.*;
import Java.awt.*;
/*
 <applet code="AppletLifecycle" width=300 height=300>
 </applet>
*/
public class AppletLifecycle extends Applet
{
  String str = "";
  public void init()
  {
    str += "init; ";
  }
public void start()
  {
    str += "start; ";
  }
```

```java
public void stop()
{
  // stop
}
public void destroy()
{
  //destroy
}
 public void paint(Graphics g)
 {
    str += "Paint; ";
    g.drawString(str, 10, 25);
 }
}
```

6.22 APPLET SKELETON

- When an applet begins, the AWT calls the following methods, in this sequence:
  1. **init( )**
  2. **start( )**
  3. **paint( )**
- When an applet is terminated, the following sequence of method calls takes place:
  4. **stop( )**
  5. **destroy( )**
- Explanation is as follows

1. init( )
- The init() method is called exactly once in an applet's life, when the applet is first loaded.
- It's normally used to read parameter tags, start downloading any other images or media files you need, and set up the user interface.

2. start( )
  - The start() method is called at least once in an applet's life, when the applet is started or restarted.
  - In some cases it may be called more than once. Many applets you write will not have explicit start()methods and will merely inherit one from their super class.
  - A start() method is often used to start any threads the applet will need while it runs.

3. **paint()**
   - The paint() method is called each time your applet's output must be redrawn. This situation can occur for several reasons.
   - For example, in which the applet is running may be overwritten by another window and the uncovered or the applet window may be minimized and then restored.
   - paint() is also called when the applet begins execution. Whatever the cause, whenever the applet must redraw its output, paint() is called .
   - The paint() method has one parameter of type Graphics. This parameter will contain the graphics context which describes the graphics environment in which the applet is running.

4. **stop( )**
   - The stop() method is called at least once in an applet's life, when the browser leaves the page in which the applet is embedded.
   - The applet's start() method will be called if at some later point the browser returns to the page containing the applet.
   - In some cases the stop() method may be called multiple times in an applet's life.
   - Many applets you write will not have explicit stop() methods and will merely inherit one from their superclass.
   - Your applet should use the stop() method to pause any running threads. When your applet is stopped, it *should* not use any CPU cycles.

5. **destroy( )**
   - The destroy() method is called exactly once in an applet's life, just before the browser unloads the applet. This method is generally used to perform any final clean-up.
   - For example, an applet that stores state on the server might send some data back to the server before it's terminated. Many applets will not have explicit destroy() methods and just inherit one from their superclass.

Example :

```
import Java.awt.*;
import Java.applet.*;
/*
<applet code="AppletSkel" width=300 height=100>
</applet>
*/
public class AppletSkel extends Applet
{   // Called first.
    public void init()
    {
        // initialization
    }
```

/* Called second, after init(). Also, called whenever the applet is restarted. */

```
public void start()
{
    // start or resume execution
}
```

// Called when the applet is stopped.

```
public void stop()
{
    // suspends execution
}
```

/* Called when applet is terminated. This is the last method executed. */

```
public void destroy()
{
    // perform shutdown activities
}
```

// Called when an applet's window must be restored.

```
public void paint(Graphics g)
{
    // redisplay contents of window
}
}
```

6.23 REQUESTING REPAINTING

- An applet writes to its window only when its update() or paint() methods are called by the AWT.

- For example, if an applet is displaying a moving banner, what mechanism does the applet use to update the window each time this banner scrolls? Remember, you cannot create a loop inside paint due the fundamental contraints imposed on an applet - An applet must quickly return control to the AWT run time system.

- Providentially the people who designed Java foresaw this predicament and included the repaint() method. Whenever your applet needs to update the information displayed in its window, it simply calls repaint().

- The repaint() method is defined by the AWT. It causes the AWT run time system to call to your applet's update() method, which in its default implementation, calls paint().

- Again for example if a part of your applet needs to output a string, it can store this string in a variable and then call repaint(). Inside paint(), you can output the string using drawstring().

- The repaint method has four forms.

1. void repaint()

This causes the entire window to be repainted.

2. void repaint(int left, int top, int width, int height)

- This specifies a region that will be repainted. The integers left, top, width and hieght are in pixels. You save time by specifying a region to repaint instead of the whole window.

3. void repaint(long maxDelay)

4. void repaint(long maxDelay, int x, int y, int width, int height)

- Calling repaint() is essentially a request that your applet be repainted sometime soon. However, if your system is slow or busy, update() might not be called immediately. This gives rise to a problem of update() being called sporadically.

- If your task requires consistent update time, like in animation, then use the above two forms of repaint().

- Here, the maxDelay() is the maximum number of milliseconds that can elaspe before update() is called.

6.24 STATUS WINDOW

- In addition to displaying information in its window, an applet can also output a message to the status window of the browser or applet viewer on which it is running.

- To do so, call **showStatus( )**, which is defined by **Applet**, with the string that you want displayed.

- The general form of **showStatus( )** is shown here :

void showStatus(String *msg*)

Here, *msg* is the string to be displayed.

- The status window is a good place to give the user feedback about what is occurring in the applet, suggest options, or possibly report some types of errors.

- The status window also makes an excellent debugging aid, because it gives you an easy way to output information about your applet.

- Example of applet demonstrates **showStatus( ) is as follows** :

```
/*
    <applet code="SetStatusMessageExample" width=200 height=200>
    </applet>
*/
 import Java.applet.Applet;
import Java.awt.Graphics;
public class SetStatusMessageExample extends Applet
{
    public void paint(Graphics g)
      {

        //drawString() shows message inside an applet
        g.drawString("Show Status Example", 50, 50);

        //showStatus() will displayed in a status bar of an applet window
        showStatus("This is a status message of an applet window");
      }
}
```

Output :

Fig. 6.5 : Example of status window

6.25 HTML APPLET TAG

- The HTML <applet> tag specifies an applet.
- It is used for embedding a Java applet within an HTML document.

Example :

```
<!DOCTYPE html>
<html>
 <head>
   <title>HTML applet Tag</title>
 </head>
   <body>
    <applet code="newClass.class" width="300" height="200">
    </applet>
   </body>
</html>
```

Here is the *newClass.Java* file :

```
import Java.applet.*;
import Java.awt.*;
public class newClass extends Applet
{
public void paint (Graphics g)
  {
    g.drawString("Hello", 300, 150);
  }
}
```

- The HTML <> tag also supports following additional attributes :

Attribute	Value	Description
align	URL	*Deprecated* - Defines the text alignment around the applet
alt	URL	Alternate text to be displayed in case browser does not support applet
archive	URL	Applet path when it is stored in a Java Archive ie. jar file
code	URL	A URL that points to the class of the applet

Contd...

codebase	URL	Indicates the base URL of the applet if the code attribute is relative
height	pixels	Height to display the applet
hspace	pixels	*Deprecated* - Defines the left and right spacing around the applet
name	name	Defines a unique name for the applet
object	name	Specifies the resource that contains a serialized representation of the applet's state.
title	test	Additional information to be displayed in tool tip of the mouse
vspace	pixels	*Deprecated* - Amount of white space to be inserted above and below the object.
width	pixels	Width to display the applet.

6.26 PASSING PARAMETER TO APPLETS

- Parameters are passed to applets in NAME=VALUE pairs in <PARAM> tags between the opening and closing APPLET tags.

- Inside the applet, you read the values passed through the PARAM tags with the getParameter() method of the Java.applet.Applet class.

- Java applet has the feature of retrieving the parameter values passed from the html page. So, you can pass the parameters from your html page to the applet embedded in your page.

- The **param** tag(**<parma name="" value=""></param>**) is used to pass the parameters to an applet.

- For the illustration about the concept of applet and passing parameter in applet. The applet has to call the getParameter() method supplied by the Java.applet.Applet parent class.

- Three methods commonly used by applets :

  ➢ **String getParameter(String name) :** Returns the value for the specified parameter string

  ➢ **URL getCodeBase() :** Returns the URL of the applet

  ➢ **URL getDocumentBase() :** Returns the URL of the document containing the applet

Example :

```
import Java.applet.*;
import Java.awt.*;
 /*<APPLET code="hai" width="300" height="250">
<PARAM name="Message" value="Hai friend how are you ..?">
</APPLET>*/
public class hai extends Applet
{
    private String defaultMessage = "Hello!";
    public void paint(Graphics g)
    {
        String inputFromPage = this.getParameter("Message");
        if (inputFromPage == null) inputFromPage = defaultMessage;
        g.drawString(inputFromPage, 50, 55);
    }
}
```

Output :

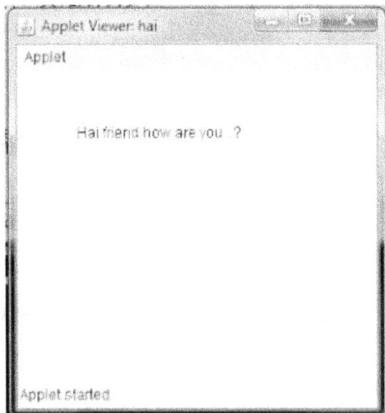

Fig. 6.6 : Example of passing PARAMs to applets

- You only need to change the HTML, not the Java source code. PARAMs let you customize applets without changing or recompiling the code.
- This applet is very similar to the HelloWorldApplet.
- However rather than hardcoding the message to be printed it's read into the variable inputFromPage from a PARAM element in the HTML.

- You pass getParameter() a string that names the parameter you want. This string should match the name of a PARAM element in the HTML page.

- getParameter() returns the value of the parameter. All values are passed as strings. If you want to get another type like an integer, then you'll need to pass it as a string and convert it to the type you really want.

- The PARAM element is also straightforward. It occurs between <APPLET> and </APPLET>.

- It has two attributes of its own, NAME and VALUE. NAME identifies which PARAM this is. VALUE is the string value of the PARAM. Both should be enclosed in double quote marks if they contain white space.

6.27 DIFFERENCE BETWEEN APPLET AND APPLICATION PROGRAM

Sr. No.	Applet	Application Program
1.	Applet is Small Program	Application is Large Program
2.	It is used to run a program on client Browser	It can be executed on stand alone computer system
3.	Applet is portable and can be executed by any JAVA supported browser.	It need JDK, JRE, JVM installed on client machine.
4.	Applet applications are executed in a Restricted Environment	Application can access all the resources of the computer
5.	Applets are created by extending the Java.applet.Applet	Applications are created by writing public static void main(String[] s) method.
6.	Applet application has 5 methods which will be automatically invoked on occurrence of specific event	Application has a single start point which is main method
7.	Main() is not Present	Main() is Present
8.	It requires some third party tool help like a browser to execute.	It is called as stand-alone application as application can be executed from command prompt
9.	It cannot access any thing on the system except browser's services.	It can access any data or software available on the system.
10.	It requires highest security for the system as they are untrusted.	It does not require any security

Contd...

| 11. | Example :

import Java.awt.*;

import Java.applet.*;

public class Myclass extends Applet

{

   public void init() { }

   public void start() { }

   public void stop() {}

   public void destroy() {}

   public void paint(Graphics g) {}

} | Example :

public class MyClass

{

public static void main(String args[])

   {

   }

} |

EXERCISE

1. What is Exception handling?

2. How can one handle Exception in JAVA?

3. Explain Nested try statement.

4. Explain Built in Exceptions in JAVA.

5. Explain Stream in detailed.

6. Explain Byte Stream and Character Stream.

7. Write a short note on Print Writer class.

8. Explain Applet Architecture.

9. Explain Applet Skeleton.

10. Write a short note on HTML applet tag.

11. Write a short note on Passing parameters to Applet.

12. Difference between Applet and Application Program.

✠ ✠ ✠

SAMPLE QUESTION PAPER – I

End Sem. Theory Examination

Time : 2 Hours   **Marks : 50**

1. **(a)** Explain Software Development Processes in detailed.   **[6]**

   (b) Write short notes on   **[6]**

       (i)   Runtime structure   (ii) Abstract semantic processor

   ### OR

2. **(a)** Explain Generic types.   **[6]**

   (b) Explain Type Checking.   **[6]**

3. **(a)** Explain programming paradigms in detailed.   **[6]**

   (b) Explain software design methods in detailed.   **[6]**

   ### OR

4. **(a)** Differentiate between C++ and JAVA.   **[6]**

   (b) Explain control statements in Java.   **[6]**

5. **(a)** What is nested and inner classes in Java? Explain with example.   **[7]**

   (b) What is Array? Explain the types of Array.   **[6]**

   ### OR

6. **(a)** What is Constructor? Explain the different types of Constructor.   **[7]**

   (b) Write a short note on

       (i)   Garbage collection   (ii)   Finalize method   **[6]**

7. **(a)** Explain Package in detailed.   **[7]**

   (b) Explain Interface in detailed.   **[6]**

   ### OR

8. **(a)** What is Exception? How to handle Exception in JAVA.   **[7]**

   (b) Explain Applet architecture.   **[6]**

✠ ✠ ✠

SAMPLE QUESTION PAPER – II

End-Sem. Theory Examination

Time : 2 Hours　　　　　　　　　　　　　　　　　　　　　　　**Marks : 50**

1. **(a)** Discuss desirable features and design issues of programming languages. **[6]**

   (b) Write short notes on **[6]**

   　　(i)　Abstract syntax　　(ii)　Concrete syntax

OR

2. **(a)** Explain Finite mapping User-defined types and abstract data types. **[6]**

   (b) What is difference between Static and Dynamic program checking? **[6]**

3. **(a)** Explain four main Programming paradigms. **[6]**

   (b) Explain different features of Java. **[6]**

OR

4. **(a)** What is JVM? Explain in detailed. **[6]**

   (b) Explain any 5 String class methods in Java with example. **[6]**

5. **(a)** What is Dynamic method dispatched? **[7]**

   (b) Explain Package in detailed. **[6]**

OR

6. **(a)** Differentiate between Method overloading and Method overriding. **[7]**

   (b) Write short notes on **[6]**

   　　(i)　this keyword　　　　(ii)　Finalize()

7. **(a)** What is Stream? Explain Byte Stream and Character Stream. **[7]**

   (b) Write short notes on

   　　(i)　Reading console inputs　(ii)　Writing console output **[6]**

OR

8. **(a)** Differentiate between Applets and Applications. **[7]**

   (b) How to create simple applet? Explain applet skeleton with example. **[6]**

✠ ✠ ✠